THE KNIGHT
ADVOCATE

By

Jason Rose

Second Print Edition January 2019

ISBN-13: 978-1985066946

ISBN-10: 1985066947

Cover images credit:

(iStock.com: sirup, oksanita)

(vectorstock.com: robuart, guarding)

(Diasi Designs)

Books by Jason Rose

The Colt Valentine Arcane Justice Series
(an urban fantasy legal mystery)

Book 1: *The Knight Advocate* – Now Available!

Book 2: *The Lycanthrope's Lawyer* – Coming Soon!

Learn more about new releases and contact me

I welcome you to visit me and subscribe to my newsletter to be the first to know about upcoming releases.

Facebook: facebook.com/jasonroseauthor

Instagram: instagram.com/jason.rose_author/

Dedication

To my beautiful wife Natasha, who is the most supportive human being on earth, thank you for constantly encouraging me to take risks, even when I'm not ready for them. I love you, baby.

I'd also like to thank my two sons Ford and Porter for completing spinning my world on its head and giving me a fresh perspective on life. Things I used to think were important—now seem silly, and things I thought were silly—now seem important.

I'd also like to thank my advance readers, including my biological father Larry, for giving insight and feedback. I know I'm stubborn and don't always take criticism well, but I appreciate your comments.

Finally, I'd like to thank my Uncle Mike, who has treated me like a son for as long as I can remember. You taught me how to throw a baseball, shoot a basketball, and most importantly, how to read. This book, my life for that matter, wouldn't be what they are without your support and guidance.

Thank you.

Table of Contents

"This is a court of law, young man, not a court of justice"

– Oliver Wendell Holmes

"I've had my first dose of caffeine and I'm ready to dole out some justice."

– Colt Valentine

Prologue

Pavo Palatinus sits at the desk in his study, swirling a thick red liquid around the inside of a heavy square whiskey glass, while he waits. The solid oak door to his study creaks open, and a long spindly being cloaked all in black crosses the room and comes to a stop in front of the desk. The being moves with a strange gait, as if uncomfortable on just two legs. Pavo's only reaction is to raise the heavy glass to his thin lips and swallow more of the crimson liquid.

The two beings stare across the desk at each other. Physically, they couldn't be any more different. Pavo is short for this century, and well-dressed in a tailored silk suit. He has an ageless face and tired, haunted, eyes. Centuries of guilt and regrets weigh heavily on his stained soul.

The cloaked being is uncomfortably tall, gangly even. His face is elongated—almost inhuman. It's as if its skin has been shrunken, dried out, and then stretched into place over his odd-shaped skull. His dark soulless eyes sparkle with intelligence, but there's no sign of humanity within. This being knows nothing of guilt and regret; it only knows fear.

Despite their antithetical appearances, they are kindred devils. The same scent of death clings to both, and both are enslaved by identical silver rings with matching blood red stones, secured to the ring fingers on their left hands.

The cloaked being finally breaks the silence, its deep and frigid voice penetrating the study like a rusty nail into pink flesh. "Does the Peacock remember his promise? Does the Peacock remember the pact he made so many centuries ago?" Pavo flinches at the sound of his childhood nickname, but doesn't respond.

"Time is short, the world is getting louder. You know what will happen if *she* wakes. *She* will *feed*, that could be ... *distasteful*. Even you must acknowledge that the human infection has spread too far; they're a danger to this world, a *danger* to us. I know you've always had a soft spot for them, but isn't it better to act now, while we can oversee a reduction? If *she* wakes ..." The cloaked one shrugs with both palms facing the sky. "Some of our colleagues have voiced concerns; they want assurances that the Peacock will honor his pact." The cloaked being pauses, waiting for a response.

Pavo remains silent while he contemplates his visitor's words. Hearing the soulless one speak confirms his worst fears; there's no turning back now—he must follow through with his plan.

Impatient with Pavo's silence, the spindly being creeps forward threateningly, and then jerks to a sudden stop as Pavo awakens from his trance and strikes the desk with his fist, his metallic ring resonating sharply off the mahogany. "I know the agreement I made, Phulcus. I've heard your words. Now, leave my house."

Phulcus hisses defiantly.

Pavo's anger rises like a tidal wave, crests, and then recedes. He strains and contorts his angry face into a controlled smile. "Leave now, before I crush you with my boot. You and your kind disgust me."

Phulcus' face rearranges; larger, sharp teeth emerge and then just as quickly retreat, settling back into his elongated inhuman face. "As the Peacock wishes. I don't need to threaten the Peacock with the consequences of betrayal; he knows the consequences." Phulcus' head tilts unnaturally to the left and he smirks, "Such a pretty daughter the Peacock has taken."

Pavo reaches down and slips his stylish, size eight Italian leather dress boot off his foot and forcefully bangs it on the top of the desk, the way a man might use a boot to crush an insect. His eyes dare Phulcus to test his resolve.

Phulcus stares at the boot, as if considering the threat. The corners of his mouth tug at a smile and then slowly, like a cornered predator, he backs out of the study, never turning or breaking eye contact with Pavo until the last possible moment.

After Phulcus departs, a beautiful woman emerges from the shadows behind Pavo and places her small delicate hand on his shoulder. "What a revolting creature."

"Yes, but a dangerous one. Don't underestimate him," says Pavo. "He's a killer."

The woman nods and then pleads, "Father, I don't like this path you've set us on. We don't need the human lawyer. We can face them together. If it comes to it, we can face *her* together. You don't have to do this. There *must* be another way."

Pavo looks up at his adopted child from his chair, his tired eyes nearly bursting with the boundless love that only exists between a parent and child. "My sweet child. We've been over this many times; there is no other path. It must be done. *He* gives the world its best chance for survival." His voice softens to an almost whisper, "and gives me a chance at redemption."

"But Fath——."

"My decision is final," snaps Pavo.

He shakes his head and sighs. Guilt weighs heavily on him, pressing him further into his chair. "I'm tired. As it is, I fear I lack the will to do what must be done. I'm afraid ... afraid I'll play the coward ... again."

Not knowing what to say, his daughter looks down at the floor. This is not the parting she imagined. This shell of a man hardly resembles the father that raised her to be fearless. She promises herself that she won't remember him like this.

Pavo gazes out the window into the dark night. His eyes fill with sadness and then resolve sets in and a grim expression takes hold. "You will do your part. *He* will need your help." Pavo turns back to his daughter, lifting her chin, and trapping her eyes with his. "You *must* promise me that you will help him."

Red tears run down his daughter's cheeks. She begrudgingly answers, "Yes, Father ... I promise. I will do as you ask."

Pavo stares at his adopted daughter's hauntingly beautiful face. He drinks in every curve, tear streak, and freckle, and smiles. He knows this will be the last time he ever sees her; and yet, for the first time in over a thousand years, he feels at peace. The guilt he's carried for more than a millennium is almost bearable. Just one more task, and his victims will finally have their justice.

Chapter One

"What a travesty!" I mutter, as I stare intently, first at the empty glass, and then at the empty bottle. It seems like just moments ago the bottle was filled with a delicious red wine, a nice pinot noir, silky smooth, rich, and easy to drink— now it's empty.

As I survey my messy apartment, I consider firing my maid. The only reason I have one in the first place is because I live alone and, without one, the bathrooms would never get cleaned. Dirty bathrooms are a recipe for a future of lonely nights and I like to imagine there's at least a possible future, where I get back on the horse again.

Clean bathrooms aside, my maid's killing me—and the environment. She mixes my recyclables. She takes all of my empty wine bottles out in the regular trash, blended in along with the Styrofoam Thai take-out-boxes, the brown-paper containers from Whole Foods and the mostly empty cardboard pizza boxes that typically litter my apartment. I thought having a maid would improve my life; instead, she's turning me into a bad person—somebody who doesn't recycle.

In my defense, although my maid's laziness may be destroying this planet, it might be saving the universe. It's entirely possible that thousands of years from now, an archeologist from a race of evil aliens, hell-bent on conquering the universe, will stumble across this empty pinot noir bottle alongside a badly decomposed pizza box, while excavating an archaeological dig site on our destroyed planet. The alien will run some sort of bio-scan and correctly conclude that the human diet consisted primarily of flour, yeast, garlic, water, pureed tomatoes, curdled milk, pepperoni, and the juice of fermented grapes. It will most likely hypothesize that our poor diet is what led to our civilization's downfall and it would probably be right. Pizza and wine, although a perfect pairing, are not the healthiest pillars of a well-balanced diet.

The evil alien will want to experience what it's like to be human. It will use its advanced technology to reengineer pepperoni pizza and red wine from my trash. Like humans, the alien will find the pairing delicious and addicting. Before it knows what's happening, it'll be eating pizza three nights a week and drinking wine with every meal.

The alien will introduce pizza and wine to its evil species. Its entire planet will become addicted. They'll start planting grapes and tomatoes on their planet and raising cows, because "fresh mozzarella is so much better than replicated mozzarella." They'll start adding bacon, and pineapple, and stuffing extra cheese inside the crusts. They'll experiment with deep dish, thin crust, thick crust, stuffed crust, pan, and flatbread pizzas, and get retired athletes to endorse the pizzas in interstellar commercials. Alien weights and cholesterol levels will skyrocket. Cattle farming will contribute to global warming on their planet, the alien civilization will crumble, and the galaxy will be saved.

Okay, my imagination might be taking this a bit far. I seriously need to stop working with the TV on in the background or, at the very least, put it on a different channel—I'm losing my mind. #SYFY+Wine=Insanity.

My gaze returns to the pinot noir bottle: long, dark, sultry, sexy, with curves in all the right places. Its birthplace, a small family-owned Sonoma farm about an hour from my East Bay home, is one of my favorite wineries. It's not too big, not too fancy, and their wine is affordable on a government salary. The farm is Sonoma's field of dreams; the winery workers play a weekly baseball game on a diamond built right in the middle of its vines. I used to visit and catch a ballgame whenever I had a free weekend or a date, both of which seem to be rarer and rarer these days. It's hard to meet people as you get older; and internet dating, and/or swiping left, or swiping right, or whatever it is the kids do on their phones these days, just isn't for me.

If I'm being honest, I haven't had a date in nearly a year. Shit, who am I kidding? Probably longer. Just thinking about my sex-life makes me want to take a handful of *Valium*. I haven't even taken my equipment on a test drive in over a year, and I'm not even sure the plumbing down there still works. I'm in my mid-thirties ... so I should be okay ... but who knows? Before any future dates, I should probably contact my doctor and get some of those little blue pills, or is it little green ones? I can never remember.

I remember when they first started advertising erectile dysfunction medications, the commercials were considered scandalous, inappropriate for children to view, and only ran on late-night television. I even vaguely remember some red-state congressmen proposing a bill to ban them entirely—it failed, of course. Big Pharma has too much money to lose.

Back then, all the commercials were of well-dressed men talking to the camera on either a boat or in the study of their home, but never in the bedroom. There was sometimes a woman in the background, presumably the wife, but all you could ever see was a silhouette. The well-dressed male actors would explain the drug's purpose and attempt to put the face of normalcy on erectile dysfunction. Big Pharma was telling you, "It's okay if you can't get it up anymore, you're not alone, let us fix your marriage." #MarriageGoals. The commercials weren't really tasteful, but they were at least informational.

Today's commercials are on at all times of the day, even during Saturday morning cartoons, and are more pornographic than educational. The new commercials are all essentially the same, a young beautiful woman suggestively lounges on a hotel bed, while a faceless man takes a shower in the background. There's always mood lighting, and the actress always looks like she's twenty years too young to be dating someone suffering from erectile dysfunction. The scantily-clad woman will look directly into the camera and say in a deep and throaty voice, "This pill makes sure you're ready ... every time I'm ready." Big Pharma is now telling you, "Take our pill and you'll bang young prostitutes in poorly-lit hotel rooms." #LifeGoals.

I can only imagine what the erectile dysfunction commercials of tomorrow will look like. Probably a live stream of a naked guy talking to the camera while he has intercourse with his robotic donkey. The actor will say something like, "I'm using erectile dysfunction medication right now and it feels great." #FearThePharmaceuticalFuture.

Scary futures aside, erectile dysfunction drugs aren't all bad. My eighty-year-old neighbor, Tom, brags he pops "ED" medication like candy. He claims they're the secret to success of his fifty-one-year marriage to the same woman. God bless him, I hope my libido's as strong as Tom's at eighty.

Tom's a conspiracy theorist; he blames the internet, big corporations, and fake news for wrecking this country—not erectile dysfunction medications. Okay, he doesn't actually say the part about erectile dysfunction medication, but you can't let the truth get in the way of a good story and it sounds like something he'd say.

Personally, I think the world's always been screwed up. I think assholes have been taking advantage of those weaker than them since the beginning of time. Murder, rape, hate, theft, betrayal, and greed are as much a part of the human condition as love, companionship, hope, honor, friendship, and generosity. They're all opposite sides of the same blade. Like the old *Married with Children* theme song says, "You can't have one without the other." Then again, I'm not much of a philosopher, I'm more of a pragmatist. I firmly believe that sometimes you have to do the wrong thing to bring about the right result.

Which brings us back to my non-existent sex life: it's sad, but it's been a while since I really thought about an erection or even talked about an erection—other than Tom's. The divorce was two years ago, not that I'm counting, and since then, I've let work consume my life. It's hard to meet someone post-divorce, especially when you're in your mid-thirties and average eighty-to-ninety-hour work weeks.

Apparently, I also prioritized work during my marriage. At least, that's what my ex, Lisa, her attorney, and the judge who oversaw our divorce proceedings, all told me, right before I was saddled with a crushingly large monthly spousal support payment. Too bad for my bank account, I didn't find out my ex was fooling around on me until after the divorce was finalized. I seriously doubt I'd have been as charitable during the asset distribution phase of our divorce if I'd known she was riding Dick.

Richard Paul Thirston or "Dick," as I call him, which he hates, is the San Francisco District Attorney. The guy's a total bureaucratic dipstick. He's the type of self-important douche-bag who works the phrases, "I'm a lawyer," and "Harvard," into every conversation. Dick's the type of guy who always uses his middle name when introducing himself and has his initials stenciled on the cuffs of his dress shirts, probably on his underwear too. In short, Dick is a dick, written in cursive, with a capital D, in permanent ink.

But don't get it twisted, I'm not mad at Dick. If anything, I feel sorry for Dick, and I should be thanking Dick. Dick's the reason that the past two years of crushing spousal support payments are finally coming to an end and I have the super tacky wedding invitation to prove it. It's one of those do-it-yourself postcards with a picture of Lisa and

Dick rolling around together on a Hawaiian beach. Pu'u Keka'a, also known as "Black Rock," is in the background. Black Rock is a lava formation on Maui's west shore that divides Ka'anapali Beach in half. Legend has it that the souls of great warriors join their ancestors by leaping from Black Rock into the ocean. I know this because Lisa and I got married and honeymooned there, and that's what the cliff divers told us. Classy of Lisa to rinse and repeat the same location from one wedding to the next.

The night I got Lisa and Dick's invitation in the mail, I drank four bottles of wine I can't afford. #BestHangoverEver.

Is it just me, or is it tacky to send your ex-husband a wedding invitation? Particularly when you're marrying the guy you were cheating on him with and you're getting married at the same goddamn resort? I'm considering pulling a dick move and actually showing up. Maybe I'll give them a canceled spousal support check as a wedding present. #WhatDoYouGiveYourExWho'sMarryingTheGuySheCheatedOnYouWith?

I tear my red watery eyes from the empty wine bottle and look across the expanse of the kitchen for the microwave's digital readout. It's 4:27 AM. The "be responsible" voice in my head tells me it is either too late or too early to open another bottle. Damn it, another glass would be nice. I have a good buzz going.

I survey the mess I made in my dining room. Papers filled with my chicken scratch handwriting and covered in purple Post-its are spread everywhere. I know the Post-its come in manlier colors, but I've only ever used purple. It's a habit I picked up from my former mentor. "Purple's the color of royalty," he'd say. "The jury responds and trusts the color purple." I don't know if that's all BS, but it stuck with me and that's the way I've always done it.

I stretch my arms above my head and fight off a yawn. Sleep is over-rated; I can do without it, but I need to sweat the alcohol out before court. I put on an old pair of broken in Under Armour cross trainers, grab my Beats headphones and jet out for a morning jog. I don't run too far, I'm not one of those sycophant runners who believes running is life; I just go far enough to get the blood pumping and get a good sweat on.

After the run, I almost feel sober. I down a protein shake and lay my uniform out on the bed: black suit, white cotton button-up shirt, red tie with a pattern, black socks, and black shoes. I shave, jump in the shower, put the lawyer uniform on, pack my briefcase and folding file cart, and head out to the garage.

I load up my simple non-descript white Honda SUV. It's the kind of vehicle you see a million times a day—it blends. There's absolutely nothing fancy about it. My mentor used to say, "The jury's always watching, even in the parking lot. Being a good lawyer isn't about being flashy or standing out; it's about telling a story and getting out of the way. The case is never about you, *dumbass.* It's about the client, so get out of the fucking way." A little crass, a bit repetitive, but sage advice.

My mentor was a self-righteous prick, but a good teacher, and a hell of a trial lawyer. Sadly, he passed last year but, don't worry, we had a really nice 'life celebration' for him at the office. We shut down for a full fifteen minutes. Somebody brought in those delicious Costco muffins. The whole thing was real classy. Apparently, the reward for thirty years of service at the Public Defender's office is an early grave and a fifteen-minute muffin break for those you left behind. I'm glad I have something to look forward to. Personally, I hope they serve pot brownies when I go. That might breathe some life into the office. I might even make a formal request of it in my will—that is, if I ever get around to amending mine. I think my ex still gets everything. I have to move that up on my someday-I'll-get-to-it list.

Once the car's loaded, I do a self-pat-down check for wallet, cell phone, and keys, and then drive to the courthouse. I have court this morning. My client's accused of raping and kidnapping a pretty young Stanford graduate. Although I don't have to go first, I probably shouldn't be late for closing arguments.

Chapter Two

Have there been times in your life when you felt obligated to clap, but it felt inappropriate to do so? When Assistant District Attorney, Brad Murphy, finally sits down, I have to physically restrain myself from clapping, not because his presentation was good, but because it's over. In general, closing arguments can be brutal to sit through, and this one was especially painful. It was worse than brunch with my ex-mother-in-law, and she hated me, and only ever wanted to talk about playing Bridge with the blue-hair crowd. ADA Brad Murphy should really do the People of California a favor and consider a career change.

Murphy's closing argument was the cure for life. He read the jury his PowerPoint slides for two straight hours. He was completely wed to his script. If it wasn't on the slide, he didn't say it. No improvisation, no humor, no spontaneity at all. Reading PowerPoint slides out loud tells the jury you don't trust them enough to read the slides themselves. It's insulting.

Even more offensive is the fact that Murphy's closing was boring and lacked soul. My iPhone personal assistant, Siri, is more engaging and expresses emotions better than Murphy. If I had to sum the experience up in a single word it'd be, "fucking-boring." I know that's two words but neither word alone accurately describes the experience. Plus, if you add a hyphen, it only counts as one word. Right? Maybe I should use a hashtag instead. #FuckingBoring.

Judge Takeda stares at me expectantly. "Mr. Valentine, are you ready to proceed?"

I glance up at Judge Takeda and then, rather than respond, turn and survey the jury. They look bored and tired. The Berkeley college student on the end, sitting in juror seat six, looks like he's dreaming about nude hipster coeds. His eyes are closed and a little bit of drool has accumulated in the right corner of his grinning mouth. He's leaning on his right hand and elbow and his left hand is actually resting on his Johnson. The retired nurse, sitting in juror seat one, who insists on wearing her uniform to court every day, even though the judge has forbidden any of the jurors from working until the trial is complete, is glaring at me with eyes that scream *you better not take too long*. It's the same look my ex used to give me during intercourse. The rest of the jurors look one part bored and two parts miserable.

The clock on the wall above the door reads 11:15. We've only been going for a little over two hours but it feels like an eternity. I glance at my client to confirm; yep, he still looks like a guilty piece-of-shit.

I continue to ignore the judge and turn around to get a good look at the rest of the courtroom. I lean against the "bar," the pony-wall divider that separates the audience, or "gallery," from the attorneys and judge. When you become an attorney, it's called "passing the bar" and it means you are now allowed to physically move past the bar in a courtroom and practice law. My law professor used to say, "The time when a student "passes the bar" and becomes an attorney is not a time for celebration, but rather a time for mourning. It's the last time that attorney will ever pass a bar without stopping." #SomeClichésAreTrue.

Most of the courtroom seats are empty. In the front row of the gallery, there's a young reporter wearing jeans, a t-shirt, and a hoodie. He's typing away on an iPad with a flat lime green plug-in keyboard attached. He probably rides an equally obnoxious colored bike. Nobody under thirty in San Francisco drives a car anymore; it's all bikes, BART, and Uber. Jeans-and-hoodie guy is lucky this judge allows electronic devices in his courtroom—many trapped-in-the-past judges don't. I wonder if anyone in his generation even knows how to use pen and paper? Do they still teach kids handwriting?

In the row behind jeans-and-hoodie reporter guy are a couple of what looks to be housing-challenged individuals. They're probably here for the free entertainment. This isn't quite Judge Judy, but a case like this does have some potential entertainment value. That is, assuming your entertainment tastes favor the dark, sick, and twisted. Still, it is a public proceeding and it's better to be in an air-conditioned courtroom than out in the heat.

Seated in the middle rows are a few of my colleagues. It's common practice for lawyers not busy in other courtrooms to watch their peers' closing arguments. Being a lawyer means constantly developing your craft, and the best way to do that is to watch others screw up. There's a reason it's called "practicing" law; invariably, we all fuck up. It's how you pivot and grow from those fuck-ups that makes a good lawyer. We also watch each other so we can razz each other. Lawyers are worse than internet trolls when it comes to professional bullying.

Notably missing from the courtroom, but not altogether unexpected, are the victim and her family. The ADA probably lost this trial when he put the victim on the stand against her will. The jury watched in horror while ADA Murphy tried to force testimony out of her. It's really difficult to convince twelve unbiased citizens that your truth, is the truth, when your own star witness won't agree with you. Murphy's overreach with the victim tainted everything he did from that point forward. He looked desperate, like he was willing to do anything to win, and juries don't respond well to desperation. Juries want to do the right thing. They want to feel good about their verdict. A lawyer's job is to give them the tools and information they need, so they can do the right thing.

Anyone who's been paying attention knows the jury has already made up its mind. My dirt-bag client's going to get off. At this point, my job is to just not do anything that might make them reconsider. Basically, just don't screw it up.

Also notably missing from the courtroom are the defendant's friends and family. Unfortunately, there's nothing I can do about that. My client's a total A-hole and doesn't have any friends. The family members I called all refused to be here. His sister told me, "I hope they give that sicko the chair." Then she had the balls to ask me to ask him, "Can I live in his house while he rots in prison?" Charming people, real salt-of- the-earth types.

Judge Takeda tries to get my attention again, "Mr. Valentine."

As I turn back towards the judge, I see a flash of lights and sense movement behind me. The back corner of the courtroom, which I swear was just empty, is now occupied by a short man in an expensive looking three-piece gray wool suit, holding an umbrella. A simple red tie and old-timey black and white Oxford wingtip shoes complete his ensemble. He's a man out of time and looks like he belongs in a *Scorsese* picture. He has one of those ageless faces; he could be thirty, or he could be sixty. I bet he gives fits to the guys who guess your age at carnivals. The umbrella's a further conundrum; it looks wet, as if he just stepped in out of a heavy rain—which is impossible, because it's Northern California and it almost never rains here. Isn't it supposed to be eighty degrees outside today?

"Mr. Valentine, any day now," says the judge.

I break my eyes away from the ageless man and focus on the judge. I probably shouldn't delay any further; it's clear from the judge's tone that he's losing his patience with me. I face the jury while I address the Court, "Judge, I think we could all use a break. I don't expect my closing argument will take all that long. I'll be done by 12:30, even with a fifteen-minute break, but before I proceed, there's a matter I need to address with the Court. Why don't we let the jury stretch their legs and get a cup of coffee? It hasn't been the most exciting morning."

That last little shot about it being a boring morning earns me a dirty look from ADA Murphy. He looks pissed, but is doing his darndest to remain quiet and not draw the jury's attention.

I made eye contact with the jury when I ask for the break, and not the judge, because I want the jury to feel like I'm on their side. I want them to believe I'm asking for a break on their behalf, that I'm their advocate. That way, no matter what the judge decides, the jury's going to empathize with me. If the judge agrees with my proposal, I look like a hero; I delivered the jury to their mid-morning coffee break. If he denies my proposal, he looks like the villain—not me. Either way, I come out smelling like roses.

Judge Takeda shrugs indifferently. "I think that's a good idea. Let's take a fifteen-minute break. Bailiff, please escort the jury out. Everyone else remain seated."

I remain standing; it's rude to sit when the jury is entering and exiting the courtroom. Contrary to what some think, the most important people in the room during a trial are the jury. The jury alone decides the case. Too many lawyers get caught up in the legal skirmishes, which are mostly heard out of the presence of the jury, or in impressing the judge, and fail to pay attention to what the jury actually observes. That's a fatal mistake.

I wait while the bailiff leads the jury into the deliberation room, which I know is stocked with coffee and donuts, because Murphy and I bought them. Budget cuts and re-worked local court rules have forced trial lawyers to step up and provide snacks for jurors out of their own pockets. It's a small price to pay for attentive and happy jurors. Once they've exited the courtroom and the door is firmly closed behind them, I address the Court, "Judge, would now be a good time to discuss the matter I mentioned?"

Without looking up from whatever he's reading, the judge answers in the same tone of voice my father used when he didn't want to be bothered, "Yes, Mr. Valentine, what is it?"

"As the Court's aware, at the outset of this trial I filed a motion *in limine* to exclude any mention that the state's witness, Miss Jones, was a prostitute, and/or that my client allegedly hired her. The Court granted that motion. Those facts are out of this case. My client's *not* on trial for soliciting a prostitute."

I pause and wait for the judge to look up; he doesn't, so I continue, "One of the slides Mr. Murphy displayed to the jury during is closing, said my client picked Miss Jones up while she was *walking the streets.* Mr. Murphy might as well have said *she was ho-ing* or *turning tricks.* The ADA effectively called her a hooker and insinuated that my client's nick-name was *John.* That's a clear violation of the Court's order and it's unfairly prejudicial to my client.

"Mr. Murphy can't unsay it and my client is entitled to a remedy. The Court should admonish the state and then read a corrective instruction to the jury. I propose the following: *This case is not about prostitution. The defendant, Mr. Silas, is not charged with any prostitution-related crimes. You are not to infer that Miss Jones was a prostitute or that Mr. Silas solicited her. You are not to consider or punish Mr. Silas for any prostitution-related crimes while reaching a verdict on the kidnapping and rape allegations in this case.* If the Court would like, I can hand up a handwritten version I wrote during Mr. Murphy's closing argument."

"Thank you, Mr. Valentine." The judge still hasn't looked up from whatever he's reading. "Please show it to

Mr. Murphy and then hand it to my bailiff. Mr. Murphy, would you like to be heard on this issue?"

"I would, Your Honor," answers Murphy in a shaky voice. "I don't think I violated the Court's ruling. The statements on the slides were factual. Ms. Jones was walking the streets when they met—"

Judge Takeda finally looks up from his papers and interrupts Mr. Murphy, "—Mr. Murphy, is the defendant charged with soliciting a prostitute?"

Murphy's shoulders slump forward and he looks down at his feet. "No, Your Honor."

"Then I see no harm in giving the instruction, but I'm not going to admonish the State for any wrongdoing. Are there any other pressing issues you two can't resolve yourselves, or can I take a break?" Judge Takeda rises up and heads back to his chambers without waiting for an answer. Takeda means warrior in Japanese. I can't help but smile and think it's a fitting name for the judge.

"No, Judge," I call after him.

Despite feeling good about how the case has played out, I am starting to tighten up. The magnitude of the situation is starting to settle in; the trial's almost over and a man's freedom is on the line. I flip my yellow legal pad over on the desk so no one can read my scribbles, and then head to the restroom myself. A million butterflies are moshing around in my stomach, my sphincter is clenching, and I have to pee something fierce.

Chapter Three

After the short break, Judge Takeda orders the bailiff to bring the jurors back in. I study the courtroom while we wait, and come to the conclusion that it lacks both functionality and charm. As far as courtrooms go, it sucks. The walls are covered in a tacky, faux wood paneling, and there's ugly, puke-colored carpeting. The counsel tables are too close together, only separated by a tiny media center, which gives you access to undersized speakers from the 1980's and a broken document projector. The no-man's land between the counsel tables and the judge's bench, the "well," is extremely small and awkward in shape.

It's generally bad medicine to enter the well without the Court's permission. The well is kind of like the White House's lawn—stay the hell off, unless you like getting tackled by security. I once saw a video where a Texas judge drew a Dirty Harry-sized .357 Magnum from under his robe and shot a man who entered his well without permission. If that's not the dictionary definition of excessive force, I don't know what is.

The jury box only has twelve seats, a design flaw shared by nearly every courtroom. Most trials sit twelve jurors, plus one to three alternates. If a juror is removed, or gets sick, an alternate takes their place. This trial is no exception; we sat fifteen—twelve jurors and three alternates. The alternates are crammed into uncomfortable metal folding chairs that are squeezed into the back row of the jury box.

Behind the bar that separates the gallery from the rest of the courtroom there are numerous rows of 1970's movie theater style folding chairs, complete with faded red cushions. Some of the cushions even have stains that look and smell like they were caused by buttery fingers. The County probably stole the seats from an old rundown theater.

The jurors file back in and take their seats. "Mr. Valentine, you may proceed," says Judge Takeda.

"Thank you, Judge."

I circle the attorney table and enter the oblong-shaped well. Fortunately, there's no gun fire. Judge Takeda is allowing us to use the well during closing arguments. It's a good thing too; I'm not wearing the right shoes for dodging bullets.

I stop when I reach the well's center and address the judge, "May it please the Court," and then the jury, "Ladies and gentlemen of the jury, good afternoon. In case you forgot, it has been a long trial, my name is Colt Valentine and I represent Roy Silas." I motion with my arm toward my dirt-bag client who's sitting next to my empty seat at the counsel table. I resist the urge to check, but I hope he isn't smiling. Roy has a really disturbing smile. It makes you want to lock all your doors, turn off the lights, and cower in the shower—with a loaded shotgun.

Roy Silas is about five-foot-seven and looks like he ate a few too many gyros. He's barrel chested, not fat, but not skinny either. Roy is second-generation Greek/American and doesn't talk much; but when he does speak, he speaks with a harsh accent he must have picked up from his parents. Other than his electric blue eyes, nothing about him stands out, but there's something not quite right behind those eyes. When you talk to him, he stares directly at you like he's trying to determine if he should use a spoon or a spork to scoop your eyes out. He's a creepy dude.

"I want to thank each and every one of you for your service. The Court, the Government and I all thank you for the time and effort you've all invested into this case." I include the Court and Government when I thank the jury, because neither entity is likely to object and it gives the jury the impression, that I am speaking with more authority than I actually am.

"We're on the home stretch," I say with a smile, "almost to the end." Some of the jurors return my smile, a good sign.

"I promise I'm not going to spend too much time rehashing the evidence in this case and I'm not going to bore you with a PowerPoint presentation." That earns me a loud chuckle from juror three, a union pipefitter, and another dirty look from ADA Murphy.

"I do want to briefly discuss the actual facts of this case, which are *very* different than the fantasy the Government, Mr. Murphy, *read* to you this morning." Nobody likes or trusts the Government, especially Californians, particularly in today's fake-news political climate. It's always a good idea to remind the jury that the Assistant District Attorney is the *Government*. In a perfect world, the law of transference will transfer any dislike the jury has for the Government to the ADA.

"It is undisputed that Joycee Baird was kidnapped, held prisoner, and raped over and over. This case is not about whether or not that happened—it happened." I pause for a moment while that sinks in. "This case is about whether the prosecution has proven beyond a reasonable doubt that my client, Mr. Silas, is the rapist—he's not. And the Government hasn't."

I glance down at my yellow pad, I don't need it, but pacing is important. "Last week you heard testimony from Officer Joe, the police officer who investigated Joycee Baird's initial disappearance. He was the funny guy who told us that defense lawyer joke. You all remember—it was something about the commonality of defense lawyers and sperm and how they both have the same chance, 1 in 30,000, of becoming a human being." Nearly all the jurors laugh at the reminder of the joke. "At least I've got a chance," I say with a laugh, and the jury laughs again.

Part of a lawyer's job is to entertain the jury. Making fun of yourself is the easiest way to do that, at least without offending anyone. It's also important to, whenever possible, try and lump yourself in with the jury by using terms like "us" and "we."

"Officer Joe told us that Ms. Baird disappeared from the tech company where she worked. Her car was left in the parking lot, nobody saw her leave, and nothing suspicious was caught on any of the surveillance cameras. She hadn't packed a bag, none of her bank accounts were accessed, none of her credit cards were used, and her cell phone was turned off. Although he tried, there was no way to track her down. Joycee Baird vanished without a trace."

I pause and slightly shift my position in the well to signal a slight change in topics. "We then heard testimony from Harold Zhou, the Good Samaritan who found Ms. Baird on the side of the road, *three months* after her disappearance. When Mr. Zhou found her, she was naked, bloody, battered, and missing large chunks of hair—the hair had been ripped out by the roots. She was talking incoherently, and she kept screaming something about a man with the head of a pig. Thank God, Mr. Zhou chose to stop and help her. Thank God, he did the right thing."

I nod as I talk about Mr. Zhou, and nearly every juror nods right along with me. I'm programming them to follow rules and do the right thing—just like Harold Zhou did. I also verbally thanked God, twice, which is always a good idea. Thanking God resonates with believers, and since it's such a common saying in our society, non-believers ignore it.

"We next heard from Doctor Smith, he told us Joycee Baird was raped and beaten severely—almost to *death*. He said Joycee had three broken ribs and that some of her teeth had been knocked out. She was suffering from extreme dehydration, malnutrition, and her vagina had suffered severe trauma. Doctor Smith said Joycee was mutilated internally, likely from insertion of something with sharp edges. Any sort of future sexual relationship will be difficult for her—painful at the very least. She'll never be able to have children. All of that happened and it's terrible. None of that is disputed or at issue in this trial."

I wipe a tear away from my cheek. "No human being should have to go through what that poor woman went through. It is unacceptable. We are failing as a species. How can one human being do that to another?" Emotion enters into my voice. This isn't acting for me. What happened to that girl is disgusting. Unfortunately, my job isn't to punish the wicked, nor is it to determine guilt or innocence. My job is to protect society by exercising the rights of those who are accused of crimes. My job is to protect the *people* of this country by making the Government do its job.

I stop and stare directly at the ADA. The jury's heads all turn in unison with mine. Everyone in the courtroom is now staring at Murphy. He swallows air and starts to turn red. It's counter-intuitive, but many lawyers hate being the focus of inquiry. By nature, lawyers are presenters; they like to scrutinize other people and things, and to tell stories about others. Lawyers make good game show hosts and bad contestants.

I continue to stare at Murphy while the silence and anticipation build to a crescendo. "We also heard from the victim, Joycee Baird, herself. You remember Mr. Murphy put her on that stand," I point at the witness stand, "and *made* her testify."

I wait while the jury reflects back on the day Ms. Baird testified. Everyone in the courtroom is remembering how it was painfully obvious she wanted to be somewhere else, anywhere else, than here. Mr. Murphy kept her on the stand for over two hours. He argued with her, badgered her, and tried to get her to identify my client, his home, his car, anything to tie my client to the crime. All Joycee kept saying over and over again was, *"I don't remember. I don't remember anything. Stop asking me questions, I don't remember."* It wasn't the finest two hours in the career of Assistant District Attorney Brad Murphy.

"We all remember her testimony, even if Mr. Murphy doesn't want us to." I might have gone too far with that last comment. It was a bit of a heavy-handed volley at the Assistant District Attorney, but it didn't draw an objection. Probably because he's distracted by all the eyeballs staring at him. Murphy's starting to get hot under the collar. He keeps tugging at his tie.

I pause to let him sweat while the jury compares and contrasts my examination of Ms. Baird with his. They're remembering I didn't press her on anything and only asked her questions for about five minutes before I politely asked the judge if she could be excused. I used her examination as a tool to adjust their expectations of me. I wanted them to see that things aren't always what they seem. The Government lawyer isn't always the good guy, and the defense attorney isn't always an ambulance-chasing-scumbag.

The key to winning a trial is winning the jury's trust. Jurors want to trust, and a good lawyer gives them reasons to trust. Contrary to what you see on television, it's rarely a good idea to beat up on a victim. It almost always blows up in the face of the attorney doing the beating. In this case, it blew up in Murphy's face—spectacularly.

At this point in my closing, I could double down, and rehash the victim's testimony. I could put the words, "I don't remember," up on a poster board or in a PowerPoint. Many other lawyers probably would. Instead, I chose to trust the jury. Sometimes testimony is so vivid and so powerful, you can't make it any better, you can only ruin it.

"What happened to Ms. Baird was horrific and what's really terrifying is that it could have happened to anyone." I pause and let the jurors imagine how they'd feel if this happened to them, their mother, their daughter, their sister. Playing with the jury's emotions like this is dangerous. I don't want them to channel their fears into punishing my client. At the same time, it's important to show the jury that you feel the same way they do. You want them to identify with you. It's like slicing prosciutto—too thin, and you can't taste it; too thick, and you have salami.

"We all agree, what happened to Joycee Baird was a terrible thing. That's not an issue for you to decide in this trial. What is at issue in this trial is the life of my client, Roy Silas." I pause while the gravity of that sinks in.

"When I'm done speaking, Judge Takeda is going to instruct you on the law. He's going to tell you that the Government, Mr. Murphy, has the burden of proof in this case. The fact that a criminal charge has been filed against Mr. Silas, Roy, is not evidence that the charge is true. You must not be biased against Roy just because he's been arrested, charged with a crime, and brought to trial. That's not the same as guilt. Roy Silas is presumed to be innocent. I'm going to say that again, Roy is *presumed*, under the law, to be innocent."

I'm using Roy's first name to humanize him to the jury, but I don't want to overdo it. If I use his first name too many times, I might draw a speaking objection from the prosecution. To avoid exposing the jury to potentially prejudicial information, lawyers are supposed to make plain vanilla objections, rather than wordy objections, and request side-bars if they want to explain the objection to the judge.

Unfortunately, there's no real consequence for making a speaking objection and it happens all the time. If Murphy was a good lawyer, he'd make a speaking objection suggesting that I'm trying to play on the jury's sympathies by using my client's first name, thereby eroding all of the trust that I've worked so hard to cultivate.

If that happened, I could complain and Judge Takeda might admonish Mr. Murphy, but the damage would already be done. The cat would already be out of the bag and, for some reason, we all know you can't put a cat back in a bag. #WTFDoesThatEvenMean? #WhoPutsCatsInBags?

"The Government must prove beyond any reasonable doubt that Mr. Silas raped and kidnapped Ms. Baird. Otherwise, you must find him *not* guilty. It's the *Government's* heavy burden of proof. Roy doesn't have to prove anything. If you were charged with a crime, you wouldn't have to prove anything. In America, you do not have to prove your innocence. The Government must prove your guilt, and they must do so beyond a reasonable doubt. This is a bedrock principle of our legal system.

"Proof beyond a reasonable doubt is proof that leaves you with an abiding conviction that the charge is true. Not possibly true, not more likely true than not true, but *true*. The evidence need not eliminate all possible doubt because everything in life is open to some possible or imaginary doubt, but it must be proof beyond any reasonable doubt. Now this is a much higher standard than the burden of proof in a civil case. In a civil case, the parties need only prove that the issue was more likely true than not true. This is not that. This is a much higher burden. The Government must demonstrate guilt beyond any reasonable doubt."

I can hear my client squirming in his chair behind me. I know I'm being a little repetitive but the burden of proof is the most important instruction in a criminal trial. It's important to sear the language into the jury's mind. You want to arm them with the phrase, "It's the Government's heavy burden," so they can be your advocate during deliberations.

"In deciding whether the Government has proven its case beyond a reasonable doubt, you must impartially compare and consider all the evidence that was received throughout the entire trial. Unless the evidence proves Roy Silas' guilt beyond a reasonable doubt, he is entitled to an acquittal, and you must find him not guilty."

I pause and spend a moment making eye contact with each juror. As I make eye contact, I nod and many of the jurors nod in return.

The judge is also going to instruct the jury on the law before sending them back to deliberate. When the judge restates the law exactly as I have, it will subconsciously reinforce the jury's trust in everything else I've said.

"Your job in this trial is to decide the facts. You must use *only* the evidence that was actually presented in this courtroom. Evidence is the sworn testimony of witnesses, and the exhibits that were actually admitted by the Court, like the negative DNA test results the lab technician Dr. Simms talked about with us on the stand yesterday." The jury nods.

"Nothing that the Government *said* is evidence. All that Government *spin*—is not evidence. Only the witnesses' testimony and their answers to questions while they were on the stand are evidence."

I pause to give the law a chance to take root in the jury's minds. I walk over to my desk and casually pick up the yellow legal pad I had previously set face down on the desk. I glance at it and then set it back down, this time face up so that my client, and only my client, can read it. It reads: "*Do not make any sounds, faces, or express any emotion whatsoever.*"

This is a crucial point in my closing. Throughout the trial, I've repeatedly told Mr. Silas he needs to keep his emotions in check. I'm about to discuss some things that

Mr. Silas is going to find uncomfortable. Unfortunately, this is not the NFL, I can't take a timeout in the middle of my closing argument to discuss strategy with Roy, or to calm him down. Through experience, I've found that a pre-planned written reminder can be a useful tool to keep a client on track, especially, when the client is himself a tool.

"Let's talk about the few facts that are actually relevant to what you have to decide in this trial. During Mr. Murphy's closing, you heard him read three words off his slides, over and over and over again: *Proximity*, *dungeon*, and *scarf*. The Government told you those three words prove Roy Silas kidnapped and raped Joycee Baird—they don't. The Government also claims global warming isn't real and there are no aliens stored at Area 51 ... you shouldn't believe everything the Government tells you." Several of the jurors chuckle.

Mr. Murphy stands and feigns his best appalled look; he starts to object and then changes his mind and sits back down.

Judge Takeda's head rises from his reading material and gives me a look, part mirth, part annoyance, and then addresses the jury, "Please disregard Mr. Valentine's last comments. Let me remind you, the arguments of counsel are not evidence nor are his bad jokes." Judge Takeda then turns and addresses me, "Mr. Valentine, the Government's position on climate change is not on trial here. Neither are the contents of Area 51—if that's even a real place. Your client, however, is very real. You might want to focus on his trial." The jury laughs again, this time at my expense. I smile and laugh along with them.

"Yes Judge," I answer. To the jury it appears as if nothing meaningful happened. In reality, the judge's comments communicated volumes. They were a warning shot across my bow that said, "Mr. Valentine, it doesn't appear that Mr. Murphy can defend himself and I want a fair trial; so from this point forward, I'm going to do whatever I have to do, even if that means doing the ADA's job for him, to keep the trial balanced. So, behave."

While Mr. Murphy should have objected and the judge should have sustained the objection, the judge should not have *sua sponte* intervened on the ADA's behalf. Judges are supposed to leave it to the lawyers to defend themselves and follow the old adage, let the players decide the game—not the referee. Judges and referees have a lot in common, nobody likes them, but we all agree we need them. Still, this was beyond the bounds of fair play.

You rarely ever want to show the jury you're frustrated. If you do, you'd better be doing it intentionally, to make a point. Outwardly I'm projecting confidence, everything is okay, everything is going as I planned, continue to trust me. Inwardly, I'm raging at Judge Takeda. He shouldn't be interfering with the trial. The judge is supposed to stay neutral and not take sides. Particularly, not the side of the Government, who already has all the power, resources, and advantages in a criminal case. Criminal defense is an upstream battle from the get-go. The default setting for many jurors is, "We wouldn't be here if the accused wasn't guilty." Although the law says innocent until proven guilty, reality dictates otherwise. A defendant in a criminal trial, always starts out behind.

In an effort to reassure the jury, I just keep on smiling— it's the only thing I can do.

"Let's talk about *proximity*." I say. "Joycee Baird was found by the Good Samaritan Harold Zhou on the Golden Gate Park side of Lincoln Way, past the Botanical Gardens, near the single digit avenues in the Inner Sunset District of San Francisco. Mr. Silas lives in Doelger City, an area in the Outer Sunset District near the Park between 27th and 39th Avenue. It's about a mile and a half from where she was found. For those of you not familiar with the area, the stylistic stucco homes in that neighborhood were all built between the 1920's and the 1940's by the same builder, Doelger; hence the name.

"Golden Gate Park is about three miles long and one-half mile wide. There are literally thousands of homes surrounding it—thousands of homes within a mile and a half of where Ms. Baird was found. She could have been held at any one of them, and there's no evidence that Ms. Baird was *ever* at Mr. Silas' home.

"Proximity, or the mere coincidence that Roy Silas lived within a mile and a half of where Ms. Baird was found, does not make him her kidnapper or rapist. Let me say it again: merely living near where Ms. Baird was found does not make you, or Roy, or anyone else a kidnapper or a rapist." I say that last part as if it were a mantra at an Alcoholics Anonymous meeting. I want the jury to personalize and remember it. I want it etched into their brains.

"Let's talk about the so-called *dungeon*. As you know, the Government called Vivian Jones—", I almost say 'the hooker', "—to the stand on Monday. Ms. Jones told us she met Mr. Silas in the Tenderloin district and he brought her back to his place and showed her his basement. No one's disputing that she called it a torture dungeon and said there were a lot of whips, and hanging chains, and even a ball gag. She testified Roy Silas had a pretty weird sexual appetite and asked her if he could tie her up. It's also undisputed that she told us she was creeped out by Roy and his dungeon and she wanted to leave.

"Now, you all remember, I asked her, straight up, did he threaten you? And she said, *No*. Then I asked her, did he try to tie you up anyway? She said, *No*. And finally, I asked her, did he let you leave? And she said, *Yes*.

"Roy didn't threaten Ms. Jones, he didn't try to tie her up against her will, and he let her leave when she wanted to. How the Government jumped to the conclusion that Mr.

Silas is a rapist based on *her* testimony is beyond me. Roy Silas may be a sexual savant, whose tastes are not the norm, and frankly are … a bit out there. I think he fancies himself as Mr. Grey and apparently wants to get his 50 Shades on." The jury laughs. Laughter is a good sign that indicates I haven't lost them. A laughing jury is unlikely to put a man in prison for life.

"Does anyone think Mr. Grey should be arrested for his perverted sexual appetite? How about people who enjoyed that movie? Come on, I know you've all seen it. I know Assistant District Attorney Murphy probably has." I hook my thumb at the ADA and the jury laughs again. "Ladies and gentleman, being into bondage does not make you a kidnapper or a rapist," I pause for comic effect, "and in Roy Silas's case, it just makes him a sad guy with an overly imaginative sex life." Many of the jurors snicker. It's better to paint Roy as awkward and pathetic than a rapist.

"Now, Ms. Jones wasn't the only witness to testify about the so-called *dungeon*. Dr. Simms also testified about the basement. Remember, he was the CSI guy, the lab technician, who scoured the basement searching for any trace of Ms. Baird's blood, hair, or body fluids. Do you remember what he said when I asked him what he found? He said, '*Nothing*.' His words, not mine.

Now does that mean there's no possibility that she was ever there? No, he didn't go that far. But Dr. Simms did tell us that, based on the condition she was found in, it's likely he would have found some trace of blood, hair, or other bodily fluids if she had been there … and he found *nothing*. Dr. Simms said it was one of the cleanest basements he'd ever been in. Ladies and gentlemen, merely having a sex-dungeon in your basement does not make you, or Roy, or anyone else, a kidnapper or a rapist."

I take a moment to survey the jury; they all seem to be listening, which is another good sign. They also all seem tired, which is a not-so-good sign. I need to wrap this up before I lose their attention.

"Finally, let's talk about the *scarf.* The police found a scarf in the trunk of Mr. Silas' car. A scarf that looks similar to the one Ms. Baird was wearing the day she disappeared. We all know this because we all saw surveillance footage from inside her workplace on the day she disappeared. Again, there was no hair, blood, or bodily fluids found in Mr. Silas' car. No DNA in the *car.*"

I emphasize the word "car" and purposefully avoid discussing DNA testing of the scarf, because it tested positive for her DNA, but the jury doesn't know that. The police misplaced the scarf for two days before it was tested, breaking the chain of custody. I filed a pre-trial motion *in limine* to exclude that evidence on the basis it could have been tampered with during the two days it went missing. The Court agreed and the DNA evidence was excluded, and it will remain excluded unless I'm stupid enough to talk about the testing—which I'm not.

"During his arrest, Mr. Silas told police he had no idea where the scarf came from. It might have belonged to his sister, or a friend; he doesn't remember how it got in his trunk. There's nothing particularly unique about this scarf; it and thousands of others just like it were sold at Bay Area department stores last Christmas. I admit it looks a lot like the one Ms. Baird is wearing in the surveillance video, but that doesn't mean this one was hers. They could just be similar scarves. Remember, Mr. Murphy asked Ms. Baird if it was her scarf, and she told us, 'I don't know.' If she can't tell if it was hers, how can ADA Murphy? I bet you all know what I am going to say now—merely having a *scarf* in your trunk does not make you, or Roy, or anyone else, a kidnapper or a rapist." A good mantra can hook a jury, and this one is catchy. I can see some of the jurors mouthing it along with me.

Now for the grand finale: "Ladies and gentleman of the jury, it's clear that you cannot convict Roy Silas. The Government has utterly failed to prove its case beyond a reasonable doubt. Because of the Government's failure, please return the only verdict this evidence demands—not guilty. Return Roy to his life, his friends, his family, and his job. Do the right thing. Do the just thing. Do what the evidence demands. Thank you."

Regardless of my internal feelings, it's always important to show deference to the Court, at least when the jury is present, so I turn to the judge, and say, "Thank you, Judge Takeda."

What I'd really like to do is tell the judge something altogether different, specifically to go to fuck himself, but I don't. I restrain myself by practicing the ancient wisdom of *if you don't have nothing nice to say don't say nothing at all*. #Woosa.

I sit back down at my desk, smile at the jury, and try to appear as if I'm paying attention while the judge instructs them on the law. Once the jury is sent back to the deliberation room and Mr. Silas is taken back into custody, the bailiff takes down Murphy's and my cell phone numbers and tells us he'll call when the jury reaches a verdict. The trial is now out of my hands and all I can do is wait.

Chapter Four

I'm sitting at the counter of a local bakery eating a turkey sandwich when my cell phone rings. It's a number I don't recognize, but it has a San Francisco area code, so I answer. "Colt Valentine speaking."

"Mr. Valentine, this is Vikram Naidu; I am Judge Takeda's bailiff. He asked me to let you know the jury has reached a verdict."

"That was fast. It's only been an hour." I pause, I'm fishing for information, hoping the bailiff will fill the silence with useful information, but he isn't biting. After a few seconds of awkward silence, I ask, "When does the judge want us back?"

"Thirty minutes from now."

"Have you let my client know?"

The bailiff answers, "Yes."

"Thanks." I hang up.

An hour is a real short measurement of time for a jury to deliberate. In a criminal case, a short deliberation usually means a guilty verdict. It means the jury went around the table and on the first pass, all unanimously voted guilty. That almost never happens with a finding of not guilty, because there is almost always at least one juror who slept through the trial and decided they were going to vote guilty, no matter what. A not guilty finding typically requires discussion, and discussion takes time.

It's both ironic and tragic; juries rush to condemn, but take their sweet time to award freedom. I've always thought society would be better off if it were the other way around, but what do I know? I'm stuck in the past. I still like Guns N' Roses, and 2Pac, and I think it's dumb to wear sunglasses at night. I am hardly a case study for progressivism.

I pay for the sandwich and coke, call my office and let them know a verdict is imminent, and race back to the Courthouse. I'm hoping to get there early enough to speak with my client before the verdict is read. I need to manage his expectation and more importantly, his behavior.

Chapter Five

It takes me about twenty minutes to return to the Courthouse, fight my way through the security line, and get to the courtroom. My client's already sitting at the counsel table when I arrive. Assistant District Attorney Brad Murphy is in the back talking with some of the other attorneys from his office. Jeans-and-hoodie guy is back in the front row, staring intently at something on his cell phone, and the ageless man is back sitting in the back row. He somehow makes the uncomfortable cinema seat look both stylish and comfortable. He is staring at me and I think he just winked. Nah, couldn't be. I must be seeing things. Maybe I imagine it? I haven't had any sleep in twenty-four hours and I'm nearing a crashing point. Hopefully, the turkey sandwich doesn't wipe me out. #TryptophanIsARealThing.

Near the door sits a young blonde girl, wearing a hoodie and large sunglasses. She's fidgeting with her ring, just like she did when she was on the stand. She looks like she might bolt at any moment. The blonde wig, baggy clothes, hoodie, and sunglasses will probably fool the reporters, but that's Joycee Baird. Maybe this trial meant more to her than she was letting on.

My stomach tightens a bit; I have a feeling she's not going to like the verdict. I walk over to my client, lean in close and whisper, "No matter what the verdict is, you are not going to show any emotion. You got that?"

Roy Silas, ever the chatty-Kathy, looks at me and grunts, not really a grunt of agreement, more of a "piss-off" grunt.

I lean in a little closer, "Roy, I want to be very clear with you. If the verdict is not-guilty, and you celebrate, clap, smile, or even take too deep a breath, I'm going to stand up, scream bloody murder, and cause a mistrial. Then I'm going to walk over to the ADA and explain exactly what he did wrong. I doubt he fucks it up on the second go-round. You're *not* going to show *any* emotion. You're going to thank the judge, thank the jury, and wait to celebrate until after you have left the Courthouse. You will *not* speak to any reporters. You will *not* say anything derogatory about Ms. Baird. You will behave. Do you understand me?"

"You wouldn't do that. You'd lose your license," he whispers.

"Yes, I fucking would. Test me."

Roy look up and stares at me with his dark soulless eyes and I stare right back into the darkness. I let my eyes convey the seriousness of my threat. Self-preservation sets in and Roy finally nods in agreement.

The judge takes the bench. "Bailiff, please bring the jury in."

Once all the jurors have taken their seats, the judge asks, "Will the jury foreman stand up?" The juror in seat ten, a stock analyst at one of the big brokerage firms in the financial district, stands.

"Have you reached a verdict?" asks the judge.

The juror stutters but manages to answer, "Yes, Your Honor." He's trembling, probably doesn't get to do a lot of public speaking. The jury as a whole look nervous, like they have a bad taste in their mouth. "We, we, the, a, jury, find the defendant *not* guilty on all counts."

Joycee jumps up from her seat and rushes out of the courtroom. The heavy courtroom door slams behind her, echoing through the uncomfortably silent courtroom. Roy Silas begins to smile; I grab him by the arm and squeeze hard enough to leave a mark. His smile vanishes.

Judge Takeda asks Assistant District Attorney Brad Murphy if he wants the jury polled. Murphy answers yes and each juror stands up and declares under oath that *not* guilty is, in fact, their decision.

The ADA and I finish making our record in case either side wants to file an appeal, unlikely, but a necessary formality. The judgment is entered and the jury is excused. I motion the Court to order my client's release. The judge asks if there is any objection. Murphy answers yes and requests a twenty-four hour hold while he confers with his dick of a boss about a potential appeal. I object to keeping my client in jail another night on constitutional grounds and demand Roy's immediate release. The Court agrees with me and orders the Government to release Mr. Silas by the close of business.

Mr. Murphy turns to me, "You just got a rapist off. How are you going to feel when he does it again?"

I consider responding to Murphy with something like, *I'm not the one who screwed up; it's your job to protect society from criminals. It's my job to protect society from you. I did my job. Learn to do your job better, Jerk,* but I don't. I don't respond at all. Part of me agrees with him. I watch while he packs his bags and exits the courtroom. It's never a good idea to pour gasoline on a raging fire.

The bailiff approaches, "Mr. Silas, I need to take you back into custody so you can be processed and released."

"Could you give us a moment?" I ask. The bailiff shrugs and walks over to the other side of the room to flirt with the Court reporter. Once he is out of earshot, I turn to Roy. "You just won the lottery. You probably don't deserve it, but you're getting a second chance. Don't blow it."

Roy's not listening, he is tuning me out. He doesn't appear to give a fuck about what I'm saying.

"Listen, scumbag," I hiss. "You're on the cops' radar now. They're going be watching you. They're going to be gunning for you. You better stay on the straight and narrow.

If you screw up again, I'm *not* going to defend you. You hurt another girl and I'll be there helping the cops shovel dirt on your coffin. Do you understand me?"

Roy leans in towards me, close enough that I can feel his warm breath, and whispers, "If you ever touch me again…" he touches his arm where I grabbed him. "I'll cut your tongue out and fuck you with it. Do you understand *me*, Counselor?"

I smile at Roy. He does have a way with words. "You'll use my tongue? Is that because you have a small dick, or because you have a hard time getting it up? I bet it's a combination of the two. Am I right?"

Roy's eyes narrow and he balls his hand into a fist. Strangely, I want him to hit me. I believe he was entitled to a good defense and I gave him the best, but I really don't want this rapist to go free.

After a moment of staring at me with his hate-filled eyes, Roy manages to calm himself, unclenches his fist, and yells to the bailiff, "I'm ready to go."

The bailiff saunters over and leads Roy away. At the door, Roy turns back to me. "I'll be seeing you, Counselor."

"For your sake, I hope not."

And like that, he's gone, hopefully out of my life forever. This isn't the movies, we aren't friends, were not ever going to hang out, watch a game, or share a beer. I never met him before I was assigned his case and I hope I never have to see him again. Bottom line, he is a scumbag and I am just his court appointed lawyer. A lawyer who did his job well, maybe too well. Yay me. I can't help thinking to myself, why am I doing this? Is this really my life?

Chapter Six

In San Francisco, the local media has agreements in place with some of the Courthouse staff where tips about the status of interesting cases are exchanged for unmarked envelopes full of tax-free lettuce. These agreements make escaping the Courthouse after a verdict without giving an interview, difficult, if not impossible.

I exit the courtroom and start swimming through the swarm of reporters who want a sound-bite, or a video for television, or a website, something to sandwich between stories about who's dating who in Hollywood and something disparaging about either the former or current president. You know, the same thing you saw on the news last night and the night before that.

A particularly attractive African-American woman wearing a short skirt, four-inch heels with crimson-colored soles, and a revealing blouse, shoves a microphone in my direction and asks, "Are you with the District Attorney's office?"

She's definitely a television reporter. Internet reporters typically go for comfort and wear flats in this hilly city, where heels are one step down the path towards a gruesome ankle injury. I think I recognize her from the local evening news; her name is Michelle, Mya, something with an M. She's not wearing a wedding ring; maybe I can leverage an interview into a drink, maybe dinner. I did just win a case, even if it wasn't a good win, and I'm feeling a bit cocky. #I'mInTheBuildingAndI'mFeelingMyself.

Then I consider how I'll feel if she shoots me down. This hallway is pretty crowded, and everyone and their mother has a tape recorder, cell phone, or camera pointed in my direction. I can already see the title of the YouTube clip: "Public Defender Crashes and Burns with Hot Reporter." I bet it gets more hits than a stadium wedding proposal gone wrong. Ultimately, I chicken out and play it straight, "No, I'm not with the District Attorney's office."

Michelle or Mya doesn't even say thank you, she just brushes past me. Apparently, I'm chopped liver and she's looking for steak.

Jeans-and-a-hoodie guy, the reporter with the lime green keyboard, approaches and asks for a statement. I know he expects me to give the proverbial "No comment," but I've found that "No comment," in and of itself, is a comment. Reporters love "No comment;" it signals you're a lying douchebag, and it's quotable on the five o'clock news. Take for example the following exchanges:

Q. Did you have sex with that woman?

A. No comment.

Q. Are you running for President?

A. No comment.

Q. Was the officiating terrible tonight?

A. No comment.

In each of the above examples, "No comment" actually provides an answer. It says, Yes, I had sex with that woman; Yes, I am running for president; and Yes, the ref sucked. If the answer was No to any of those questions, the interviewee would just say No. 'No' is easier to say than 'No comment,' it's fewer words; and answering No puts an end to any follow-up questions. Defense lawyers as a profession already have a terrible enough reputation without me contributing to it. The last thing I want is to be on the evening news, looking like a lying D-bag.

Rather than "No comment," I give a nonsense response: "I had lunch at a wonderful deli in the Mission District. Had a great turkey sandwich, it was crantastic," and I keep swimming towards the elevator.

A few years ago, I realized I could stay out of the news by giving reporters unquotable responses, or by answering different questions altogether. I started off by answering every reporter's question with a plug for my favorite Italian food restaurant. If I was asked, "Do you believe the judge fairly applied the law?" I'd answer, "They have the best meatballs at Tony's." If I was asked, "Are you going to appeal?" I'd answer, "I love the cioppino at Tony's."

No newsroom editor will play a video where the interviewee is shamelessly plugging a restaurant. Even if they did, the public would just think the newsroom was up to some shenanigans. They'd ask themselves, "What bozo would answer a question like that?" and conclude that it must be the editing. #FakeNews.

Sure, the reporter knows I'm being an evasive dick, but the public doesn't. Most of the public would still think it was fake news, even if the reporter released the raw footage; and even if they did, no one would care. I'm just a piss-ant Public Defender. No one cares what I say.

Unfortunately, about three years ago, I got in trouble and was suspended for a week without pay for an ethics violation related to this practice. I've been "retrained," and according to the press release, I now know that talking to the media falls within the job duties of a public defender, and also that Government employees are not supposed to endorse private businesses while acting within the scope of their employment. My bad; I've now been sufficiently rehabilitated and have promised not to make that exact same mistake again.

So now I just talk about food generically without specifically mentioning the name of any specific restaurants. My boss still doesn't like it, but screw him; I'm not violating any ethics rules and I hate giving interviews.

Despite my brush-off, jeans-and-hoodie guy keeps pace with me on the way to the elevator. To make matters worse, some of the other reporters begin to follow us. Even the pretty girl in crimson bottomed shoes joins the chase. They're like bloodhounds chasing a rabbit, and I'm the rabbit. A tired and slow rabbit. The hounds overtake me en masse at the elevator. Feeling boxed in and seeing no viable escape route and still having a bad taste in my mouth from my last discussion with Roy Silas, I decide to give a statement. Maybe I can shine a light on his neighborhood and issue a subtle warning.

I turn towards the gaggle of reporters, "Look I'm not going to take any questions, but I will make a brief statement." I wait for the reporters to get their cameras, cell phones and microphones pointed at me.

Just when I'm about to launch into my statement, the pretty reporter interrupts me, this time with a practiced smile. "Um, who *are* you?"

Before I can answer, jeans-and-hoodie answers for me, "The Public Defender who tried the case, Colt Valentine."

The pretty reporter frowns and says under her breath, just loud enough so I can hear it, "Isn't he a bit young to try a rape and kidnapping case?"

She isn't wrong but the comment still deflates my ego a little. Most murder trials, in most counties, get assigned to geriatrics with decades of experience. I've been fortunate, or unfortunate, depending on your point of view, to work in an office where nearly all of the senior, better paid attorneys, are regularly laid off due to budget cuts. It's funny how the District Attorney office always finds funding to keep their experienced attorneys, while the Public Defender's office repeatedly gets screwed. Some might argue the system is designed to skew in the governments favor.

I take a deep breath, shake off the pretty reporter's insult, and address the crowd, "Look folks, my name is Colt

Valentine and I represented the accused Roy Silas. The jury found Mr. Silas *not* guilty of all charges. He is going to be released later this afternoon and will be returning to his home in the Doelger City neighborhood." It's not a breach of the attorney-client privilege to disclose where my client lives; it's public record. It's perhaps done in poor taste, but it's not a breach of any ethical duty, and under the circumstances, it feels like the right thing to do.

"Although today was a good day for Roy Silas, let's not forget that Joycee Baird's rapist and kidnapper is still on the loose. Everyone, particularly those who live near the Park, need to look out for one another. If you see something suspicious, please call the SFPD. Keep your eyes and ears open. Thanks." I'm saved from most of the awkward follow-up questions by the ding of the arriving elevator.

The rude reporter works her way right up next to me. "Makayla Hill, from Local News. Is it true that Mr. Silas has a *dungeon* in his basement?"

Makayla, huh, I knew it was an M name.

I step into the elevator, turn, and hit the close door button. Strangely, none of the reporters, not even Makayla, enter the elevator with me. I smile at my good fortune. They're probably afraid they'll miss their chance with the Assistant District Attorney if they leave the floor. An ADA is a better grab for a reporter, better for ratings. Joe public doesn't want to hear what some scumbag defense attorney has to say. These vultures, apparently don't realize that Murphy snuck out of the courtroom before they descended on the hallway and I'm sure not going to clue them in.

From inside the elevator, I make eye contact with Makayla Hill and decide to answer her question, "Yes, he does." Maybe my public identification of his neighborhood, and public acknowledgment that he has a dungeon in his basement, will make the five o'clock news. Maybe it'll prevent another kidnapping. Even if my words are unlikely to make any difference, I feel better having said them. The elevator door shuts and I exhale deeply while unbuttoning the top button of my shirt and loosening my tie. I can turn the lawyer persona off. It's been a long day and I need a bottle of wine.

Chapter Seven

I unlock the driver side door of my Honda and then freeze. Something isn't right. Someone's been inside my car, which should be impossible; the doors were locked, no windows are broken, the alarm appears to be working, and I have the only key. But none of those things change the fact that someone's broken into my car and placed a small black jewelry box onto my driver's seat.

I scan the underground parking garage for anything out of the ordinary, but nothing seems amiss. There are no creepy-looking individuals in trench coats, no vans with blacked-out windows, no flickering lights, nothing that directly jumps out at me.

After satisfying myself that no one is hiding in the shadows waiting to kidnap me, I begin to study the box without touching it. There are no visible writings or markings on it. It's the kind of small, plain, black, velvety ring presentation box you might use to propose to your girl.

After a few minutes of intense staring, I finally gather the courage to pick it up, half expecting it to explode—it doesn't. I feel like an idiot for even entertaining the thought. I really need to get some sleep.

Inside the box, where a ring would fit, is a folded-up yellow Post-it note. I unfold the note; it has a time, 9:00 PM, and an address in the Fruitvale neighborhood of Oakland written on it. Fruitvale's a mix of old industrial buildings, dilapidated houses, and apartments. During the day, artisans and entrepreneurs work out of the eclectic warehouses. At night, pimps, prostitutes, and drug pushers roam International Boulevard, the main drag that pierces through the heart of Fruitvale. It's not really my first choice for a late-night rendezvous. Not exactly my scene. Too much like my day job. Same cliental.

I run through my mental Rolodex, searching for a potential suspect, someone with a grudge or someone with the skillset to break into my car undetected, and draw a complete blank. All I'm left with are burning questions and a burning urge to piss. Why didn't I go before I left the Courthouse? I glance down at my phone, it's a little after 4:00 PM, five hours until the meeting. I make a snap decision to go home, pour myself a glass of wine, piss, and take a short nap, and not necessarily in that order. When I wake up, I'll decide if I'm going to participate in this ring-box chicanery.

Chapter Eight

After a piss, a nap, two glasses of red wine, and a bacon, lettuce, provolone cheese and tomato sandwich, I hop into an Uber and head to Fruitvale. I've decided to play along with this secret message charade, at least until I figure out who the players are and what game we're playing. Having defended multiple DUI suspects, and seen firsthand the carnage alcohol-related accidents can inflict on families, hiring an Uber is a no-brainer. It also gives me the freedom to ride my buzz. I'm trying to maintain that perfect alcohol equilibrium between euphoria and dulled senses. I call it dullphoria. My personal dullphoria rule: as long as I know my name, the name of the current president of the United States—which I can verify with the closest bartender—and my address, I'm allowed to have another drink. #Dullphoria.

The Uber, a Toyota Prius, pulls up to the Fruitvale address—a three-story brick warehouse. I thank the driver, a father of two, who's working nights to make extra money to pay for his kid's braces—at least that's the sob story he is going with—and step out into the brisk Bay Area night. The building's typical for the neighborhood; nothing about it stands out in any measurable way. It looks deserted. The building's address, its sole identifying feature, is painted in white above a red metal fire door. I double-check the numbers against the Post-it—they match. I'm in the right place. I try the handle—it's unlocked. The door opens revealing a dimly lit bar. I'm not really surprised. Finding an unmarked bar in a seemingly abandoned warehouse is not such an uncommon experience in the Bay Area; it's the new-school trendy thing. #BlindTigers.

As I step through the doorway, a large tattooed Samoan bouncer looks me up and down, sticks his long tongue out in the air as if he's using it to smell me, and then begrudgingly waves me in. I hope that deodorant really does "last all day long;" otherwise, that weirdo got a mouth full of B.O. I scan the bar for familiar faces and find only one. The ageless man I saw at the Courthouse today is sitting by himself at an empty table in the back. He doesn't look like the breaking and entering type, but he's the only face I recognize, and must be my bride.

I don't wear a watch anymore; nobody under the age of forty except rappers, fitness geeks, and douchebags does. Watches have evolved into tacky and unnecessary jewelry for men. They've become the city-slicker version of driving a lifted truck. I have it on good authority from a peer reviewed scientific journal that watch face size inversely correlates to penis size. #BigWatch=SmallPenis. Your phone contains all the information you'll ever need, including a dictionary, an almanac, a ruler, and the time. Mine tells me its 8:50 PM, which means I'm early and have time to get a drink.

Because of the proximity to Napa, you can typically trust Bay Area bars to pour good house wines. The bartender's an extremely large and hairy fellow. He kind of looks like a balding bear. He's literally covered in hair and despite the fact that he's dressed sharply in dirty overalls and a wife beater, there isn't much skin showing—it's all hair, except for the top of his head, which is as bald as the nether region of an unnaturally tan New Jersey housewife.

I order the house red and ask for a refill for the fancy guy in the back corner. The bartender gives me an odd look and shakes his head while he pours my wine. He probably thinks I'm about to try and pick the ageless guy up—either that, or he's not fond of the moniker, "fancy guy."

The bartender goes into the back and returns with a heavy whiskey glass filled with a velvety crimson syrup. The glass is warm to the touch. I look to the bartender for some indication of what it is—he gives me a non-committal shrug, picks up a dry rag, and begins to polish glassware.

Above the bar is a large sign with three B's painted on it. "What's the Triple B stand for?" I ask.

The bear of a bartender half answers, half growls, "Billy Bob's Bar."

I chuckle, "You're a hillbilly and you opened a bar in Oakland and named it after yourself?"

The bartender sets down the glass he was polishing, places his disturbingly large hands on the cedar bar, and leans his massive frame towards me until we're almost nose to nose. I can feel some of his gruffy facial hairs poking me. "It's named after my dead Pa. I'm Billy Joe."

His breath smells like a combination of bratwurst, moonshine, and dog-ass. I decide this might be a good time for diplomacy and manage to eke out, "Beautiful name; my condolences on your ah, Pa."

Billy Joe leans back and gives me a terrifying grin. "I'm glad he's dead. Pa was a mean old grizzly." I do the best I can to form my lips into the shape of a smile, grab the full glasses, and quickly step away from the bar.

When I reach the back table where the ageless man is sitting, I set his glass down and take a seat across from him. He doesn't speak or even look up from his phone. I glance at mine; it's 8:59 PM. I loudly clear my throat—there's no reaction. The ageless man continues to ignore me. I know this game, it was one of my ex's favorites, everything was always on her schedule. I lean back in my chair, take a sip of wine, and begin swiping through e-mails on my phone, no sense in wasting a minute.

After nearly a full minute of silence, at 9:00 PM exactly, the ageless man looks up from his phone and asks, "Mr. Valentine, what is the difference between law and justice?"

I set my phone down onto the table and study the ageless man. There's an edge to him, a sadness. I wasn't really planning on getting into a philosophical debate with a stranger, albeit a well-dressed one, but sure, I'll play along for now. I rattle off a typical academic answer: "Laws are standards or principles that are set by either man, God, or self, to govern behavior. Laws are not always *just*. They're often as flawed as their makers. Justice is a transcendent principle of fairness, righteousness, and morality. It has a universally experienced quality, like love, goodness, and beauty. Some might argue it's one of Plato's forms. It's something we all know and recognize. You can't really define the concept, pardon my pun, but it *just-is*."

The ageless man smiles. "Was what happened today in court … justice?"

The question stings. Rather than answer, I sip my wine and ask, "What do you want?"

The ageless man stares intently into my eyes, silently moving his lips and commanding me to answer the question.

I snicker and mockingly wave my hand in front of the well-dressed man's face, "These are not the droids you are looking for. Are you trying to Jedi mind-trick me? Don't bother, that never works on me. Ask my ex-wife." In a more serious tone, I say, "I'm tiring of this charade. Who are you?"

The ageless man finishes the glass of red liquid he was drinking, carefully sets it near the edge of the table, and grasps the replacement I brought him. "My name is Pavo Palatinus." Pavo searches my face for any sign of recognition. Although I recognize the name, I do my best not to give any indication either way.

"Interesting, no rise in body temperature, no increase in heartbeat, no eye movement, no micro facial expressions; you remain a blank canvas to me. I'm almost impressed," Pavo quietly mutters more to himself than me.

Did he suggest he can monitor my heartbeat and body temperature? Is this guy cray-cray?

"Does the name Palatinus mean anything to you?" He asks.

By the inflection in his voice, I can tell he already knows the answer. Is he testing me to see if I'll tell the truth? I see no reason to lie ... yet. "Yes, it was my mother's maiden name, but you already knew that—didn't you? Are there any other questions, that you already know the answer to that you want to ask me anyway?"

Pavo smirks, "You now know my name. I'm not a reporter. I'm not recording this conversation and no one else is within human earshot. Please humor an old man and answer my question. Was what happened today in court ... justice?"

I act as if I'm pondering the question, when really I'm buying time. I'm trying to determine if Pavo has any resemblance to my mother—none that I can see. My mother was tall and beautiful. Pavo isn't exactly ugly; some might even consider him handsome, I guess, but his features are hard and he's short. He looks nothing like my mother. "Yes and no," I answer.

"Please explain?"

"What I did was just. However, the outcome was not."

Pavo nods.

Seeing an opening, I ask, "Are we related?"

"Yes," Pavo answers with a smile. "Do you believe it is *just* to provide the accused with a defense?"

"Yes," I respond. "I think all men deserve a defense. Particularly, from flawed laws." I take another sip of wine. "How are we related?"

Pavo sighs, "It's complicated, but I assure you we share the same blood." Pavo plays with the silver red gemmed ring on his left hand, spinning it back and forth. "Is justice served by defending the guilty?"

"Absolutely. Everyone deserves a defense." I answer.

"Why?"

"There are lots of reasons."

"Give me one."

"Okay: for one, our legal system's sentencing guidelines are absurd. Part of my job as a Public Defender is to ensure the guilty receive appropriate punishments. Under our laws, you can spend more time in jail for non-violent drug crimes than assault or battery. More prison time for rape than murder. I knew an old defense attorney who specialized in rape cases. He used to tell his clients, "Leaving your victim alive is the surest way to spend the rest of your life in jail. If you're going to rape someone, you better kill 'em." It was disturbing advice, but accurate when it comes to the application of our flawed laws, which are a product of our flawed political system.'"

This is a familiar topic for me, a familiar rant—one I've perfected over many a beer. "Politicians run for office on *tough-on-crime* platforms. Once they're elected, they need to fulfill their campaign promises or they won't be in office for long. They typically pick a crime, preferably something in the news, and pass a new law that takes sentencing discretion away from judges and increases the punishment. This cycle repeats over and over. We're at the point where the punishments for many crimes far exceed what is fair or just.

"Justice is *only* served when and if a criminal is given an appropriate punishment. I think it's important to do everything in my ability to ensure my clients get justice." I exhale and then ask, "My mother always told me we were the end of the Palatinus line. Was she mistaken?"

"Your mother was correct. You are the last." Pavo pauses, as if making a decision. "We are distant ... *relatives*. She was unaware of me. There are no others."

Pavo takes another sip of his warm red liquid. "Is it true that you convinced the judge to exclude evidence that would have proven your client's guilt?"

How does he know that? It was a sealed hearing. "Yes," I reply. "The DNA match on the scarf was excluded."

"Why?"

I sigh, "Because of a procedural error by the police."

"A kidnapper, and a rapist, goes free because a police officer made a procedural error? Is that *justice*?" Pavo asks. His smile grows wider as if he just took my queen with his knight.

Although I believe in justice, I also wanted to win, and the ethics associated with my position as a defense lawyer require me to zealously defend my client. If I hadn't moved to exclude the scarf based on police misconduct, I would have been committing malpractice. Sure, I can hang my hat on the age-old excuse that we need to hold the feet of the police to the fire in this case, in order to protect society and to ensure precise police work in every case, but that doesn't change the fact that here, today, a rapist went free, and his victim fled the courtroom in tears. Is that really justice? Suddenly, I'm stone-cold sober and feeling pissed off.

Pavo, as if sensing my mood shift, doesn't push for an answer and instead asks, "What if you could do more? I want to offer you a chance to do *real* justice."

"Are you offering me a job?" I ask in disbelief. "All this skullduggery is about a job? I have a j—"

"No," Pavo interrupts as he slams his hand down on the table. "I'm offering you salvation. An opportunity to save humanity."

"If this is a recruitment pitch, I think you're laying it on a little thick," I quip. "I'm not trying to be Captain America."

Pavo reaches into the black leather briefcase sitting on the floor beside him, retrieves an iPad, and slides it over to me. "Mr. Valentine, do you believe in monsters?"

Chapter Nine

My right arm is numb and my head is pounding. I vaguely remember soloing a bottle of wine after my meeting with Pavo—a necessary form of self-medication. I flip the pillow onto the arctic side and roll over onto my side. Blood and feeling start to return to my right arm, but my head still feels like it spent twelve hours pressed against the speakers at a Slipknot concert.

I rub open my eyes. I'm wearing the same suit from yesterday, jacket and all, and I still have one shoe on. My remaining shoe careens off the dresser, with a loud thud. It doesn't sound like it broke anything—I must have angels looking out for me. #AngelsIntheOutfield.

Thank God, it's Saturday ... God, *is* it Saturday? I *hope* it's Saturday. No ... it is Saturday. "Fuck," I need aspirin and coffee.

I stumble into the bathroom, raid the mirrored medicine cabinet, and make my way to the kitchen. I grab a generic coffee pod and slap it into the single-serve coffee maker that my work-mother, Trudy, bought me for Christmas last year, and press the single 12 oz. cup button. The digital readout reads, "ERROR." I sigh, "Fuck," I shout, much louder than the prior fuck. For some reason, probably because I'm cheap, I keep buying generic coffee pods that don't have QR codes and don't work in my "big-brother" coffeemaker. Why did I ever throw out my old-school coffee pot?

I flip open the top of the pod coffeemaker and tape a pre-cut QR code, stolen from an old expensive pod, to the new cheap generic pod. I shut the lid and wait patiently while the hot dark coffee pours into my oversized Reese's Peanut Butter Cup mug, where a splash of vanilla flavored creamer is already waiting. I know the mug is super douchey, but my best law school buddy, V, bought it for me after we watched a story on *Last Week Tonight* with John Oliver, about the end of net neutrality and how consumers are being screwed. The mug is V's way of making fun of me and how I refuse to directly answer media questions. Basically, she's comparing me to the head of the FCC and calling me a douchebag. The only viable response to V's teasing is to double down on the mug, and use it all the time. #Pride'sABitch. #NetNeutrality.

The coffee and aspirin are doing their jobs, the heavy metal concert in my head is quieting and I can feel my body returning to life. The view from my kitchen table usually centers me—but not this morning. All I can see this morning are the disturbing images from the video Pavo showed me last night, playing over and over in my head. Despite having visual evidence that monsters exist, I'm having a hard time believing Pavo. The things he told me are impossible. Monsters aren't real. They can't be. But what other explanation is there? I've seen a lot of crime scenes during my career, a lot of sick shit, and that video looked real, but that's impossible. Isn't it?

I run all of the alternative possibilities through my head: student film, Hollywood movie, CGI; nothing seems to fit. The video's raw, it looks like it was shot with an iPhone set on a makeshift tripod, or maybe just leaning against something on a table. I can't see any edits, it's one long continuous shot, which is really hard to fake. I don't like where this line of thinking is taking me. I don't want to believe the things Pavo told me are true—because, if they're true, I won't be able to sleep … ever again.

As I think back to last night's meeting, I realize that the only thing I'm sure about is that Pavo's holding information back. He Mambo No. 5'ed around my questions, like a retired athlete on *Dancing with The Stars*.

After our philosophical discussion about justice, Pavo told me monsters existed, and the world was a lot larger and more dangerous than I knew. I told him he was on drugs. And then he pushed the iPad towards me and pressed play.

Pavo didn't watch the video; he watched me. After I played it twice, he looked deep into my eyes, like we were on a romantic date, nodded and said, "You've already made your decision, you just don't know it yet. Keep the iPad, and meet me back here at Billy Bob's Bar tomorrow night at 7:00 PM." Before I could respond, he was gone. He didn't exactly disappear, I watched him leave. He just moved so fast—faster than I would have expected for a man of any age—unnaturally fast.

I take another sip of my coffee and come to a decision. I instruct my phone to "Call Wilson Scarborough." Wilson's my friend, a tall wiry ex-military guy with kind of a hippy surfer thing going on. He was an investigator for the Public Defender's office, until he was arrested for breaking into the home of a dirty cop who planted evidence on some of my clients. In exchange for burying the evidence that Wilson turned up against the cop and avoiding an embarrassing news cycle for the city, I was able to get the District Attorney to drop all charges against him. Unfortunately, Wilson still lost his job. The last I heard he was doing some freelance work for some products liability defense firm. Shady stuff, but it pays the bills.

Wilson answers on the third ring, "Boss? Is that you?"

"Yeah buddy, it's me. I need a favor."

"A favor, shit, it's Saturday. The only reason I answered was because I thought you might be calling to invite me over for a beer. You know, like we used to. The only thing I can figure is that your phone must be broken, because you ain't called me once since I got canned." Although he's speaking with bravado, it doesn't mask the hurt beneath.

I grimace; has it really been six months? That's a real dick move. Wilson doesn't have a lot of friends other than me. I should have checked in on him. "Yeah, sorry about that, buddy. Work's been crazy. I hate to ask, but I still need a favor, and it's time sensitive."

"Of course, it is. It's probably gonna' ruin my weekend, right?" Wilson snarks.

"Yeah, sorry about that too."

"You're a real dick. I'm surprised your ex-wife ever left you since she loves Dick so much," Wilson says in a smart-ass tone.

I laugh, relieved we're back to our old banter. The mere fact that he's joking about my ex-wife is a good sign. A sign I haven't completely ruined our friendship. "Yeah, she does love Dick. That's why you never had a shot."

I can hear him snicker through the phone, "Alright, what do you need? You're gonna owe me a twelve pack and some tri-tip."

"I need you to find out everything you can about a guy named Pavo Palatinus, and I need it by 6:00 PM tonight."

"Palatinus, isn't that your mom's maiden name?"

"Yeah, how do you know that?"

"I know everything about your mo—."

"—Hey, hey, watch it. You're close to a line."

"Yeah, yeah. Are you and this Pavo guy related?"

"Maybe."

"Ok, play it close to the vest then. You need anything else? Or is that all?" he replies in an incredulous tone. "You sure you don't need me to find Jimmy Hoffa's body or help wax your bikini line?"

"I'm sorry about the short turnaround. Just do the best you can. And nope, I could care less where Hoffa is buried, and I don't wax, I shave."

"Yeah, yeah, I got you," he says between chuckles. "Is this for work?"

I'm relieved he's agreeing to help me. "No, it's a personal thing." I stop and consider how deep I really want to involve him. I decide, probably incorrectly, balls deep. Wilson's top notch, and I need his opinion. "Wilson, I'm going to send you a video file. I want you to take a look at it, and when you get here, I want you to let me know what you think. Don't show it to anybody."

"Sure. Let me guess, you're thinking about posting a sex tape of you and your ex-wife and you want me to critique it—be the straight-man voice in the room. Am I right?"

"No, jackass. Just watch the video, find out what you can about Pavo Palatinus, and meet me at my place around 6:00 PM."

"Will do. You better have a twelve-pack waiting for me."

"Yeah, yeah." After I hang up, I wonder if I should've involved him at all? I have a feeling the lives of anyone who sees this video are going to be changed forever. It's too late to change my mind. I grab my Beats headphones, running shoes, and hit the pavement. I need to think, clear the cobwebs from my brain, and I think best when I sweat.

Chapter Ten

After my run, I watch the video a few more times, and do some internet digging. Strangely, my searches don't turn anything up. It's as if the ageless man doesn't exist. Wilson arrives early and makes a beeline for the fridge. He looks shook. He struggles with a Mexican beer, finally popping the cap off with a lighter, and then pounds it like a desperately thirsty man. He grabs two more beers from the fridge, and tosses a manila folder down on the table in front of me.

"Where the fuck did you get that video?" he demands while trying to open the second beer. There's a slight tremor in his hand, he's having a hard time getting the edge of the lighter under the lip of the beer cap. The video must have upset him as much as it upset me.

I hand him the combination beer and wine opener I keep on my kitchen table for emergencies. He uses it to pop the top off and downs his second beer.

"I just watched the video in my truck. What the fuck, Colt? You could have warned me. There's a little kid, a baby, in that video."

"I'm sorry. I know, it's messed up on an epic scale. It's like watching a Rob Zombie movie. I'm sorry for not warning you, but I needed an unbiased opinion. I'm guessing you think it's real?"

Wilson sips his third beer and considers the possibility it's a fake. "I think it's real. There are no visible edits, nothing looks like an added after-effect. It doesn't look like makeup or animatronics and I can't see any video filters or overlays. The *blood* ...," he takes another sip of the beer. "It just looks and sounds *real*. I mean other than the guy, the *thing*, the whatever. I don't know, man. It looks fuckin' real."

I nod. "That's what I thought too."

Wilson mutters something incoherent about poisons and exterminators and this not being fucking Australia and that they're not supposed to get that big. He eventually makes eye contact with me. "I know a girl who works over at the San Francisco Academy of Art College—she can tell us for certain. She's gifted with movies and makeup and shit. She was on that TV show about monster makeup artists. She'll know if it's real or not."

I grab a fourth beer out of the fridge and hand it to Wilson. "No, I don't want anyone else involved until I know more."

Wilson nods.

I open the folder Wilson brought; there are only a few pages inside. "Well, looks like it's not quite the mother-lode of info," I say, dripping with sarcasm. "What did you find out about Palatinus?"

"Practically buttkiss," answers Wilson. "The guy's essentially a ghost. He owns some properties in high-rent areas, a small building in Oakland, and a house in Sausalito. Probably has property outside the state as well, but I didn't have time to run that to ground. He appears to be wealthy as shit. The building and house are owned outright, no mortgage records, he paid cash."

Wilson takes another pull on his beer. "According to the DMV, he's seventy-nine and the registered owner of half a dozen cars. It's strange, but I can't find a birth certificate for him. Even stranger, he has a passport, but there is no record of him ever using it. Not exactly normal behavior for a rich guy."

"Maybe he doesn't like to fly?" I suggest.

Wilson shrugs. "Maybe. Professionally, he's a licensed lawyer. Passed the California bar exam forty years ago. No bar complaints. Always pays his dues on time. Clean as a whistle, which means he's d—."

"—dirty as shit." I finish Wilson's sentence for him.

Wilson smiles for the first time since he arrived at my home and passes me a Berkeley yearbook photo. "He does have a twenty-eight-year old adopted daughter, Sinn Palatinus. She is hot as shit on a Texas sidewalk. Girl makes me want to sin over and over again. Adoption records state she's the biological daughter of two Thai immigrants who were killed in a car accident in Chicago shortly after her birth. I couldn't find out anything else about her parents; it's as if they didn't exist before the car accident. The daughter's also a lawyer. She graduated Berkeley Law last year."

Wilson ignores the three empty chairs surrounding the kitchen table and instead sits on my counter. "Palatinus and his hot daughter run a small law practice out of his Oakland building. It's weird, but there's no record of any other employees—must be a small office. It gets weirder. I can't even tell what type of law they practice. I can't find a record of any court case where either were named as counsel of record. I can't find any news stories on them, nothing on the internet, no website, no social media and, get this, the answering machine just says leave a message and then beeps. Yeah, you heard me right, they have an actual answering machine. That's pretty much it. Like I said, the guy's a specter. I got buttkiss."

"It's bupkis, not buttkiss, moron," I say.

"Bupkis?" Wilson says in a mock confused tone. "Why would I say I got Yiddish beans? That makes zero sense. I didn't find beans, I found *buttkiss*."

I sigh, "You're an idiot. Thanks for the help. I got to go. I have an appointment with the *specter*. Take the rest of the six-pack with you."

"One beer? Gee thanks. You still owe me six more and some BBQ." Wilson's tone becomes serious, "You need backup tonight?"

For a second, I consider saying yes. I might need a guy who can handle himself, plus Wilson's smart and observant. Then the guilt from not calling him for six months rears up. I'd feel like a real ass if he got hurt doing me a favor. "No, I'm good," I answer.

Wilson's face takes on an almost fearful expression. "Colt, what is that thing in the video?"

"I don't know, but I aim to find out."

Chapter Eleven

I take another Uber, another Toyota Prius, to Billy Bob's Bar, which as far as I'm concerned will forever be known from this day forward as the Triple B. I refuse to tell people I frequent a bar in Oakland called Billy Bob's. I'd lose all my street cred.

The Triple B looks and smells the same as it did yesterday. The same bartender is working, and the same big tank top-wearing Samoan is guarding the door. Today's tank top has a giant cartoon turtle on it. It looks ridiculous, like something a parent would dress their infant in. Especially ridiculous, when you factor in the snake scale tattoos that cover most of his body.

As I walk by, the Samoan with anaconda sized arms, flicks his serpent-like tongue out as if tasting my scent. What a frickin' weirdo. #OnlyinCali. I quicken my pace and try to put as much distance as possible between myself and the big, scaly, turtle tank-top-wearing, escaped mental patient.

When I reach the bar counter, I look towards the back table where we sat yesterday, and note that Pavo hasn't yet arrived. It's 6:45 PM. I'm early again. Good. When negotiating, you should always arrive first; you want to set the field, and dictate the battle. In this case, I want to set the field with copious amounts of alcohol. I raise my hand to get the bartender's attention. "Billy Joe, I'll have a glass of the house red. What's the deal with your bouncer? Is he in a Samoan Kiss tribute band or something?"

Billy Joe's responsive grunt almost sounds like a laugh. "Pili? He is just trying to determine what you are." Billy Joe pours me a glass of red wine from a plain dark green wine bottle. It doesn't have a label, which isn't necessarily a bad thing. "No label" sometimes indicates shitty wine; other times, it indicates that the bar has entered into a blind distribution agreement with a high-end winery.

In order to increase sales volume and profits, high-end wineries sometimes agree to supply a restaurant or bar with "house" wine in unlabeled bottles at much-reduced prices. In return, the bar or restaurant agrees not to disclose where their amazing, high-end "House" wine comes from. It's a win-win for everyone involved, especially the customers. Having tasted this wine yesterday, I think Billy Joe has a blind distribution agreement with an extremely high-end winery. This stuff is really good, Screaming Eagle good.

"What I *am*?" I ask in disbelief. "By tasting the air? Like if I'm a vegetarian, a Capricorn, or a Raiders fan?"

Billy Joe's oddly-colored black eyes meet mine, and with a completely straight face, he says, "Yup, he thinks you smell funny." Billy Joe pushes a glass of the warm red liquid that Pavo was drinking yesterday towards me, and then heads to the other side of the bar to help a buxom young lady. I sarcastically mutter, "Oh thanks, that sure clears everything up," while I grab the two beverages and turn towards the back corner.

As my eyes reach the back table, I realize Pavo somehow slipped past me and is already sitting and waiting for me, and he's wearing another classic 1920's-era pin-striped three-piece suit. The only people who dress like that in this neighborhood are straight pimps, and that's not a euphemism. Despite the casual setting, I feel underdressed in jeans, a button up and sneakers.

Pavo's sprawled out, reading something on his phone. If I didn't know better, I'd think he'd been perched there for hours. How the hell did he get past me? Is he a roaring twenties ninja? Is there another entrance? I shake my head and chalk it up as another mystery to add to the enigma that is Pavo, the seventy-nine-year-old who looks like a forty-year-old, and moves like his name is Usain Bolt.

As I approach the back table, I notice a pair of mismatched misfits eyeing me from across the bar. The tall one has a hooked nose and a face not even his grandmother could love. The fat one's face is so bloated that it's hard to distinguish facial features. It's like a giant blob, with eyes and a mouth. I can't tell where the nose ends, and the cheeks begin. I'm guessing he's a big fan of super-sizing everything.

Both miscreants are wearing black jeans, white sneaks, and matching black T-shirts with a cheesy-looking logo—an outline of a profiled upside-down pig with X's for eyes. Both seem more interested in me than in their beers and the empty bar-snack bowls stacked at their table. I mockingly wink at the twins as I sit down at Pavo's table. They immediately lose interest and make a hurried exit. Hmm? My wink must be terrifying. Note to self, don't wink at any potential lady friends.

I push Pavo's glass towards him and open my mouth to ask about the video when he interrupts me, "—What do you know about our family's history?"

Not what I expected him to say. I really want to grab him by his waistcoat, turn him upside down, and shake him, until he tells me everything he knows about the video, but I have a feeling threats aren't going to get me very far. It's probably smarter to play along, at least for now.

"Not much," I answer. "My mother told me she was a second-generation Italian American. Her father came over as a boy, and grew up outside Indianapolis. He spent his life working at the International Harvester engine foundry. She met my dad while visiting grandpa at the plant; he was on grandpa's crew. Dad was a college football star, but never was very good at school. She said it was love at first sight. The only thing she ever told me about her side of the family was that they were all dead. She did mention once, after a few too many glasses of white zin, that Grandpa fled Italy. I assume she meant he fled the Nazis."

Pavo nods, a momentary glimpse of melancholy washes over him, and his eyes gloss over as if he's replaying a memory in his head. "Our family is all dead. You're the last in the bloodline of the once proud Palatinus family. We were a family of knights, protectors. Our family's complex history goes back centuries. Before the night's over, I'll tell you what you need to know." Pavo looks up from the glass he's clutching tightly in his hands and says, "But first, I need to rid you of your preconceived notions about what is, and is not, real."

Pavo opens his mouth wide, displaying a set of large sharp fangs. "I am a vampire."

I almost fall out of my chair laughing. "Sure, whatever. Not my scene, but I have no problems with alternative lifestyles. Go ahead, let your freak-flag fly. By-the-way, those fangs are amazing. They almost look real. Is that Ronnie's work? Up in the Mission District? He does good work, very natural. You're not the first so-called vampire I've met. I'm a San Francisco Public Defender; you wouldn't believe the crazies I've defended. They come in all flavors."

Pavo smiles, clearly amused. "I've walked this earth for nearly sixteen hundred years. I have seen newborn babies grow into old men, wither, and die. I've seen empires crumble, and rise anew. I've taken the lives of kings and peasants alike. I've murdered thousands, and bathed in the blood of my enemies. I assure you, I am a true vampire."

"O-kay," I say in my most sarcastic tone. This guy is clearly off his meds. I wonder if I need to give him the whole *Please don't confess any future crimes you're planning to commit, first I don't want to know, and second, future crimes are not protected by the attorney-client privilege* speech? As I take another sip of the house red, my eyes are drawn to Pavo's glass and the thick red liquid it contains. Is that supposed to mimic blood? Is that real blood? Did I buy him a glass of *blood*? Where the hell do they get the blood? Is it animal blood? That can't be sanitary. I might have to anonymously report Billy Joe to the health department.

"Look, nice speech. Your outfit's great. The warm tomato juice, or whatever, is a nice touch. I don't care if you think you're a vampire, a cross-dressing alien, or the Pope—it's all good. This is the Bay Area—live and let live. I just want to know everything you know about that video. There is some pretty disturbing shit going on in that video. Is the thing in that video real? What is it? An alien? A government experiment gone wrong?"

Pavo's face remains unreadable, "Where is the last place you vacationed?"

"Are you hitting on me? Is this all some elaborate set-up to get me to go on vacation with you?"

"No. Answer the question."

Bristling with irritation, I respond, "I don't remember. I'm a workaholic. Vacations are for lotharios and family men, and I'm neither. And, what the hell does my last vacation have to do with you being a vampire? I mean other than the obvious that both words start with the letter V?"

Pavo, clearly unperturbed by my shit talking, continues to ask dumb questions. "You were married once?"

I sigh, "Sure, and I've got the bullet holes in my bank account to prove it."

"Where did you go on your honeymoon?"

"Hey, you're not going to drop this, are you? Fine! We went to Maui, to the resort attached to Black Rock. The food and scenery were great, the company sucked."

"Black Rock." Pavo shares a smile with himself, clearly remembering a better time. "I know it well. It's a place of great power."

"Sure, whatever. I just remember it was a place of great expense."

Pavo pulls a vintage ornate silver pen out of his inner jacket pocket, stands up and walks to the back wall. The pen is beautiful. It looks like the old-fashioned kind, the kind you'd have to dip into ink in order to write with. Pavo presses the pen against the wall, and silver glowing ink begins to flow from the tip. He draws a door on the brick bar wall, complete with a door handle, and then places the pen back into his jacket pocket. With the index finger and thumb of his right hand, Pavo grasps the ornate silver ring with a blood-red stone on his left hand, and chants something under his breath. I can't quite make out what he is saying. I'm not even sure he was speaking English.

Pavo reaches into the wall, grasps the glowing door handle, and pulls opens the door. I nearly drop my glass. My face must look the same way a child's face looks when it is first introduced to the game of peekaboo. I'm dumbfounded, and my brain actually hurts.

"Holy shit! That is some Criss Angel level magic!" I exclaim. I look around the bar. Nobody else seems to be paying any attention. "How did you do that? And why don't you have your own TV show?"

Pavo patiently waits by the open door. "Are you coming?"

"Through there?" I ask suspiciously.

Pavo nods. Before I know it, I've jumped up out of my chair and I'm moving towards the door. I finally gain control of my body, and force myself to pause, inches before entering the shimmering light, while I listen to the responsible voice in my head urging me not to go through the door with the strange little man who thinks he's a vampire. Unfortunately, the responsible voice in my head knows it's arguing a losing proposition, and barely puts up a fight. I have to know where the door goes—I'm going. I take a deep breath and step through the door into ... *paradise*. Or, as close as one can get.

The cool ocean breeze brushes across my face, and I taste salt in the wet air. I smell acidic volcanic rock, and I hear the heavenly sound of a ukulele from the hotel bar across the beach. There's no mistaking it, I'm standing on Black Rock, staring out into the Pacific Ocean. I'm on the Maui shore. How the hell am I in Maui? How is this possible? When I'm finally able to tear my eyes away from the ocean, I realize the door's gone.

"This can't be real. Is this like that trick in *Now You See Me 2*, with Woody Harrelson, where they "magically" slide down a garbage chute and end up in China? Did you slip a mickey into my drink?" I ask, half-hoping he answer yes. A drug induced fantasy would be so much easier to accept than the alternative.

Pavo smiles and pulls the pen back out of his jacket pocket and waves it at me like a wand. "It's magic. The pen is a tool every Advocate is given. If you accept the job, you'll have one too. The pen, although it has other uses, can open a door to any place you can picture in your head. Before the internet, that meant you had to have been there before. Now a video or a picture is usually sufficient, so long as you concentrate. The pen pretty much eliminates frequent flier miles; you're not going to be popular with airlines."

I can't take my eyes off the pen, thinking about all its possible uses. "How come no one at the bar seemed to notice the glowing door?" I ask.

"When active, the pen projects a sort of don't pay attention spell on both sides of the gate. Most people don't see it, or ignore it. The spell also defeats video cameras. Don't ask me anything beyond that—I'm a vampire, not a witch or mage. I am not exactly sure how it works, or what the radius is, or anything like that. I just know it works. Frankly, I've never been all that interested in learning how it works. The fact that it does work is good enough for me."

I nod, signifying some level of understanding. In actuality, I don't understand at all. The whole thing is too fantastic to be real. He must have drugged me. That is the only reasonable explanation. You know Occam's Razor and all that shit. The simplest explanation is the most likely explanation.

Pavo steps towards me. "Now just for a moment, try to put aside everything you think you know and open yourself to the possibility that monsters and magic exist. I have a lot to tell you, and not a lot of time to do it in. Things will go quicker if you have an open mind. Do you think you can do that?"

I find myself giving the same answer *The Little Engine That Could* would give, "I think I can."

Pavo nods, "Good, let's return to Billy Bob's Bar. I'm thirsty and everything here has a disgusting coconut flavor to it—even the blood."

Chapter Twelve

The trip back to the Triple B takes longer than expected. Pavo has to wait for me while I climb down the cliff face to the beach below. It turns out the gate pen only works on flat surfaces. Black Rock is many things—flat isn't one of them. Rather than help me, Pavo leaps the thirty yards from the cliff down to the sand, and then lounges on a beach chair and watches with a disapproving look as I slowly navigate the treacherous cliff.

I make the descent guided only by moonlight and music from the poolside resort bar. I can hear someone singing, Israel "IZ" Kamakawiwoʻole's, *What a Wonderful World.* I know the song well. I heard it about a million times when I honeymooned here. As I climb down BlackRock, I can't help but think it won't be so wonderful if I fall and crack my head. When I reach the beach, I'm flooded with relief, but before I can even catch my breath, Pavo's up and walking towards the resort, urging me to follow.

Pavo and I find a flat wall in an empty hotel corridor. Pavo draws a door and handle on the smooth stucco, grabs the ring on his left hand with his right index finger and thumb, mutters, "Billy Bob's Bar" under his breath, and then reaches inside of the stucco wall, grabs the magical door handle, and opens the door back to our table in Oakland. I'm again overcome with amazement. Magical doors aren't a bad way to travel; no delayed flight, long lines, or lost baggage. I could get used to this.

Billy Joe must have known we'd be back, because he refreshed our drinks while we were gone. I sip my wine and play with the bowl of bar snacks Billy Joe left on our table while I wait for Pavo to check something on his phone.

Pavo finally looks up and says, "Why don't we start with the video?" I perk up at the mention of the video; it's all I've been thinking about for the past twenty-four hours.

"The creature in the video is a werespider—a man that can transform into a spider. Although some might argue it's the other way around. Werespiders typically embrace their spider side and shed all emotions associated with being human. This particular werespider is named Lycocide. He's a young and particularly vile wolf-spider."

"Werespider?" I ask.

"Yes, part man, part spider. They're tough to kill and should *never* be underestimated. Fortunately, there aren't that many of them. All werespiders start off as humans and are rebirthed, possibly through a sexual act with the queen, at least that's the rumor. I have never witnessed it myself. Supposedly, during the rebirth, the spider queen chooses the type of werespider they'll become. If she chooses a type of werespider that already exists, the newly born werespider will seek out his brother or sister and fight them to the death. They really got that whole "*there can only be one*" of any one type of werespider at any one-time vibe going on. In my sixteen hundred years, I've known three different werespiders that went by the name Araneidae, or Orb-Weaver. They were all killed by their successors."

"You're telling me that thing in the video, drinking blood from an infant, while it tortured the baby's mother and father, is a werewolf-spider? This is a joke, right?"

Pavo frowns. "Not a werewolf-spider. I thought you're supposed to be smart."

I purse my lips and give Pavo a one finger salute.

Pavo ignores my colorful sign language and continues his lecture, "There are werewolfs and then there are werespiders. There are also weretigers, werelions, and werepanthers, among others, but that's not important right now." Pavo points towards the hefty bartender and whispers, "Werebear."

"Seriously?"

Pavo nods. "A dangerous one. Now, where was I? Oh, yes, Lycocide is a werespider that happens to be of the wolf-spider variety. He just as easily could have been of the tarantula or recluse variety. That's why I gave you the orb-weaver example. Lycocide is not a *werewolf,* he is a werespider. You got it? Or do you need me to explain it again, maybe *slower*?"

"Yeah, I got it." I do, I just don't know if I believe it, and I can't stop staring at Billy Joe. He is one massive mamma-jamma and hairy as all hell, except for the bald spot on the top of his head.

"Can he really turn into a bear?" I ask.

Billy gives me a full-toothed grin from across the bar. He has way more teeth in his mouth than I would have thought possible. On an instinctive level, his smile makes me want to climb a tree and pee myself. With all those teeth, I wonder if his dentist charges double.

"Yes, he can turn into a bear if he wants to," answers Pavo with a grin. "And in case you're wondering, I have it on good authority that werebears have great hearing."

"Thanks, Grandpa," I sarcastically respond. "Just what I need, a bartender that turns into a giant bear pissed at me."

"You're welcome," Pavo smiles as he sips his beverage.

"How did you get the video? And why do you have it?" I ask, changing topics.

"It's complicated," says Pavo.

"Cliffnotes version is fine."

"Cliff's Notes? Who is Cliff?" asks Pavo in confusion.

"Cliff is, cliffnotes are, er, never mind, please just give me the abbreviated version."

Pavo slowly spins his heavy whiskey glass. Each turn makes a low-pitched carving sound as he works the heavy glass against the wooden table. "I'm an Advocate. My job is to enforce the laws of the Magna-Concordat and to protect the rights of its citizens."

"What is the Magna-Concordat?" I immediately fire off the question as if I'm examining a witness.

"It's an agreement that was entered into in the Fourth Century, right before the fall of Rome. It's a set of laws. Nearly all the intelligent races on Earth: weres, vampires, witches, goblins, djinn, sirens, mages, shifters, and many others, are signatories. More than a thousand years ago, the leaders of each race signed the agreement in blood, thereby making all of their kind Concordat citizens, and binding them to the laws of the Magna-Concordat. These races have their own kingdoms, their own laws, but the Magna-Concordat treaty regulates interaction between the races. It prescribes methods for dealing with criminals and resolving disputes. All signatory races are governed by the Magna - Concordat treaty."

"Why would any of them sign a treaty?" I ask.

"The Magna-Concordat was a prophylactic response to the rise of humanity. Humans bred much faster than most other races. Humans were also developing better, more lethal weapons, and were becoming dangerous, efficient killers. The non-human races realized they had to unite or risk extermination. For the humans, it was a path to peace, no more fear of things that go bump in the night."

"Humans were a part of the Magna-Concordat?"

"Initially yes, all humans were represented by the Roman Church during the initial treaty negotiations. However, Rome fell and humans were not part of the final treaty, unless you consider mages and witches to be human—and they don't." Pavo sips his syrupy beverage.

"In the centuries since the treaty was signed, a divide has formed within the Concordat regarding the best way to address humans and their exploding population in this shrinking world. Some feel the human population again needs culling, while others feel we should pursue less drastic solutions. I fear a confrontation is coming. I fear for the future of humanity."

"What do you mean *Again*? You've culled the human population in the past?"

Pavo pauses, strategically choosing his words, "Various Concordat factions have, in the past, utilized various techniques to engineer human population reductions like war, famine, and disease outbreaks. These past actions haven't all received official Council approval. For the magnitude of what I foresee coming, Council approval will be needed."

I nod. This is a topic we are definitely going to revisit but I can live with his political half-truth, at least, for now. "How many Concordat citizens are there? Hundreds? Thousands?"

"I'm not sure anyone has actually counted or performed an official census," Pavo says dryly. "Citizens aren't partial to filling out surveys, but my guess would be millions."

"Shut the fuck up!" I exclaim, louder than I intended. I can literally feel my blood pressure rise along with the volume of my voice. "You're telling me there are millions of werespiders running around drinking the blood of infants?"

Pavo shakes his head. "No. I said there are millions of Concordat citizens, but not all citizens are as vile or reckless as Lycocide. Most citizens just want to be left in peace. Werespiders are a very small and vile segment of the population."

Despite the fact I haven't caught him in a lie yet, I'm having a hard time believing everything he's selling. I know a doomsday profiteer when I see one; I lived through Y2K, and this guy's hiding something. "Okay, putting aside the terrifying possibility that there are millions of monsters running around the world, what's an Advocate?"

Pavo takes a deep breath, "During the great ratification, it was decided that the Magna-Concordat would be maintained and enforced by a council of twenty-four. The council was chosen from many different races and they were called Advocates. An Advocate is like a cross between a lawyer and a Roman Republic Senator.

"On one hand, Advocates perform a service like a modern-day criminal prosecutor. They investigate crimes, serve complaints on suspected violators of the Magna-Concordat, and try cases before panels of judges made up of their peers. Advocates can also act as personal representatives of Concordat citizens who are either involved in civil or criminal disputes. Much of the human practice of law was copied from our Court.

"On the other hand, Advocates have a legislative function. They vote on proposed changes to the laws of the Magna-Concordat treaty. Changes or additions to the Concordat can be made, but only by two-thirds majority vote of the twenty-four Advocates. As you can imagine, changes are rarely made. Citizens can also propose changes or additions to the treaty, but citizens do not vote. Only Advocates vote. Advocates also vote on policy decisions that affect Concordat citizens, such as going to war."

"Or mass murdering billions of humans?" I ask sarcastically.

Pavo nods and answers, "Yes," in an uncomfortably serious tone.

"Do the Advocates rule over the other citizens?" I ask.

Pavo gives me a strange look. "I hope you don't have dreams of becoming a king. Advocates are essentially glorified public servants. An Advocate doesn't rule. An Advocate serves."

"You said Advocates settle disputes between races. What did you mean?"

"There are numerous forms of government amongst the different individual Concordat races: covens, packs, democracies, monarchies, and others. Regardless of the type of government, the Magna-Concordat treats them all equally and generically defines them all as kingdoms. All kingdoms of Magna-Concordat citizens fall under the umbrella of Magna-Concordat law."

I wrinkle my brow in confusion.

"Think of it this way: the Magna-Concordat is like the Federal Government, and the various kingdoms are like states. The kingdoms are all free to govern themselves as they please, so long as they don't run afoul of Magna-Concordat law or objectives. If a dispute arises between kingdoms, or citizens of different kingdoms, Magna-Concordat law is used to resolve it. It's just like how Federal Law is used to resolve disputes between states, or citizens of different states."

"I think I understand," I answer.

"Good, I was starting to worry you were an idiot," says Pavo.

"Fuck off! You're lucky, I'm even sitting here listening to your looney sales pitch."

Pavo smirks as he casually reaches into his jacket pocket and pulls out his phone. He opens an app and sets the phone in the center of the table. The phone disperses a soft buzzing sound.

I raise my eyebrows quizzically.

"I just activated a spell app," answers Pavo.

"A what?"

"It's a magic spell programmed into my phone. It works like any other phone app, except it affects the world around the phone. The Guild is doing some really interesting stuff, combining magic and technology."

"The Guild?" I ask.

"The Mages Guild."

I nod, not understanding at all. "What does it do?"

"This particular mage app creates a sphere around us, which allows outside noise in but traps and prevents noise from within the sphere from escaping. It's like one-way privacy glass. You and I can hear each other, and hear what's going on outside the sphere, but nobody outside the sphere can hear us."

"How d—."

"—Don't ask me how it works, I have no idea. Now pay attention, this part is important."

I start to say something else, but Pavo silences me with a hand gesture and continues his lecture. "Being an Advocate is both a great honor and a great responsibility. It can also be a difficult job and a dangerous one. Each Advocate is given three items of great power to assist them in their tasks. These items are enslaved to the Magna-Concordat and the Advocates they serve.

"Each Advocate is given a ring ..." Pavo points to the silver ring with the blood red stone that he wears on his left hand.

"a gate pen ..." Pavo places on the table the old-fashioned silver pen he used to draw the door to Maui.

"and a book of laws." Pavo reaches into his jacket and pulls out a small thin paperback-sized leather-bound book with a silver inlaid cover.

"These gifts are to be used to enforce the laws of the Magna-Concordat and to protect the rights of Concordat citizens."

I can't take my eyes off the ring; it's as if it's calling to me. "What does the ring do?" I ask.

A sad look crosses Pavo's face. "Each ring has its own personality. They affect everyone differently. My ring allows me to feel, to forgive, and to love. It reminds me what it meant to be human. I think it knew … that's what I needed most."

Sadness grips Pavo, he stares off into the past, and then he snaps back, straight-faced, emotions buried, "I've heard others claim it made them stronger, faster, and more powerful. I don't know what it will do for you."

"What about the book?" I ask, finally managing to tear my eyes away from the ring.

"The book holds all the laws of the Magna-Concordat. If a law is changed, the book magically updates. It rewrites itself to include the updated law. It was really impressive a couple centuries ago. In my day, you had to have a whole new book copied by hand every time there was an update. It was tedious work. My daughter calls the Book of Laws the world's first Kindle Fire. It also translates the writings into whatever language the Advocate reads. Don't worry, English is currently the universal language used to conduct Magna-Concordat business. For centuries, it was Latin, but nobody speaks Latin anymore, and English is the easiest of all the widely spoken languages to learn.

The book and pen are bound to the ring's magic. They can't be used without it and if you lose them or they're stolen, the ring will help you find them."

"That's handy," I say.

"It is. Now back to your original question," says Pavo. "As an Advocate, I have the power to investigate citizens whom I suspect are breaking the laws of the Magna-Concordat. The video is part of an investigation into Lycocide, which brings us to you. I want you to take my place and become an Advocate. You'll be able to help more people than you can imagine. You can continue my investigation and bring Lycocide to justice."

I frown. This is not at all how I imagined this conversation going. "Putting aside the facts that I'd have to be crazy to say yes, and that I'm too old to go back to school, what would I have to do? —And I'm not saying yes. I just want to know what's involved. Do I have to go to a Monster Advocacy Academy, or some shit like that, and hang out with a bunch of teenage-monsters? This whole thing feels like a bad television show. Isn't "teenage-monster" an oxymoron? Aren't all teenagers, monsters?"

"No schooling involved." Pavo leans forward, wearing a serious expression, and looks deep into my eyes, "You just have to kill me."

Chapter Thirteen

"Are you crazy?" I shout. "I'm not going to kill you!" I press both hands onto the wooden table, push off, and rise to my feet.

"Sit down and listen," Pavo barks. "I am tired of your childish outbursts."

For the first time in decades, I feel like a scolded child waiting for Dad's belt. I sit back down and find myself reactively adopting the posture of a defiant teenager. Despite my self-awareness, I'm too prideful to correct my posture and cease the childish body language.

Pavo's about to say something when his phone vibrates. I can read the name "Sinn" on the caller ID. Pavo glares at me, daring me to move, as he picks up his phone from the center of the table and answers it.

"Yes ... I see ... text me pictures. We've been over this ... my decision is final." His tone then becomes softer, "Che gli dei possano salvaguardartie proteggerti, dolce figlia mia. Ciao Caro." I barely speak any Italian but I understand enough to know he's saying goodbye to someone he loves.

Pavo ends the call and turns to me, "I'm afraid time is running out. I'm going to talk very quickly and you are going to listen. Do you understand me?"

I want to say go screw yourself; instead, I find myself nodding.

Pavo's phone vibrates again and he skims the incoming text message. Without looking up, he says, "You're going to kill me, because if you don't, a girl will be raped, and possibly killed, by the man you set free yesterday. Her blood will be on your hands." Pavo turns his phone so I can see a pic of Roy Silas carrying an unconscious girl over his shoulder. The picture is geographically generic; I can't make out any landmarks, but it's definitely Roy.

"The photograph was taken about five minutes ago. As you know, he likes to play with his victims. Isn't that how he got caught in the first place? A victim got away? If you hurry and kill me, you'll have plenty of time to save her. If you don't—she will die."

As if anticipating my next thought, he says, "Of course, calling the police is another option, albeit a poor one. Mr. Silas is not at his home and finding him will probably take days, if not weeks, if at all. By that time the girl will either be dead or damaged beyond repair. You know what he's capable of. You're the only chance she has to make it out of this alive and relatively unharmed."

Although my mind is running through different possibilities at a million miles an hour, I feel like time has slowed. Pavo is talking slower, everyone in the bar is moving slower. I swear I can see the beating wings of a fly hovering over the bowl of bar snacks. I'm not sure why, but I have always been at my absolute best in high-stress situations. That's probably why I became a trial lawyer.

After careful consideration, it's clear to me. I don't have any choice but to take Pavo at his word. I have no idea where Roy is taking the girl, and Pavo's right—the police might take days, even weeks, to find her. That is, assuming they even believe me. The only evidence of the kidnapping is on Pavo's phone and, after witnessing the cliff stunt, I doubt I'm strong enough to take his phone by force. Despite his advanced age, he's definitely stronger than me.

I don't see any good options other than playing along. I already have enough guilt on my conscience from Roy Silas; I don't need any more. I'm not going to let Roy kill or rape another girl. I'm going to do everything I can to save her, but I can't kill someone. I don't care if it is a vampire, I am not a killer. Maybe I can convince Pavo to help her, by agreeing to give him what he wants.

"Please," I plead. "Just you use your pen to open a gate and we can save her together! Or have whoever took the picture stop Roy, or call the police and give them his location. I'll take the job. I'll be an Advocate … whatever you want. Please, help the girl!"

"What I want is for you to kill me."

"I'm not going to kill you."

Pavo leans forward and snarls, "The girl's life means nothing to me. She's food. I'm a vampire. I kill for pleasure. She is but one human. I'm giving you the opportunity to save billions. If you succeed in killing me, that alone will save hundreds of humans from my bite. Whether you realize it or not, you will take the job; you will become an Advocate; and the only way to do that is by killing me."

Pavo leans back and his tone softens, "Please understand this, I can't just give you my job—you have to take it. Being an Advocate is a lifetime position—it must be earned. We must fight. If you kill me, the ring, the pen, and the book are yours. You can use the pictures on my phone to open a gate and you can save the girl. You can continue the investigation into Lycocide, and you can ... there is much more you can do. If you fail to kill me, you will die. I will not hesitate to kill you. I do not care that we are family. Only one of us can leave this bar alive."

Pavo pauses and takes another sip of his beverage. "If you succeed in killing me, my daughter Sinn will help you in all things. You can trust her. Do you understand everything I've said to you?"

I'm backed into an impossible situation and I'm not seeing any viable options. I can't kill anyone, not even a two-thousand-year-old vampire, but I'm also not going to let the girl die. He's not going to kill me in front of all these people, is he? I need to buy time, while I come up with a better plan than murder, to save the girl. If agreeing to fight him to the death buys me time, so be it. I can always back out.

"Yes, I understand."

Pavo reaches into his briefcase and pulls out a dagger, a Pugio, and sets it in front of me. It's sheathed in a beautiful silver inlaid scabbard decorated with a single golden rose. It's breathtaking. I'm far from a weapons expert or anything like that; my youth was spent playing basketball, football, and baseball, not fencing or training with swords. I only know it's a Pugio because a tour guide at the Roman Coliseum once let me hold one; well, a cheap replica anyway. The name stuck with me because it sounds more like an exclusive wine label than a knife.

I wrap my right hand around the handle of the dagger and place my left hand on the scabbard. Just as I'm about to free the blade from the scabbard, the door to the bar bursts open, and the twins from earlier, wearing the black t-shirts with the white outline of an upside-down dead pig with X's for eyes on it, enter the bar, led by a large creature.

The creature is also wearing black jeans, and white sneaks; but instead of a t-shirt, it's wearing a sleeveless black hoodie with the dead pig logo on it. The creature is about six-and-a-half feet tall and well-muscled. It's constructed like an athletic NFL Defense-End, not bulky, but lean and strong, built for straight line speed. The perfect body type for killing quarterbacks or lawyers. It has a flat face and a wide snout and resembles more pig than human. Its visible skin is a dark grayish-pink color, and its eyes, although farther apart than a human's eyes, are the color of a starless night sky. It's holding a wicked-looking wooden baseball bat wrapped in rusty barbed wire in its left hand. The creature doesn't look like he has much of an imagination, or much of anything, going on upstairs—I doubt it's a Mensa member. I wouldn't be at all surprised if it named its bat. #Lucille.

As the creature enters, Pili stands and carefully pushes his stool to the side. He turns to Billy Joe for some sort of signal. Billy Joe turns and looks in our direction. Pavo sighs and stands in obvious annoyance. He motions with his hand for me to remain seated. He makes eye contact with Billy Joe and a silent communication passes between them. Billy Joe turns back to Pili and shakes his head no. Pili nods and then slides the stool back into its rightful place and places his large rear end back down on top of it. The stool creeks under Pili's weight, but holds.

Pavo walks towards the disgusting pig creature and his two flunkies at a speedy pace, faster than walking, but slower and more graceful than a jog. He stops a few feet short of the creature and addresses it in a language I don't understand. Pavo isn't exactly a tall man, but next to the pig-creature, he looks comically small, like Carey Elwes next to Andre the Giant.

The creature responds in rough English, "I know who you are, *Peacock*. I am not here for you. You go. This is not your business. I am here for the human law—yer. I will teach the human law—yer a lesson." He points the barb-wired wrapped bat at me. "He made threats against one of my piglets. I cannot allow." The creature steps forward.

His piglet? Who the fuck is he talking about? I've never seen this thing before in my life, unless it was an extra in the *Lord of the Rings* movies, in which case Peter Jackson gets way too much credit for the special effects.

Pavo holds his ground. "I know why you're here, but you can't have him. I'm doing you a favor. He would kill you. He is not what you think. You should leave, while you still can."

The creature tosses his head back and snorts. Snot flies through the air. I'm equally fascinated and disgusted. If that's how it laughs, I definitely don't want to see its O-face. I feel sorry for its wife, or girlfriend, or boyfriend, assuming creatures like him have voluntary partners. I involuntarily shiver just thinking about it. Yuck, I need a shower.

Pavo shouts at the creature loud enough for everyone in the bar to hear, "You have to the count of three to turn around and leave this bar of your own free will."

"Or what, little *peacock*?" says the creature. "I am not afraid of you, *lit—tle* vampire." The creature steps forward again, dragging the bat behind him. He stops about a bat's length from Pavo. The twins fan out to the creature's sides. The three stand in an arrow formation, aimed right at Pavo.

"One," counts Pavo.

The creature cocks back the barb-wire wrapped baseball bat above his head and readies himself to swing in a downward striking motion. Like a homerun hitter, the pig-faced creature's fingers waggle as they grip the bat.

Pavo remains calm and stands proud and defiant before the large creature and its deadly looking bat. He's either got the biggest pair in the world, or he knows something I don't—probably both.

I stare in amazement as Pavo's fingers stretch and elongate into deadly claws. He definitely knows something I don't. "What the fuck? I got to get out of here," I whisper to myself.

"Two," counts Pavo.

The creature swings the barb-wire wrapped bat in a downward arc aimed at Pavo's head. Pavo side-steps, just out of the bat's swing path, and then, as quick as a cobra, plunges his right claw into the pig creature's chest and rips out its beating heart. Blue blood gushes from the wound. The whole exchange is over in less than a heartbeat.

Pavo holds the pulsing heart up in front of the creature and slowly enunciates, "Three."

Confusion fills the creature's eyes, and then, recognition of what has just happened takes root. It loosens its grip on the bat, which crashes to the floor, the metal wrapped bat clanging against the tiles. The creature's companions, the twins, stand slack-jawed, and the bar patrons collectively hold their breath. It feels like an eternity passes before the creature collapses to its knees and then smacks, face first, into the blood-covered floor, with a loud sucking sound.

Pavo waltzes over to the bar counter, reaches up, and grabs a water goblet from an overhead rack. He holds the still beating heart of the creature above the goblet and he squeezes. Warm blue blood oozes from the heart, between his fingers, into the glass, and down its sides. Once the goblet is full, he tosses the now deformed and discolored heart onto the floor near the creature's body. Pavo reaches across the bar counter and spears an olive with one of his claw fingers. He dips the olive into the glass and then drinks all the blood down in a single gulp. Streams of blood run from the corners of his mouth, down the creases of his cheeks. He uses his claw to toss the now blood-dipped olive into the air and catches it in his mouth, savoring it, as he chews. Pavo slams the empty glass upside-down onto the bar counter and dramatically spins, until he's facing the twins.

Grinning like a rabid killer, he says, "You have to the count of three."

The twins bolt towards the exit. The skinny hooked-nose one just edges out his tubby companion and makes it out the door first.

Pavo watches them go and shouts loud enough for the entire bar to hear, "That was a legal kill under the Magna-Concordat. The Orog provoked me. He swung first. Does anyone dispute that??"

The bar remains silent. After a few seconds, Billy Joe growls, "Ay, it was a clean kill. Nobody disputes that he swung first. It was legal. Ain't that right?" Billy Joe shouts to his bar patrons.

The bar patrons collectively mumble their agreement. A good rule of thumb, never disagree with the man who serves your drinks, especially when he can turn into a giant fucking bear.

Billy Joe turns to Pavo and gives him a full-toothed smile. "That is, unless there is a law against killing idiots. In that case, friend, you're fucked."

Pavo chuckles.

"Pili, get a mop and clean this pulled pork up," orders Billy Joe.

Pili reluctantly raises his massive frame from his stool, grabs the dead Orog by the foot and drags it into the kitchen. If I wasn't seeing this with my own eyes, I wouldn't believe it.

Billy Joe turns back to Pavo and says in a good-natured, but threatening tone, "Thanks for not wrecking the bar, but if you ever reach that claw of yours behind my bar again, you'll have to grow a new one."

Pavo gives Billy Joe a respectful nod and then addresses the bar with his outdoor voice, "I've challenged Colt Valentine," he points at me with his sword-like fingernails, "to a duel to the death. He's accepted. Any resulting death is legal under the laws of the Magna-Concordat. No *one* ... is to interfere." The last bit, the warning about not interfering, was said in a violence-promising tone.

For the first time since I met Billy Joe, his devil-may-care attitude is gone. He seems uneasy, surprised, and maybe even a little afraid.

Chapter Fourteen

Watching Pavo effortlessly rip the heart out of the Orog, whatever the fuck an Orog is, has crystallized my situation—I am completely and utterly fucked. I think Hudson, Bill Paxton's character in *Aliens*, said it best, *"That's it, man. Game over, man. Game over! What the fuck are we gonna' do now?"* What am *I* gonna' do? I've stupidly agreed to duel with a sixteen-hundred-year-old vampire who is going to kill me and drink my blood—I am fucked.

If a miracle happens and I somehow manage to kill this vampire psychopath, my prize is the chance to save a girl, and become one of twenty-four Advocates who decide and enforce the laws that govern the millions of monsters that roam the earth eating babies for breakfast. I imagine they're not going to be too happy about having a human as a member of their club. Screw my life. How do I get myself into these things? I should have been an accountant. Accountants never have to deal with shit like this, I've seen the t-shirts, "Accountants do it with double entry." I'm not exactly sure what that means, but it sounds more appealing than being eaten by a monster.

Pavo walks back towards our table with his claws extended. I move to position the table between us. I am many things, a lawyer, an out-of-practice lover, a certifiable asshole, but I am not a fighter. I prefer to grapple with my words, and think my way out of violent confrontations rather than rolling on the floor and wrestling. I have absolutely no interest in fighting an ancient Roman vampire with Freddy Kruger claws. If given a choice, and I don't feel like I am being given one, I'd rather talk it out, hug it out, play a competitive game of badminton, or do just about anything—other than fight.

I deeply exhale to keep from hyperventilating. This is really happening. He's going to kill me—that is, if I don't kill him first. And these yahoos—I look around at the twenty or so bar patron looky-loos—are going to sit around, sip their beers, munch on their bar snacks, and watch me die. I might as well be a free pay-per-view match, the newest schmuck fed to Tyson in his prime. Well, screw that. Today, my name is Buster Douglas. I want to live, and in order to do that, I need to kill this Cosa Nostra suit-wearing Nosferatu-looking motherfucker—but how? Okay, breathe and then think. Treat it just like you would a legal problem; brainstorm, and use your critical thinking skills. How do they kill vampires in the movies?

Sunlight? It's two in the morning. Unless I can get him to delay the fight five hours and move outside, sunlight is probably not a viable option.

Wooden stake to the heart? I guess I could snap off a table leg and wield it like a stake. Even if I managed it, how would I make it sharp enough to stab through his chest plate and into his heart? I've seen autopsies, the chest cavity is harder to cut through than you'd think.

Cut off its head? In *Highlander*, Sean Connery did say, "If your head comes away from your neck, it's over." Wait, those weren't vampires. Didn't they turn out to be aliens? Regardless, I think cutting off a vampire's head is supposed to kill it. I do have the dagger, although it's not really ideal for cutting—it's more of a stabbing weapon. It could work; then again, I have my doubts that Pavo will hold still long enough for me to saw through his neck.

What about silver? Isn't silver supposed to burn vampires? The Pugio looks like it's made of silver, then again, so does the ring he's wearing, and he doesn't seem to be suffering any ill effects from its contact with his skin. At least, his hand hasn't burst into flame or anything—silver's probably out, at best it's a maybe.

Pavo is stalking closer. I'm running out of time.

Shit, what else? Aren't ultraviolet rays supposed to burn vampires? I wonder if my cell phone's LED flashlight is ultraviolet? Probably not, that would be really cool, though. Death by cell phone flashlight, how has that not been in a movie?

Fire? Maybe I could try and burn him? In the movies fire always kills vampires. Unfortunately, I don't have a lighter, or matches, and there are no candles on the tables. I've watched that show *Naked and Afraid*; it's fucking hard to make fire from scratch. Fire also has a habit of getting out of control and there are innocents here.

Maybe I can run? Then again, maybe not. Pavo's standing between me and the door and he's a lot faster than I am. He also has the gate pen. I'm not going to be able to get away and, even if I do, it won't be for long.

Pavo's getting closer. He's dragging his claws across one of the wooden tables, making a screeching sound. I can barely hear the sound of my knees knocking with fear over the noise.

Crosses? I could use something to make a cross but crosses don't kill vampires, do they? In the movies, crosses almost never work, and when they do, they just repel them. I don't feel like being mocked by this long-tooth blood drinker for trying to repel him with a cross. Plus, that plan has the same problems as running—it merely delays the inevitable.

Holy water? That's another no go. I don't see any priests and I'm certainly not pious enough to bless water.

Quick, what else? What about a shotgun blast to the head? It seemed to work well for Tarantino in that Mexican bar where he lived out his cinematic Clooney is my better-looking brother fantasy. Selma Hayek was so hot in that movie—Colt, focus! The painfully obvious shortcoming with the Tarantino plan is—I don't have a shotgun. I wonder if I could call timeout and go buy one. Maybe Amazon will deliver? There is probably an app for that.

Shit, he's getting really close.

Maybe I can distract him? Wasn't there something in the movies about vampires having severe obsessive-compulsive-disorder? I seem to remember someone throwing a handful of seeds at a vampire, which compelled it to stop and count them. That sounds ridiculous, but I'm running out of ideas.

Fuck it, this brainstorming session is getting me nowhere, except closer to death. I've got to do something. I free the pugio's blade and use the scabbard like a hockey stick to slap the bowl of bar snacks, like a hockey puck, at Pavo. It misses ... badly, but bar snacks fly everywhere. Unfortunately, Pavo doesn't hunch over the spilled bar snacks and frantically count them like in the movies. Rather, he tilts his head to the side and asks, "Did you just throw pretzels at me?"

My cheeks turn red. "I think it was Chex mix."

"Are you daft, boy? Did your mother drop you as a child?"

The embarrassment I'm feeling over my failed plan is rinsed away by the anger aroused by his insult. I think about insulting his mother and then I remember, his mother is probably my great-great-great-great aunt, or something. Instead I say, "Whatever, short-stuff." In retrospect, probably not my best insult ever.

Pavo circles around the table until we're separated by less than a table length of empty space. I take a step back and to my left into the aisle between tables to give myself more room. I stagger my feet shoulder width apart and point the scabbard I'm holding in my left hand towards Pavo's chest. I intend on using it as my jab, my lightning, to keep the distance between us. I cock the dagger in my right hand back into a stabbing position. I intend to use it as my counter-attack, my thunder. For some reason, naming my attacks gives me some comfort. #VideoGameGeneration.

"Come get some!" I yell. I know—I sound silly, I feel silly, but I'm more interested in surviving than looking silly, and action heroes always yell something before a fight, and heroes always survive, so there must be something to it. If yelling something, even something idiotic, increases my odds of survival, even a little, then I'm going to yell. "Come get some of my thunder and lightning!" I scream. God, I sound like a moron.

Pavo's normally unreadable face oozes sadness, "Boy, I am sorry we didn't have more time together. I had so much more I wanted to tell you." His voice has a sad calmness to it; it's the voice of a man who has accepted and made peace with fate. The voice a suicide-bomber uses to order a cup of coffee fifteen minutes before he sets off his payload.

"Remember, you can trust Sinn," he says. Then, faster than I would have thought possible, Pavo steps towards me and strikes me with a closed fist uppercut, launching me skyward. I crash into a neighboring table, collapsing it under my weight. Pain rushes into my body as all the oxygen escapes.

As I lay on top of the broken table, gasping for air, I take inventory of my situation. I hurt everywhere, but I don't think anything is broken. Come to think of it, I don't think I've ever broken a bone in my body. Life is funny, isn't it? I'm lying here, about to die, and all I can think about is how I've never broken a bone. Guess that makes me a near superhero, Willis-like. #Unbreakable.

My lightning is gone. I must have lost it in the fall. Fortunately, my right hand still has a death grip on the handle of my thunder. It's a miracle I didn't stab myself during my fall. Seriously, what am I doing fighting an ancient vampire? #I'mNotAVanHelsing. If there's a God up there, I could use a little help. Please?

Pavo takes a step forward and then leaps into the air with his chest puffed out in front of him, fangs bared, and both claws extended and cocked back behind his head. I can't help but marvel at his gracefulness and geek out about how much he looks like a well-dressed Wolverine or Sabertooth, jumping through the air in one of those comics I loved as a kid. His deathblow is unnecessarily flashy, but there's no doubt in my mind, I'll die if his claws reach me. I wonder why the Orog kept called him "Peacock?" He looks more like a jungle cat to me.

Time slows to a crawl as Pavo soars through the air towards me—just like when I'm in a courtroom. I can't move any faster than normal, so I have no hope of moving my collapsed body out of Pavo's path, but my mind is free. I watch in awe as Pavo's powerful form inches toward me. It's fascinating to watch your own death approach in super slow motion. Spit and blood fly from Pavo's mouth and nails as he inches closer. It's like watching the world's most 4K, 3D horror movie.

An admittedly pathetic thought invades my consciousness, I haven't been laid in over a year–I don't want to die without having sex, at least one more time. I'd even be okay with mediocre sex. I can't die yet, I have to do something. The dagger in my right hand is already pointed towards the sky; if I can shift it, aim it at his heart, I might be able to survive this or at the very least, cut him. That's at least something.

Contrary to what you might have learned in grade school, the human heart is not located in the left side of your chest. It's located in the middle, with its apex pointing to the left. The dagger's in my right hand, so I don't have to move it that far to position it such that it should strike true. I aim the dagger, millimeter by painstaking millimeter. It's a race between Pavo's soaring body and the dagger. I make a quick mental calculation and it appears fortune favors me. It's going to be close, but I think I'm going to be able to get the dagger in position before Pavo reaches me.

I lock the dagger into place and brace for impact. Then, something unexpected happens. The dagger begins to glow, a little at first and then more intensely. It gets warm and then hot—so hot it begins to burn my flesh. I want to let go, but I can't open my hand. The glow keeps intensifying until it erupts into a blinding bright white light and the heat continues to build until I'm screaming in pain. The dagger momentarily cools as its tip pierces Pavo's chest and a volcano of energy erupts out of the blade into Pavo. There is an explosion of heat and burning white light and then blackness.

Chapter Fifteen

I awake to screaming ... it takes me a moment to ascertain that it's me. I'm the one who's screaming. I feel like a newborn who's just been torn from his mother's embrace—disoriented. Where am I? I choke down air and try to self-soothe, but my body doesn't cooperate; it's frozen with terror. After my third deep breath, the screaming stops and my pounding heart begins to slow. I count backward, "ten, nine, eight"... it's a calming technique I sometimes teach my clients who are facing prison time ... "seven, six, five," ... isn't it amazing how something as simple as counting can change your entire outlook ..."four, three, two" ... my heart and breathing rates normalize, my eyes open, and I begin to orient myself ... "one."

The counting works. I begin to regain power over my facilities. I'm lying on the floor in the Triple B. I have a death grip on the Pugio, which is thankfully no longer glowing or burning my hand—it's actually cool to the touch and it feels ... empty? Or spent. It's hard to describe. I've never felt this sensation before. It's like I can feel inside of the blade.

As I sit up, I realize there is a swath of destruction radiating out from me. It looks like a bomb went off, and I'm sitting in the epicenter. Chairs and tables have been flung to the far corners of the bar. Staring bar patrons have congregated along the edges of the radius of destruction. I ignore the patrons for now and search for Pavo or his body, but it's nowhere to be found.

My mind is flooded with painful questions: What the heck just happened? Why am I not dead? What was that white light, and where did it come from? Did I really do that? The more I stress about my circumstances, the more my head hurts. I think I have a concussion.

A slight tingling sensation starts in my left hand and starts moving up my arm. I search for the source of discomfort and realize that Pavo's silver ring, with the red stone, is wrapped around my ring finger. "Shit," I say aloud. Does that mean I killed him? How did it get on my finger? I try to remove it, by twisting, yanking, and pulling, but it's stuck and won't come off. I start to panic. The dagger clatters to the floor as I urgently try to wrench the ring off—it won't budge. It's like the ring is fused to my skin, like it's a part of me. I have a feeling no amount of lotion or oil is going to make any difference. "Shit!" I scream in frustration.

My mind begins to race again as it sifts through the millions of unanswered questions that plague me, and then it hits me—the girl. I scramble to my feet and search the wreckage. I find Pavo's phone beneath an overturned table, but there's no sign of the book, pen, or even Pavo's body for that matter. I thank the heavens his phone is neither locked nor broken. Although relieved, I can't help but think critically of Pavo. It's really stupid to leave your cell phone unlocked.

I scroll through Pavo's text messages; there aren't many, it looks like he wiped his phone before our meeting. There's only one contact, Sinn, and a string of cryptic messages from her. The phone is otherwise clean, even of apps, except for one called SoundSphere, which I assume is the mage crafted sound barrier app. The photo Pavo showed me of Roy carrying an unconscious girl has been deleted. I have nothing to give the police except a fantastic story that's sure to get me locked up in a mental institution. The last message from Sinn is a photo of some old houses. I instantly recognize them as the "Painted Ladies."

The Painted Ladies are tri-colored Victorian houses that became famous when they were included in the opening scene of a popular 1990's television show based in San Francisco. After that show, they became a must-see, and a must-take-selfie stop on every San Francisco tourist's must-do list. I'm pretty familiar with the area. I can't tell you how many weekends I've spent playing a San Francisco tour guide for a visiting friend or one of my ex's family members.

The picture was taken from within Alamo Square Park, which is right across the street from the houses. At this time of night, the park will be empty, except for the homeless who call the park home. I can't tell from the picture which house Roy took the girl to, so I don't have enough information to call the police yet, but at least I have a place to start looking. I also have Sinn's cell phone number. Maybe she's less of a dick than dear old dad, and maybe she'll be willing to help. I press the call button and it goes straight to voicemail. *Damn it.*

I have no choice but to go myself. I pray that Sinn is waiting for me, but first I need to find Pavo's gate pen. Without it, I'm never going to make it in time to save the girl. Even at this time of night, when traffic is negligible, it would take over an hour to get an Uber and drive across the Bay Bridge. A lot can happen in an hour … I need that pen. Unfortunately, the last time I saw the pen, it was in Pavo's jacket pocket—and his jacket, like his body, is missing.

Wait, didn't he say something about the pen being linked to the ring? This whole thing is crazy, but what do I have to lose? I place my right thumb and index finger onto the ring, just like I saw Pavo do, and I close my eyes. I don't know what I'm supposed to do exactly, but asking the pen to come to me seems like the natural thing to do. After a moment or two of visualizing the pen appearing before me on the floor, I open my eyes and I'm stunned—it actually worked. Pavo's beautiful vintage ornate silver pen is on the floor in front of me.

The pen is cool to the touch. After a moment, it begins to warm in my hand and it keeps warming, until it's nearly burning my flesh. It begins to melt and transform its shape from Pavo's beautiful vintage ornate pen into something else altogether. My first instinct is to fling the mass of molten silver as far away from me as I can, but I can't—the ring won't let me. It tells me I have to hold on to the mass of molten silver until its metamorphosis is finished. It's as if the metal is merging with me, pairing itself to me. The seemingly living metal begins to take a new shape, one that resembles one of the more modern pens I prefer to use. One with a fat cylindrical barrel and a cap with an elegant clip. A beautiful ribbon of ornate etching circles the meeting place of the pen cap and barrel. The intricate band pattern looks like flowing water and appears to move as I watch—it's mesmerizing. The final product looks like a silver Sharpie, the most elegant and ornate Sharpie ever made. I can't help but think of Sméagol/Gollum, and jokingly whisper to myself, "My precious."

Someone's approach snaps me back to this screwed-up reality in which I'm sitting in the middle of a bomb blast in a blackened and burning Oakland bar. Instinctively, I cradle the Sharpie with two hands, shielding it from potential danger. Once I know it's safe, I look up and make eye contact with Billy Joe, who is nonchalantly navigating the bar carnage towards me.

"Sorry about the mess," I stammer.

Billy Joe shrugs, "Pavo has an open tab with me ... it goes back a few months. I assume you're good for it?" Billy Joe pauses and spits some of the sunflower seeds he is chewing into a rocks glass. "And I assume you're good for the damage?"

"Are you seriously hitting me up for money right now?" I ask in my practiced outraged lawyer tone. A tone every lawyer has perfected by the time he graduates law school. "Pavo's body isn't even cold."

"What body?" Billy Joe asks in his slow hick matter-of-fact country drawl.

He has got me there. "Well ... whatever," I say. "If there were a body, it wouldn't even be cold."

Billy Joe's expression reads, I would rather be fishing with dynamite than dealing with your bullshit. He spits some more seeds into the bar glass. "Actually," he says, "if you're talking about Pavo, the ancient *vampire*, his body was already cold. The guy's been dead for hundreds of years. He just didn't have the courtesy until now to check out, or pay his bar tab, which you're going to pay. ... right?"

"Wasn't he your friend?" I ask in the same outraged tone.

Billy Joe just keeps staring at me, while chomping on his seeds.

Finally, I say, "Can we do this later? All I know is that I need to open a gate or a girl's gonna' die."

Billy Joe shrugs again and starts walking back towards the bar. He shouts over his shoulder in a smart-ass tone, "Don't leave that knife on the floor. Someone else might fall on it and kill themselves."

"What a prick," I mutter, as I search the rubble for the knife's decorative scabbard. I find it under a chair, and I use it to clothe the naked blade. I can't help but think it's strange that there's not a single drop of blood on the blade ... or handle ... or floor for that matter. Don't vampires bleed? Where does all the blood they drink go? A mystery that will have to wait for another time. Right now, I have to go see about a girl.

Instinctively, as if I've done this before, I make for the back wall where there is a flat surface I can draw on. I'm not the best artist, but I should be able to draw a door. I press the silver Sharpie to the wall and begin drawing. Magic silver ink flows for me, just as it did for Pavo. When I finish outlining a rectangular door, I draw a round doorknob and I tuck the pen away in my pocket. Then, just like I saw Pavo do, I grab the ring on my left hand with my right thumb and index finger. I close my eyes and visualize the park across from the Painted Ladies and say, "Alamo Square Park." I open my eyes and reach for the doorknob, to my surprise, I'm able to grab it. It feels solid, cold, metallic to the touch. I swear I'm holding a real silver doorknob. It even has weight to it. It's amazing. I slowly turn the knob and pull the door open.

"Holy shit!" I exclaim. It worked. It actually worked. I just opened a door to Alamo Square Park. I can see trees and grass on the other side. I'm standing in an Oakland bar, looking through a magic door into a park in the middle of San Francisco. It's probably not the most dignified reaction, but I can't help myself. I shout, "David Blaine can suck it!" #ThisIsRealMagicBitches.

Just as I'm about to step through the door, it hits me. The euphoria I was feeling from performing magic is buried under the weight of a new terrifying world. A world where magic is real, monsters are real, and my life is never going be the same. I hold my breath, the way I did as a child when my dad drove us through a tunnel, and step through the magic door into an uncertain future.

Chapter Sixteen

Before I'm even able to gain my bearings, or clear the gate light from my eyes, a foot solidly connects with my groin. I wince, double over in excruciating pain, and nearly collapse. I somehow manage to balance myself in a bent over position with my legs spread and my hands protectively cradling my balls. Those yoga classes I took to meet chicks are finally paying off. I brace for a follow-up blow that never comes.

Finally, I compose myself enough to look up. Standing before me, with her arms crossed, and an unimpressed look on her face, is one of the most beautiful women I've ever seen. She's not voluptuous, but fit. She clearly takes care of herself. Not weightlifter fit, but triathlon fit. Her pale brown skin seems to glow and sparkle under the Alamo Square Parks halogen street lamps. The picture Wilson showed me doesn't do Pavo's daughter justice. Her oval-shaped face, delicate chin, almond-shaped brown eyes, and dark hair unmistakably mark her heritage as Thai. Wilson said the records indicate she's twenty-eight years old—I'm having a hard time believing that. She looks more like she's twenty-one. As I stare, I realize, twenty-one isn't right either; there's something older, much older, lurking behind her eyes. Is she a vampire? Pavo never said one way or the other. It'd make sense, though. Did I mention she looks unimpressed with me? If looks could kill, my balls wouldn't hurt anymore because I'd be dead.

After a few moments of sucking air, I manage to squawk out, "Hi, I'm guessing you're Sinn?" There's no response. "I'm Colt." Still, no response. "You kick like a mule."

Her tough exterior momentarily cracks, and a pride laced smile peeks through as my icebreaker lands. Then, as quick as it appeared, the crack disappears, the hint of a smile is gone, and her steely death stare is back.

"My father's dead?" She not quite asks and not quite declares. There's anguish and just a sliver of cynical hope in her voice. She knows the answer already, but wants to be wrong, prays she's wrong.

"Yes," I answer in the most empathetic tone I can muster, considering my balls are throbbing. I elect not to mock her or his memory by apologizing. I'm not sorry that I'm still alive, however, even though Pavo was kind of a dick and forced me to kill him, here, now, looking at Sinn, I feel terrible for the role I played in his death. I consider trying to explain the circumstances surrounding his death—to justify killing him. I know blaming him will make me feel better, but this isn't about me. This is about a girl mourning her father. It won't matter to her that I feel I was justified in stabbing him, so I keep my excuses to myself. It's better to let her process his death in her own way.

Sinn's jaw clenches when I answer "Yes," but otherwise she remains a statue. Rather than discuss the kick to my junk, which I assume was her way of coping with the fact that I killed her dad and she's now helping me, she says, "If you want to save the girl, we need to go—now." Sinn turns and starts walking in the opposite direction of the Painted Ladies.

Apparently, she isn't much into sharing her feelings. That's fine by me. I always say it's better to bottle them up and never talk about them. Even better to drown 'em with wine. Sinn's all business. I respect that, because I'm positive I'd act the same way if our roles were reversed. Under the circumstances, I decide to let her blast to my balls go. #Bygones. Still, I follow a few paces behind her. I want to give her plenty of space. The further her feet are from my nuts the better. I may want kids someday after all.

Chapter Seventeen

Sinn stops in front of an old dilapidated Victorian home situated about two blocks from the Painted Ladies, on the far side of the park. The leaded white paint covering most of the house is severely weathered and chipped. Boards cover the windows and there's an old construction sign staked in the front yard. The illusion that it's a "fixer-upper" and being restored probably keeps the neighbors at bay, but this is a project that will likely never be finished. This house looks nothing like the beautiful Painted Ladies in the photograph Sinn sent Pavo. As if reading my mind, Sinn volunteers, "I sent a picture of the Painted Ladies to Pavo so you'd have something familiar to anchor the gate to. Pavo told me using the pen can be difficult, especially if you don't know where you're going. I thought a familiar location might make it easier for you, and every Bay Area native knows the Painted Ladies."

I nod in understanding. She's smart and beautiful. If I hadn't just killed her father, she might be at risk of me hitting on her. Shit, she might be at risk anyway.

"Your client took her in there," she points at the old dilapidated home.

I mumble "Ex-client," under my breath.

"Do try to be careful. That's a Dead Pigs flop house," she adds.

"Dead Pigs?" I ask.

Sinn looks at me angrily, "You really don't know anything." It was a statement—not a question. "What does ... *did* ... Dad ever see in you?" She shakes her head in disgust. "The Dead Pigs are a gang of psychotic rapists and killers. They're low rent for the most part, mostly weak bloods. Basically, a bunch of pansies playing clubhouse, but in sufficient numbers they can be a pain. Try and be careful.

Some of their shot-callers are dangerous—nothing a Palatinus shouldn't be able to handle."

"Wait, what?" I say. "What's a weak-blood?"

"You really are stupid, aren't you," she snaps. Again, it was a statement not a question. My annoyance with this chick is beginning to exceed the sympathy I'm feeling for killing her father.

Sinn continues in the tone a first-grade teacher might use with her students, "Weak-bloods are individuals that are more than 50% human, but less than completely human."

Apparently, the glazed-over look on my face encourages her to explain further. "Many races have compatible biology with humans and over the centuries have mated—sometimes forcefully—with humans. The children produced by these unions are mixed-blooded; they typically look more human than their non-human parent, and many of these children inherit their parents' more than human traits, although at diluted levels. These are called mixed-bloods. Mixed-bloods are generally less dangerous than their parents, but still dangerous."

"Are you a mixed-blood?" I ask.

"No, I'm a vampire. There's no such thing as a mixed or weak-blooded vampire. You're either a vampire or you're not. Vampires are made—not born. Vampires can't breed with humans. Now pay attention, and stop asking stupid questions; I'm not going to go over this a second time."

I nod to placate her; I want her to keep talking.

"Mixed-bloods sometimes mate with humans, or other mixed-bloods, and produce offspring with even more diluted blood, which look even more human, and have even weaker non-human traits. These are called weak-bloods. Weak-bloods are often cast off by their parents as abominations."

"Why?"

"Because they're weak–practically human."

Sinn pauses long enough to shoot me a frustrated look, "You only qualify as a citizen under Concordat law if you are 50% pure-blooded or higher. Citizens consider all blood other than human blood to be pure. In other words, if you're between 1 and 50% human, you are a mixed-blood, and a Concordat citizen. If you are between 51 and 99% human, you're a weak-blood and not a citizen. Weak-bloods are essentially outcasts—outsiders, not accepted by either the human or monster world. It's not uncommon for weak-bloods to band together for protection and form blood gangs like the Dead Pigs. Unfortunately, blood gangs are often exploited by pure or mixed-bloods. Some weak-bloods even worship pure-bloods like gods."

"Seriously?"

"Seriously."

"Okay. What do you know about the Dead Pigs?"

"The Dead Pigs are a powerful east coast blood gang, mainly made up of weak-blooded cave or sewer dwellers. Pitiful creatures that prefer dark dank places—hardly worth the effort to kill. Their shot-callers are a different story. They're mostly pure-bloods, dangerous ones. I'd heard a rumor that the Dead Pigs had expanded their territory to the west coast, but I hadn't run into any, until now. This dump has their markings all over it."

"Markings?"

"Like human gangs, blood gangs identify themselves and mark territory, with colors or symbols. Throughout history, symbols have been used to unify the angry and disenfranchised. They are often misused to control the weak minded. The Dead Pigs identify themselves with a symbol, the outline of an upside-down pig with X's for eyes." Sinn points at some tagging on the side of the home.

"I've seen that before," I say.

Sinn looks unimpressed with my observation.

I don't see any harm in being honest with Sinn, "I think I met some Dead Pigs today. Charming fellows, Pavo killed one."

Sinn's eyes fill with grief at the mention of her father's name. "What do you mean Dad killed one?"

"There were two guys at the Triple B who were eyeing me—"

"—The Triple B?" Sinn asks.

"Billy Bob's Bar," I explain. "The Triple B's a better name."

Sinn nods in apparent agreement.

"They were both wearing shirts with that symbol," I point at the tagging on the house. "When they saw me sit down with Pavo, they immediately left the bar. I thought it was strange at the time, but people at bars do strange things, so I didn't give it a second thought. About an hour later, they returned, with a big ugly mother in tow. Something Pavo called an orog."

I see recognition in her face and pause and wait for her to explain. Finally, after what feels like an eternity, Sinn relents, "An orog is the offspring of an ogre and an orc. They're rare. Ogres are aggressive lovers. Other species rarely survive mating with one. I've only met one orog—it was fat and had a head like a pig." Sinn gets a faraway look in her eyes, "Nasty creature, not something I want to spend any more time with."

I nod. "This one also had the head of a pig, but it wasn't fat. It was fit. It looked like an NFL Defensive-End. The orog and Pavo had a disagreement that ended when Pavo ripped its heart right out of its chest and drank its blood. Its two companions fled." I don't mention the part about it threatening me.

A red tear slowly traces Sinn's cheek as I talk about her father. Sinn looks away and coldly says, "Time's a'wasting. Think about what your client is probably doing to the girl. You'd better go."

I don't need her to remind me of the obvious. I know time is ticking, but I'm afraid to go in there by myself. I need Sinn's help. "You're not going to help?" I ask.

"You're a Palatinus. You don't need my help to deal with some weak-bloods."

Sinn wipes her tear and hands me a bloody business card with an Oakland address on it. "Be here Monday morning. It's your new office. I promised my father I'd help you in your duties as an Advocate, and I intend to fulfill that promise. Now if it's all right with you, I'm going to go and mourn my dead father." Sinn turns and takes a step back towards the park.

"Wait!" I shout. "I do need your help. I can't fight a gang by myself!"

Sinn turns back towards me, and with an even more annoyed and incredulous look on her beautiful glowing face, which I didn't think was possible, says, "Did you not kill my father?"

"Well ... I guess ... yes," I finally stammer. Although I can't help but think Billy Joe had a point. Did I really kill Pavo or did I simply hold the knife while he impaled himself? In retrospect, I'm beginning to think I was a prop in an elaborate suicide.

"Are you not a Palatinus?" she asks.

"Yes, my mother was a Palatinus. Why do you keep asking me that? What does my mother's maiden name have to do with the price of tea in Bangkok?"

I realize after I say it that it might be early in our relationship to be using racially charged metaphors. Fortunately, Sinn doesn't seem to notice or care. Rather than anger, a confused look crosses her face. Unlike Pavo, who was an emotionless statue, Sinn wears her emotions. "It's not the name," she says. "It's what the name means. It's what you are."

"What I am?"

If possible, she looks even more confused than I feel. "Are you trying to trick me, Colt?" It's the first time she has called me by my first name; it rolls off her tongue like fresh 100% Vermont maple syrup. Hesitantly, she says, "You are a paladin?" This time it's more of a question than a statement.

"A what?" I ask. "A paladin? What does that even mean?"

The seeds of anger take root in the pupils of her eyes and grow. She steps towards me, balls her right hand into a fist and swings at my head. Just like when Pavo was flying through the air at me, time slows to a crawl. The punch approaches in matrix-like slow motion. Having experienced this before, I quickly acclimate to the time slow, shift my weight to my back foot and, inch-by-inch, begin leaning back out of the path of her fist. A quick mental estimate tells me she's going to miss—barely. As I lean back, I raise my right hand in a defensive posture—just in case she follows her first punch with a second. After what feels like an eternity, her punch sails by, barely missing my chin. Once I'm out of danger, time speeds back up. What is happening to me?

"I am tiring of this charade," she says. "You're clearly a paladin. What game are you playing?"

"What game am I playing? Are you fucking kidding me?" My indoor voice evolves into an outdoor voice, "First off, stop trying to hit me. You're starting to piss me off. I let the kick to my balls go. I figured, I killed your dad, you kicked me in the balls; we're even-Steven. Well, close to even-Steven. Regardless, I'm warning you, you swing at me again and I'm going to swing back. I don't care if you're a girl. The whole 'don't hit a girl' thing, doesn't apply to hundred-year-old vampires with superhuman powers." I take a breath and lower my voice, "Now what the fuck is a paladin and why do you think I am one?"

Sinn doesn't immediately respond to my outburst. She takes the measure of me, studies me with her exotic eyes. Finally, she says in an almost non-mocking tone, "I am *not* a hundred years old. It's clear to me that you know even less than I was led to believe. We don't have time for a fireside chat, but I'm not risking my life until I know you can handle yourself. Answer me quickly, what do you know about the history of the Palatinus family?"

"Nothing, really," I answer with a shrug. "My mother told me her side of the family was all dead. Her father emigrated from Italy, he was fleeing something. I always assumed it was the Nazis."

"Didn't Pavo discuss your family history with you?" asks Sinn.

I shake my head. "We ran out of time."

Sinn looks up at the heavens and sighs, visibly frustrated with her father. "Your family has many enemies. Your ancestors wielded great power; they were knights, feared by many of the Concordat. They fancied themselves the champions of humanity—the Christian God's chosen saviors. A fat lot of good that did them. Their arrogance led to their destruction and near extinction. You're all that remains, and you don't even know what you are." Sinn pauses for a moment "There is much you need to know, but not now, not here."

I'm getting pissed off that everyone keeps telling me there are things I need to know, just not right now. If not now, when? After I'm dead? I start to protest a further can-kick-down-the-road when Sinn interrupts, "—When you're in combat, does it feel like the world slows down? Is that how you were able to avoid my punch?"

"Yes," I stammer. "I mean, I'm not in combat all that often—almost never. I'm a *lover*—not a fighter." Albeit, an out of practice one, although I don't mention that part. Despite my most charming smile, Sinn doesn't react at all. Slightly wounded, I continue, "Time does slow for me sometimes. It happens mainly in stressful situations, like when I'm in court, or when you tried to punch me." I don't mention that it also slowed when I killed her father.

"Fascinating. It manifests outside of combat?" she says more to herself than to me. "I haven't read anything like that in your family journals."

"Journals?" I ask.

She ignores my question. "Your ancestors called your gift Battle-Sight. It was common amongst your family, although not all had it. Gifts, and the strength of gifts, varied amongst your family, and not all Palatinus' were born with gifts. It was ... difficult for those of your blood who were born without gifts. Your kin weren't the nicest people." She wipes more red tears away with her forearm.

"According to your family's journals, Battle-Sight allows you to slow time; at least your perception of time. Time doesn't actually slow, and you don't actually move any faster. It's all perception. The gift gives you more time to think and react. A fight is all about timing—when to block, when to dodge, when to strike. Battle-Sight gives you the ability to perfect your timing. It made your family nearly invincible on the battlefield, at least when fighting other humans, and it gave them a chance when fighting things that are ... more than human. Faster than human."

"Like vampires," I quip.

Sinn frowns. "Colt, there are things much more dangerous than vampires in this world."

"Like female vampires?"

Sinn's frown mostly fades, but a hint of a smile pokes through her defenses. I think she is warming up to me. "Do you have any other gifts?" she asks.

"I don't know," I say. My thoughts drift to the ornate dagger I carry and how it now feels empty to me. I think about the explosion of light and release of energy that occurred when it penetrated Pavo. I decide it's probably not a good idea to mention that right now. I don't even know if that was me, the dagger, or something Pavo did, and I really want to avoid discussing the details of Sinn's father's death with her. Talk about uncomfortable. #ThingsI'dRatherNotDo.

"Most of your family members had multiple gifts," Sinn says. "At least with your Battle-Sight you won't be completely worthless. Are you sure this girl's worth saving? You don't even know her. She's just another human girl. You don't owe her anything. Human girls all over the world will be raped and will lose their life this night. Why save this one?"

"Because it's the right thing to do. I'm going to save the girl, whether you help me or not." I say that last bit with as much conviction as I can muster. Outwardly, I may be portraying myself as altruistic, but that's not really why I have to do this. I'm not that guy. I'm no hero. My motto is help where you can, but stay out of the line of fire, and don't take unnecessary risks. I suspect guilt, not altruism, is the driving force behind my sudden charitable tendencies. I can't shake the feeling that I owe this girl, that it's my fault she's in trouble. If I hadn't defended Roy, she'd be home with her family, boyfriend, girlfriend, whatever. Her blood is on my hands.

"I'd prefer you helped me. I think I have a considerably better chance of not dying if you help. If I die, I doubt I'll make it to work on Monday. Won't that make it hard to honor your promise to your father?" I don't like weaponizing the death of her father and using it to manipulate her, but a girl's life is at issue.

Sinn closes her eyes for a moment. A cool breeze brushes her hair away from her face. "I guess I have to help you then." Her eyes open and she begins to study the house. "I can't let you die on your first night as an Advocate. Dad's spirit would haunt me to the end of days." Sinn pauses, and grins wickedly as she glances over at me, "And maybe you'll trip and hit your man parts on my foot again."

While Sinn chuckles to herself, I shiver. I'm going to have to keep my head on a swivel around this one.

"After you, Sir Paladin," Sinn says, while making a sweeping gesture towards the front door with her arm. I shake my head and start climbing the dilapidated stairs to the front door of the old Victorian home. At least she can't kick me in the balls from behind.

Chapter Eighteen

Despite the home's shoddy outward appearance, the front door's sturdy, and the lock's new. Fortunately, whoever last entered, forgot to lock it, or ... left it unlocked on purpose. I hope it's the former, but something feels off about this place, and I have a feeling it's the latter. My senses are screaming *danger, danger, run from the creepy house, run directly to the nearest church, and take a bath in holy water*! What am I doing here? I'm not a hero, or knight. I don't really owe this girl anything—do I? I'm just a lawyer, and all I did was do my job. Storming dilapidated mansions to save girls from gangs of monsters really isn't my forte.

For a moment, I consider packing it in and heading home to my warm bed. It's a long-shot, but maybe I can convince Sinn to join me. Don't sex and grief go hand in hand? Then my conscience weighs in arguing, It's my fault the girl's in danger, *blah, blah, blah*. Do the right thing, *blah, blah, blah*. Consciences are buzz-killers.

I reconsider calling the police, but I'm not sure they're really equipped to handle situations like this, and I'm positive they'll lock me up in a mental institution if I tell them to prepare to fight a gang of monsters. I could lie and say it's a drug den, but in this age of budget cuts and crank calls, the police would probably send a single patrol officer to check it out, and then I'd have his death on my conscience too. No, I've got to do this myself. Fuck, I think I just lost an argument with myself—how embarrassing. God, this is a stupid idea. I'm an idiot. I'm going to die and my ex-wife is going to get all my stuff. If I make it out of this alive, I have to update my will. No more perpetually putting it off until next week. If I have to watch my ex-wife inherit my shit from the afterlife, I will come back from the dead, just so I can kill myself.

The old house smells like squirrel piss and wet dog. I battle my gag reflex, swallow my fear, hold my nose, and push forward. As I cross the threshold and enter into the formal sitting parlor, I look back at Sinn, "Do I need to invite you in or something?"

Sinn lets out a genuine full-throated laugh. "You've been watching way too many teenage-vampire-shows."

"It's not my fault I like cheerleaders," I answer.

"I was a cheerleader ... once," says Sinn with a flirtatious grin.

My jaw drops as I try and picture Sinn in a cheerleading outfit.

Sinn shakes her head, obviously aware of what I'm thinking, and waves her hand at me, urging me to continue into the house. I add vampires to the ever-growing list of things I need to research; that is, if I get out of this alive. I'll admit it's comforting to know that vampire women are as much an enigma to me as human women. The more things get weird, the more they stay the same.

The parlor opens up into a formal dining room leading to an empty kitchen. The furniture is old, but surprisingly well kept. An old, unsigned, creepy oil painting of a large pig being hung at the gallows by villagers with pitchforks and torches hangs over the fireplace. The painting is mesmerizing; the artist clearly had exceptional skill. The longer I stare at it, the more real it seems to become.

"It's a mage painting." Sinn whispers.

"A what?" I ask.

"This painting was done with magic. Some mages can use their magic to look back into history. It's a kind of remote-viewing. The mages who can do it channel their magic and with ink or paint transcribe what they're witnessing. It's rare. This is only the second one I've ever seen."

I nod, not really knowing what else to say, and continue searching the house. I wonder if I could get a mage to transcribe the JFK assassination? I've always wanted to know how many shooters there were.

This level of the house appears unoccupied. There are two additional stories above us and a ground level cellar below us. There are two staircases, one leading up and one leading down. "Up or down?" I whisper.

Sinn shrugs indifferently.

I sigh, "Don't you have like super vampire hearing or something?"

Sinn stares at me like I just won an award for being the world's biggest moron. After waiting a few seconds, I realize she's not going to answer me. "Do you hear anything?"

Sinn curtly responds, "Only your heavy breathing and annoyingly loud voice announcing our presence to the entire neighborhood."

I stare at Sinn dumbfounded. Apparently, input and advice aren't part of her definition of help. If I get into serious trouble, I wonder if she'll help at all? Something tells me she's not going to risk getting her well-manicured nails broken unless she has to. Why am I trusting her anyway? I don't want to admit it, because I don't like the answer, but I know why—I'm afraid. Fear makes smart men make bad choices, and I can't think of a night in my life where I made more bad choices than this one—and I'm not even drunk.

I was the type of kid who always ate all his vegetables first and saved his macaroni and cheese for the end. My instincts tell me the vegetables are in the basement, so we go down. I draw the dagger from its scabbard, take a deep breath, and start descending the wooden staircase.

The basement's as dark and cold as an Alaskan winter night. About three steps down, I begin to shiver. I turn on the always handy flashlight app on my cell phone. The LED beam cuts through the darkness like a hot chainsaw through ice. I can't help myself, I have to know, I turn and shine the LED beam up the stairs at Sinn. The light reflects off her eyes causing them to glow. I search for any sign that the light is causing her harm, like spontaneous combustion, and see none. All I see is her impatient gaze, and the back of her raised middle finger, encouraging me to continue down the stairs. So much for using my cell phone flashlight as a weapon against vampires. Despite its real-life ineffectiveness, I still think it'd make a cool weapon in a cheesy sci-fi movie.

I locate a light switch at the bottom of the stairs. Halogen lights slowly kick on, one by one, and flood the basement with an eerie yellow glow. The basement's huge, but other than some couches arranged in a semi-circle around an actual circle that's painted on the floor, and a giant Dead Pig banner on the back wall, it's empty.

I wonder what they use the circle for? I sure hope it's for human or monster fight club, and not dog or animal fight club. "If it's used for dog fighting, I'm going to go Henry E. Hudson, times one thousand, on their ass!" I shout, more to myself than Sinn. I know I should be quiet, but people that hurt animals really piss me off.

"Who is Henry E. Hudson?" Sinn asks.

"He was the righteous federal sentencing judge in the Michael Vick dog-fighting case." I answer tripping with sarcasm. "Remember the headline, '*Vick received twenty-three months and a lecture*'; it was a travesty. All those poor dogs and all he got was twenty-three months? That's why I'd go Henry E. Hudson, times one thousand, on their ass."

Sinn shakes her head. I'm not entirely sure if it's in reverence for the knowledge I just dropped or just in annoyance.

As I pace the room, I notice there's a cold draft coming from the back wall where the giant banner is hanging. I slide the banner aside like a shower curtain to reveal the opening to a large tunnel sloping down into the darkness.

"I doubt they got a permit for this," I mutter. "Well, it's either go back upstairs and search the second and third floor or search the scary tunnel? Lady's choice." I give Sinn my best flirty grin.

Sinn continues to ignore my attempts to lighten the mood. "No reason to go upstairs, there's nothing up there."

I raise one eyebrow quizzically. After I saw the Rock do it in *Be Cool,* the sequel to *Get Shorty* with John Travolta, I taught myself how. I spent weeks practicing in my bathroom mirror every morning while I shaved. I've earned my black-belt in the single eyebrow raise.

Sinn gives me a quarter of a smile. "Super vampire hearing or something like that," she quips.

"You're funny," I answer. "Then it's down the monster hole we go. Ladies first." I imitate Sinn and make a dramatic sweeping gesture with my arm, like she did at the house's entrance.

"No," Sinn says while crossing her arms. "Stupid father-killing assholes first."

I cringe. I thought she was warming up to me. "I'm guessing you don't like car doors opened for you either?"

Sinn punches me in the shoulder, not gently, but not too hard.

"Ouch," I say in mock pain. "I warned you about hitting me again. Keep it up and see what happens, vampire girl."

Sinn raises one eyebrow at me; she does it almost as good as I do. The Rock would be proud. I'm actually really impressed right now, and maybe a bit hard. I think I'm in love. "Touché, I guess I'll go first." I take another deep breath, and begin to sing as I enter the tunnel, "Hi ho, hi ho, it's down the tunnel we go." It's hard to be scared when you're singing.

Chapter Nineteen

About a hundred feet into the tunnel, we reach a fork and discover a wooden sign, one of those cheesy ones that a toothless guy in overalls will make you at the county fair for ten bucks. It reads 'DEAD PIGS' with an arrow pointing down the left tunnel. Come to think of it, the smell down here reminds me of the county fair.

"Trap?" I suggest.

Sinn shrugs. "I doubt it's for us. You've been an Advocate for all of ten minutes. You really think they had time to make a sign just for you? It may hurt your ego to hear this, but not everything has to do with you. It's probably just a wooden sign. I bet they figure if anyone gets this far, they're either supposed to be here, or not worth hiding from."

"You've been an Advocate for all of ten minutes," I repeat in the voice of a whiny thirteen-year-old-girl.

Sinn shakes her head in disgust. "What are you, twelve?" and then starts down the left tunnel.

"No ... thirteen," I mumble, as I follow her down the tunnel.

The tunnel snakes and, after a particularly sharp corner, opens into a large cavern. Like the basement, the cave has a large circle painted on the rocky dirt floor. Unlike the basement, the cave isn't empty. Twenty or thirty goons, all wearing the Dead Pigs symbol somewhere on their persons, surround the empty circle. At the edge of the far end of the circle is an oversized accent chair. I wouldn't call it a throne exactly; it's more of a sitting room chair on steroids, the type of casino lobby novelty chair you and four friends took a drunken selfie in after you got killed at the tables. #ICanOnlyAffordPennySlots.

The oversized chair is occupied by another one of those pig-headed orog creatures. This one's skin is the color of dark mud and its body shape has more in common with "Fat Bastard" from the Austin Powers movies than an NFL defensive-end. I thought Sinn said they were rare? This must be my lucky day. This is the second one I've seen in as many hours.

In the back corner of the cave, a poorly built wooden pen holds three of the largest hogs I've ever seen. The inhuman squeals emanating from the pen send shivers through my bones. A pile of rotting bodies, likely losers from the blood-soaked fighting circle, are stacked next to the pen, one on top of the other. The losers are being fed to the giant hogs. I'm not sure what smells worse, the rotting flesh or the piles of pig shit.

Along the far wall, tied in the same manner a cowboy ties his horse to a hitching post outside his favorite saloon, are four human girls. I immediately recognize Joycee Baird—Roy's victim from the trial. She must be the girl he was carrying in the picture. Joycee is sitting in silence, a dead look in her eyes, the same look I've seen in the eyes of death row inmates—hopelessness. The other girls are sobbing, clearly afraid, but trying not to draw attention to themselves.

Standing on one side of the oversized carnival chair, grinning from ear-to-ear, is Joycee's tormentor, my former client, Roy Silas. On the other-side of the chair, stands Blob Face and Hook Nose, the twins from the Triple B. All eyes in the room, other than Joycee's, are fixated on me. I feel like the jerk at one of those fancy parties, where everyone's supposed to be nicely dressed in all white, who shows up in blue jeans and a ripped red t-shirt.

The sea of hoodlums parts, clearing a path to the center of the ring. The dagger is useless against this many adversaries—at least, in my hands it is. I can't help thinking that a grenade would be nice right about now—maybe next time. I understand I'm probably better off acting confident than pissing my pants and curling up in a ball on the floor screaming for mommy, which is what I want to do, so I do my best to hold my pee inside my body. Not seeing any other options, I sheath my dagger, tuck it into my waistband, and walk purposefully into the center of the circle to stand before the fat orog.

Sinn enters the circle with me and takes position half a step back and to my left. I can't tell if she's strategically positioning herself in case of a fight, or if she's simply trying to keep a safe distance from me. Maybe she's just trying to avoid flying shit. My father always said don't stand in front of flying shit, and I have a feeling shit's about to fly in my direction.

The orog ignores me and focuses on Sinn, its lustful eyes slowly massaging her lithe frame. I'm not sure why, I hardly know Sinn, and it's only been about twenty minutes since she kicked me in the nuts—not that I'm counting, but I don't like how he's looking at her.

"My dear Sinn, it is so nice to see you again. My, how you've grown. I wish your father had let me keep you when you were a child. Such pleasures you would have given me.'Tis a shame you've grown fangs. No matter, fate has brought you back to me." The orog speaks with the flair and pomposity of a bad American actor, method acting the part of an eighteenth-century English dandy, complete with a bad accent and wild theatrical hand gestures. If I wasn't so terrified, I'd find the entire setting hugely comical.

Sinn defiantly meets the orog's stare, "Colt, this is George, the shot caller of the Chicago branch of the Dead Pigs. George, it looks like you put on some weight since the last time I saw you. Why are you here?"

Sinn's insult strikes cleanly and danger flashes across the dandy's face, "Such ugly words coming from such a pretty mouth. I can think of all sorts of things I'd rather see go in and come out of that dirty mouth," George laughs and shouts in an excited tone. "But to answer your question, expansion! The Dead Pigs are expanding!" George raises his arms and the crowd of thugs cheer.

George slumps back into his chair and becomes almost melancholy. His mood changes as quick as a Kardashian's outfit. I don't think this pig's playing with a full rack. "I admit it, I've gained weight. It's been such a dull year, and I may have ... overindulged. It's hard to be George. I'm always so bored." His mood shifts again, and he says in a peppy voice, "But things are looking up since you arrived. Perhaps my pretty little lotus flower can help me work off some of this extra weight?"

Sinn cringes in disgust.

George laughs and gives Sinn an entirely inappropriate smile, with way too much tongue. He'd be in big trouble if someone from Human Resources saw that. And did he just call her a pretty little lotus flower? I guarantee he's earned himself a swift kick to the nuts. I wonder if I should warn him? Nah, where's the sport in that?

Sinn clenches her fist; it looks like she's having a hard time suppressing her anger. I decide to intervene before she does something I'll regret. "Georgie," I say, putting extra emphasis on the 'gie.' "It appears you have something that doesn't belong to you—well, *four* somethings. I'd like you to give them to me and then we'll be on our way, and you can get back to playing clubhouse with your friends." I give Georgie my best and brightest used car salesman smile.

The heat from Sinn's disapproving stare warms the side of my head. I barely know her, and yet I know exactly what she's thinking. Specifically, that we came here for one girl—not four. Well tough-titties, I'm not leaving any of these girls behind with Fat Georgie and the Cosby kids— we're rescuing all four.

George furrows his brow, appearing to notice me for the first time. He seems perplexed about something. I seem to be getting that reaction a lot lately. "Mr. Valentine, I want to thank you for coming. When I saw you enter our mansion, I thought, What a bother, I'll have to have the carpets cleaned again. Then my favorite pet," he affectionately strokes the top of Roy's head, "told me you were the one responsible for his freedom, and I just had to meet you. I so hoped that you'd find your way down here to me. I even had Roy hang a sign."

"The sign was for me?" I ask.

"I just told you it was."

"How thoughtful," I say with feigned earnestness as I turn and smile at Sinn, who rolls her eyes and makes a gagging sound.

George continues, "I understand you had the pleasure of meeting my brother Henry today." George pauses, "I heard a nasty rumor that Sinn's father murdered my brother. Is this true? Is Henry dead?"

I recognize the question for what it is—a trap. He already knows the answer. It's hardly a rumor; his lackeys were there, and they watched his brother die. Regardless, I don't see any advantage to lying, and I don't like how this pig was talking to Sinn, so I might as well rub the death in his face.

"I'm sorry for your *heart*-ache, but you heard right. Your brother started a fight he just didn't have the *heart* to finish." I symbolically place both hands over my heart and do my best not to smile.

George flinches and stares off into the distance. "Mother would be so upset if she were still alive. Henry was her favorite. Her golden boy. He could do no wrong."

George jumps up from his chair and spins and leaps like a dancer over to where the four human girls are tied. He's extremely graceful for such a large creature. The sheer strength and dexterity required to move his massive frame in such a manner is unsettling. This is not a monster to underestimate. George grabs one of the girls by the neck and forces her mouth open with his large fat fingers. He carefully inspects her teeth, similar to the way a trainer would inspect a horse. "Such beautiful teeth."

The girl cringes, but dares not move for fear of reprisal.

George looks back at me and smiles as wide as he can, his nasty decaying yellow teeth on full display. "Human teeth are a passion of mine. I like to grind them up and sprinkle them on my food. One might say I have a sweet-tooth." George chuckles and then turns back towards the girl and continues to probe her mouth with his fat fingers.

"Uhmmmmm," I clear my throat. "Georgie dear, as I said, those four do *not* belong to you. I'm taking them with me. I'd appreciate it if you didn't damage them any further."

George spins towards me, flinging the girl to the ground. "How very interesting. You seem to think they belong to you, and yet they are here in my home. Very curious. These humans were hunted in the normal course of such things. No Concordat laws were broken. I see no slave markings on them. How do I know they're yours? … No, I don't think they're yours. I think you're trying to steal from me."

The crowd of miscreant Dead Pigs start chanting, *"Feed the pigs. Feed the pigs. Feed the pigs."*

George smiles with his large yellow plaque-covered teeth, while he quiets the crowd with a gesture. "Perhaps ... we can come to an agreement? I am a gentleman, after all."

"I'm listening," I say.

"Is she your lover?" He gestures towards Sinn. "That would make this so much more interesting." George rubs his hands together like an over-excited child. Neither Sinn nor I respond to the inquiry. "No matter, keep your secrets." George turns and addresses the crowd, "The father of this beautiful lotus flower killed my brother. What should we do with her?"

The crowd resumes their chanting, *"Feed the pigs. Feed the pigs."*

George silences the blood gang with another hand gesture and says, "I never liked my brother. He spent too much time playing with his *bat* for my taste." George gets a faraway look in his eyes. "Mother ... Mother loved him dearly. If she were alive, she would demand that I avenge his death." In a snotty tone, George adds, *"And mommy always gets what she wants."*

George slips back into his dandy caricature, "So, you see, I also have a problem. Perhaps we can make a trade?"

Sinn starts to say something, but I put my hand up to shush her. She gives me a dirty look, but holds her tongue. With my eyes, I do my best to communicate, "Trust me" to her. I don't know if she understands, but she seems content to wait, and watch to see what I do, at least for now.

"What exactly are you proposing?" I ask.

George is giddy with delight, like a child on Christmas morning. "I want her." George points at Sinn. "Four human girls for one teeny-weeny vampire girl—seems like a fair trade to me."

I can sense Sinn tensing beside me, preparing for a fight.

"No deal," I say with as much conviction as I can muster. Despite her having kicked me in the balls twenty-five or so minutes ago, I'm growing attached to Sinn, and even if I wasn't, I wouldn't trade her to this loon. No one deserves that. Plus, I need her. I still don't exactly understand what I've gotten myself into and she's my only lifeline.

"Bor-ing!" Shouts George. "I could just kill you both!"

The chanting starts again, *"Feed the pigs. Feed the pigs."*

I dig my nails into my palms to keep my knees from shaking. I'm starting to worry that this is too far over my head, and I'm going to end up pig food; and then a Sun Tzu quote pops into my head, *"Appear weak when you are strong, and strong when you are weak,"* and my lawyer training kicks in, "You could try," I say, in the middle of a planned yawn. "You wouldn't succeed."

George squints his eyes. He seems perplexed by my behavior.

"Isn't there something else you want?" I ask.

George raises his fist to his chin and assumes the thinker pose. For a moment, the cave is silent, and then he smiles, and twirls on one leg, like an overweight ballerina. *"Mommy* must have her revenge. If you won't trade *her* to me, I want you to kill *her* Daddy." George points at Sinn with one of his sausage like fingers. "In return, you can have these pathetic creatures." He indifferently motions at the tied up human girls, and then points at Joycee. "That one's broken anyway."

George is almost floating as he elegantly spins and dances his massive body back to his oversized chair. He's clearly enjoying the circumstances; at least, as he understands them. His minions fled the bar before Pavo and I fought. He must not know that Pavo's dead. I can work with that.

Roy whines, "Master, she belongs to m—"

"Silence!" George screams at my former client. Roy flinches, the way an abused puppy flinches when a stranger tries to pet it. I almost feel sorry for the little twat … almost.

"Mr. Valentine, I apologize. My pet needs to learn his place."

"Think nothing of it. Your proposal intrigues me, Georgie. However," I point at Sinn, "her father is a very old vampire and an Advocate. The death of such a person is worth more than you offer. Perhaps if you were to sweeten the deal, we could come to an arrangement."

Sinn squirms beside me. I'm guessing she doesn't like this plan.

"Oooh, I do love a good barter." George rocks in his chair in delight. "What do you propose, Mr. Valentine? We do want to be fair. You are such an interesting man. This is *sooooo* much fun."

Before I can respond, George undergoes another mood shift, leans forward in his chair, and in a suspicious tone asks, "Why does she not strike you down? Sinn loves her father and you're openly plotting his death?"

"That's none of your business, but if you must know, she does not strike me down because she belongs to me and is sworn to protect me."

"Interesting," says George. He stands and studies me from my head to my toes. "Mr. Valentine, what are you?"

"A Sagittarius and I like long walks on the beach," I answer. "Do you want to hear my terms or not?"

George sighs, "Yes, terms. Go on."

I smile, knowing a deal is imminent. "I'll show you proof of her father's death in exchange for the freedom of the four human girls, and your word that no member of your gang will ever bother them again. You will further agree the girls are, and will continue to be, under the protection of your gang, and you will do everything in your power to ensure their safety—*without* bothering them. Do we have a deal?"

George gleefully claps his hands together like an overexcited toddler. "I agree to your terms."

"Then it's agreed. Please have the girls untied—we're leaving."

"No," says George forcefully. "Mr. Valentine, they do not belong to you … yet. The humans are still mine to do with as I please, until *after* you have killed *her* father. But alas, I think it's more likely that Pavo will kill you. He is a vicious blood-sucker. A killer of killers. Maybe he'll rip *your* heart out too. Perhaps Sinn would like to wait here with me for news of your death. I would certainly enjoy her company."

Georgie turns to Sinn, "Would you like to induluge in my company, my flower."

Sinn makes another gagging sound.

"Georgie, you are a really creepy bastard, aren't you? Can you even help yourself or is it a genetic thing?"

Anger flashes across George's face. "My name is George, not Georgie!" he yells.

"—Georgie, we have a deal. It's time for you to pay up. I'm taking the girls—now. You're not breaking your word, are you?"

George pauses, and then slips back into his terrible English dandy persona, "Of course not, Mr. Valentine. I don't break deals, but you cannot take the girls until you fulfill your part of the bargain. Until then, the humans are mine to do with as I please. I am getting bored with this conversation. You'd better hurry, I can't guarantee there will be much left of the humans when you return. You should have bargained better." George laughs maniacally.

I interrupt his laughter, "—Georgie, Georgie, *Georgie*, you really don't get it. Pavo is already dead. I killed him before I came here. The bargain's fulfilled. I'll be taking the girls, *now*." I should stop there, but I can't help myself and, in a poor English accent, I say, "You should have bargained better." For a hot second, I consider adding an exclamation point, and imitating his maniacal laugh … and then I think better of it. He's a four-hundred-pound orog that moves like a gymnast; it's probably not smart or safe to continue antagonizing him.

Steam begins to rise from George's nostrils. Can orogs breathe fire? God, I need to do research before I get myself into any more of these situations.

"Proof! You must show me proof of his death!" George screams.

"Of course. A deal is a deal." I raise my hand and display my new ring to George and his gang. "Georgie, you know what this is, don't you?"

George stares in disbelief.

"It's Pavo Palatinus' Advocate ring. The only way you get one is by killing the owner. Shortly after your servants," I point at the twins, "left the bar with their tails firmly tucked between their legs, Pavo challenged me to a duel." I pause for dramatic effect, and then in the most intimidating voice I can muster, I say, "He lost. Untie the girls. We are leaving"

"No, this cannot be!" George whines. He looks to Sinn. "Is this true? Is your father dead?"

Sinn nods.

"It's true. Accept it," I answer. "Do not welch on our bargain. Ask your man what Pavo told your brother about me."

George and Sinn both turn and look at the twins. They look at each other and then the hooked nosed one steps forward and squawks, "He said that one," Hooknose points at me, "is not what we think. He told us to run if we wanted to live."

George looks at me again and thoughtfully says to himself, "He looks like a human, but vampires fear and serve him; He kills, killers of killers; What is he? It's a riddle. What *are* you Mr. Valentine?"

I smile, but ignore the question. "Free the girls, honor our agreement. I tire of this place. It smells. I get your going for farm yard sewer chic, I'm just not really partial to the pig sty decor. It's just not my style."

George shrieks in frustration, but stays true to his word, and instructs his gang to "Free the human slaves. A deal is a deal." Several members of his gang look at him curiously, but two begin to untie the girls. I signal to Sinn to collect them. I don't want to break eye contact with Georgie until the last possible moment.

George's frustration is replaced with a mischievous look. "As I said, the girls may go, but you may not leave … *Advocate*. You are trespassing on Dead Pig land. You must pay a toll. You must fight in the circle."

I meet George's smile with one of my own. "I don't think so, Geor*gie*. Good try, though; you get an 'A' for effort. I'm not a trespasser. You told me, in front of all these witnesses, that you invited me here. Didn't you have your pet hang a sign for me? I can't be a trespasser—if I was invited. Now, can I? Thanks, for the warm hospitality. We should do it again sometime. We'll be going now."

Sinn, the girls, and I all start walking towards the tunnel entrance. George screams, "*No*! I never invited *her*! I never wanted the vampire here! *She* cannot leave!" George points at Sinn and Dead Pigs move to block the exit.

I take a deep breath as I turn back and face the orog. I try my best to appear annoyed rather than afraid. I'm dreading the fight that's coming, but I've suspected since we got here that we weren't going to be able to leave without a fight.

"Okay, Georgie, you win. I'll fight. One fight, one-on-one, in your circle, on one condition. When I kill your champion, we all leave. No more games. No more tricks."

George doesn't even hesitate, "Yes. Agreed. Goody, goody, I cannot wait to see how you fight. I wonder … what champion I should choose to match up against the killer and enslaver of vampires?"

Sinn's nails dig into my arms and worriedly whispers, "What are you doing? You should have let me fight. You're untrained. You might die!"

I smile reassuringly. "Trust me, I have a plan. I intend to fight in my own weight class."

"Georgie, Georgie," I say in a sing-song voice as I walk over to Roy. I stop when we're almost nose to nose. "Your pet is beautiful, isn't he?" I ask mockingly.

"Yes, he is beautiful. He has brought me much pleasure and entertainment. Thank you for returning him to me."

"Ah, now it all makes sense," I say.

A moment of silence passes and then Georgie takes the bait. "What makes sense?"

"Roy's dick-whippedness," I answer.

George is becoming visibly agitated. "Mr. Valentine, I don't understand what you're saying."

"You know exactly what I'm talking about. I was Roy's lawyer, and in confidence he told me things ... things about you."

"Liar!" spits Roy.

"It all makes sense now that I have met you and seen you together. You said it yourself; he brings you much pleasure."

Steam begins to rise from George's nostrils again.

Roy pushes me. "Master, let me gut this fucker! Please."

I laugh and continue to goad the orog, "Georgie, surely you won't risk the life of *your favorite pet.*"

Some of the other gang members seem to be shifting uncomfortably and begin muttering amongst themselves. Although homosexuality is completely normal, particularly in the Bay Area where it is both common and mostly accepted, I know from my work as a PD, that many street gangs have an extremely prejudicial view of homosexuality outside of prison. I'm playing a hunch that the same stupid stereotypical misguided machismo carries over to non-human gangs.

Roy pleads, "Master, let me defend your honor! Let me kill him!"

George reads the room and recognizes the corner he's been backed into. I don't know if they really are lovers and, frankly, I don't care; it's none of my business, but he can't deny it now. A denial would just reinforce the claim. He'd look like a liar, and lying indicates weakness. A guy like Georgie can't bear to look weak in front of his goons. After what feels like an eternity, he finally says to Roy, "Do not fail me."

I smile at Sinn, hoping for a nod of encouragement, maybe a gold star for a job well done. She shrugs, clearly not impressed, and whispers, "You got the fight you wanted; you'd better win, or you'll set the world record for shortest-ever tenure as an Advocate, and you'll break the promise I made to my father. Don't screw up and die."

Note to self: Don't count on Sinn to be your cheerleader, although I bet she'd look amazing in a cheerleading outfit—something I'll certainly never witness if I die today.

Chapter Twenty

One of the Dead Pigs, a large one with huge muscular arms, begins to beat on a war drum with what looks like a pair of human femurs. A steady and captivating pulse surges through the cave. The drum beat has a raw animalism to it. The rhythm awakens my senses, raises my testosterone levels, and readies my body for battle.

Roy enters the circle across from me and takes off his shirt. He's in much better shape than I thought. For a short, fat, middle-aged Greek man with a double chin, he sure has a lot of muscle. One of the gang members hands him a wicked looking meat cleaver. Roy expertly spins the cleaver in his hand, while he grins at me across the circle. He looks like a demented butcher.

I need to reevaluate my life choices. I'm about to engage in an underground circle fight with a mad Greek wielding a meat cleaver, surrounded by a mixed audience of humans, monsters, and a vampire, who all probably want to see me bleed, and this isn't even the scariest duel I fought in the last two hours. #FML. Next weekend, I'm staying in, ordering a pizza, opening an expensive bottle of pinot noir, and watching some Netflix. Maybe I can convince Sinn, or that reporter with the red heels, to Netflix and chill with me.

I untuck the ornate Pugio from my waist and free the blade from its sheath. I hand the sheath to Sinn and take a few awkward practice swings. Yep, I have no idea what I'm doing. My matrix power or what did she call it, Battle-Sight, better kick in, or I'm going to bleed. The blade still feels empty, but with each swing, I begin to feel something, a trickle of something, building in the blade. It's hard to describe, but it's as if the blade is being filled with liquid energy, one tiny drop at a time.

George raises his hand, signaling silence, and the drumbeat stops. Stillness, and the anticipation of death, fill the cave; and then George addresses the audience, "My fellow Dead Pigs, and guests. Today is a special day. Today an Advocate is given the opportunity to die in our fighting circle."

The audience cheers for my death.

"There are three rules in the fighting circle." George looks directly at me and says, "Rule One: Two enter the circle and only one leaves." The crowd chants the rules along with George. "Rule Two: There are no rules in the circle. Anything goes. Rule Three: The audience may not use weapons, but they may participate, as long as their feet remain outside the circle. Be careful when navigating the edges of the circle; danger may come from anywhere."

I look to Sinn and mouth, "What the fuck?" Sinn replies with her now patented shrug, which loosely translates to, "You're the idiot who got yourself into this mess, now deal with it."

George introduces Roy, asks him if he consents to the fight, and whether he has any final words before the match begins.

Roy consents to the fight and then addresses the crowd, "Master and brothers, I will bring you glory." He then turns to me and says, "I'm going to kill you, but don't worry, Counselor, I'll honor your death. I'm going to cut your tongue out and rape Joycee with it. You and I can both be inside her at the same time."

Out of the corner of my eye, I see Joycee shudder. It's the first emotional response I've seen from her, and it gives me hope that she's still in there and will be able to come back from this.

George then asks, "Mr. Valentine, do you consent to this fight to the death?"

"I do."

"Mr. Valentine, do you have last words before the match begins?"

I think about insulting Roy or taking another verbal shot at Georgie, but realize there is no getting out of this. Further insults aren't going to improve my shitty circumstances. Instead, I turn to Joycee and gently call out her name: "Joycee." She doesn't look up. I call it out again, a little louder this time: "Joycee." Her eyes twitch in my direction. I signal to Sinn who gently turns Joycee until she's facing me.

"Joycee, with your permission, I'm going to kill this monster. I'm sorry the Court system failed you yesterday. I'm sorry I failed you. Please let me be your instrument of justice. Let me be your champion. Do I have your permission to kill this sick fucker for you?"

Joycee takes a deep breath. Tears begin to roll down her cheeks. She manages to mouth the word, "Yes."

I give Joycee my most reassuring smile, and then the other women embrace her and they all cling together for support.

I turn back and face George. "I'm ready."

George looks at me for a moment and I see a flicker of doubt. George drops the dandy bit and says in clear-as-day plain American English, "Mr. Valentine, I see you, I hear you, but I don't know what you are ... yet." He then climbs into his oversized chair and screams, "Fight!"

Roy bursts across the circle like a sprinter out of the blocks, and swings his cleaver at my head. My Battle-Sense kicks in, and I'm able to easily parry the cleaver with the edge of my dagger. Not precisely how the dagger is intended to be used, but it works in a pinch.

Roy is much faster and better skilled than I. If it wasn't for my Battle-Sense, I'd be dead already. We fall into a routine; he attacks, I parry. This pattern repeats over and over again. He is relentless in his aggression and too skilled for me. I can't counter-attack without leaving myself vulnerable. The Battle-Sense doesn't make me faster; it just slows things down so I can better plan my defense and gives me room for error. Neither of us seems to be gaining any advantage. It's a stalemate—at least for now. I wonder how long can he keep this up? I'm already starting to tire. The dagger is getting heavier. My muscles are stinging from the repeated blows.

There is something building in the dagger. It's still a trickle, but it calls to me. It grows with each parry, begging to be set free.

A particularly savage attack pushes me to the edge of the circle. I hear Sinn yell a warning, but I can't make it out over the loud cheering of the bloodthirsty crowd. As Roy gathers himself for another swing, I'm blindsided by a punch from someone standing at the edge of the circle. The punch spins me and Roy rushes in to take advantage. I see the cleaver approaching in slow motion, I'm never going to be able to get my blade up in time to deflect the blow. He is going to cut me and I'm going to bleed. I realize this is the moment the fight ends—the end of our stalemate.

Instead of trying to block Roy's cleaver with my blade, I meet it with my left forearm, thereby shortening the length of Roy's swing and reducing its power. The cleaver bites deep into my arm. Blood sprays, and my ears ring with the cracking sound of blade meeting bone. I bite down as hard as I can and try not to pass out from the pain. I need to end this fight, and Roy's strike has left me an opening. My right arm pushes the tip of the Pugio toward Roy's now exposed throat. Time slows as I use my Battle-Sight to maneuver the dagger into a perfect striking position. The power that had been growing in the blade releases, sending destructive energy out in all directions. Roy's head is obliterated into a fountain of blood and brain matter. The energy release is much less powerful and more controlled than the one that engulfed Pavo, but it feels similar. This time, I know I'm the one who is doing it.

Roy's headless body's grip on the cleaver slackens, and then releases, as his body crumbles to the cave floor. The cleaver remains embedded in my arm. I'm afraid I might bleed out if I remove it. I turn towards George and awkwardly bow. "Thank you for your hospitality."

Before George can reply, I turn and usher the girls toward the exit. I hear a commotion behind us, but we don't stop to investigate. I know if I stop, I'm going to pass out from the pain. When we reach the fork in the path where the sign hangs, we take the right tunnel, rather than the tunnel back to the dilapidated mansion, just in case someone's following. The pain is unbearable—only my fear for the lives of the girls is keeping me on my feet. Once we're out of sight of the fork, I reach into my pocket and pull out my magical Sharpie. Sinn allows me to lean against her for support. I manage to draw a door and a handle on the tunnel wall in magical silver ink. I visualize the living room of my apartment, mumble the magic words, and open a gate.

The four girls, Sinn, and I step out of the dark tunnel into the bright light of my apartment. I immediately collapse to the floor. I keep thinking there is a cleaver stuck in my forearm; someone needs to get it out. Someone calls my name, and then there is only silence, darkness, and forever nothingness.

Chapter Twenty-One

I awake in my own bed to the mouthwatering smell of frying bacon. Why do I smell bacon? The blinds are drawn, my alarm clock's unplugged, and my cell phone is missing from the nightstand where it charges while I sleep. What time is it? Is it morning? Night? Why is the alarm clock unplugged? I consider opening the blinds, but they seem so far away. Instead, I rub the sleep from my eyes, stretch my arms above my head, and arch my stiff back. I hurt everywhere.

As I stretch, I realize I'm naked, which is weird, because I always sleep in boxer briefs, even when I have coed sleepovers. When I was a kid, our house caught fire— nothing too serious, the house didn't burn down or anything—but I ran outside naked, and all the neighbors saw me. I was so embarrassed. Dad just laughed and laughed. Said it served me right for not sleeping in the PJs he spent good money on. Everything was always about money with Dad.

That bacon smell is delicious. I wonder who's cooking? I'm famished. I feel like I haven't eaten in a week. Maybe I got lucky last night? Too bad I can't remember. I hope I wasn't so drunk that I failed to perform adequately. I hope it's that hot reporter, and I was amazing, and that she's making me breakfast as a reward for my sexual prowess.

I grab a pair of boxer briefs from my dresser drawer, nice ones, not ones with holes, and step into them. I crack my neck, first to the right, and then to the left; it hurts, but in a good way. God, I need coffee, but first I have to piss. I come to a complete stop when I reach the master bathroom mirror. I look like a zombie. I'm pale, gaunt, and have dark circles under my eyes. What the hell did I do last night?

I turn on the sink faucet and let the water run until it's warm. The splash of water on my face feels amazing, and then it hits me; images of vampires, gangsters, pig-headed monsters, and a crazy cleaver-wielding Greek dance through my head—I remember everything. I grab my arm where I was cut by the cleaver, but there's nothing there. The skin is smooth, no wound, no scar, nothing at all. How is that possible? Did I dream it all? Was I drugged?

The memories are so vivid. I start to panic when I see that I am wearing the silver ring with the red stone. I frantically pull and twist, and apply liberal amounts of soap, but it still won't come off. "Fuck!" I shout in frustration. Then I remember the girls. I rush into the main living area of my open concept apartment, hoping to see the girls, but it's empty except for Wilson.

Wilson's sitting at my breakfast bar, eating eggs and bacon, and nursing a Corona. Between bites, he manages to say, "Sleeping Beauty finally wakes."

"What are you doing in my apartment?" I ask. "Is anyone else here? Are you having beer for breakfast?" I scan my apartment for signs that anyone else might be here, but find none.

Wilson continues to shovel food into his mouth. "I'm eating. No, and no."

"What?" I ask in confusion.

Wilson looks up from his breakfast. "You look like the undead, but to answer your questions: I'm eating, nobody else is here, and I'm not having a beer for breakfast—it's lunch time." Wilson winks at me and takes another pull on his beer.

"Where are the girls?"

"At their homes, I suspect."

I shake my head in frustration. "Why are you here?"

Wilson answers with a mouth full of food, "Taking care of you. A little gratitude wouldn't kill you."

I consider throttling him, but decide I need coffee first. I pop a pod with a taped on QR code into the coffee machine, and mix in some creamer as the single serve coffee maker fills my mug. I sniff the coffee, smells like bliss, and then take a sip, ahhh, tastes like Nirvana. After a few moments of personal meditation with my coffee, I ask, "Is there any bacon left?" I think I need a full stomach to deal with Wilson's shit.

Wilson almost looks guilty. "Ah, no. Sorry, Boss."

"I'll just have eggs then," I murmur, as I walk toward the fridge.

"Um, there are no more eggs either," Wilson says in between bites.

"What the fuck? I just bought eggs. There was a full carton in there. How can I be out?"

"I ate them."

I open the fridge; sure enough, it's empty. "You ate an entire fucking carton?"

Wilson sheepishly says, "Yes, but not at once. I'm not a monster."

"What do you mean *not at once*?"

"Maybe you should sit down. You look peakish."

"I don't want to sit down. Answer my question!"

"Well … I ate them over several days." Wilson takes another pull of his beer. "While you got the fridge open there, will you grab me another beer?"

I slam the fridge closed without grabbing Wilson a beer. "What do you mean you ate them over several days?"

"Boss, you have been on ice for four days. It's Wednesday."

"Bullshit!" I shout. "It can't be Wednesday—it's Sunday! What do you mean it's Wednesday?" I grab my cell phone off the counter to check the date, but the battery's dead. I slam it down on the table in frustration and reach for the television remote.

Wilson walks over to the fridge and pops the top off another brew. "Boss, it really is Wednesday. You know, the day *after* Tuesday, the day *before* Thursday."

"I know the days of the week, asshole."

Wilson shrugs as if his smart-assery was a courtesy and I'm the one being the asshole.

I cycle through the cable menu and sure enough it says it's Wednesday. I feel a migraine coming on. "Why did you let me sleep for four fucking days?"

"I wanted to wake you, but that scary Asian chick, your new law partner, told me not to. She said you'd be fine, and that if I woke you up, she was going to ... Boss, the things she said she would do to me were disturbing and not in a good way. I don't scare easy, but she scares me."

I nod in understanding. Sinn scares me too.

"Boss, I'm thinking about contacting HR at our new firm and complaining about that crazy lady. You are going to hire me, right? Do I get medical coverage? I have this thing on my ... anyhow, I need to get it checked out, but I haven't had good insurance since I got canned by the PD."

"Wilson, focus. You're rambling. I need you to start from the beginning and tell me everything."

"Sure thing, Boss."

Chapter Twenty-Two

On Saturday night, after I declined his assistance, Wilson waited in my parking lot for the Uber to arrive and tailed me to the Triple B. As long as I've known him, he's been superstitious and always trusts his gut. It's what got him in trouble when he worked at the PD's office. It's also what makes him such a good investigator. I'm not mad at him for following me, even if it's a little sketchy. I know he's loyal to a fault and a better friend than I deserve.

At closing time, when I didn't come out, he went in. Billy Joe told him I left through a back exit. With no way to track me down, Wilson returned to my apartment and parked out front. Said he wouldn't have been able to sleep until he knew I got home safe. I'm not sure if that's creepy or sweet; for the sake of our friendship, I'm going with sweet.

Around 3:00 AM, Wilson noticed movement in my apartment, but something didn't look right. He said he tried to sneak in, but Sinn discovered him, and they "reached an understanding." He flinched when he said "reached an understanding." I have a feeling that "understanding" involved him getting kicked in the nuts.

Sinn had Wilson drive the girls home and when he returned, I was already in bed. Sinn must be the one who undressed me. In retrospect, it would have been a bit weird if Wilson had removed my clothes—not because he's a man, but because he would have essentially stalked me, broken into my home, and removed my clothes while I was passed out. We're friends, but that sounds like date rape—without the date. I like my friends without a side of Hollywood producer.

During the four days I slept, Wilson never left my side, not even to go shopping. Under the circumstances, I really shouldn't be mad at him for eating all the eggs and bacon, but I am. I had to eat a bowl of instant apple cinnamon oatmeal for breakfast, the kind you pour into a mug, add water, and put in the microwave for two minutes. It's barely edible and doesn't hold a candle to eggs and bacon.

I am not sure what else transpired while I was passed out. Wilson wouldn't say, but he admitted that he and Sinn had at least one animated discussion about taking me to the hospital. Wilson was concerned about all the blood. Sinn told him not to worry, that I'd be fine. She said I was probably going to sleep for a while, gave him a card with her phone number on it, and told him to call her if there was a problem, or I woke up.

I can't tell if Wilson likes Sinn very much. He won't call her by her name, he insists on calling her the scary Asian, which is borderline racist. If I'm being honest, she is scary, and she is Asian. Maybe scary Asian is more descriptive than racist. Under the circumstances, I don't think he means any harm; I'm going to give him a pass.

Wilson said the wound on my arm was healed by the second day. Its miraculous improvement was the only thing that kept him from taking me to the hospital. He said the scary Asian stopped by to check on me each of the last three nights. With each passing night, she seemed more anxious that I hadn't awoken. Last night she brought him a twelve pack of Corona, a peace offering of sorts, and told him I should awaken soon. I am going to have to ask her how she knew that.

The biggest shocker for me is the fact that Wilson seems completely unfazed by the revelation that there are monsters in the world and it's now my job to enforce their laws. He believes absolutely everything I told him. I'm still struggling to believe it myself, and I saw it with my own two eyes. This whole situation is nuts. I wish I was half as well adjusted as him.

I'm headed to my office at the Public Defenders. I need to turn in my resignation letter and clean out my desk. I'm guessing my boss is wondering where the hell I've been the past three days. I still haven't decided how I'm going to play it: drunken binge after my victory, new girlfriend, kidnapped, sick? None of those excuses feel right. Maybe I'll just tell him the truth, that I fought a duel to the death with a sixteen hundred-year-old vampire, traveled through a magic door, infiltrated the clubhouse of a gang of half monsters ruled by a pig-headed orog, and then fought and killed my former client, whom I just saved from prison on Friday, all so I could save four girls and impress another. I wonder if he'll believe me? Nah, probably not. Instead, that would get me 5150'd and shipped off to the looney bin. I'll probably just go with the ever popular, "I need a change in my life for mental health reasons." Isn't that the vogue excuse for quitting these days?

After I deal with my soon-to-be-former employer, I'm going to meet Wilson at Sinn's building. I haven't called Sinn yet, and I made Wilson promise not to call her either. I'm not sure why, but I want my first trip to my new office to be authentic, not staged. I still don't completely trust her. I want her a little off-balance. I think there is a lot going on that she isn't telling me, and I plan on getting to the truth. I have so many questions; most pressing, why did I heal so quickly? And why aren't I dead? Sinn better have answers for me. I have a feeling today is going to be an interesting day.

Chapter Twenty-Three

I take the old rickety elevator up to the Public Defender's office. I can't help but get a little nostalgic. I'm going to miss this place. This office and building have been a part of my life for nearly a decade. It's been like my second home. At times during my failed marriage it felt like my only home. I can't even count the number of times I slept under my desk after a bad fight with Lisa. I am so glad I finally divorced her.

The office is just as busy as it ever is. The chaotic Courthouse scene before me is strangely comforting—just a typical Wednesday in my old life. Scores of clients and their families nervously wait in the lobby for a chance to talk to their Government-appointed attorney. Children cry, clients yell, and Public Defenders frantically jump from well to well, trying to do as much good as they can within the confinements of the law and budget approved by the county.

Most of these poor souls have convinced themselves that they're innocent, but will spend time in jail anyway. The maxim, "Innocent until proven guilty," is known and believed by every red-blooded American. The concept is so revered, you'd think the words were spoken by God himself. If they were, they were never recorded in the Bible, nor can they be found in the Declaration of Independence, nor even within the United States Constitution. Those lovely words are a sweet lie. Justice ain't free; somebody always pays.

A more truthful maxim would be, "If you're charged with a crime, just accept it; you're doing time." The wheel of the American justice system turns quickly and crushes all, innocent and guilty alike, who fall within its path.

Trudy, the office receptionist/manager, waves me over to the front desk. Trudy's been with the Public Defender's office for nearly forty years. She's more like the office den-mother than a receptionist; her hands are in everything. The County's been trying to promote her into a new position for decades, but she keeps turing them down. She tells them she'll accept a raise, but not a new position. She's an amazing woman and, frankly, I don't think the office could function without her. She means a lot to me. She's always treated me like family. The only wrong she ever did to me was giving me that God-forsaken single pod coffee maker. Trudy's smile infects those around her with unabashed cheerfulness. I can feel the corners of my mouth responsively tugging into a smile as she nears.

"Colt, there is a sassy little number in your office. I think I have seen her on television. Says her name is Makayla Hill. You two would make the cutest babies."

"Stop it, Trudy," I say with a smile.

"Colt, you got to move on, child. Put that nasty divorce behind you. You are too fine a man not to have a woman in your life. If I were thirty years younger and not happily married—"

"*Trudy.*"

"Yes, Colt," she replies in her most mock innocent tone.

"What does Ms. Hill want?" I ask.

"I don't know. I tried to tell her you weren't here. The hussy ignored me and then helped herself into your office. Said she was gonna' wait. Never even asked if you were expected back today. It ain't my job to keep pretty girls out of the barracks," Trudy says in a jaunty tone.

"Actually, it is," I correct her. "Keeping strangers out of my office is exactly what you're paid to do."

Trudy shrugs. "I didn't see that in no hand book."

I sigh, "Ms. Hill will have to wait a bit longer. First, I need to speak with the big boss. Is he in?"

Trudy nods. "In his office. You want me to let him know you're coming?"

I shake my head no and walk towards the big boss's office.

"He's in a good mood, Colt. Don't you go and ruin it," Trudy calls after me.

The big boss is an ironic title we use for Jeff Green. He runs the office here, but there ain't nothing big about him. I've been told he has six brothers and five sisters and they're all six-foot-four or taller, a Viking family. Sadly, Jeff isn't six-foot-four—he barely stands four-foot-six.

Jeff tells anyone who will listen that he was born with a heart deformity and underwent open heart surgery as an infant. He claims that his growth was stunted in proportion to the amount of time his chest was open on the surgeon's table. Jeff likes to tell the same joke over and over about how thankful he is that the surgeon smoked in the operating room during the surgery, because he'd only be three feet tall if the surgeon had taken an outside smoke break. I didn't laugh the first time I heard it, either.

What Jeff lacks in stature he makes up for in agreeableness. He never was much of a trial attorney, but he's an effective manager. He treats his staff fairly and never puts his ego ahead of the job. We're not friends, but I respect him, and enjoyed working for him. He gave me a lot a rope, which let me grow into the lawyer I am today, or was. I don't know *what* I am anymore.

I knock on Jeff's door.

"Come in!" he shouts.

I enter the large corner office and close the door behind me. Jeff sits at his modern monstrosity of glass and metal desk that nearly swallows him whole. A Montblanc prominently rests on a stylized pen holder next to his sleek oversized laptop. The desk is otherwise clear of clutter. The office is clean and well organized, designed to make an impression. The oversized window looks out onto a striking view of City Hall. It's a Hollywood office, meant to impress new associates and the lard over at City Hall; nothing about it screams actual working lawyer.

Jeff looks up at me from his oversized chair. "Colt, I'm glad you're here. We need to talk. Great job on the Roy Silas trial. That was really good work. I understand you have been out sick for a few days?" He phrases that last part like it's a question; he's trying to provide me an out.

"Something like that," I say.

He nods, electing not to push.

"Thanks. I don't really deserve much credit for the trial. Brad Murphy basically gifted the verdict to me. He spiked the questioning of the victim; from there, I just tried to stay out of my own way."

Jeff nods again, this time in apparent understanding. Although, I'm not really sure he does.

"Jeff, I have enjoyed my time here. I want to thank you for the opportunity. I learned a lot, but I think it's time I moved on. I want you to accept my resignation. I don't have any active cases; you cleared me for the trial. I don't have anything to hand off."

Jeff's eyes widen in surprise. "Is it the money?" he asks. "The budget is tight, but I can try and work something out. Maybe I can get you more vacation time? Or send you to a legal convention in an exotic location? I think there is a death penalty convention coming up in Tampa. Do you like Florida?"

Do I like Florida? I smile to cover up the urge to vomit that surges through my body at the thought of spending a week in Florida with other lawyers arguing about whether the death penalty is a form of cruel and unusual punishment. Screw the death penalty; sending me to a death penalty convention in Tampa would be a cruel and unusual punishment.

"I don't want to lose you, Colt. You're a good attorney. You'd be hard to replace. Why don't you take a week or two of vacation and think about it?" At least, he's honest and admits he thinks I'm replaceable.

"I appreciate that, Jeff, I really do. It's not the money, and I'm not going to change my mind. Working here was never about the money. Fate has intervened and my life is headed in a new direction, one that doesn't involve me working here."

Jeff looks at me funny, but nods in acceptance. "Colt, I can see you've made up your mind. I am sorry to see you go. You were a great Public Defender. A great lawyer." He says that last bit like my life is over—and maybe it is.

"Thanks, Jeff. If it's alright with you, I'm going to go clean out my office now. Trudy can forward any paperwork to me at my home address."

"Sorry, I can't let you do that, Colt. There's a new County policy. Whenever an employee quits, management has to go through the employee's office and box up all their stuff for them. We have to make sure the employee doesn't accidentally take any files or Government property home with them. It's nothing personal; you know how it is. Identity theft is a hot topic in the news. All our client files contain personal information, and if any of that information got out, it would be a nightmare for the County. I'm sorry, Colt. We'll have all of your stuff sent to your house." Jeff can tell by the go-fuck-yourself look I'm giving him, that I'm not thrilled with the new policy.

"Look, I'm supposed to have security walk you out," says Jeff. "Here is what I can do. I can wait five minutes before I enter your resignation into the system. Why don't you swing by your office really quickly and grab any valuables or anything that might be embarrassing for us to find … like booze." He winks at me. "We'll get the rest to you later this week. I'm sure Trudy will take good care of your things. You know you're one of her favorites. She's going to miss you. We're all going to miss you. See, I can be a nice guy. Are we good?"

Jeff stands up from his chair and reaches his short arm across his desk to shake my hand. I grab his small hand and give a good firm shake.

"Thanks, Jeff; we're good."

I shut Jeff's door behind me and walk down the hall to my office. My office isn't very big and it doesn't have a view, no windows in fact. It's more like a walled-off cubical with a door than a lawyer's office. I don't even have seating for guests. It's wall to wall files, books, purple tabs, and yellow legal pads filled with my chicken scratches; it's a truly worked-in space. If I have to meet with clients, I do it in one of our tiny conference rooms. In all the years I've worked here, I don't think anyone other than Trudy and the nightly cleaning staff have ever been in my office, that is until today.

As I approach the open doorway, I see Ms. Hill is seated at my desk, banging out an e-mail or a text message on her phone. She's probably following up on a lead or harassing somebody. Isn't that what reporters do? Probably shouldn't lead with that, its not exactly the strongest opening line. How should I play this? I noticed an ankle tattoo at the Courthouse the other day. It wasn't exactly a butterfly. Looked more like a black spade. She looks like she's into bad boys. I think I'm going to try being the charming scoundrel.

I lean against my office doorway in what I think is a sexy fireman calendar pose. "Ms. Hill, I know you find me attractive, but stalking me at my place of employment seems ... well ... a bit desperate." I flash her a roguish grin.

Makayla stands up a bit flustered. She really is an exceptional beauty. I actually feel a little weakness in my stomach as I stare at her. She is way out of my league. Wait ... that's not nerves, that's the oatmeal I ate for breakfast. Damn Wilson and his bacon pilfering.

Makayla does her best to take control of the conversation and put me on the defensive. "Mr. Valentine, are you aware no one has seen Roy Silas in three days?"

"No one in the entire world has seen him in three *whole* days?" I ask incredulously. "You had the time to interview everyone in the entire world? Impressive. Must be a slow news week. I would hate to see your cell phone bill. Don't you media types just make things up if you can't find a real story?" #Fakenews.

Makayla ignores my baiting, and continues her interrogation, "Mr. Valentine, I spoke with his neighbors, his sister, and his employer, and none of them have heard from him since Saturday. I stuck my card in his front door jam on Sunday morning; it's still there, which means he hasn't been home. Do you know where he is?"

The card in the door-jam trick is something cops do, although cops usually use a pizza coupon or Chinese food takeout menu. It tends to freak people out when they find a cop's business card jammed in their door. I wonder if she has a cop-dad, or cop-brother, or cop-boyfriend? All three are warning signs, but I hope it's not a cop-boyfriend. This woman is resourceful and beautiful; I think I'm falling in lust. Looking at her now, I can't stop thinking about gently grabbing her by her long braids, sitting her up on my desk, and feeling her well-manicured nails rake across my back. Snap out of it, Colt, the way you're staring at her is starting to get a little creepy, and it's bordering on sexual harassment.

"I don't know where he is," I coolly say. My motto is, stick to the truth when possible. What I said is technically truthful. I really don't know where he is. Hell? Maybe Valhalla? No, that's not right. Where do Greeks go when they die? Purgatory? I'm going to have to look that up. I'm not even sure where his body is. If I had to hazard a guess, I'd say in the bellies of those giant hogs, but I don't know that for a fact; I'm speculating.

"Why do you want to know?" I finally ask.

"I want to interview him for a news story I'm working on. It's something big, something my viewers are going to want to hear." A mischievous gleam shines in her eyes.

I don't think I'm going to like the answer, but I ask anyway, "What story is that?"

"I think you're going to like it," she says. "It's a story about a public defender with a crisis of conscience. He's so overcome with his own guilt after winning his guilty client's freedom that he confesses everything to a classy reporter."

"Sounds like a fairytale."

"Could be. Isn't it true that after the trial, Mr. Silas and you argued, and then you made a public statement all but admitting his guilt? I think it's got potential to be made into a Hollywood movie; maybe Denzel or Clooney will play you? Why don't you tell me your side?"

"Aren't they both a little old to play me? I think Justin Timberlake or Michael B. Jordan would be more age-appropriate? Maybe that Jesse Williams guy from *Grey's Anatomy*. But, before we get ahead of ourselves, I think we should hit the pause button on casting, and discuss the plot. The whole thing sounds pretty fantastic. I don't think anyone would believe it. Maybe we could co-write a romance story about a reporter who falls head over heels for a ruggedly handsome Public Defender instead?"

Makayla shrugs. "That sounds terrible, I don't think I'd watch it." She continues her examination. "Judge Takeda's bailiff said he heard you and Mr. Silas threatening each other after the verdict. Is that true? If so, why did you threaten him?" She sets her cell phone on the desk between us and it begins recording.

The fucking loud-mouthed bailiff was apparently more interested in our conversation than he let on. Shit, I need to manage this situation and put an end to this story before it gets off the ground. I've killed two people in the past week and my life seems to be getting more complicated by the day. I don't need my name in the news or the scrutiny that comes with that. I certainly don't need Denzel or Clooney playing me in a movie.

Damn it, I'm not seeing any good outs. So, I do the unexpected and burst into laughter. "That's a good one. Did the bailiff put you up to this? Am I being *punked*? Are there hidden cameras in here?" I feign looking around the office. "Clooney, Denzel, you're fucking hilarious. Haha, guys, you can come out, joke's over!" I shout. "Is Roy in on this? Roy, are you hiding somewhere?"

"Why were you fighting, then?" asks Makayla in a defensive tone.

"Look, I don't know what you've been told, but we weren't fighting. It was an emotional day. We might have been talking in elevated voices—I don't remember. But we weren't fighting. Nobody threatened anybody. I just told him to stay out of trouble because the cops, and reporters like you, would be gunning for him. I think I really got through to him. I don't think he will have any more issues with the law." I almost add, *I don't think anyone will ever see him again.*

"What about the statement you made to the media?"

"What, that the rapist was still out there? That's true. I hope the Golden Gate Park community looks out for one another. I would have made that same statement even if the jury had found Roy guilty. I don't want anyone to get raped. You think I'm heartless? Do you want people to get raped? That's cold. You got a real *if it bleeds, it leads* mentality, don't you?"

Clouds of doubt roll through Makayla, her pupils dilate, and there is a slight tremble in her lower lip. Laughing and answering her questions is clearly not the response she was expecting. She probably expected me to invoke attorney-client privilege or say no comment. Both responses would have convinced her she was on the right track and pushed her in a direction that would eventually cause me stress. Answering her questions on the record has thrown her for a loop.

Now for the coup-de-grâce; time to make her hate me, make her think I'm a real scrub. She won't want to report on a story making me look like a saint with a conscience, if she thinks I'm a creep. I sigh. I am going to regret this. She is so hot.

"Makayla, baby, I'm actually headed to a joint right now to have a drink with some friends. I just resigned here, took a job at a new law firm, I'm gonna' get paid. Why don't you come with me to the club and we can continue this conversation; we can celebrate and we can work, work, work, work, work." I sing the last little bit like it's the chorus of a popular Rhianna and Drake song, and gyrate my hips. "Maybe get to know each other better—you know what I'm saying, girl?"

Makayla gives me a disgusted look, similar to one my wife used to give me when I was trying to get fresh. My wife used to say, "You're not sexy. When you try to look sexy, you look constipated." Everybody's a critic. #HatersGonnaHate.

This may seem childish and harsh, but I have to do it. I can't have Makayla thinking my quitting has anything to do with Roy Silas. If she left today without knowing I quit, and then found out later, she'd assume my quitting had something to do with her theory, and that she was on the right track. It's better to get out in front of this potential landmine early, with a plausible explanation; mainly, that I'm just another playboy douchebag lawyer who sold out for money. When you're trying to convince someone of something, it's important to present your case in a way that aligns with your audience's natural biases. It's easy to convince someone of something if all you're doing is reinforcing their expectations or world view. Believing a lawyer is a douchebag sellout doesn't require mental gymnastics; it's a story easily sold.

"No, thank you Mr. Valentine. I'm leaving. Please let Mr. Silas know I'm looking for him." Makayla coldly pushes past me on her way to the elevator.

The angry look on Makayla's face says it all; crisis averted and my *no-sex* streak is intact. Her story is as good as dead and buried. I can't help but feel a twinge of regret as I watch her go.

Childishly, because I need the last word, I call after her, "Does this mean no movie deal?" Makayla doesn't dignify my cat-calls with a response. She doesn't even turn around inside the elevator until after the doors are closed.

I sigh and take a final look around my office. I realize as I stand there in the doorway, staring at the desk where I spent the majority of the last ten years of my life, there's nothing left for me here. Any regrets I thought I might have about quitting are gone. The only thought running through my mind is, why not sooner? I've fantasized about quitting this job for years. I've agonized over the decision. I was irrationally afraid that I wouldn't get another job, and that quitting would be the biggest mistake of my life. If I'm not a Public Defender, what am I? I still don't know, but I do know one thing; this office is my past. I flip the light switch off for the last time and head for the elevator. It's time to embrace my future. Time to get answers.

Chapter Twenty-Four

On the way to Pavo's building, my new office, I call Wilson but it goes directly to voicemail. So much for our plan to confront Sinn together. Well, I'm not waiting. I want to know, need to know, everything she knows about: my family, my new abilities, this ring that I can't take off, my new job, and most importantly, monsters. I want to know their strengths, weaknesses, even their favorite fucking colors. I want to know it all. I'm tired of getting bushwhacked. I want to be prepared for the next thing that threatens me, smells me, or tries to kill me. I don't like feeling vulnerable. I like being the most prepared person in the room. My mother used to say I have a touch of OCD. My father used to laugh and say, "A touch, that's one way of putting it. Another would be, the kid's nuts." Yeah, Dad was a sport.

I pull into an empty parking spot across the street from my new office: an old, naked, faded red brick, two-story building, with voussoir-arched windows, and oversized decorative keystones. It's breathtaking. I took some architecture classes in college, so give me a break on the nerd terms. The building reminds me of my childhood. It looks a lot like the buildings I grew up around in Indianapolis. There's something about brick buildings that calls out to a man's soul. They perfectly embody man's ability to build with his hands. Building with bricks doesn't require fancy equipment, or a crane; all you need are bricks, mortar, and willpower. It's the type of building I always imagined running my own law office out of—it's perfect.

A black limo pulls up and illegally parks in front of my brick building, partially obscuring my view, and completely interrupting the perfect moment I'm having. A massive muscled meathead, wearing an old fashioned driver's uniform, complete with white driving gloves and a tiny hat, emerges from the vehicle and ambles around the side of the limo to the passenger door. His muscles are so massive, it makes walking look awkward and painful. The driver opens the door for two similar-looking women wearing nearly matching dark-colored pant suits. The women exit the vehicle without so much as a thank you to the driver and enter my building through the front door. The driver shuts the door and then leans his Venice-beach body up against the limo.

After the week I've had I can't help but wonder, are these good people, bad people, in-between people, village people? Maybe they're just regular old clients? Nah, with my luck, they're bad people, itching for a fight. The women probably turn into dragons, and the meathead probably shoots lightning out of his ass. I hate being unprepared. I didn't even bring the knife; it's sitting on my nightstand. I wonder if there's a back entrance. I'd like to get into the building without alerting the two women, or lightning-ass that I joined the party. Maybe I can eavesdrop and actually learn something.

I'm just about to circle the building, to look for a back entrance, when my pocket starts to vibrate. It's a text message from Wilson:

SORRY I MISSED CALL IN REDDING FOLLOWING LEAD
LOTS TO DISCUSS
WILL CALL LATER
IF YOU DON'T HERE FROM ME BY TOMORROW COME
FIND ME I MUST BE IN TROUBLE
YOU OWE ME A LOT OF BEER

Redding, California, that's about four hours north from here. Why would he have gone there? He spelled "hear" wrong, what an idiot. I hope he's not doing anything stupid. My phone vibrates again, with another text message; this one reads:

P.S. YOUR XWIFE LOVES DICK ... XOXO

Wilson always knows how to make me smile.

My phone vibrates a third time; this time it's a picture of a sleazy motel. This must be the hotel he's staying at. Smart, he's following protocol. At the PD's office, we instructed our investigators to continually text photographs of all field investigations to a handler—just in case. It gives us a record of the investigation and a place to start looking if someone goes missing. It almost never happens, but it's always good to prepare for the worst-case scenario. Whatever he's doing, I'm sure he'll be fine. Wilson's a professional. He can handle himself.

Which brings me back to my problem: how do I get into my building without being seen? After a moment of contemplation, I come up with a plan. I circle around to the backside of the stucco building I parked in front of, just outside the muscle-bound meathead's line of sight, and draw a door and a handle on the wall with my magic Sharpie. I grasp my ring and visualize the top of my building, while I chant, "Office rooftop." I reach into the wall, grasp the door handle, pull it open towards me, and step through the shimmering doorway.

The rooftop looks a lot like one would expect the top of a 1940's era brick building to look, except there's no rooftop access into the building. "Well, this blows," I mutter to myself. Anyone that lives in a city knows rooftop space is boss. It's good for BBQs, chilling, smoking, drinking, hooking up, whatever. This rooftop is wasted space. We're going to have to remodel.

I look over the edge of the building, but I can't see a way to safely lower myself to the fire escape that connects to a second-story window and, even if I did, there's a good chance I'd be seen by the meathead below. I've been in buildings like this before; all the action is on the ground level. The second stories are typically used for storage. I'm spit-balling here, but I wonder if I can use the pen to open up a hole in the roof, and jump down through the ceiling to the second floor?

If this works, there's a chance I'm going to fall ten or fifteen feet from the ceiling to the second story floor. That's going to make a lot of noise and it has the potential to cause me pain. I wonder if my Battle-Sense will kick in? Will I fall in slow motion? Maybe I can contort in midair like a cat and land on my feet. That would be so cool. My other option is to use the front door. That's probably the smarter play, but where's the fun in that?

I draw a square shaped door on the roof with a half-moon shaped rope handle. It looks like one of those wooden trap-doors you see in video games. I close my eyes and visualize the door opening to the ceiling on the other side of the roof, which is harder than you think, because I don't know what the room below looks like. Is it brick or drywall? Is the room empty or packed with boxes? I visualize an empty room with brick walls and stacks of banker boxes. "Please open to the other side," I say in a less than confident tone. "Oh, and if you're taking requests, please make the fall not hurt. No fall would be even better." I'm not sure who I'm talking to, but it can't hurt to ask, can it? Somebody might be listening.

I grab the rope handle and pull the door open. There's now a glowing hole where there used to be gravel and tar paper. It takes me a moment or two, but I finally gather up the courage to step through the glowing hole in the roof.

As I experience the sensation of flight, I recognize I've made an error in judgment and regret not using the front door. I soar fifteen feet down through the ceiling and impact the floor with a loud crash that echoes through the building. So much for my cat-like reflexes theory. Let's just say, I don't land on my feet. After a minute or so spent lying on the floor feeling self-pity, I pick myself up and check for permanent injuries. Fortunately, other than my red ass, both literally and figuratively, I seem to be all right.

I dust myself off and look around. It's just as I suspected—this room is used for storage. It's stacked floor-to-ceiling with banker boxes. Of course, I somehow managed to fall through the ceiling in the one box-free section of the room—I'm just lucky, I guess. The door to the storage room is open and I can see out into the hallway. At the end of the hallway is a door with a sign indicating there's an enclosed stairwell going down. There are other rooms on this floor, but I'll have to explore them later—I hear raised voices arguing below. There's no sense in sneaking around at this point; they must know somebody's up here. They'd have to be deaf not to have heard my fall.

About halfway down the enclosed stairwell, I hear Sinn's voice cut through the musty air, "I don't have the ring. Look at my hands—do you see a ring?" Sinn and the two women sound more interested in their argument than investigating the crash upstairs.

A high-pitched women's voice snaps, "One way or the other, you're going to tell us where the ring is."

"Are you threatening me, Witch? I'll rip your throat out!" shouts Sinn.

She sounds pissed; maybe I should stay out of this? It's dangerous to get in the middle of two pissed off women. Maybe it's a witch-vampire thing? For all I know, they're arguing about a different ring. Maybe an engagement ring? Right, and Santa Claus is real.

I hear the high-pitched voice again, "Touch me and the Coven will end you, bitch."

Another woman's voice, a deeper, more controlled voice, weighs in, "We're not going to leave until you tell us where the ring is. Sinn, I always liked your father, I don't want to hurt you. You know how important that ring is. It can't fall into the wrong hands. It's unfortunate that he didn't pass it on to you; that would've made things so much easier. Please tell us who has it. Is there something you want in exchange for the information? Money? Revenge on your father's killer? Name your price."

There's an uncomfortably long silence. My heart starts to beat rapidly. I'm not sure why—I barely know her, and she is a vampire for God's sake—but the thought of her selling me out upsets me. After what feels like an eternity, Sinn says, "That information's not for sale."

I exhale with relief, dance down the final few steps, slip my hands into my pockets, and exit the enclosed stairway into a surprisingly well-designed office space. The ground floor of this building has an amazing open concept floor plan with exposed wooden beams, a large wooden table, oversized desks, a beautiful seating area, and even a professional full-sized restaurant quality cappuccino machine. I'm in love.

Sinn intercepted the witches near the front door and is blocking their path into the office. She looks ready to lay a beat down.

Up close, the witches look a lot alike. Sisters, maybe? Both are decked out with a mess of jewelry. Multiple rings, earrings, necklaces and a ton of visible piercings decorate their persons. I can only imagine what's underneath the clothing. Neither are wearing an Advocate ring.

The younger one is wound up tighter than an eight-day clock. If I don't intervene, violence isn't far off. The older one is giving me freezer burn. She's as cool as an Antarctic penguin eating a popsicle and wears an icy expression that says, "I've already calculated how to kill you; you just haven't realized you're dead yet." She's scary.

"Good afternoon, ladies, how much are you offering?"

The two witches turn and face me while Sinn relocates her position a bit to the left of where she was standing. There's now a direct line of fire between myself and the two witches. Sinn did the same thing in the Dead Pig's lair. Is she trying to get out of the way, or is she strategically positioning herself in case a fight ensues? After we get out of this, we need to have a talk.

The older woman studies me, her eyes lingering on the pockets where I'm storing my hands, and shielding the ring from her view. I can't help myself, "Excuse me, my eyes are up here."

Sinn smirks.

The older woman is rattled, but quickly recovers. Her gaze rises until she's looking me directly in the eyes. "My name is Arianna Soot, and this is my daughter Vanessa. What did you say your name was?"

"Mother-daughter, huh?" I would have bet good money they were sisters. "I didn't say," I reply.

Sinn smirks again.

Arianna shoots Sinn a threatening look, and then asks, "I assume you want cash; how much do you want?"

"How much do you have on you?" I ask.

Arianna looks perplexed. She can't decide if I'm dangerous or not and it's bothering her. "What should I call you?" she asks.

Persistent, isn't she? I think it's safest for everyone, especially me, if I keep this killer penguin off-balance. "Sir is fine. I always liked sir. It reminds me of older times. Times when people still had manners."

Arianna frowns but decides to indulge me. "Just name your price and we will get it to you, *Sir*."

"I don't want to wait for payment. How much cash do you have on you right now?"

Arianna's perplexed look begins to mature into an annoyed look. "I don't carry cash on me."

I shrug and turn to her daughter Vanessa. "How about you, kiddo? How much cash do you have on you?" They really do look a lot alike—not exactly classic beauties, but they've got that whole sexy suicide-girl thing going on.

Vanessa looks to her mother for guidance and receives none. Her mother's too busy studying me. I feel like a first-time performer at a peep show. Finally, Vanessa pulls a small wad of cash out of her jacket pocket and counts it. She hesitates and then says, "I have eighty-three dollars on me."

"Sold to the young witch!" I dramatically shout like she just won a prize on a game show. "Please hand the cash to Sinn so we can conclude the transaction."

Vanessa looks stunned. "Are you proposing that I give Sinn eighty-three dollars and then you'll tell us where the ring is?"

Arianna continues to watch me like I'm on stage dancing at a Thursday afternoon lingerie show.

"Yep," I answer.

Vanessa's face reads I don't believe you. To her credit, she ignores her intuition and hands Sinn the cash. Sinn takes the money while grinning and shaking her head in disbelief. She counts it, nods at me confirming it amounts to the agreed-upon price, and then slips it into her pocket. "I'm going to keep this," she says. She's clearly enjoying the spectacle.

"I wouldn't expect anything less," I reply with a flirtatious smile.

Sinn gives me an awkward smile-frown. She's still uncomfortable with my flirting. I should probably give her a break. It's only been four days since I killed her father; I doubt she's forgiven me.

Arianna watches me and waits for my next move.

After I count to ten in my head, just to let the tension build, I remove my hands from my pockets and display the Advocate ring with my palm down and fingers spread, the way I have seen newly engaged women show off their shiny new diamond rings. Arianna doesn't seem surprised at all, but Vanessa looks pissed. "I have the ring. It's beautiful, isn't it?"

Neither of the witches responds.

I shift to a more serious tone of voice, "Now you can go. I don't plan on giving it to you, and neither of you are powerful enough to take it." My words linger in the air, while the witches study me, trying to assess my threat level.

Growing bored with the situation, I turn my back on the witches, and walk over to the cappuccino machine. Showing my rear end is a calculated risk, but I'm trusting Sinn to warn me if they try anything. The cappuccino machine is just like the one I used during my college bartending days. I grab the filter handle like an old pro, untwist it from the group-head, and set it on the counter. I grasp the silver cannister labeled *Ground Expresso*, and scoop espresso out with a spoon, and load and pack the espresso down into the filter. I then reattach the loaded filter onto the group-head, grab an espresso cup off the rack, set it below the group-head, and press the button with the sticker indicating espresso. I patiently wait while the screaming machine fills with steam and then slowly drips espresso into a small mug, also known as a demitasse. The tension in the room rises with each agonizing drip.

When the screaming stops, I grab my demitasse, and turn back to face the ladies, while I calmly sip the hot espresso. "Is there a reason you haven't left?" I ask. "Is there something else I can do for you?"

Vanessa looks as if she is about to blow a dial. Arianna reassuringly places a hand on her daughter's shoulder and then takes a step towards me. "What makes you think we can't take it from you?"

It's a clever question, not really a threat and easily retreated from. It's designed to enrage me into revealing my strengths, but I'm not stupid. I don't really want to get into another physical altercation with something more than human, so I need her to think I'm more powerful than I actually am. A bluff will likely achieve more than a show of force.

"Well, you couldn't take it from Pavo or you would have," I answer. "I killed Pavo and I've bound his vampire daughter to my service. Frankly, my dear, I don't think you want to test me." A good measured response if I don't say so myself. I didn't really give her any new information, at least nothing she hadn't already guessed, and I put the ball back in her court.

I take another sip of my espresso; it's delicious, only a bit bitter. It could use a single sugar packet, but I'm not going to add one now. Turning around, walking back over to the espresso machine and adding a sugar packet would break the careful illusion of control I've crafted. And adding sugar would make me less intimidating. I mean, would you be afraid of someone who adds sugar to their espresso?

Arianna calculates the odds as she looks from Sinn to me. She's trying to determine if I'm bluffing, or if I'm really dangerous. Finally, her eyes settle on me and her face contorts into an almost smile. "Congratulations on your new position, Advocate. The Coven looks forward to a fruitful relationship with you. Do you have a name, Advocate?"

"I do have a name. Thank you for asking. And thank you and the Coven for the warm welcome," I say with a Cheshire-like grin.

Sinn snorts as she tries to hold back her laughter.

Arianna takes a step towards me. "Forgive me for asking again, but what is your name, Advocate?"

You have got to respect her persistence. "I'm sorry," I say. "I'm not in the business of giving things away for free, especially information. I think we've already established that you and your daughter are out of cash."

Vanessa's jaw drops to the floor. I can see anger rising behind the cold calculating eyes of Arianna. I wonder what witches can do? Can she turn me into a toad? Put me to sleep for a thousand years until Prince Charming wakes me with a kiss? I hope not. I'm not really a fan of either scenario. Frogs are gross, and one thousand years of sleep sounds like a bore.

"Thank you two for stopping by," I say. "Now if we don't have any other business, I really do have other appointments to get to." I dismissively turn and start walking away from the witches, back towards the largest desk, which I assume used to be Pavo's. Hopefully, they leave before I get there, otherwise I'm going to look foolish. I don't actually have anything to do at his desk.

The two witches look at each other for a moment and then sensibly move towards the exit. They must realize they've been outflanked, and Arianna doesn't look like the type to wade into a fight without knowing the outcome. When they reach the door, Arianna stops and calls out to me, "*Sir*, we will meet again. You can count on that, *Sir*."

I turn back towards Arianna, and quickly respond, "Be sure to bring cash next time. Hundreds, ones, I take all denominations. Oh, and one more thing, please warn your muscle-beach reject that if he ever parks illegally in front of my building again, I'll have him towed." It then occurs to me that I might not want to alienate every single Concordat member, so I add, "Do come back if you have any legal trouble. Thanks for stopping by."

Vanessa starts to say something, but Arianna pushes her out the door. Once the door slams shut behind them, Sinn falls to the floor in laughter.

"What are you laughing at?" I ask with a smirk. "We have a lot to discuss. You are going to finally give me some answers. First ... I'm hungry. Do vampires eat?"

Chapter Twenty-Five

We step through the gate onto a dirt parking lot decorated with all manner of reclaimed signs, license plates, and colored string lights. A restaurant, sort of an indoor-outdoor shed with picnic tables constructed of old junk and scrap, stands in the forest clearing before us. A long line of people are waiting for their chance to order food at a wooden counter with two old cash registers. Intoxicating aromas of black pepper, brown sugar, apple cider vinegar, smoke, and slow-cooked BBQ fills the air. The delicious smells cause my stomach to rumble.

"Where are we?" Sinn asks.

"Mississippi, East of Biloxi," I respond. "The BBQ here is amazing, at least it used to be. I discovered this place in college. Some friends convinced me it would be a good idea to spend Spring break in Biloxi, the *Vegas of the South*—it wasn't. I don't remember much about that trip, other than BBQ. I have always wanted to come back, but there haven't been a lot of opportunities in my life to just up and travel to Mississippi for BBQ. Last time I checked, even without traffic, it's a long drive from California."

Sinn gives me a sidewise glance, I'm guessing she's put two and two together and is, at least, suspicious that I have an ulterior motive for picking this place. She's right, I do. I picked this place for a couple reasons. First, it's far out of the way, so I doubt we will run into any trouble. Second, it's far out of the way, which means Sinn is dependent on me to get her home. I'm going to be able to control the conversation, at least when it starts and when it stops. We are not leaving until I get the answer I need. And finally, because I'm craving good BBQ.

Sinn and I stand in line and read the menu to ourselves while we wait. I order meat four ways, pulled pork, brisket, ribs, and sausage with a side of baked beans. Sinn orders brisket and a Caesar salad. Salad at a BBQ joint? Blasphemy. On general principles, I consider canceling the salad order, but ultimately refrain. I don't want to start a fight … yet. We get our food and our sides of house BBQ sauce from the condiment counter, and sit down across from each other at one of the empty wooden picnic tables.

"So, vampires can eat?" I ask awkwardly, hoping to start the conversation off with something non-controversial.

Sinn bites into her perfectly cooked brisket and with a full mouth says, "This is amazing. Yes, we can eat, but we shouldn't eat very much. Our bodies don't need nutrients from food anymore, and it's uncomfortable when it passes through us. Vampires are more in tune with their bodies than humans; we actually feel the food as it is digested and travels through our stomach, intestines, and colon. It is not a pleasant sensation."

"That's *gross*."

Sinn frowns at me, but keeps chewing the brisket. The BBQ is incredible, the sauce is fantastic, it has just the right amount of vinegar and sugar, with a hint of heat. It's just as delicious as I remember.

"I've always wondered if vampires go to the bathroom? They never show it in the movies. If not the toilet, where does all the blood go?" I ask.

Sinn's eyebrows raise. "Are we really having potty-talk during dinner?"

I nod between bites.

Sinn sighs, "Yes, vampires occasionally use the bathroom. Female vampires shit fluffy white clouds and piss rainbows." Sinn smirks as she takes another bite of the delicious brisket. "I'm not dead, if that's what you're thinking. Vampires are living creatures. I've run tests, even sequenced my DNA. Almost everything about my condition is explainable scientifically. As far as I can tell, vampirism is a disease, like cancer. Do you know what the definition of cancer is?"

"Sure," I answer between bites. "I took biology in college. Cancer is the loss of controlled cell growth."

"Close enough," she says. "Normal cell growth involves the division of a healthy cell into two identical daughter cells, in a controlled manner. Controlled is another way of saying on a schedule. Different cells types divide on different schedules. Cancer cells are cells with genetic errors in them. When a cancer cell divides, it transcribes, or copies the errors, into each of its daughter cells, which then divide into additional cancer cells, and so on and so on. Are you following?" she asks.

I nod.

"When the error involves the P53 cancer suppressor gene, the cell loses its ability to self-regulate, and it begins to divide in an uncontrolled way at unscheduled times, often rapidly. Rapid, unscheduled cell growth often results in tumors, which interfere with other cells and systems in the body, causing illness and death. It's the interference with the body's other systems that usually causes death, and not the cancer itself. Cancer is like real estate—it's all about the location, location, location."

I chuckle at the cheesy analogy. At least, I'm not the only one guilty of using them.

Sinn ignores my chuckle. "Vampires have what I'm calling a kind of anti-cancer. Unlike cancer, where cells are dividing out of control and interfering with the body's systems, vampire cells remain frozen in the exact state they were in when the disease was contracted. They don't change, and they don't divide—except to heal, which means vampires don't age. If a vampire is injured, its cells temporarily activate and holistically regenerate the vampire, by cell replication and division, until the vampire is returned to the exact state it was in when it first contracted the virus."

"Fascinating," I say, and I meant it. This is the first glimpse I've had into who Sinn really is. She's smart and has a passion for science. This conversation is the first time I have seen her genuinely happy; she lights up when she talks about science. She is beautiful.

"It is, isn't it? Did you know vampires can actually regrow a limb?" she says.

"Wow, sounds painful. Can they un-crush crushed limbs?" I ask while protecting my manhood with both hands.

Sinn frowns at my dick joke. "There are some things I haven't figured out yet," she says between bites. Sinn forks some pork off my plate.

"Like what?" I ask.

"You know how vampires are stronger and faster than humans?"

"Yes." I saw Pavo in action, and there's no doubt in my mind he was stronger and faster than any human that ever lived.

"I can't explain why. I think it has something to do with adrenaline, but it's only a hypothesis. I need to run more tests."

"What do you mean?" I ask.

"I'm sure you've seen videos on the internet where someone performs an impossible feat of strength and lifts something unbelievably heavy like a car, or a boat, in order to save a child or a loved one?"

"Sure," I answer.

"Most of the time when you see or hear about something like that, it's a hoax or an exaggeration, but it's been documented enough times that scientists believe it's a real phenomenon. Currently, the scientific community believes that short-term increased strength can be caused by a massive adrenaline dump. I think vampires are on a 24/365 adrenaline high. I think the virus triggers an adrenaline dump when it infects the body. Since all the cells in the body become frozen, vampires are frozen in the middle of a continuous adrenaline dump, which would explain the increased strength. That's my theory anyway, but it doesn't explain everything. It doesn't really explain our speed or our other abilities."

"Other abilities?" I ask.

"I'm not going to give away all my secrets on the first date." Sinn winks at me. "Anyway, it's just a theory, a work in progress really." Sinn takes another bite of her brisket. She still hasn't touched her salad.

"I always wanted to be a scientist," Sinn says. "I believe everything can ultimately be explained by science."

"Even monsters and magic?"

"Yes, even monsters and magic. We just need to use modern science and medicine to study the monsters. Magic is nothing more than a word we used to describe things we don't yet understand." Sinn gets a faraway look in her eye. "Dad never believed the answers to the important questions could be found in science. He used to say my scientific pursuits were a waste of time. He would say, "*Sinn, there are some things you can't learn with a microscope.*" He never supported my interests and pushed me into law school. He had me convinced I would be an Advocate someday—it was all a lie." Crimson drops of sorrow pool at the corners of her exotic brown eyes.

I barely know this girl, and she's probably the last girl on earth who needs my protection, and I'm probably the last person on Earth she wants protection from, and yet, seeing her in pain bothers me and makes me want to protect her. "Do vampires need to drink blood?" I ask, changing the subject.

The moment of sadness passes and she continues her lecture, "Vampires need blood to maintain and repair cells; it's the fuel that maintains their stasis. Vampires regularly need to replenish their blood supply or they get weak and can die. Blood starvation is one of the cruelest ways to kill a vampire. Cutting the head off is a bit dramatic, but also works. It's hard to function without a head. Come to think of it, very few things can live through a beheading. You should probably write that down." Sinn reaches over and stabs one of my sausages with her fork.

"Anything else?" I ask.

"A dramatic injury to the heart." A strange look crosses Sinn's face. "Don't be weird and make a joke about how you're not going to break my heart."

I put my hands up in mock innocence. "I wasn't even considering it." In actuality, she had me pegged. Am I that transparent? #INeedNewGame.

Sinn continues, "Without a functioning heart, a vampire cannot properly disperse blood throughout its body. Without fuel, the vampire dies."

"What about sunlight?" I ask.

"Only affects young vampires; something in the ultraviolet rays interrupts the virus and prevents it from maintaining stasis. There is a mage I know, Tolliver; he believes ultraviolet rays can be used to cure vampirism—if you catch it early enough. Of course, Tolliver's never been able to prove his theory. He's never had a young enough vampire to experiment on. I offered to turn him, in the interest of science, of course, but he declined."

"Interest of science, right. That sounds perfectly reasonable." I mumble, perfectly understanding why Tolliver declined the offer.

Sinn smiles and takes another bite of sausage. "Over time, vampires develop an immunity to sunlight, and once you get to be my age, it's harmless. I spent an entire month last summer tanning on a beach in Phuket; it was heaven."

"How old are you?" I ask.

Sinn stares at me for a moment and then just keeps eating meat off my plate. I guess that rule about not asking a woman her age also applies to female vampires. I've always thought that was a dumb social rule. As a lawyer, I advise all my clients, especially the female high school teachers who seem to have a hard time keeping it in their pants these days, to make sure you know how old they are before you sleep with them. #MakeSureThey're18. #Don'tSleepWithYourStudents.

"This is all fascinating, particularly the mental image I now have of you in a bathing suit." Sinn's cheeks rosed up a bit. "And I have about a million sciencey follow-up questions, but first, I want answers about my family. Who were they? What am I? How did I heal so quickly? Why does everyone want this fucking ring?" I flash the ring at Sinn. "And most importantly, what has your father gotten me into?"

Sinn looks uncomfortable. Her eyes frantically search the restaurant for something, probably an exit or a distraction.

"There is no exit," I say. "No emerging crisis that is going to postpone this talk. I brought you sixteen hundred miles to the middle of nowhere Mississippi to get answers, and you're going to give them to me."

Finally, Sinn relents, "Where do you want to start?"

"At the beginning. Tell me about my family."

Chapter Twenty-Six

Sinn takes a deep breath, "Your ancestors were great knights; the Emperors of Rome called them paladins—"

"—You keep using that word paladin. What exactly do you mean?"

Sinn's brow furrows. "You don't know what a paladin is? You're practically a man-child. Are you telling me you don't play video games? Or watch movies?"

"Man-child? I'm a grown-ass man, you better ask somebody. And yes, I know conceptually what a paladin is. I don't live in a shack in the woods. I have cable. And yes, I've been known to play a video game here and there."

Sinn smirks, clearly not believing I only play video games "here and there."

"Paladins are essentially white knights with limited magic powers and a magic sword," I continue.

Sinn shrugs. "There you go; other than being racist, your description is mostly accurate."

I give Sinn an eye roll that would make Anderson Cooper jealous.

"The Palatinus family dates back to the beginning of the Roman empire. In the early days of Rome, your family was rich and powerful, but they didn't possess any abilities. It wasn't until around the time of Christ's death that your family became something else. I'm not saying the two events were related; I'm also not say they weren't. I really don't know."

I consider interrupting her and telling her a juvenile Jesus joke a priest once told me when I was a child, *What do you call holy bread? Jesus crust,* but I bite my tongue. I finally got Sinn talking and I don't want to derail her.

"Servius Palatinus was the first in your family to develop abilities. He was a great general and a master of hand-to-hand combat with no equal. Servius was not a rear-guard General. He rode into battle and fought at the front of his armies. His soldiers loved him. In a time when a soldier's average lifespan could be counted on his dead fingers and toes, Servius lived and fought for more than a century. He fought not only men, but also monsters. He was the world's first paladin.

According to your family journals, Servius had three abilities. These core abilities are the ones most commonly associated with paladins. Most if not all paladins that came after him had at least these three abilities. The first was Battle-Sight, of which you are familiar. The second was the ability to heal. The third is called Light-Bringer.

Light-Bringer is described in your family journals as the ability to release the energy stored in inanimate objects. A small release causes a sword to glow. A large release creates an explosion. Servius would charge into battle wielding a glowing sword, and men would cower in fear. This is likely the genesis of the concept of magical weapons in today's books, movies, and video games, but there's nothing magical about it—it's just energy."

"What happened to him?"

"In the year 101 CE, while on a diplomatic mission to Dacia, Romania today, on behalf of Emperor Marcus Ulpius Traianus, Servius was ambushed. He and his twelve guards were attacked by more than two hundred men. Servius fought bravely and single-handedly killed nearly a hundred men before he was overwhelmed. He was one-hundred and sixteen years old at the time of his death. Fortunately for you, he left behind a large family."

"Yeah, lucky me."

As per usual, Sinn ignores my commentary. "During his lifetime, Servius fathered twenty-six children with three separate women. It's tragic really, your family is long-lived; all of the members of your family are destined to watch their loved ones grow old and die, while they remain young."

"How long do we live?" I ask, suddenly very interested.

Sinn shrugs. "Until you don't."

That response earns Sinn another Anderson Cooper eye roll. "Are you saying I need to put more money away for retirement? My current retirement plan only budgets for me to live to age seventy-five. After that, I am out of money and will have no choice but to convince some guys at the old-folks home to rob a bank with me."

Sinn gives me an eye-roll of her own. "I really don't know. Your family has made a career of dying young and violently. I don't know if retirement is a realistic concern."

"Brutal. Your telling me I should expect to die young?"

Sinn shrugs indifferently. "How should I know when you're going to die? I just know that historically, most of your family members, other than . . . Pavo, didn't have the longest life spans."

"I guess that actually makes sense. I can see how fighting monsters isn't really conducive to living a long life. Look at how many times I've almost died, and I've been doing this for less than a week."

Sinn's eyes crease and her lips pucker, as if she's tasting rotten milk. "Most of Servius' children developed abilities, as did their children, and so on down the line. As I indicated before, not every child of your bloodline developed abilities. Occasionally, a child would be born without any gifts. Those children lived tough lives, often shunned by your family. The Palantinus could be ruthlessly cruel."

I nod. I know exactly how cruel family can be.

"Despite spending decades researching your family, I've been unable to uncover any records that accurately detail how Servius gained his abilities. I have discovered stories, rumors really, but there is no census."

"How do you know all this stuff anyway?" I ask.

"Pavo was secretive and never liked to talk about his family. Sure, he told me stories as a child, but it was always at his whim, and he refused to answer my questions. My family was killed when I was very young and Pavo took me in. He was my hero. I wanted to learn everything I could about him; so, I started doing research. As I got older, I realized Pavo had many enemies, which meant I had many enemies. In order to protect him, I needed to know why. Since Pavo wouldn't answer my questions, I had to find out on my own. I've spent decades researching your family's history."

"Why do you keep calling it my family? Isn't it your family too?"

"No! Pavo was my family—not your fucked-up ancestors. I am a Palatinus in name only."

I nod again, not quite understanding the hostility she has for my family. "Tell me some of the rumors about how my family acquired abilities," I ask.

"I have heard three different theories about how your family gained its abilities—the Churches, the Mage Guilds, and my favorite, the one Pavo used to tell me as a child, the Witches' curse."

"Let's save that one for last. What does the Church believe?"

"Before the fall of Rome, the Roman Church believed that Christ chose your family to be the protectors of humanity. They believed that upon his death, a portion of his soul bound itself to your family. They believed your family's abilities were Christ's gift to humanity and that your family was a weapon of light to wield against the darkness."

"Christ's soul?"

Sinn nods. "That's what the Church believed. Before the fall of Rome, your family were treated like living saints."

"And after?" I ask.

"After Rome fell, the Church distanced themselves from your family. Today the Church curses your family name and denies that paladins ever walked the earth."

"Seriously?" I ask.

"I never actually asked, but that's what I have heard. Pavo hated the Church. Couldn't stand to be near priests."

"Isn't that normal for a vampire?" I ask.

Sinn shrugs. "I don't mind priests. I find them interesting and I admire their self-discipline."

"You mean when they're not fondling little boys?" I ask.

Sinn sighs. "Do you always go for the low hanging fruit?"

"I do. It tastes the best."

Sinn sighs again and shakes her head. "Pavo once told me there's an ancient library below the Vatican. He said it contains the history of the world and all the secrets of the Church, the Concordat, and Ancient Rome. I wanted to break in, but he forbid it. He said it was too dangerous, and then refused to talk about it further."

"Interesting," I say to myself. I wonder if I can use the ring to break in. The library might be a good Plan B if Sinn continues to hide information from me.

"What do the mages think?" I ask.

"They claim your ancestor Servius stole a rare artifact from them. For centuries, they petitioned your family and demanded the artifact's return. They think this artifact is the source of your family's abilities. Strangely, none of the records I've seen ever identify what the artifact was or even what it looked like. I once asked Tolliver, my friend the mage, what it was, and he said he didn't know. It's simply known as the artifact."

"Weird," I say.

"There is something else you should know."

"What?"

"Your family doesn't exactly have the best relationship with the Guild either. In 434 CE, the Mages Guild went to war with your family; unfortunately for them, they gravely miscalculated your family's power. It was a slaughter. Your family nearly eradicated all mages from the face of the earth. An uneasy peace was eventually reached, but trust was eroded, and a hatred between your family and mages persisted for centuries. Pavo said the mages eventually broke the peace and assisted in the eradication of your family. The Mages Guild of old was ruthless. The Guild of this century, the Guild I know, is made up of scholars and scientists—not battle mages. I think they could be our allies, but Pavo was stubborn; he refused to trust any of them other than Tolliver and his master."

I nod. Things just keep getting better and better. My list of potential enemies continues to grow. I wonder if there's anyone who actually likes my family.

"My favorite legend about how your family gained its abilities is a love story. It's the tale of Servius' mother Dulcia, and how she fell in love with a god, and how their forbidden love caused your family to be cursed. When I was a little girl, I used to make Pavo tell it to me every night before bed." A single red tear streaks down Sinn's cheek.

"Dulcia was an exceptional beauty, wanted by every man who met her. Her father, a poor fisherman, married her off to a rich nobleman. This was not a love match, but rather a marriage for position and comfort. Dulcia's father loved his daughter dearly, and wanted her to have a life of luxury, something a fisherman could never give her. At first, Dulcia was happy; her husband gave her the finest silk dresses and the most beautiful gold jewelry and he treated her with kindness. But then, as time passed, he grew bored with her and began to beat her, and treat her with cruelty. Her only escape from her husband's torment was the long morning rides she took in the woods.

One morning, on a particularly long ride, her horse stepped into a hole and broke its leg. Dulcia was thrown and sprained her ankle in the fall. A god, disguised as a man, happened upon the scene and offered his assistance. Dulcia was reluctant to accept it; she had heard stories of brigands in the woods and was afraid of what the man might do to her, but she didn't have much of a choice. She couldn't walk and her horse was badly injured; it would never walk again. The man insisted on helping and she finally relented.

After wrapping her ankle, the man knelt beside her horse, whispered softly into its ear, and took its pain away with his knife. Dulcia recognized this for what it was, an act of kindness. The man then offered to carry Dulcia back to her estate. She offered him payment in coin for his kindness, but the man refused. He said the only payment he required was her company on the journey.

During the long walk, Dulcia and the man talked and laughed. Dulcia found herself confessing things to the man she had never told anyone else. She even told him about the abuse she suffered at the hands of her husband, something she had never shared with another soul.

The man likewise found himself sharing secrets with Dulcia. He confessed that he was also married; his, also an arranged marriage of position. He told Dulcia he was a minor god and had been forced to marry a much more powerful goddess, a cruel goddess who enjoyed torturing and abusing all who were unlucky enough to find themselves in her presence.

Dulcia and the god comforted each other and fell in love, but it was a despondent love. Dulcia and the god knew they could never be together; their spouses would never allow it. The god feared there was nowhere in this world they could go where his cruel wife wouldn't find them. Theirs was a hopeless love. They decided they could never see each other again.

Dulcia fell into a deep depression when she returned to her husband. The only thing she had to hold onto was the memory of one perfect morning in the woods. That is, until nine months after that perfect morning in the woods, when Servius was born.

On the day of his birth, Dulcia was visited by the cruel goddess. The goddess told Dulcia that the god had confessed to his adultery, and she had tortured and killed him for his betrayal. Dulcia was heartbroken and consumed with fear for the life of her child. The goddess had planned on killing Dulcia and the baby, but seeing her husband's offspring in the flesh overwhelmed her with anger. How could he have preferred a human to *her*? Instead of killing the child, she cursed the child and his bloodline. She prophesized that the last of the child's bloodline would stand atop a burning kingdom and know that a price had finally been paid for the crime Dulcia and the god committed one perfect morning in the woods."

"I'm part god?" I ask.

"Don't let it go to your head," answers Sinn with a laugh. "Most gods I've met are dicks."

"Touché'," I say with a smile. "So, my family's abilities were genetically passed down from a god?"

"Not really," she says. "It's more complicated than that. Witches believe magic requires balance. For example, if you raise someone from the dead—another must die."

"Witches can raise the dead?" I ask.

"You're missing the point," Sinn says. "Witches believe there is balance in all things; for every desired action there is a reaction or consequence."

"I got it."

"When I was a young, I had a sleepover with a young witch. I think Pavo was dating her aunt. Pavo was at times … a bit of a ladies' man."

"Really?" I smirk.

Sinn rolls her eyes at me and continues. "I begged Pavo to tell us the story of Dulcia's curse and he finally relented. After we were tucked in bed, lying there in the dark, the young witch told me her grandmother had told her the same story. Her grandmother believed your family's abilities come from the curse itself; it was an unforeseen side-effect of the curse, a counter-balance."

"Okay, but what about the traits passed on from Servius' father?" I ask.

"I don't know who the gods in the story are," answered Sinn. "If Pavo knew, he never said. They might not have been gods at all. They might have been something else. Many things were once called gods. Regardless, Pavo always described the god as weak, and your family was anything but weak. If the abilities were a genetic trait passed on by Servius' father, they would have gotten weaker with each subsequent generation as the bloodline was diluted, but that's not what happened. Your family's abilities increased with each generation."

"Okay, what do the witches believe?"

"They believe your family's powers grow stronger as destiny and fulfillment of the prophecy grows closer."

"You're telling me my abilities came with a price, and that price is the end of the world?"

Sinn laughs. "Colt, it's just a story, a fairytale for children. In real life, everything is explainable with science, even your abilities ... I just haven't figured them out yet. Anyway, why believe the witches' prophecy over the Church's theory that your family is the protector of humanity, or the mages' theory that your family stole an item of power? Frankly, the mages' theory seems most plausible."

"Because the witch's prophecy sounds the worst. In my experience, whenever I've been presented with alternative theories as to what happened, the worst-case scenario *always* turns out to be true."

"Colt, that's because the two scenarios you're presented with are typically those of your clients, and the cops; and your clients always lie," argues Sinn.

"Not always," I reply. "Sometimes the cops lie."

"Colt, you're being ridiculous. Do you really believe that your great-great-great grandmother slept with a married god whose scary goddess-wife cursed your family to destroy the world?"

"When you put it like that, it does sound ridiculous." She may be right, but something about that story creeps me out. It feels true. I know that doesn't make any sense; something can't feel true—it either is true or it isn't, but that doesn't change the fact it *feels* true to me.

"You said my family's abilities got stronger with each generation—what did you mean?" I ask.

Sinn takes another bite of my brisket and then responds. "Each generation of your family was stronger than the last. The variety of ability also grew with each new generation. For example, Servius' ability to heal was relatively weak. According to the journal, he could only heal himself, and the process was slow and took a lot of energy. The journal describes an instance when he was stabbed in his side during a battle and it took him more than a month to heal. Later paladins could heal similar wounds in weeks, and some were able to use their abilities to heal others. Your wound healed in mere days; there isn't even a scar. Your healing ability is much more powerful than anything described in the journals."

I unconsciously touch my arm where Roy Silas cut me.

"How does the healing work?" I ask.

"I don't know," answers Sinn. "I will give you the journals, and you can search for the answer yourself. Or we can cut you again and see what happens? I would love to run some tests."

"Thank you, I'll pass," I answer with conviction.

Sinn shrugs indifferently.

"You're really going to just give the journals to me?" I ask in disbelief.

"They're your family's journals," she says. "Why wouldn't I give them to you? I need you to survive. Hopefully, the information in the journals helps you do that. I can't allow my father's death to be a waste."

"Tell me more about Light-Bringer," I ask, changing the subject from Pavo's death.

"I don't know much about it," she says. "Only what I read in the journals. I have never had a paladin to experiment with. From what I read, it sounds like basic physics. Every time an object moves, it creates energy and some of that energy is trapped. The more an object moves, the more energy that gets trapped. Your ancestors could somehow touch and manipulate the trapped energy. The example used in your family's journal involves an ax. Each time the ax was swung, more and more energy would be trapped inside the ax. Your ancestors could reach into the ax, release a little energy, and make the ax glow. Or they could release a lot of energy at the point of impact, and an ax could fell a tree in a single blow. When the ax was drained of energy, they would recharge it by swinging it again and again. The journals claimed they could do this with any object, a rock, a pot, a pan, anything."

That explains the explosion that happened when I fought Pavo and the glowing blade when I fought Roy Silas. "So, the dagger Pavo gave me isn't magical?"

"No. Priceless, but not magical. That dagger was a gift to Dad from Romulus Augustus."

"The last Emperor of Rome," I exclaim in surprise.

"Yes, try not to lose it," suggests Sinn. "It's irreplaceable."

I knew it was old but it's an actual piece of history. It should be in a museum, and I left it on my nightstand. #IHopeILockedMyDoor.

I have been beating around the bush for long enough. Time to ask the awkward questions. "Why did your dad want me to take his place?"

Just as Sinn is about to answer, we're interrupted by the buzzing of my phone. The screen reads, 'WILSON CALLING.' I point at Sinn as I stand up and step away from the picnic table. "You're not off the hook. I expect answers when I get back." I want privacy so I head towards the parking lot. I'm coming around on Sinn, but I still don't completely trust her.

"What's up?"

Wilson sounds nervous, "Colt, I might have gotten myself into a tiny bit of trouble."

"What kind of trouble?" I ask.

"You know, nothing I can't handle, but since you asked, it's the big scary baby-eating kind."

"Where are you?" I demand.

"In a bar in downtown Redding. I'm okay for now, but I'm not sure I can leave without getting into a fight. The thing in the video is following me."

"Don't leave the bar. Sinn and I will be right there. Text me the address."

"What?" Wilson asks in surprise. "You're in Redding?"

"No," I answer.

"You know Redding is at least a four-hour drive from Oakland, right?"

"I'm aware," I answer.

"Where are you?" Wilson asks.

"A BBQ shed outside Biloxi."

"Biloxi, Mississippi? You're in Mississippi? Bullshit. Are still trying to razz me about your fucking Sharpie? Colt, I don't believe you can draw magical doors on the wall. You're full of shit. It may have been my birthday yesterday, but I wasn't born yesterday."

"It was your birthday yesterday?" I ask in surprise.

"Yeah, prick," he says.

God, I'm a terrible friend, I really need to make a better effort; I feel like a huge dick. Wilson spent his birthday watching over me and all I did was yell at him about eating all my bacon. "Just text me the address and I'll be there shortly. Don't leave the bar. Don't even go to the bathroom."

"Colt, it's 7:30 PM here and this ain't the City. The bar closes at midnight. Are you sure you're gonna' get here in time? I'd rather not end up like the people in those videos. I may have to exterminate a spider."

"What do you mean videos, *plural*?" I ask.

"It's a long story, I'll tell you when you get here—and Colt?"

"What?"

"I just took a shot of tequila to take the edge off and I'm nursing a Corona. I'm going to have to pee soon. Colt, someone is playing Creedence Clearwater Revival's *"Have You Seen the Rain"* on the jukebox. I can't stop thinking about flowing water."

"You're an idiot," I say. "Just ..." I think about reassuring him and telling him everything will be alright, but that seems weird. Instead, I say, "Stop being a little bitch. Just hold it."

I hang up my cell phone before Wilson can respond. Hanging up first is the easiest way to get the last word in. As I start to jog back to our table, I notice Sinn walking toward me carrying a Styrofoam takeout box. I give her a questioning look, and she says, "I'm ready to go home."

Before I can respond, my phone vibrates again; it's a message from Wilson with the name and address of the Redding bar. I quickly Google the bar and search for a picture I can use to open a door. I find one of an old man in overalls posing out in front of the bar with an age-inappropriate date; she must be forty years his junior. I say 'date' rather than 'relative,' because his hand is cupping her breast. #DifferentStrokesDon'tJudge. At least, I hope it's his date.

When Sinn reaches me, I say, "We're not going home. We're going to finish our conversation, but first we're going to help Wilson. He says a werespider is stalking him."

Sinn looks genuinely surprised. "A *werespider*? Colt, werespiders are formidable. Even Dad wouldn't tangle with one unless he had to. There aren't that many and the old ones are really dangerous. Do we have to save Wilson? Can't you just get another investigator?"

"No, we have to save Wilson," I reply.

"Fine, but let's try and do it without putting you at risk," she says. I'm touched. I think I hear genuine concern in her voice.

"Are you telling me you really don't have any idea why Wilson might be following a werespider?" I ask.

"Nothing comes to mind," she says, while nervously playing with a strand of her hair.

I watch her closely for any further signs of deception. "Your dad didn't show you a video of a werespider torturing two people and eating a baby?"

Sinn vigorously shakes her head. "No. I don't know what you're talking about."

I'm usually pretty good at reading people, and she genuinely looks perplexed about the video. I think she's telling the truth about that, but she does know something she's not telling me.

"The first night I met your dad he showed me a video of a werespider doing unimaginable things to a couple and their child. It was disturbing." Just thinking about the video causes me to shiver and break out in a cold sweat. "Pavo said I could help people like the family in the video—if I agreed to become an Advocate. He pitched it as my first case and said the werespider in the video was a wolf-spider named Lycocide."

Sinn looks relieved. "I don't know what you're talking about. Dad didn't tell me anything about a video, but thank God!" she exclaims. "I've never met Lycocide, but I've heard of him. He's a baby spider, still dangerous, but in comparison to some of his siblings, let's just say we're lucky. What did Wilson do to piss him off?"

"I don't know. But we're going to find out."

Chapter Twenty-Seven

Sinn and I step through the portal into a damp and cold Nor-Cal autumn night. The outside of the honkey-tonk dive bar looks exactly the same as in the online picture, so I know we are in the right place. The sun has already set, but light still dances across the gray sky. The sound of Lynyrd Skynyrd's *Simple Man* spills out of the bar and runs with the breeze.

A dozen sets of eyes turn and stare at Sinn and me as we enter through the swinging saloon doors. I suddenly feel self-conscious that I'm wearing a suit and wish I had changed. I'd sure feel more comfortable in jeans and a t-shirt. The attention doesn't seem to bother Sinn; then again, people would be staring at her even if she wasn't dressed in a work blouse, skirt, and expensive heels. Constantly being stared at everywhere you go is one of the burdens of being beautiful.

My eyes sweep the bar, which looks like it hasn't actually been swept in years; sawdust on the floor doesn't even begin to describe this place. I'm not sure there's even an actual floor beneath the dirt and grime. Wilson's sitting on a bar stool, warming a Corona with his hands, while drooling over a busty blonde bartender and chatting with an old timer. There are at least ten empty shot glasses stacked between them. I'm sure they're having a productive discussion about the economy, climate change, immigration, and such. I recognize Lycocide from the video. He's sitting in a corner booth watching Wilson. His eyes are the only ones that didn't look up when we entered, but that doesn't mean he didn't notice us.

Sinn and I join Wilson at the bar. I position myself so I can watch Lycocide. I want to know if he tries to leave. He and I are going to have a talk before this night is through.

Wilson is stunned to see us. "It's only been five minutes. How did you ... you weren't lying about the pen thing were you?"

"No, I wasn't, but you were lying about how much you've had to drink."

Wilson gestures at the empty shot glasses. "These...these...aren't...well, some of them aren't mine."

Sinn asks the bartender for a glass of water and pushes it toward Wilson.

With a big grin, Wilson exclaims, "I can't believe the pen works. Colt, we're going to Aruba when we get out of here. The women in Aruba ... oh, Boss, you don't know nothing about that!"

"Wilson, what's going on here?" I demand. It comes out a little gruffer than I intend. I'm feeling anger, maybe frustration. I'm not sure if it's because I had to interrupt my interrogation of Sinn, or if it's my close proximity to Lycocide, or maybe it's the fact that Wilson's life was in danger and he thought it was good idea to take tequila shots.

Wilson spies the BBQ to-go box. "Is that from the Mississippi BBQ shed? Is that for me?" he asks hopefully. I look at Sinn and she shrugs indifferently.

"You can have the food after you explain to us why the fuck you drove up here and why that psychopath is following you?"

Wilson licks his lips in anticipation. "I found him, the guy in the video. I took initiative and I found him." Wilson takes a tug on his beer. "I think I deserve a raise."

I'm not sure if Wilson can read my facial expression, but if he can, he knows it says 'You're not getting a fucking raise.'

"Maybe a bonus?" Wilson suggests.

My expression doesn't change.

Wilson sighs, "Nobody appreciates initiative anymore." He takes another tug on his beer and continues with his explanation. "I had a friend look at the video. She was able to trace it back to an IP address. Said something about information being embedded into the file. Real amateur hour. Don't look at me like that; I don't understand it either. Anyhow, she hacked his computer and discovered Lycocide had posted thirty-seven other videos, on a peer-to-peer, video sharing website."

"There are thirty-seven more videos? Did you watch them?" My blood begins to boil.

Wilson knows me well enough to recognize when I am angry. "Boss, calm down. I didn't watch them all."

"How many more victims?" I ask.

"I don't know," he says, while refusing to make eye contact.

"How many?" I demand. My voice is getting loud enough that other bar patrons are starting to pay attention.

"A lot," Wilson meekly answers.

"How did you find him?"

"My friend narrowed the computer's IP address down to a one-mile-square radius here in Redding. She said all the houses within that area were sharing the same internet cable. We were lucky it's a rural area without a lot of houses. I checked on Google maps and there were only five potential houses within the area. So, I drove up here and staked them out. I found the itsy-bitsy-spider back there," Wilson jerks his thumb over his shoulder at Lycocide's booth, "at the first house I stopped at. The problem is, he found me too. He saw me spying on him, chased me off his property, and started following me. I figured you wouldn't want me to get in a fight with that thing, so I drove to a place where I knew there would be people. I hoped he would back off—I was wrong. He's been sitting in that booth staring at me for over an hour. God, I have to piss something fierce."

"Are there more children in the videos?" I ask.

Wilson doesn't answer, but the look on his face and his silence confirm my suspicion.

Sinn places her hand on my shoulder. I shrug it off and turn towards her.

"Explain to me the process of charging a Concordat citizen with a crime," I demand.

"I don't think you should do this right now. I think you're—"

"Answer me."

Reluctantly, Sinn says, "First, you inform the citizen in person that you are accusing them of a crime. You tell them they must appear at the Concordat Central Courthouse at sun-up seven days hence, and then you mark them with your ring. The other Advocates will be given notice by their rings that a citizen is being accused of a crime. I'm not sure how that part works; I think you have to have a ring to understand it. Dad just seemed to know whenever it happened. The rings will select three Advocates to sit as judges for the trial. Again, I don't know how that's communicated; Dad just seemed to know when he was selected. At the trial, you will be required to present your case against the citizen and then he will have to plead or—"

"That's enough," I say. I push away from the bar and start walking towards Lycocide. Sinn grabs my shoulder. "Wait, don't do this. You don't understand."

I spin away from her; she's strong, but I'm seeing red, and I'm not going to be stopped. "I understand enough," I say.

When I reach Lycocide's table, I take the seat across from him. I tuck my ring hand under the table and stare Lycocide in the eyes. Sinn hovers nervously behind me.

I couldn't tell in the video, but up close Lycocide looks to be of Mexican descent. He is tanned and has some bulk to him. He clearly spends time at the gym. Lycocide has a thick goatee with clean edges, the kind that doesn't connect up, and he has a shaved head. There is something about his shaved head that just doesn't look right. It's a little too large and misshapen, kinda' similar in size to a certain prolific Bay Area home run hitter. He has no visible tattoos, but the exposed skin on his arms looks off. It's stretched and discolored.

Lycocide looks first at me and then at Sinn and then says with a thick Spanish accent, "I'm not into mixed-raced threesomes, especially with vampires. The señora is too skinny, anyway. I would break her."

Sinn cracks her knuckles behind me. "Well, you got it half right," I reply. "I'm here to fuck you, just not in the way you're thinking. Tell me, why did you make the videos?"

"What?" he asks, confused.

"The vid - e - o's. Why do you make them?" I ask again.

"I don't know what you're talking about, and I don't like how you're talking to me." Lycocide rises up out of the booth.

"Sit your ass down, Lycocide." I punctuate the command with his name, hoping it throws him off his game.

"Fuck you, mayate, I don't take orders from humans. You better watch your mouth." Despite running his mouth, Lycocide sits back down.

I lean forward across the table until my face is only inches away from his. "Why did you make the videos?"

Lycocide stares right back at me with absolutely zero fear in his eyes. His mouth shifts; giant fangs grow and protrude past his lips. "Because I like to," he says. "I like to watch them over and over again. I look for that moment when hope departs. That moment when they accept, that they're going to die. Sometimes you can actually see hope exit their body. Their heads droop, their shoulders slump and their eyes dull—it's beautiful. I've never weighed them before and after, but I've always wondered—how much does hope weigh? Maybe we can find out together?" Lycocide smiles, his large fangs on full display.

"Why do you post them online?" I demand.

"I like to share with others. I'm a giver, mayate. Do you want some?" He snarls, opening his fangs even wider.

I refuse to retreat or back down. We continue our staring contest, practically nose to nose, my face inches from his fangs. "Lycocide," I say, using his name again. "Do you know who I am?"

Lycocide pauses; my question appears to have thrown him, maybe he's not as undisciplined as he looks. He retracts his fangs and leans back into the booth. His thoughts run across his face, like a stock ticker on the bottom of a news channel—*Who is this guy? Have I met him before? Should I know who he is? Am I going to be in trouble if I kill him?* He must suck at poker. After a long pause, he says, "You ain't nobody. Just another soon-to-be-dead human."

"Ehrrrgh! Wrong answer. Try again!" I bellow in my best game show host voice.

"Why do I care who you are?" he asks, uncertainty in his voice.

"Maybe you're not as dumb as you look. I didn't think spiders had brains; they must have that wrong on Wikipedia."

Lycocide grips the table with his claw-like fingers.

As I stare at this real-life monster before me, I suddenly realize that we're in a bar full of innocent people and I'm acting reckless and cavalier with their lives. I'm angry and I want justice for that poor baby and his family—for all of them, but I would never forgive myself if any of the people in this bar got hurt because I'm acting like an ass. I need to wrap this up before somebody does get hurt.

"You should care because my name is Colt Valentine and I'm here to get justice for all those people you tortured and killed." I raise my hand from under the table and display my Advocate ring to Lycocide. "Do you know what this is?"

Lycocide stares hard at the ring. He clearly recognizes it, but he doesn't move or make a sound.

Sinn puts her hand on my shoulder again. "Colt, I think we should talk about this first. You don't—"

I raise my right hand in front of her face. Frankly, a dick-move, but I know what I'm doing. Pavo put me on this path and I'm going to follow it to the end. There is no backing out, no playing it safe. I never had a choice here, and I think Pavo knew that.

"Lycocide, I, Advocate Colt Valentine, accuse you of crimes against the Concordat. You must appear at the Concordat Central Courthouse at sun-up seven days hence. Give me your wrist and accept the marking of the ring." I'm not sure how I know the right words and that I must touch the ring to Lycocide's wrist to complete the notice ceremony, but I do. It's like I've always known or, more accurately, like the ring, which is now a part of me, has always known, and it's speaking through me.

Lycocide jumps up and yells in anger, "¡Vete a la mierda!"

Other bar patrons are starting to take notice of our conversation. Fortunately, Lycocide's spider fangs have retracted. Otherwise we would have panic and possibly unsolicited gunplay from the locals.

Sinn steps forward and asks Lycocide, "Are you refusing to accept the complaint? You know the consequences. You forfeit your right to a hearing, are presumed guilty, and are immediately stripped of your rights as a Concordat citizen, which means we are then within our rights to exterminate you with prejudice."

Lycocide stops his retreat as he weighs Sinn's words. Finally, he steps forward with a sneer and presents his wrist. I touch his wrist with the ring. A slight burning sensation courses through me, and a black rune appears on his wrist. Lycocide's eyes never leave mine as he backs out of the bar through the swinging doors and into the night.

Wilson whistles loudly to get the bar's attention. "Folks, I apologize for interrupting your evening. My friend here," Wilson places his hand on my shoulder, "just served that gentleman with divorce papers." A collective groan wafts through the crowd. Clearly many of these folks have been through that experience and aren't fond of process servers. "That jackass beat his wife and kid up pretty badly. He was a real dick and deserves whatever's coming to him," preaches Wilson. "To make it up to you for the inconvenience, my friend has agreed to buy the next round."

The crowd's groans turn into cheers. Wilson's quick-thinking distraction seems to have done the trick. It's going to cost me a couple hundred dollars, but I'll take that out of his next paycheck for acting like an idiot and coming up here without backup in the first place. Tom Petty's *Free Falling* comes on the jukebox and meanders through the bar, quickly changing the mood. Before you know it, my confrontation with Lycocide is a distant memory to the bar patrons.

I thought I would feel better after serving Lycocide, like I'd taken a step towards justice on behalf of that baby, its parents, and all of his other victims, but I don't feel anything other than anger. Even if I get this killer off the streets, it's not going to bring those people back. I place two hundred dollars on the bar for the round of drinks, and turn and look at my team. Wilson looks concerned, and there is worry written all over Sinn's face.

"Let's go back to the office," I say, as I walk towards the swinging saloon doors. "I don't want to be around people anymore. I have a feeling it's going to be a long seven days until the trial."

Chapter Twenty-Eight

It looks like it's going to take a little longer than expected to get back to the office. Wilson drove his truck to Redding and refuses to leave it. He says it's sentimental and he'd never forgive himself if it was stolen. I lean against the wall of a deserted building next to the bar and wait while he and Sinn retrieve it from a parking lot down the street. Despite having served Lycocide with a notice of his pending court date, and having watched him leave with my own two eyes, I don't like the idea of letting Wilson drive home on his own, particularly in his semi-drunken state.

I say semi-drunken, because it turns out Wilson isn't as drunk as he was letting on. The bar has a wall mounted breathalyzer and, for a dollar, you can blow into it to see if you're above the legal limit. Wilson bet me gas money that he wasn't legally drunk. I donated a dollar to the machine and, against all odds, Wilson blew a 0.07, which is just below the legal limit.

Wilson claims the Tequila shots were a ruse, intended to lower Lycocide's guard in case they got into a physical altercation. He says after the first one he asked the bartender to substitute water. I'm having a hard time believing he only had one shot. I know Wilson can be sneaky; that's why he is such a good investigator, but I can't figure out how he passed the breathalyzer. Maybe he had a penny in his mouth? I've heard that can mess with the reading.

When Sinn and Wilson return with the truck, we resume our debate about leaving it overnight.

"Why don't you draw a bigger door with your *magic stick* and I'll drive my truck through it?" asks Wilson.

Although crude, I have to admit it's a good idea. "Sinn, have you ever seen Pavo do anything like that?"

"Drive a truck through a door he drew with his *magic stick*?" she asks.

"Yes." I answer, irritated with her mocking tone.

"Never."

I sigh in frustration and Wilson chuckles.

As I draw the truck-sized door on the wall of the abandoned building, I would be lying if I didn't admit I'm a little concerned it won't work. Fortunately, my worry is for naught. The door opens without a hitch and Wilson drives his truck straight through from the quiet streets of Redding to the mean streets of Oakland.

As soon as we arrived back in Oak Town, Wilson jumps out of his truck and starts screaming, "I am the greatest driver ever! Nascar ain't got shit on me! I just set a Guinness world record for the fastest drive from Redding to Oakland, ever!"

"No, you didn't."

"Yes, I did!"

"Do you have any video evidence? Do you have three witnesses who will sign declarations under oath?" I'm not sure Guinness requires either video evidence or declarations, but I doubt Wilson checks, and I'm having too much fun raining on his picnic.

"No," he says, disappointedly.

"Then you didn't set a record," I declare, stealing the wind from Wilson's sails. I almost smile at Wilson's disappointment, but the amused feeling is fleeting. I am much to pissed off for it to have a lasting effect.

Once we're inside the office, Sinn gives me a dirty look and excuses herself to the powder room, and I begin ransacking the office for something, anything, that contains alcohol. I check the desks, the cabinets, even behind the espresso maker. After about five minutes of searching, I give up. What kind of law office doesn't have a booze stash? This is unacceptable. Half the reason I became an attorney in the first place was so it was socially acceptable for me to be a drunk during the day, and socially expected for me to be a drunk at night. I dejectedly saunter over and sit in the middle of the long rectangular wooden conference table that occupies one side of the first floor of my new office, and begin sifting through e-mails on my phone while I wait for Wilson who's parking his truck, and Sinn, who's still in the bathroom.

Once my inbox is clear, I trace the patterns in the wood grain of the dark walnut-colored reclaimed wood conference table with my finger and ponder my recent conduct. I'm not exactly proud of how I acted at the bar, especially towards Sinn. I should have listened to what she had to say before making a decision. I doubt she could have said anything that would have changed my mind, but I need us to work as a team, which means we need to trust each other. Dismissing her opinions out of hand isn't great for morale and doesn't build trust. I was just so enraged. After I heard there were more videos, more victims, more dead *children*, I saw red and acted impulsively. Some might characterize my conduct as passionate; then again, others might just say I was a jackass. #Tomato/Tomatoe.

If I'm being completely honest with myself, and nobody ever is, I'm not handling all of this Advocate stuff in the smartest way. It's not fair. I liked my life. I didn't ask for this. I never wanted to be a paladin or a monster prosecutor. This job was forced on me by a two-thousand-year-old vampire claiming to be family, and no one screws you quite like family. My life is spinning out of control and I don't know how to stop it. A man who turns into a giant spider wants to kill me, a gang of monsters is moving into my city and, according to some fucked-up prophecy, I'm cursed to bring about the end of the world. #MyLifeIsSoFucked.

Wilson skips into the office, carrying the Styrofoam container Sinn gave him. He sits down at the conference table across from me and greedily opens the container like a child opening a present on his birthday. The joy on his face turns to anguish as he stares slack-jawed at the open box. Finally, he looks up at me, clearly upset. "What the fuck, Colt? Salad? Are you kidding me? You brought me back a fucking salad?"

I laugh so hard I nearly fall out of my chair. I forgot Sinn ordered a salad. In hindsight, it makes sense that the container had a salad in it, as we ate nearly everything else. I feel bad for Wilson; he looks like someone just peed in his Cheerios, but after the day I have had, this is funny, hilarious even. Once I get my laughter under control, I manage to say between breaths, "Wilson, I'm sorry, man. I didn't know. I thought there was BBQ in there." Wilson doesn't acknowledge the apology—he just keeps staring at the salad in disbelief.

Sinn exits the bathroom; she looks a shade or two lighter than normal and is holding her stomach with one hand. "I haven't eaten that much food in decades," she says, "maybe ever. Why did I eat so much?"

Wilson immediately snaps, "You're getting no sympathy from me. You pricks went to Mississippi for BBQ and all you brought me back was a fucking salad. I hope you are sick. I hope both of you get food poisoning." Wilson crosses his arms and continues to pout like a child.

Sinn smiles at Wilson. "Chin up. While I was in the bathroom, I used an app to order you a pizza. I hope you like pepperoni."

Wilson looks up in surprise. "Thank you. I love pepperoni." He jumps up and starts walking towards her, arms outstretched.

Sinn points back at the bathroom. "You can use the bathroom now."

Wilson continues towards her. "No need," he says. "I pissed in the alley." Just as he reaches her, Sinn deftly dodges his embrace with vampiric speed and says, "Disgusting, don't touch me with those dirty hands. Go wash them."

Wilson shrugs it off with a goofy smile and walks towards the bathroom singing to himself, "I'm getting pizza...I'm getting pizza."

Sinn yells after him, "Use soap!"

I can't help but smile to myself; they barely know each other and they're already fighting like brother and sister. Life's funny like that. Some people bond effortlessly; others don't. Sinn sits at the far end of the conference table and levels me with her eyes. Any warm fuzzies she may feel towards Wilson clearly aren't reserved for me.

"Colt, you should not have done that. That was impulsive and stupid."

Without being specific, we both know she is talking about bringing charges against Lycocide at the bar.

"It's done," I say. "There was no point in dragging it out. Your father showed me the video for a reason. He knew I wouldn't be able to let it go. Lycocide is a murderer and he is going down. I don't care if this ruffles feathers."

Sinn shakes her head in frustration. "You think I care about ruffling feathers. You're an idiot, Colt. All I care about is your life."

"What are you talking about?" I snap.

"Have you read the book yet? The Concordat Book of Laws?" Sinn asks in a sarcastic tone.

"You know I haven't had time," I reply in frustration.

"You might want to; just a suggestion, your royal ass-holishness." Sinn gets up from the table and starts walking towards the exit.

"Wait," I say. "I'm sorry. Don't leave."

"Apology accepted, but I'm not leaving, idiot. The pizza is here."

"I didn't hear a knock."

She scoffs, "God you're a moron. There wasn't one. I have super vampire hearing, remember?"

I stare, dumbfounded.

Sinn opens the front door and surprises the pizza guy mid-knock while Wilson plops down in the seat beside me.

"You two just need to screw already; there's way too much tension in here. Just get it over with. If not for yourself, do it for me. You're creating a hostile work environment. It will probably only take you ten, maybe thirty seconds. I doubt she'll even feel a thing."

"I heard that!" Sinn yells over her shoulder.

"Just shut up," I say in a hushed and frustrated tone. I'm mad, mostly with myself. It has nothing to do with sexual tension or Wilson's poor attempts at levity.

Wilson gives me his big goofy grin. "God, I missed working with you, Boss."

My body language reads #SMH.

Sinn returns to the conference table and passes the pizza to Wilson, who disgustingly starts scarfing it down. He makes what he calls pizza sandwiches. He places two pieces on top of each other, cheese to cheese; that way there is crust on top and crust on the bottom. He then slathers ranch dressing between the slices, like Miracle Whip on a turkey sandwich.

When he bites into the pizza sandwich, cheese, ranch dressing, and red tomato sauces squeeze out the sides of his mouth and get everywhere. How does this slob ever get laid? The look of terror on Sinn's face as she watches him eat confirms we share the same opinion about Wilson's pizza-eating manners. At least we have some common ground, even if it's just being disgusted by Wilson.

Once I fight off my gag reflex, I turn to Sinn. "Let's pretend I *had* read the Concordat law book—what would I have learned?"

"First and foremost, you would have learned that you're an *idiot*," she responds. "What law is it you think Lycocide broke?"

"Murder!" I say with conviction. "I watched a video of him killing a baby, for God's sake, and we have thirty-seven other videos just like it. I take it you're telling me with that smug look of yours that murder isn't a Concordat crime?"

"Murder is a crime under Concordat law," Sinn answers. "But killing humans is not. Humans are not Concordat citizens. Concordat law defines murder as the unlawful killing of another Concordat citizen, without justification, with malice aforethought."

The blood rushes out of my face as a feeling of betrayal sets in. "What?" I ask, although it's less of a question and more of a statement of disbelief.

"Concordat citizens can kill all the humans they want. Lycocide may have tortured and killed all of those people, but he didn't commit a crime. At least, not in the eyes of the law," continues Sinn. "And that's not even the worst of it—" she says in a tone that's not quite gloating, but definitely emphasizing the fact that I should have listened to her at the bar.

"—That's bullshit!" I shout, interrupting Sinn. "Are you telling me human life is worthless. We don't mean anything to you monsters? We're just food?"

"Fuck you, Colt. We're not all the same."

I admit it's not really fair of me to have lumped them all together, but this is bullshit. Why would Pavo convince me to be a part of a system that discounts human life entirely? Was it just a game to him, one last cruel joke to play on his would-be killer? I stand up from the table and walk out of the office into the brisk night. Neither Wilson nor Sinn try to stop me.

I'm too angry to think rationally. I need to calm down. As I walk, I stare up at the waxing crescent moon, barely visible through the fog, and allow myself to get lost in its beauty. I stop on a street corner and close my eyes and breathe in the scents and sounds of Oakland: lilacs and jasmine, exhaust fumes, urine and marijuana smoke, car horns, music, people shouting, and the beeping of a crosswalk. After a moment, the sounds and smells fade away and I'm completely alone with my thoughts.

What can I do? How can I change an arcane justice system that's designed to screw humans? I'm just one man. I stand there in silence, feeling sorry for myself, and then I hear my father's voice calling out to me from a memory. "Son, one day you'll learn life isn't fair. Quit crying and man up."

Nearly all of my memories of my father involve him telling me to "quit crying and man up." Maybe Dad had a point. The Concordat laws are what they are and, for now at least, I need to accept them, and work within their confines. Maybe I don't have to change the system to win this case. Maybe I've been asking all the wrong questions. Instead of asking why murdering humans isn't a crime, I should ask why Pavo put me on to Lycocide in the first place? Why give me the video? He must have had a plan. Nothing I've learned about Pavo thus far indicates he wants me to fail. If anything, he's done everything he can to help me, including making his own daughter promise to protect me.

There must be something I'm not seeing, a puzzle piece I'm missing. Come on, Colt, "quit crying and man up." This is what you do. You're given impossible tasks and you find solutions. Stop whining and form a plan. This is no different than thousands of other cases you have worked on. Just apply the facts to the law. It sounds easy-peasy; now I just need to learn the law.

After the meditation, I feel better. More centered. When I get back to the office, Wilson's working on what looks like his third pizza sandwich and Sinn is still patiently sitting at the table looking uncomfortable. She doesn't look surprised that I returned; then again, she probably heard me coming.

"Sinn, you're right, that was unfair. I'm sorry. As far as I can tell, you have absolutely nothing in common with that monster Lycocide. I really am sorry. Now, you said there was a worse part? Please tell me what you called the worst part. Give me the rest of the bad news."

Sinn unfolds her arms and, after what feels like an eternity, responds, "As I was saying at the bar, there is a procedure that must be followed when prosecuting a criminal complaint against a citizen. First, you inform the citizen that you are accusing them of a crime and then you mark them with your ring. At the trial seven days later, you will be required to present your case against the accused to three judges, and the accused will then have to enter a plea. The accused can (1) plead guilty, in which case the three judges will immediately pass down a sentence; or (2) plead innocent, in which case, he can either present his defense immediately, or request additional time to respond; or (3) elect Ordeal by Combat. If the accused chooses Ordeal by

Combat, you as the accusing attorney have to either fight him to the death, or you can withdraw the charges."

"I see. Is there anything else I need to know?"

Sinn pauses and frowns; she's mentally wrestling with something. "Yes, one more thing; Pavo told me the ring will punish you if you lose a trial. I don't know what that means. Pavo never explained it and I never knew him to lose a trial, but that's what he said."

"Thank you for telling me. I appreciate your help."

The disapproving frown on Sinn's face recedes a bit. "You're welcome."

"I need some sleep, and I need to read the book of Concordat laws. If I have learned anything in all my years as a lawyer, it's that there is always a way. If we can't prove murder, we'll prove something else. He is guilty. We're going to get those people justice. I need you two to trust me. We're going to find a way."

Wilson and Sinn both nod.

"As far as the fight to the death thing, we'll address that problem once we figure out what our case is against Lycocide. One problem at a time."

"Wilson," I look directly at him, "I want those videos tomorrow, and I want to meet the expert, your friend the computer whiz. Please have them both here in the office at 1:00 PM sharp."

With a full mouth, Wilson says, "Will do, Boss."

My gaze shifts to Pavo's daughter. "Sinn, get some sleep, drink some blood ... do whatever it is you do to relax. Tomorrow we get to work. I don't want you in the office before noon."

Sinn nods.

I give Sinn and Wilson my biggest smile. "Seriously, you two get some rest; everything is going to be alright."

Chapter Twenty-Nine

Everything is not alright. "We are fucked!" I shout to an empty apartment. It's seven in the morning, and I'm sitting at my pecan-colored dining room table, drinking coffee from my oversized novelty mug, reading the book of Concordat Laws. "This is bullshit!" I shout, as I slam my fist down onto the table. The criminal law section isn't very thick; I've now read it, cover to cover, six times. Each time I reach the same conclusions: (1) We have absolutely no case against Lycocide; and (2) humans have no rights under the Magna-Concordat, and are valued less than property or animals. No matter how I try to stretch or bend the laws, I can't come up with a shape that's going to hold enough water to drown Lycocide.

I probably shouldn't find it surprising, but many of the Magna-Concordat Laws aren't all that different from human laws. The subject matter of some of the laws are arcane and sometimes absurd, but the laws themselves, their form and function, are similar. For example, you can find many human laws that put a limit on the number of spouses one may take, but they typically, not always, draw the line at one spouse. Apparently, the Concordat draws the line at two?

Trigamy: *The condition of having three spouses simultaneously is unlawful.*

I can't imagine why? Nor can I imagine the levels of pain and frustration that two wives could create in a man's life. I could barely tolerate my life when I had one.

And then there's:

Possession of a Dragon Seed: *It is unlawful to be in possession of a dragon seed.*

I don't know what the hell a dragon seed is? Or even if dragons are real? That's a terrifying thought, but there are many similar human laws that prohibit possession of one thing or another: drugs, fireworks, firearms, etc.

And:

Royal Forest Trespass: *It is unlawful to trespass against the vert or the venison in a Royal forest.*

Trespassing laws like this one are also extremely common under human laws. I recently had a client charged with breaking a law very similar to this one. He was caught stealing roses from the gardens behind City Hall. There is a whole chapter of these weird, but familiar, criminal laws—none of which seem helpful in building a case against Lycocide.

There is also a chapter on more standard crimes, like:

Murder: *the killing of another Magna-Concordat citizen, without justification, with malice aforethought is unlawful.*

And:

Rape: *the carnal knowledge of a Magna-Concordat citizen forcibly and against their will is unlawful.*

And:

Larceny: *It is unlawful to misappropriate another Magna-Concordat citizen's property by means of taking it from their possession without consent.*

I'm already familiar with the definitions of each of these crimes as they are nearly identical to their English "common law" counterparts, these just don't apply to humans.

In the Western human world, "common laws" have largely been replaced or codified by "statutory laws," which are laws drafted by monarchs or legislators. They are sometimes just a copy of the common law, but for hundreds of years "common laws" were, and in some cases still are, enforced. "Common sense laws," as they are often called, arose from real-life disputes. A judge would hear a complaint and then issue a fact-specific ruling. These rulings would become the law of the land and were relied on by future judges. When a future judge encountered a similar factual situation, he would apply the law of the prior case.

I suspect early English judges were heavily influenced by the laws of the Magna-Concordat, which would explain the similarities. Then again, some concepts like murder, rape, and theft exist across cultures. It's possible that English judges and Magna-Concordat Advocates simply came to the same conclusions about what the definition of these crimes should be.

Interestingly, there are also modern criminal laws included in the Concordat Book of Laws, which means they make an effort to adjust with the times, like:

Treason by Disclosure: *It is unlawful for any Magna-Concordat Citizen to intentionally disclose the existence of the Magna-Concordat or its citizens to humans, without justification, in a way that endangers the Magna-Concordats or the lives of Magna-Concordat citizens.*

And:

Cybercrime: *It is unlawful to use a computer as an instrument to further illegal ends against another Magna-Concordat citizen, such as committing fraud, or theft.*

There is also a section on criminal procedure, which includes this gem:

Ordeal by combat: *Instead of pleading guilt or innocence, an accused may elect Ordeal by Combat and challenge his accuser. If elected by the accused, the accuser must either consent to the Ordeal by Combat or withdraw the charges. Once an Ordeal by Combat is accepted, the* *parties are to immediately fight to the death. The winner is triumphant and righteous in the eyes of the law.*

Sinn was right, I can't win a fair fight with a werespider. I almost died fighting Roy Silas, and this thing is much more dangerous. If Lycocide elects ordeal by combat, I'm absolutely screwed, but, I can't worry about that right now. That's a problem for tomorrow. Today, I need to build a case, and despite there being hundreds of laws in this book, I can't find a single one that is going to be useful against Lycocide.

"Damn it!" I slam the book shut. I'm beginning to feel overwhelmed. I need to clear my head. Maybe a long run will inspire me. I always think best after a good sweat.

Chapter Thirty

It's one o'clock in the afternoon when I arrive at the office. I feel a little better after my run, but I'm no closer to making a case against Lycocide. I'm still waiting to get hit by a brilliant epiphany. Fortunately, I have six days—an eternity to a lawyer. I'm sure I'll think of something ... I'd better.

Sinn is talking on the phone at what must be her desk in the back of the office. The desk is extremely organized, clutter-free, no photographs or trinkets, not even a name plaque or a fancy pen. Its lack of warmth collates perfectly with the robotic personality she projects to the world. It must be hard to be the person she thinks she needs to be.

Wilson's leaning against the wall eating a burger and drinking something out of a thermos, which I'm willing to bet contains some sort of alcoholic beverage, while he watches something on an oversized monitor. He must have set the monitor up on the conference table this morning, because it wasn't there last night. The alcohol in the thermos bit is a test. Wilson abhors authority, even if it's me, and feels it's his duty to push boundaries. He brought the food and alcohol in just to see if Sinn or I would say anything. He's trying to provoke a reaction. He acts like an overgrown adolescent ... but I've got to admit, I missed working with him.

Behind the monitor, I discover a young woman with short blonde hair, rapidly punching a keyboard with the tenacity of a honey badger. This must be Wilson's computer expert. The woman seems familiar to me, but it takes me a moment to recognize her. The last time I saw her, four days ago, she had long brown hair and was nearly catatonic. I was afraid she might never recover. It's hard to believe this woman before me is that same comatose girl. This woman not only looks alive, but looks fierce and confident at that computer, ready to take on the world; there's no mistaking it—it's Joycee.

When Joycee sees me, she jumps up from her chair and embraces me. I look to Wilson for guidance and he just shrugs. I'm not much of a hugger, but under the circumstances, I'm going to let this go. When she finally unburies her head from my chest, Joycee touches my arm where I was cut, and says, "Mr. Valentine, you're alright? I was so worried! Wilson told me you were alright, but I didn't believe him. Oh, it's all healed! How is that *possible*? There was so much blood!"

"I'm fine, it's just a flesh wound!" I say in my best Black Knight impersonation voice.

Joycee looks at me like I'm crazy.

"You've never seen *Monty Python and The Holy Grail*?" I ask.

"Monty who? And the what? Mr. Valentine, is that a TV show?" asks Joycee.

"Colt, you're old," says Wilson while laughing and choking on his burger. "Really old."

"It's a movie, a good one, but don't worry about it—I'm fine. I heal fast and it looked worse than it was. And, please stop calling me Mr. Valentine. It makes me feel old. It's just Colt," I say to Joycee while non-verbally communicating, "Go fuck yourself" to Wilson.

"You are old," mumbles Wilson between bites.

"Ok, Mr. Val—er, Colt," answers Joycee. "Thank you. You know … for what you did. for ..." Joycee tears up and hugs me again. "Thank you."

I turn red on the inside, probably a little on the outside too. I've never really been good at accepting gratitude, it makes me uncomfortable. "Thanks, Joycee. It's not really a big deal. I just did what anyone in my position would have done."

"That's not true," says Joycee. "You saved us. You fought that monster and you saved us. You're a h—"

I interrupt her, "—Let's not go overboard now."

"Come on, *hero*, let the girl thank you," chimes in Wilson.

I grab a green highlighter off the table and chuck it at Wilson, who somehow manages to duck underneath it without dropping either the burger or the thermos.

Wilson chuckles, and defiantly takes another drink from his thermos.

"Sorry about that," I say to Joycee. "What are you doing here?" I ask in an obvious bid to change topics.

Joycee's smile is erased and a confused look crosses her face. "I thought you wanted me here?" Joycee looks over at Wilson apprehensively.

Wilson smiles reassuringly at Joycee. "That's right, he told me to have you here at 1:00 PM today. I just do what I'm told. He might have forgotten. You know how it is with old people."

Joycee places her hand over her mouth and fake-coughs—a poor attempt to suppress a laugh. While Joycee tries not to laugh, Wilson and I silently converse with our eyes. Our conversation goes something like this:

"Grow up."

"Never."

"WTF, your expert is Joycee? I never would have approved that."

"She's a computer expert and wanted to help. She already knows about monsters so she seemed like the logical choice, and I thought giving her a task and keeping her busy might help keep her mind off of what happened to her."

"Okay, I admit, you make good points."

"I told you so."

"Despite your good intentions—it's a dumb idea. I want her out of this life."

"That's not your choice. It's hers."

"Fine, but I don't like it."

The entire silent exchange happens in the blink of an eye. It can be frustrating working with people who know you as well as you know yourself, but it sure cuts down the amount of time we waste arguing.

I take a deep breath as I say to Joycee, "Of course, my mistake. Yes, I want you here. Thanks for coming. What can you tell me about the videos?"

Joycee starts talking; I think it's English, but I sure don't understand much of it. From what I can gather, she somehow traced information she found embedded in the original video file back to Lycocide's internet address. She then hacked into his computer, through his internet connection, and determined from his web history that there were two websites he regularly visits that are outside what she considered "normal internet-behavior."

The first is a chatroom for spider lovers, where Lycocide, also known as Wolfspider666, regularly posts non-supernatural spider videos, and chats with other members. She read me a sampling of some of his recent video posts: *Spider Eats Cat*, *Australian Web Storm*, *Deadly Spider Infestation*, and *Giant Spider In Bathroom*. Although disturbing and, in Joycee's words, "super-creepy-duper," I don't see anything illegal about these posts under either human or Concordat laws.

The second is a peer-to-peer video sharing site called X-change. Joycee says the site is popular with the dark web crowd and a favorite for individuals sharing things that will get you put in jail. I asked for examples and she said, "Child pornography, murder, and torture videos." #NSFW.

Joycee says X-change programming is genius level and the website is impossible to hack. Surprise, surprise, it's managed from somewhere in Russia. The United States Government knows about it, but they can't get in, and they can't shut it down. Its cyber security is just too good. You can't even get access unless the webmaster gives you an encryption key, and you can't get a key unless you're a member, and you can't become a member unless you share something illegal.

According to Joycee, Wolfspider666 is a member, and has uploaded and shared thirty-eight videos over the past five years. All thirty-eight are similar, at least in subject matter, to the one Pavo gave me. Joycee watched all thirty-eight in fast-forward, and counted fifty-three victims in total, including five children. Most of the videos involve a single victim, and most of the victims look homeless—easy targets because nobody will miss them. Joycee says the video Pavo gave me is by far the most graphic, and the only one involving an infant.

"So, let me get this straight," I ask. "Anyone can download these?"

"No," answers Joycee. "You have to be a member of X-change. You need a key."

"How did you become a member?" I ask with concern.

"I didn't," she answers defensively. "I logged in as Lycocide, and used his key. The idiot has a folder on his computer named, 'PASSWORDS.' If you want, we can log into his bank account and steal all his money."

"No. We're supposed to be the good guys. Let's not start committing cyber-crimes … at least, not yet."

"What if he miraculously donates it all to cancer research? Or a home for orphans? That's not really stealing, is it?" Joycee asks.

"I like where your head's at, but let's hold off on that for now."

Joycee looks disappointed, but nods in agreement.

"Thanks for doing this. This is great work." The compliment has the desired effect, and Joycee perks back up. "How many hours of videos are there in total?" I ask.

"About forty," she replies. "The videos vary in length; some are a couple hours; others are only a minute or two."

I nod. "Is this set up for me?" I ask, pointing at the computer and oversized monitor.

"Yes." she says. "Wilson asked me to make it as easy to use as possible for you."

"I told her to make it *idiot*-proof," volunteers Wilson.

I rip the thermos out of Wilson's hand and dump it out in the sink next to the cappuccino machine. It smells like straight vodka, no chaser. Wilson doesn't complain and instead dons a goofy smile, the kind a boy gives his father when he catches him looking at pornographic magazines. Although he abhors authority, the ex-soldier in him craves discipline. The man is an enigma.

When I return from the sink, Joycee hands me some headphones and shows me where she saved the files. I thank her again and let her know I'll be in touch. I still feel uncomfortable allowing her to get involved, especially after what she has been through. Shouldn't she be running *from* danger—not towards it? I wish Wilson had consulted me before deciding to involve her. I would've said *hell no*. She'd be better off as far away from me as possible. Then again, who am I to make a decision for her? I can barely make decisions for myself. Maybe Wilson's right; maybe facing your fears is the best way to overcome them. I don't know. All I know is that the world is a whole lot more complicated today than it was a week ago.

After Joycee leaves, I instruct Wilson to do some digging on the victims. "Identify the ones you can. I want to know when they disappeared and from where."

"Yes sir," he responds with a mock salute on his way out the door. I smile at his insolence. Wilson does his best work when he's complaining. It keeps him sharp.

I glance over at Sinn's desk. She's still on the phone. I wanted to speak with her, I guess it'll have to wait. I slide into the chair facing the large monitor, slip on the headphones, and press play on the first video.

Chapter Thirty-One

I'm startled when Wilson pulls the left headphone away from my ear, and then lets go, causing it to snap painfully against the side of my head.

"What the fuck?" I shout, ripping the headphones off, and standing up. Unfortunately, my legs are asleep and I fall right back into my chair.

Wilson snickers as he sits down next to me and hands me a fresh cup of coffee. There's concern in his voice, "Boss, do you know what time it is?"

I grab my cell phone off the desk in front of me—the battery's dead. I look around for a wall clock but there isn't one. I finally find the time on the lower right corner of the computer monitor. It reads 8:23 AM. Holy shit, I've been sitting at this table for nearly nineteen hours.

I've gotten through most, but not all of the videos. They're all similar in scope. Lycocide strips and restrains his victims with rope. I wonder if werespiders can even make webs? He then makes them watch while he changes into a half man, half spider. He seems to get off on terrorizing them. He then slowly tortures them, stabbing them with his claws over and over again. He screams in ecstasy each time he makes a new cut. Only after the victim has stopped screaming, after their hope is gone, does he drain them with his spider fangs. From the look of the corpses, he drinks more than just their blood. When he's done feasting, all that remains is a dried-up skin bag of bones.

Wilson places his hand on my shoulder and gently shakes me, bringing the room back into focus. "Boss, you need sleep. You need food. Go home. You're no good to anyone like this."

I nod and stand. This time I'm ready for the tingling in my legs; I brace for it and I manage to stay up. After a few moments, the blood flow recirculates, and I start limping towards the front door. With each step it gets a little easier to walk.

Wilson calls out, "Boss, don't forget your coffee, and don't drive. You're in no condition to drive. Just make a doorway."

Wilson's probably right, I shouldn't' drive. I don't know why I'm so tired. I've pulled plenty of all-nighters in my lifetime and I have never felt this groggy. It must have something to do with the healing. That reminds me; just as soon as this case is over, I need to get my family journals from Sinn. I grab the coffee off the table and use my Sharpie to draw a gate that leads directly to my bedroom. I step through the gate and lie down on my bed. The second my head hits the pillow, I sleep.

Chapter Thirty-Two

I awake to a burning sensation and not the kind that you get on a trip to Tijuana. The Advocate ring is burning my finger. I think it's warning me. I'm not sure how I know that's what it's doing—I just do. It's communicating with me, but not with words; rather with pain, and it's telling me, "I'm not alone." I'm starting to think the ring is alive, which is an unsettling thought, one to ponder later when I'm not in danger.

My hand searches the nightstand for Romulus Augustus' dagger. As my fingers wrap around its decorative hilt, a sense of confidence fills me, like I can handle anything; and then it turns to guilt, as I consider the possibility of damaging the dagger. I haven't had it appraised or anything; it's not like I have Christie's or Sotheby's on speed dial. Still, I'd be willing to bet it's worth more than my apartment, and I live in the Bay Area where you have to a sell your soul to afford a 300-square-foot dump—that's why I rent. The dagger should be in a museum, or at the very least, inside a safe. I definitely shouldn't be stabbing people with it—I don't know if I could forgive myself if I broke it.

I search the room for another weapon or something with a sharp edge. The only real contender is a leather belt with a heavy metal belt buckle. It's part of a cowboy costume I wore one year for Halloween. I dressed as Woody, and my ex dressed as Jessie. Don't judge—it was a difficult period in my life. I didn't have a lot of self-respect. I consider trading the dagger for the belt, and then decide better of it. Call me superstitious, but the belt gives me a bad vibe. It brings up bad memories. Violent memories of dear old dad using his heavy leather belt to whip my ass. It's hard to feel confident when you're remembering how helpless you felt bent over dad's knee catching a beating.

The ridiculousness of my circumstance suddenly hits me and I have to choke back laughter. There's an intruder in my home, possibly here to kill me, *probably* here to kill me, and I'm more concerned about damaging the dagger of a long-dead emperor than losing my life. #FML.

Don't I value my life as much as some stupid dagger? Sadly, that's a question I'm seriously pondering. I wonder what the result would be if I asked an economist to perform a forensic economic comparison of the value of my life to the value of the dagger. On one hand, the dagger is a piece of history and likely priceless. On the other, I'm pretty attached to my life. On second thought, I probably don't want to know the results. My ego probably couldn't handle knowing my economic value. Shake it off, Colt; find your way out of this mental quagmire. There is an intruder in your home—at least I think so; either that, or I need to see a doctor about this burning sensation.

I sit up in bed, and listen for intruder sounds. I don't hear anything out of the ordinary, just the hum of the refrigerator's engine working overtime. I really need to replace it before it craps out on me. Despite the lack of tell-tale intruder noises, whatever those are, the hairs on the back of my neck stand straight up. I'd bet an egg-salad sandwich someone's in my living room waiting for me. I can sense them, or the ring can, which is kinda' creeping me out. I hope I'm not turning into one of those hippies who carry crystals around, claiming they can read your energy.

I slide out of bed and creep on the balls on my feet towards the living room. I think about putting clothes on and then decide against it. I'd be too loud, take too much time, and it would definitely announce my presence to the intruder. I'm not exactly excited about confronting an intruder, in boxer-briefs, with an antique knife. Then again, I don't think wearing clothes, or chainmail for that matter, would increase my excitement level very much. I don't like the idea of confronting an uninvited guest—under any circumstances.

I slowly open my bedroom door as quietly as I can, inch by painstaking inch. I visualize surprising the intruder, such that he or she or it flees—once he or she or it realizes they've been discovered. Even better, I fantasize that there isn't any danger at all. Instead, my house is being invaded by a scantily clad college coed or that reporter Makayla Hill. Maybe she's seeking a late-night interview? Maybe she's waiting for me in the living room, wearing nothing but a notepad and a pen. My fantasy is interrupted by a strange sensation. I look down … great, I am starting to get wood. The tight boxer briefs I'm wearing accentuates my situation—as if confronting an intruder could get any more awkward. My little man points the way as I step through the crack in the open doorway, out into the living room.

It turns out I'm half right. Someone is waiting for me. Unfortunately, it's not a coed, but rather an older gray-suited Korean man with short dark hair and a long goatee. A samurai sword—at least, that's what it looks like, I'm not sure there were feudal samurais in Korea; I'll have to Google it—is strapped to a belt secured around the intruder's waist. He's definitely not my type, not even after a few beers. The intruder appears to be waiting for me; at least he doesn't seem surprised to see me awake. Then again, it's almost noon; he's probably surprised I'm not dressed. I take a good long look at his long sleek samurai sword, and then I glance down at my short fat dagger. I'd be lying if I didn't admit I felt a little inadequate.

Before, I can say something witty like, "You're not a busty coed," or "I didn't order any Korean shish-kabob," the intruder introduces himself, "Good evening, Mr. Valentine. My name is Whanung. I think we have something in common." He holds his ring finger up for me to see. His Advocate ring is an exact match to mine. "I would like a moment of your time to talk."

"Great, make an appointment with my assistant and I will consider taking a meeting," I reply as I adopt a non-aggressive stance to match Whanung's laissez-faire demeanor. "You're interrupting my beauty sleep and, trust me, I need all the sleep I can get." Self-deprecation can be a useful tool in high-stress situations like trials, first dates, even home invasions.

After a few seconds of awkward silence, during which he stares at me, I decide to take a different tack. "What's the deal with the one-name thing?" I ask. "Are you like a singer? Korean pop star? Let me guess, you and Psy kick it on the weekends? Do it Gangnam style?" When self-deprecation doesn't work, insulting your adversary is a useful alternative, one guaranteed to get results.

Whanung remains composed, the kind of composure that is achieved only with practice, lots of practice. His breathing remains perfectly constant. There's an unnatural rhythm to it, as if he inhales the bare minimum amount of oxygen necessary to live, and part and parcel, exhales an equally minimum amount of carbon dioxide. Breathing is purely mechanical to this guy.

Nearly faster than I can track with my eyes, his hand reaches into his pocket, retrieves a small object, and snaps like a wet towel, launching the object through the air at me. Time slows, as my Battle-Sense activates. I immediately recognize the object as a small black velvet pouch. Rather than tip my hand by using my abilities to block or catch it, I allow the pouch to hit me square in the chest. Thankfully, it's soft and falls to the floor after impact. I don't give my intruder the satisfaction of seeing me flinch. Rather, I stay perfectly still, before, during, and after the impact.

After a silent count to five, I dramatically yell, "Ouch! I've been hit! It's bad ... I don't know if I'm going to make it! If I don't make it ... tell your mother I loved her."

Whanung's demeanor still doesn't change. He completely ignores my theatrics and yo-mama crack. I can't tell whether I gave the reaction he expected—or not. He's inhuman, like a robot statue, impossible to get a read on.

After an awkward thirty seconds of Whanung staring at me, like I'm a prize pig at the state fair, he finally says, "Interesting, you aren't what they think you are. You're something else entirely. Something this world hasn't known in a very long time. Something this world has forgotten. Something this world will learn to fear again." Whanung smiles as if experiencing a memory from long ago, "Even in death, nae chingu Pavo is full of secrets." Whanung nods at the black velvet pouch, "It's tea; please make me a cup."

"You just broke into my house, threw a pouch at me, and then ordered me to make you tea? *Wang*, I'm sure I'm pronouncing that wrong, but I really don't give a damn. *Wang*, have I fairly summed up our interaction thus far?"

"You have," he answers. "It's pronounced, *Wa–nung*. I like a little honey with my tea. Oh, and don't mind me, feel free to put some clothes on. Your generation has the strangest sleeping habits. It's nearly noon and you're still in bed. In my youth, we got up with the sun and—"

"—Yeah, walked uphill to school both ways, through the snow, et cetera. I get it. Your generation was the best. Yada-yada."

He doesn't respond to my outburst, but Whanung's face almost has an annoyed look on it—almost.

On general principle, for breaking into my home, throwing a pouch at me, and ordering me to make him tea, I consider throwing my knife at him, but I'm afraid I'll look foolish doing it, and worse, I'd probably break something. The Pugio isn't designed to be thrown, and I think the Cleveland Browns have better odds of winning the Super Bowl than I do of throwing and hitting Whanung with it.

I also consider just straight-up attacking him. He is an intruder in my home, and an impolite one at that. I know California doesn't have "stand-your-ground" laws, and technically, if I'm charging him, I'm not standing-my-ground, but that's a minor detail. #Semantics. One that could be easily adjusted during my post-fight interview with the police. I doubt I'd get convicted for defending myself from an intruder who brought a sword into my home. I do know at least one good lawyer.

All that said, he does have a ring. Sinn warned me that pretty much everyone with a ring is a major badass. I don't really want to start a fight I'm going to lose, and I don't want to die on a Friday. I always imagined I'd die on a Tuesday. Tuesday is definitely the worst day of the week. A lot of people say Monday, because you have to go back to work on Mondays—those people are wrong. On Mondays everyone's hung over from the weekend and nobody gets anything done. People come in late and go home early. Nobody really expects anyone to get anything done on a Monday. On Tuesdays, however, you're expected to work hard and get shit done. And it's four days until the next weekend. Tuesdays are the real first day of the work week. #TerribleTuesdays.

I next consider continuing with my sharp wit, and hurling some more insults at him, but I don't do that either. Whanung seems nearly impervious to my wit and, frankly, I'm tired. I'm going on a little over two hours of sleep and, after reflection, it just seems easier to give the guy what he wants.

I throw on some black sweatpants, and a gray wife beater, and head to the kitchen to make this jackass some tea. I tuck the dagger into my sweatpants. It's not exactly comfortable, and I doubt I'm going to need it. This guy is definitely dangerous, but I don't think he's here to fight me. I don't leave it on the nightstand because I don't like the idea of him being the only one armed. I'll admit it—it's a dick measuring thing.

The black velvet pouch is full of dried foul-smelling leaves. I don't have a kettle, nor do I have an infuser for loose leaf tea. Fuck it, I'm not making this. I toss the black velvet pouch onto the counter, open my cupboard, and grab a green tea pod and a mug. I use my pod coffee maker to make him a single serve cup of green tea. I set it on the counter in front of where he is standing, watching me. I open another cupboard, and grab the sugar from the top shelf next to a jar of honey. I leave the cabinet open long enough for him to observe that I have honey, and then I set the sugar in front of him. Fuck this guy; I'm not giving him any of my honey. I admit it's childish, but this asshole broke into my house carrying a sword, for God's sake.

I make myself a cup of black coffee, and then turn back to my intruder. He has an amused look on his face. I'm glad I fucking amuse him. What am I, a clown? After a few sips of coffee, I ask in my most annoyed tone, "What do you want to talk about? Why are you here?"

Whanung calmly answers, "I understand you served the werespider, Lycocide, with a criminal complaint."

"I did," I answer.

"I would like to know what crime you intend to charge him with? And what evidence you have against him?"

Now this is starting to make sense. This guy is on a fishing expedition, but why? And for whom? Is he a potential ally or a potential enemy?

"I'm sorry," I respond. "I'm not really comfortable talking about an ongoing case. I don't think it's appropriate. You'll have to wait until the hearing. I'm sure you understand."

Whanung remains a robot statue. If he expected a different answer, he's keeping it close to the vest. After a few moments, he responds, "I do understand." He momentarily pauses, "I had another reason for coming here today. I respected Pavo; there was a time ... when we were ... friends. When I heard that a human had bested him in a duel, and claimed his ring, I had to confront you. I owed Pavo a debt. Now that I'm here, I can see ..."

"—What can you see?" I ask defensively, not liking where this conversation is headed.

Whanung ignores my question. "Our fraternity of Advocates is rather small and is delicately balanced. It's rare we get a new member. Some will be concerned that you will upset the balance. Some are afraid of change and they will be afraid of you."

"Are you afraid of change?" I ask in a slightly sarcastic voice.

"No," he answers. "Fear is an illusion. A distraction from things that will either be, or not be, and there is no point in being afraid of things that will either be, or not be."

"Sounds like a fortune cookie," I respond.

Whanung bows slightly. "It has been a pleasure to meet you, Mr. Valentine. The world is about to get interesting. A storm is coming."

"What do you mean by that?"

Whanung smiles as he withdraws an elegant black-lacquered-handled brush from his pocket, and draws a door and a handle on my living room wall. His gate pen is beautiful, a piece of art. He reaches into my wall and opens the gate without ever touching his ring with his index finger and thumb, and without saying any words. I wonder if those were just tics that Pavo had?

Before he enters the gate, Whanung turns back to me and asks, "May I offer you a piece of advice?"

"Nobody's stopping you," I respond.

"Werespiders are nearly impossible to kill in their full spider form, even for a paladin. If you have to kill one, do it quick, and do it while it's in its human form." Whanung takes one step into the open doorway and then stops and turns back to me again. "Mr. Valentine, I shall tell no one that we spoke today. I leave it up to you to decide whether to disclose this meeting to anyone or not." With that, the gate closes and he's gone.

That was ... interesting. I don't think I made a friend, but I don't think I made an enemy either, and I didn't get run through with a samurai sword. I'm going to chalk that one up as a win. How does he know I'm a paladin? I probably should have been more hospitable, and pumped him for information. I wonder what he was? I wish I'd asked. The more information I can gather about others and their abilities, the better my chances of survival.

I look at the clock on the wall; it's a little after noon. Now that I drank an entire cup of coffee, I'm not going to be able to get back to sleep. I might as well take a shower and head back to the office. There's still a lot of work to be done.

Chapter Thirty-Three

When I arrive at the office, the doors are locked and the lights are off—it's empty. It's the middle of a workday; closed for business is not a good look for an active law firm, even if its primary area of practice is Magna-Concordat law. What if somebody stops by—a potential client, or a process server? We're going to need to hire a full-time secretary to man the store during business hours. Come to think of it, how do we make money? Do I get paid for this Magna-Concordat gig? How am I going to pay Wilson? How am I going to pay rent? I need to remember to ask Sinn what the deal is with finances. Pavo made it sound like money wouldn't be an issue, but money is never an issue unless you don't have any. In other words, money has always been an issue for me.

I find a typed note from Sinn on the conference table.

Dear Colt,

I mailed out all the requisite paperwork and filed a copy with the Concordat Clerk's office. Yes, Colt, there is still paperwork involved with the practice of law under the Magna-Concordat. I'll be gone for a day or two. There is a personal matter I need to take care of. I'm also reaching out to other Advocates to try to figure out who was selected to sit on the panel of judges for Lycocide's case. While I'm gone, please figure out what you're planning on charging Lycocide with. Or better yet, let's withdraw the complaint. This whole thing is stupid and risky. One other thing, don't die while I'm gone. That would be irritating.

Sinn

My death will be irritating? Really? I doubt I'll care much about her irritability if I'm dead. She'll be irritated? I'm irritated right now. I'm irritated that she's handling personal business when we should be working together to build a case against Lycocide. The hearing is less than a week away and we only have five days to figure out how to get his victims justice. What is she thinking? I shake my head in frustration. I hope she has a shitty weekend, and the guilt of not being here working on the case eats at her.

I make an espresso to relax myself, sit down in front of the large monitor that Joycee set up for me on the conference table, open the file containing the videos she downloaded for me from X-change, and play the next video in order, picking up where I left off yesterday; and after the first one, I play the next, and the next, until I have watched them all. They're all pretty much the same, Lycocide terrorizes, tortures, and then drains each victim. He has a sick routine and sticks to it.

I watch most of the videos in fast forward. I'm not really sure what I'm looking for, or if I'm looking for anything at all. All I know is that I have to watch all of them. I owe it to the victims; their deaths need to be witnessed. #AllofLycocidesVictimsMatter. Watching the videos doesn't change anything; those poor people are still dead, but I want those people to know I saw. I saw what happened to them, and I want them to know I'm going to fight for them.

It's around six thirty when the last video ends. For a moment, I stare at the now dark monitor. Nothing's changed. I don't know what I thought would happen if I watched them all, but this isn't it. I don't feel better. I just feel dirty, depressed, and afraid. Not afraid for my own life, but afraid that I'm going to let those people down, and afraid for all human life. What can humans do to fight monsters like Lycocide? What hope do we have? I need a shower. I need to wash off the darkness.

I shut the computer down, turn the lights off, and make sure the office is locked up tight. I draw a door with my Sharpie and step through the portal into my waiting bedroom. I manage to get my clothes off and make it to the shower before self-medicating. I nearly scrub my skin raw, trying to get the evil out. I find myself weeping; tears of sorrow race down my cheeks, and mix with the shower water, as I mourn fifty-three unfinished lives, on the cold marble tiled floor of my bathroom.

Once I pick myself off the floor, I open a bottle of pinot noir, which I quickly ditch in favor of stronger, brown liquor. I think about trying to eat something, but elect not to waste the food. I doubt I can keep anything down.

I spread out on my couch in front of my seventy-inch television and flip through the hundreds of worthless cable channels I never watch, searching for anything that doesn't involve murder or spiders. #SizeDoesMatter. I settle on one of those home-remodeling shows and then turn my attention back to my glass of brown liquor.

My therapy is interrupted by the sound of my phone vibrating against the glass coffee table top. I flip it over so I can see the screen. It's a text message from Wilson:

BOSS, C U AT 10 AM. SOMEWHERE WE NEED 2 GO. WEAR COMFORTABLE CLOTHES.

I respond with the "ok" emoji and then lose myself in mindless television. Before you know it, the whiskey bottle is empty and I'm passed out with one leg hanging off the couch while visions of refinished wood floors, shiplap, and marble countertops dance through my head.

Chapter Thirty-Four

It's Saturday morning, I'm sitting at my kitchen table, sipping on my third cup of coffee, and re-reading the silver inlaid Concordat Book of Laws. I feel better this morning, ready to work. Suddenly, the latch on my front door clicks unlocked, and the door thumps open against the door jam, as if someone pushed it a little harder than they intended. I consider standing, searching for a weapon, maybe a knife from the kitchen. But the ring isn't warning me that I'm in any danger, assuming that's what the burning sensation means, and it's almost 10:00 AM, so, instead, I remain seated and await my guest. As I suspect, it's Wilson. He strolls into my apartment wearing camo pants, a black t-shirt with the punisher logo on it, and an old beat-up gone-fishing hat. He's carrying a powdered sugar donut in one hand, and there's a stack of files, an old book, and a firearms case pinned against his body with the other.

"Wasn't my front door locked?" I ask.

"Yeah. So?" answers Wilson with his patented goofy look.

"Did I give you a key to my house?" I ask in an accusatory tone.

"No," answers Wilson as he bites into the white donut, dropping crumbs and powdered sugar onto my floor, all the while balancing the files, book, and firearms case.

"How did you get in, then?" I ask with annoyance.

"You just saw me walk through the front door," says Wilson, while pointing at the front door with the donut.

"No shit," I snap. "How did you open the front door?"

"With the handle," Wilson replies in a sarcastic tone, while still sporting that stupid goofy smile.

"Alright dickwad, how did you unlock my door?"

"Boss, for a lawyer, you're not very good at this whole question and answer thing." I didn't think it was possible, but his grin widens even further. He clearly thinks he scored a point with that dig.

At least there's one constant in my life—Wilson is a constant ass. I take a deep breath and rather than scream in frustration, my first instinct, or throw my coffee cup at him, my second instinct, I calmly ask, "Wilson, how did you unlock my door?"

Wilson sets the files, the old book, and the gun case down on the table, and walks towards the refrigerator. "I used a key," he answers. His head is buried in the fridge and his back is to me, but I'd bet a turkey and avocado sandwich he's still sporting that stupid cocky grin.

"Where did you get a key?" I ask, hoping the answer isn't too creepy. Please don't be creepy.

"I made one," he answers with his head still buried in the refrigerator.

Fuck, it's creepy. "When?"

"Last week, when you were recovering from your stabbing. Remember ... I was here, taking care of you." He laid the last bit on a bit thick; I can tell he's really going to try to milk this for all it's worth. "I had a locksmith stop by and upgrade the locks. These new ones are practically impossible to pick—they're extra strong. I switched out the key on your keychain and kept a copy for myself—just in case."

"Okay," I answer, realizing I've only used the front door twice since my coma, and apparently, I didn't notice the new locks. "Thanks ... I guess."

"Your security is for shit. I think we should put in some cameras."

"I'll consider it."

"I already ordered them. They should be here in a few days."

"You what?"

"Don't worry, I ordered them with our credit card."

"Of course, you did," I say while choking down my real feelings on the subject. Wilson smiles, apparently pleased with himself. The monkey thinks he did good. What I really want to do is stick a banana in his tailpipe. I don't like anybody, even Wilson, making decisions for me.

"Wilson, you knew I was going to be here this morning. Why didn't you knock?"

Wilson looks at me with confusion, "I didn't want to bother you. I figured you'd be at the table working and I didn't want to make you get up."

"You thought it would be better to surprise me? You thought it was a good idea to enter my home unannounced? You do realize that in the last week I've been in a fight with a two-thousand-year-old vampire and a crazy knife-wielding ex-client gang member, and I had a fucking werespider threaten to kill me?"

"Boss, if you want me to knock next time—just ask. Stop being so dramatic."

I shake my head in frustration. What did I do to deserve this imbecile in my life? "Next time, knock."

"Sure thing, Boss. All you got to do is ask." Wilson retrieves a vitamin water from my refrigerator and starts gulping it down like he just returned from a hike through Death Valley. I watch in disgust as he drinks the entire bottle and lets out a massive belch.

I want to punch him. Instead, I change the subject, "What's in the folders and why did you bring the guns?"

"The folders contain all the information I could find on the video victims. So far, I've been able to identify thirty-one of the fifty-three victims," answers Wilson.

"That's amazing. How did you do it?" I ask.

"Missing person's files at the Shasta County Sheriff's department. Joycee printed me screen grabs of each victim's face. She also gave me rough height and weight estimates. She used Lycocide as a comparison. There was almost always at least one shot in each video where he was standing next to his victims. Then I made nice at the Sheriff's department and the secretary gave me access to the county's missing person files. I spent all day yesterday trying to match faces, heights, and weights."

"The secretary gave you access, huh? Full access I bet."

"You're sexist," Wilson replies. "You automatically assume the secretary was a woman. Well, you're wrong. The secretary was a nice young man. So, get your head out of the gutter. By the way, you owe me a hundred bucks and gas money. I had to pay for access."

"You're the sexist," I reply. "I never implied the secretary was a woman. And don't you always have to pay for it?"

"Fuck you, Colt. It was one time. One time I paid for it—and I told you that in confidence. And you know I only like girls."

"Now you sound desperate, sexist, and homophobic," I reply with a smile.

"Seriously, Colt, you're an asshole."

I nod in agreement, "Yes I am. During your date with the secretary, did you find anything useful? Any patterns or similarities between victims?"

Wilson uses his middle finger to send me the international greeting of brotherhood. "Not really. Most of the victims were homeless or out-of-towners visiting Shasta County for hiking or camping. As far as victim profiles, Lycocide's all over the map. If there's a pattern, I don't see it. The only thing that they all had in common was that they all went missing in Shasta County and they all got eaten by a spider."

"No kidding, Columbo. Where did you get the book?"

"Sinn gave it to me."

That piques my curiosity. "Is it like a self-help book?" I ask with a smirk.

Wilson ignores my slam. "It's one of your family journals. From what I can tell, it's kinda' like a monster compendium. Did you ever play D&D?"

I shrug, not knowing exactly what he is talking about. I play video games, not pen and paper role-playing games. Although as a kid I used to love the Saturday morning *Dungeons and Dragons* cartoon and as an adult I love that show *Stranger Things* on Netflix.

"Think of it like a monster encyclopedia," continues Wilson. "Your family took notes, a lot of notes, about things they hunted. This journal has a section on werespiders."

"Well, what does it say?" I ask.

"It's in Latin," answers Wilson.

"Then I'm guessing you have no idea?" I mumble as I thumb through the missing persons folders.

"It says wolf-spiders don't create webs to trap their prey; instead they stalk and overpower their prey with brute strength. They also don't produce venom and they're not usually all that clever, but your family recommends avoiding close quarter fighting with them—up close they're deadly. Your family's preferred method for killing a wolf-spider was to incapacitate it with a shitload of metal crossbow bolts, and then decapitation. Your family liked silver, but the notes indicate any metal will do. In general, most were-species are allergic to silver; it makes it difficult for them to shapeshift, and it takes a long time to heal from a silver wound," lectures Wilson smugly.

"You don't speak Latin," I state in disbelief.

"Of course, I do. … Don't you? Didn't they teach you Latin at that fancy law school you went to? How much did you pay for that piece of paper you framed and hung over your desk? Maybe you should think about asking for a refund. Or maybe you're just not as smart as you think you are—Counselor." Wilson is able to keep a straight face for all of about fifteen seconds before he starts laughing.

"Fuck you," I say with a smile. "You don't speak Latin."

"No, Boss, I don't. I found a Latin professor at Oakland Community College and asked her to read it to me."

"You showed her my family journal without asking me?"

"Don't worry, I told her that some rich Silicon Valley geek had put together an elaborate fantasy role-playing scavenger hunt for his rich friends. I told her this was one of the obscure tasks we had to complete to get the next clue. That, and I paid her to read me anything in the book about wolf-spiders. Oh, you owe me a hundred for that also."

"Right. And she bought that?"

"Yes, apparently she's a gamer. When you think about it, who else but a gamer would want to learn Latin?"

I shrug, not really understanding his logic. "Did she say anything else?"

Wilson pauses for a moment, presumably, searching his memory, "Nothing I can think of. She said there was a lot of other stuff about different types of werespiders in there. Nothing else specific to the wolf-spider variety. She offered to translate the whole thing; seventy-five dollars an hour, said it would only take her a couple weeks."

"I'll think about it," I reply. "Hold off for now. Before we start handing my family journals over to strangers, I want a complete picture of how many there are. I'm going to want it all translated and probably all by the same person. Maybe there's a high-tech solution?"

Wilson looks thoughtful for a moment. "I'll look into it. There might be a computer program or something."

I nod, thinking the same thing. I wonder how Sinn's reading the journals? And I wonder why she didn't mention they were in Latin. She probably speaks Latin and assumes I do as well. Mysterious, hot, and smart—I really hate her.

My eyes drift to the gun case. "What's in the gun case, and if you say guns, I'm going to throw you out. Never mind, I withdraw that question. I'm going to assume there are guns in that case. Why are their guns on my table?"

Wilson gets a big grin on his face. "Because we're going shooting."

I frown. "You know I'm not really a gun person. I prefer to use words to solve problems and grocery stores to get meat."

As usual, Wilson ignores my smart-ass comment. "Boss, you need to learn to protect yourself. Sinn's agreed to train you in hand-to-hand combat techniques. She's a badass in multiple disciplines. I think she'd destroy the current MMA women's champion—even without her vampire powers. Probably the men's champion too. I can't wait to watch your sparring sessions. She is going to fuck you up."

I don't think I have ever seen Wilson happier. The thought of me getting my ass kicked really revs his engine.

Wilson continues, "I agreed to teach you guns and knives. We think it's important that you're competent with a mixture of weapons and fighting styles."

"When did you see Sinn fight?" I ask in genuine curiosity.

Wilson looks down at the floor. "Let's just say we had a disagreement about who should teach you to fight. The, ah, discussion, didn't last very long."

I smile. "She kicked your ass, huh?"

"She's gonna kick your ass, too."

"We'll see."

Wilson grins from ear to ear. "Yes, we will. But today, we're going teach you how to shoot."

Chapter Thirty-Five

I arrive home from Wilson's beginning Fire Arms 101 class around 8:00 PM, and immediately jump in the shower. Despite the fact my professor is a dill-weed, I'd be lying if I didn't admit I had fun, and Wilson seemed happy with my progress.

Wilson brought two different semi-automatic pistols for me to practice with. A Beretta M9, which he called the "World Defender" and told me is the pistol favored by the United States Military since 1985, and the Walther PPQ. Wilson said the Chinese favor the Walther PPQ as do many police forces around the world. The Berretta felt better in my hands and had a slightly softer recoil, but I was slightly more accurate with the Walther PPQ, and its three dot sights, as opposed to the Beretta two dot sights. Overall, I preferred the Beretta.

Wilson took me to an indoor/outdoor gun range northeast of Sacramento. We started off indoors, firing at a stationary target from a two-handed firing stance, and progressed to more exotic outdoor firing stations. He ran me through a variety of different skill exercises. After firing at stationary targets, bottles, and cutouts of bad guys from a traditional firing stance, he had me practice firing one-handed, which is harder than you might think. We started with my dominant right hand, and then switched to shooting with my left hand. I was terrible with my left hand; I couldn't hit water if I fell out of a boat.

We also practiced shooting while walking forward and sideways; by the end of the day, I actually got pretty good at moving and shooting at a stationary target.

We then progressed to moving targets: a metal rabbit would run across my field of fire, and Wilson would yell at me to shoot it, and I would miss, of course.

Finally, Wilson had me practice with a blindfold. He said it would simulate what could happen in a fight if the lights go out, something gets in my eyes, or I get blinded from a flashbang grenade. When I pointed out that I have no plans of visiting Afghanistan anytime soon, and I doubt I'm going to come into contact with any flashbang grenades, Wilson just gave me an eye roll.

The blindfold drill was really hard. With the gun at my side, I would scan the field of fire, which was littered with numbered targets, and try to memorize where the targets were located. Wilson would then make me put on blacked-out sunglasses and call out targets by number. I would raise the gun and try to hit the target from memory. I only hit the target once out of like twenty-five tries, and I think I got lucky that one time.

My shoulders ache all over. I'm surprised at how sore I am. I never realized how exhausting firing a gun could be. Muscles that I didn't even know I had, hurt. I always assumed shooting a gun involved little to no physical ability. I thought you just point and shoot, like a video game. I was great at Duck Hunt, that game with the orange and gray plastic gun, and I never felt tired after marathons of that as a child. Based on how good I was at that, I figured I'd be at least decent at shooting a real gun—I was wrong. Lesson learned. #VideoGamesAreNotRealLife.

After a long hot shower, I uncork a bottle of pinot and, for like the fifteenth time, start pouring over the Book of Laws. Maybe this time, I'll discover something new or get smacked by an epiphany—I'm due. There are only four days until Lycocide's hearing and I still have no idea what I'm going to do. If I don't come up with something soon, I'm going to have to withdraw the complaint. Premature withdrawal, like premature ejaculation, is not ideal. Losing my first case wouldn't be a very good start to my career as an Advocate. I hate losing, and Lycocide's victims deserve justice. I can't think of a worse way to die than alone, afraid, hopeless, and then drained by a giant spider. I need to find the equivalent to a big can of Raid in this book.

Chapter Thirty-Six

It's a little after 7:00 AM when I arrive at my office. The drive only took about twenty-five minutes, not bad for a Monday morning. I know I don't have to drive anymore; call me crazy, but I like the morning commute. It gives me time to think, mentally prepare myself, and plan my day. I also enjoy listening to the local morning sports shows. It's the only way I can stay up-to-date on our local teams. Sitting in morning traffic, drinking a thermos of hot coffee flavored with hazelnut creamer and listening to sports radio, is my pre-game. The commute home on the other hand—blows, and I could do without it.

I spent all day Sunday pouring over the Concordat Book of Laws, searching for any crime I could prove Lycocide committed. I think I got something—it's weak, but colorable. That's another way of saying it's a long shot, but at least we got a shot. I'm going to run it by my team this morning; it won't work if they're not on board.

I didn't hear a peep from Sinn over the weekend. I know it's only a job, and she has a life outside of work, but this case is important. I expect my team to work nights and weekends when there's an approaching trial. Work has got to take priority over personal life. Sinn and I are going to have to discuss her commitment.

As I enter the office, the burning sensation in my finger returns, either warning me of an STD or imminent danger. Sinn is standing near the conference table in a defensive position; her legs are shoulder-width apart, and her hands are in front of her, ready to scrap. She doesn't look happy. She's having an animated conversation with a tall spindly being cloaked all in black. I don't need it to turn around to know it's both an Advocate and a werespider—it's definitely the source of my finger pain. If you close your eyes and imagine what a man who turns into a spider looks like—that's this guy. He's Ichabod Crane—and I'm not talking about the Johnny Depp version from the Tim Burton movie—on meth.

The Ichabod Crane looking motherfucker senses my entrance and spins to face me. He's unexpectedly quick for a being with such gangly proportions. Now that I have a better look, I can see his face is elongated, almost inhuman; it's as if his skin has been shrunk and then stretched into place over his odd-shaped skull. His dark colorless eyes shine with malevolence, and he stands precariously, as if uncomfortable on just two legs.

"You are the human that bested Pavo the Peacock?" he asks in a shrill inhuman voice. "I find it odd … that Pavo's adopted daughter would choose to work with the man who killed her father."

"I guess I'm just lucky," I answer.

The werespider stares first at Sinn and then at me. He seems to be thinking, possibly making a threat assessment. After a moment, he turns towards me and steps forward.

Suddenly, my mind is under attack. The creature seems to be emitting some sort of field of fear. I can feel him probing my conscience, searching for entry. He pulls and prods at me from all directions, urging me to let him in, to drown in his cold embrace. I do my best to hold firm, like a cliff against the rising ocean. I'm steadfast in my resolve not to give in to the fear.

And just as quick as it began, the terror attack ends and the penetrating fear dissipates. A warm and tingly sensation of relief courses through my body. That must be what a fly caught in a web feels like, and this must be what it feels like when the fly unexpectedly breaks free.

I smile, trying not to let on how close I was to breaking, and step forward towards the creature, offering my right hand so we can shake, like proper lawyers at a proper meeting. "Good morning, my name is Colt Valentine. Welcome to our office. Sinn didn't warn me we were having guests this morning or I would have had the maids clean up better. I apologize for the mess; there are cobwebs everywhere. It's an old building and we have been having a hard time eradicating all of the eight-legged pests. I hate spiders, find them disgusting. Every time I see one, I just want to stomp the shit out of it." I give the creature an even wider, toothier grin, and leave my hand extended. I'm not going to be intimidated by this skinny deformed freak.

The creature frowns, momentarily hesitates, and then grasps my hand so we can shake. He has a strong grip. I squeeze with as much force as I can muster and give him the old presidential shake. He either forgets or more likely chooses not to introduce himself. It seems that not even werespiders are impervious to being thrown off their game; either that, or he just lacks basic manners.

Sinn finally jumps in, "Colt, this is Phulcus. He is a—"

"—An Advocate and a werespider. I'm aware. Thank you." A surprised look crosses Sinn's face and is then replaced by a thoughtful one. I think she is reevaluating my spider killing comments in light of the information that I knew what Phulcus was. Phulcus remains unreadable, but I can tell he is studying me with the eyes of a predator.

I release his hand, nonchalantly shift my weight, and take a step to my left, strategically positioning myself so that he can't see both Sinn and me at the same time. Phulcus has to focus on me, giving Sinn freedom of movement, in case violence ensues. I hope to avoid violence, particularly with anyone wearing an Advocate ring, but it pays to prepare, and I want him as uncomfortable as possible. His mere presence is disturbing the Feng shui in my office.

"It's nice to meet you. Phulcus, that means you're a daddy-long-legs?" I ask. I give him an opening, but he doesn't respond, so I continue driving the conversation.

"I've been reading about spiders on the internet. Phulcus is Latin, right?" I know from my reading that Phulcus is the Latin name of the genus of the cellar spider family, which Google says are commonly called Daddy-long-legs. "I didn't think Daddy-long-legs were real spiders at all?" I add just to irk him. Now that I'm on a roll, I can't help but keep going. "Do the other werespiders call you Poppy-Long-Strider?"

Phulcus seems perplexed. Whatever expectations he had about this conversation have been completely blown. I'm guessing he imagined his mere presence would intimidate me. I don't think he planned for my passive-aggressive stance, and his pathetic attempt to fish for information regarding my relationship with Sinn was effortlessly countered. To his credit, Phulcus has remained calm and tight-lipped. Most people, when thrown off their game, begin to crack. When they crack, they talk and talk, usually to their detriment. Phulcus may be a little off balance, but he's not spilling secrets; he's thinking and readjusting his strategy. This spider is clever, and clever equals danger.

Finally, he says, "I see you have been doing your homework. I'm a skull spider, sometimes called a cellar spider. Let me assure you, Mr. Valentine, I am a spider." Phulcus smiles and sharp fangs descend from the roof of his mouth. "And no one calls me Poppy and lives."

"Not even the ladies?" I ask with tongue firmly planted in cheek.

"No one," he answers.

I place two fingers on my wrist, miming a pulse check, not so subtly indicating that I'm still alive. From the look Sinn is giving me, she doesn't approve of my antics.

Phulcus pauses for a long moment. I'm not sure if it's an intentional dramatic pause, or if he's merely taking a moment to select phrasing. He's very difficult to read. His mannerisms and pattern of speech are wholly alien. Phulcus is a spider in a man's body. There don't appear to be any remnants of the human being Phulcus once was inside of that thing.

Phulcus makes his word selections and continues, "I want you to withdraw the complaint you served on my clutter member. Killing humans is not against Concordat law. You won't win at trial and even if you did, you wouldn't want to. You would regret it. Do the smart thing."

So, he went for the straightforward approach, no bullshitting; I can appreciate that. What the fuck is a clutter? Is a group of spiders really called a clutter? Like a gaggle of geese, a pack of wolves, a murder of crows? A clutter is a stupid name for a bunch of spiders. The word clutter only strikes fear in the hearts of maids and moms of messy teenagers.

"I'll consider it," I answer. "I can promise you this; if your *clutter* member didn't break the law, he has got nothing to worry about. Anything else I can help you with?"

I went with the diplomatic response. I wasn't overtly rude. I didn't even tell him to go fuck himself, well ... not directly. Admittedly, "I will consider it" is lawyer-speak for "go fuck yourself." But it's the nice kind of "go fuck yourself." It's the make sure you use lotion while you fuck yourself, so you don't get chafed, of "go fuck yourselves."

Then again, I did punctuate "go fuck yourself" with "if your clutter member didn't break the law, he has got nothing to worry about." Which is a nice way of saying your clutter member is fucked with a capital F, and has every reason to worry, because I'm going to stomp the shit out of him—he's gonna be a puddle of spider guts when I'm through with him.

Phulcus takes his time considering my response, carefully contemplating his next move. Patience is a powerful tool for sharks and lawyers—two creatures that are often mistaken for one another. It's a tool I often forget to use. I'm more of a take immediate action type of guy, a get-shit-done guy. I prefer to err on the side of recklessness/awesomeness. #FortuneFavorsTheBold.

Phulcus continues to study me; I'm starting to feel like a grasshopper that's been thrown in a terrarium with a tarantula. "Mr. Valentine, I don't know what you actually know, and what you are pretending to know, and I don't care. You're a mere inconvenience, and one I'd be happy to dispose of. I have been encouraged to reach out to you and seek a diplomatic resolution. I represent a faction of powerful like-minded individuals within the Concordat. You don't want to cross us. Your friends and family wouldn't like it." He glances over at Sinn, who shivers under his gaze.

I consider interrupting Phulcus with a witty comeback, something along the lines of, "Let me tell you what I actually know; I actually know you're a dick and it sounds like you're part of a clique of dicks, and you and your clique should beat it." I'm pretty sure a group of dicks is called a click; if not, it should be. It's a travesty of the human language if it isn't. Instead of dropping that awesome line, which I'm definitely saving for later, I bite my tongue. I finally got him talking and I'm finally learning what the heck is going on. It sure would have been nice if Sinn had clued me in on Concordat politics before I was ambushed by Ichabod's anorexic brother.

"The group I represent had an understanding with Pavo. A transaction was made. We own his council seat. We want your assurance that nothing has changed. It would be unwise for you to rock the boat. A pebble cannot stand up to a river."

I start to respond, but Phulcus shushes me, "—Shush, little human. Save your words." He tosses a black thumb drive with a red hour glass decal on it onto my conference table. "I brought you a present. I think it will help clarify things for you. Do reconsider withdrawing the complaint." With that, Phulcus strides out the front door, his long legs moving rapidly. Spiders always seem to know when to scurry.

There are a number of questions I want to ask Sinn right now, but my eyes are locked on the thumb drive. My stomach tightens at the thought of what might be on it. Sinn watches silently as I plug it into the USB port of the conference table computer. There is only a single file on the drive, a video file, and it's short, only three minutes and thirty-seven seconds in length. My heart skips as I move the mouse icon over the play button.

Chapter Thirty-Seven

The video was taken inside of an apartment; the camera's pointed at an empty kitchen. Someone off camera, it sounds like a woman, is screaming in pain. The date-stamp in the bottom left corner of the video reads yesterday's date. For the first two minutes of the video you see an empty kitchen, and you hear screaming, and then at the two-minute mark, the camera slowly pans until it's framing a naked blood-covered woman tied to a chair. I involuntarily seize up, it becomes hard to breathe. I know the victim. Sinn places her hand on my shoulder reassuringly.

For nearly a minute of video, I watch in terror as the woman struggles against her ropes. Blood flows from more than a dozen cuts on her body. She is still screaming, but the screams have lost their volume. Her eyes have glazed over. She has the look of someone who has given up. Someone who no longer believes anyone will hear her and knows her torture can only end one way.

At the three-minute-and-seven-second mark of the video, Lycocide in his half-man, half-spider form, scurries into frame and, like plucking a grape off of a vine, uses two of his large spider appendages to violently pop the victim's still screaming head off her body. Lycocide buries his fangs in the geyser of blood spraying from her neck and drinks. After he satiates himself, he turns and looks directly into the camera, blood dripping from his giant fangs, "See you soon, Valentine," and the video ends.

I push Sinn's hand off my shoulder, stand up, and wipe the tears from my face. "I knew her. Her name was Trudy. She was my work-mother at the Public Defender's office. She took care of me. Looked out for me. She had a family. She was a good person! She didn't deserve to die alone and afraid! Trudy didn't deserve this! Her poor husband, her children, her grandchildren, will be devastated. How can I even tell them? This is all my fault." Tears flow down my cheeks.

Sinn remains silent. She awkwardly shifts her weight from one foot to the other, not knowing what to do.

"Lycocide is going to pay for this!" I shout. "Phulcus and his whole fucking group of like-minded individuals are going to fucking pay! If they wanted my attention—they got it! Get Wilson and Joycee here, *now*. We have a trial to plan." I grab Sinn by the shoulders and pull her close so our faces are inches apart. "When this trial is over, you and I are going to have a chat. No more games. No more half-truths. You're going to tell me everything. Or you're going to get the hell out of my life. Are we clear?"

Sinn nods. From the look on her face, I can tell she's sorry. Sorry isn't going to bring Trudy back. It may not be Sinn's fault that Trudy's dead. She couldn't have predicted this, but it's her fault I'm constantly in the dark. This cloak and kingmaker shit, has got to end. Either Sinn is going to start cluing me into what's really going on, or I'm going to do this without her. I need to be surrounded by people I can trust.

I may not be able to bring those people back, but I can make sure that sick son of a bitch Lycocide pays for his crimes, and that's what I'm going to do. One way or another, I'm going to deliver justice.

Chapter Thirty-Eight

It's Wednesday morning, trial day, T-Day, and I'm sipping an espresso, waiting for the rest of my team to return to the office, so we can gate to the Courthouse together. Over the past two days, the four of us hunkered down and put in work. The team really stepped up. A few hours ago, I sent everyone home for a shower and a change of clothes. They needed it—especially Wilson. I'm the first one back at the office, which isn't really unexpected; I do have the ring.

I may not have slept in the past forty-eight hours, but I did shave, shower, have some breakfast, and get suited up. I'm dressed in my typical trial uniform: black suit, white shirt, and a red tie. Romulus Augustus' Pugio is strapped to my waist. Sinn insisted that I arm myself. I think I look absurd. Carrying a knife isn't really comfortable, either; it slaps against my thigh when I walk. When I bitched about it, Sinn told me to "quit crying and man up." I wonder if she knew my dad? Then she explained—something my dad never would have done: every other Advocate would be armed, so I'd better be.

It feels strange to carry a weapon to court. That type of anti-social behavior would ensure a second court date in California and it would probably get you shot in Texas. I have a feeling there are going to be a lot of other dramatic differences between Concordat court and the courts I'm used to.

The last forty-eight hours were a whirlwind. After the meeting with Phulcus, I gathered the team and presented my game plan. They didn't like it. Frankly, I don't like it either. It's a last resort—a hail Mary. Unfortunately, nobody had a better plan. That means, by default, my plan's going forward. My team and I spent the past two days busting our asses and getting everything ready for the hearing. My plan will either work or spectacularly fail. There's nothing more we can do to prepare; we're as ready as we're ever going to be.

The biggest debate we had over the past forty-eight hours was about what we were going to do if Lycocide invokes his right to Ordeal-by-Combat. Sinn wanted me to spend the little time we had remaining, training in hand-to-hand combat. It took some convincing, but she finally agreed it was impossible to teach me how to fight in forty-eight hours, and that the time was better spent preparing our case.

Ultimately, we decided we would just have to cross the Ordeal-by-Combat bridge when and if we reach it. Sinn explained that per tradition, once an Ordeal-by-Combat is invoked, the person it is issued to can take up to twenty-four hours to decide to accept. Once accepted, again per tradition, the parties typically agree to a time and place for the duel. Bottom line, if it happens at all we'll have time to sort shit out. Secretly, I hope Lycocide is too afraid to invoke his right. I know it's probably wishful thinking, but let a guy dream.

Sinn, Wilson, and Joycee all shuffle back into the office at about the same time. Wilson and Joycee look tired and, per the usual, Sinn looks worried. The corners of my lips turn up into a smile. This is how a trial team should look: exhausted, nervous, and on edge. It's a good sign. I don't know if we are going to win today, but I believe this team rose to the occasion and did everything possible to get ready. I won't tell them until after the trial, but I'm proud of how we've come together.

"Do you think Lycocide is even going to show?" I ask, more to pass the time than anything else. There's no doubt in my mind he'll be there, I can feel it.

Sinn gives me an odd look. "I sometimes forget how new you are to this. I think it's because you're such an ass. Rookies are usually wide-eyed—not ass-eyed."

"Ass-eyed isn't even a word," I respond with a goofy eye roll.

Sinn returns the zippy look. "It isn't? It should be. It describes you perfectly. You should put it on your business cards, Colt Valentine, the ass-eyed Advocate."

I give Sinn my biggest toothiest fuck-off grin.

Sinn returns the smile and continues her explanation, "He doesn't have a choice to show up or not. You marked him when you served him. Remember the rune you placed on him? Whether he wants to appear or not, the rune will transport him to the Courthouse at the prescribed time. He'll be there. That is, unless he found a mage to break the rune. Which is unlikely—most mages know better than to mess around with the law."

Interesting, so that's what the whole rune thing was about? I probably should have asked before now. I probably should have asked a lot of things. I probably shouldn't have served Lycocide at all—at least, not until I had a better grasp of the basics. I'm like a blind man trying to cross a freeway during rush hour. Sinn's been right the whole time. I've been reckless and acting like an ass. Maybe I *am* ass-eyed.

"Have any of your contacts gotten back to you about who the judges are?" I ask.

"Answer is still no," replies Sinn. "Nobody seems to know, or is willing to say. It's really strange. We'll just have to find out when we get there."

I look around at my team. Wilson's wearing a camo backpack and carrying a black briefcase with a rusty-looking metal lock. It looks like something Gordon Gekko carried in the 1980's, and then donated to Goodwill in the 2000's; they threw it out, and then Wilson dug it out of the trash. It might have been nice once, but now it's faded, scratched up, and looks like somebody dropped it off the roof of a building into a river, and then it got run over by a truck. I assume it has the victim files in it—either that, or Wilson's transporting drugs. The briefcase is so nasty, I doubt security would even want to touch it without first getting a tetanus shot.

Joycee's carrying a modern black composite fiber literature-bag with wheels. I saw her pack it with a projector and her laptop. She's also carrying a collapsible projector screen. Wilson offered to help her with the screen, but she got testy. Said something about jackass men always thinking women need to be saved, as if women don't have arms of their own. I didn't quite catch it all. Wilson seemed to have gotten the message, though. He elected not to help her and moved all the way to the other side of the room.

I'm concerned about Joycee, concerned that this is going to be too much for her, but we really don't have any other options. Sinn pulled me aside yesterday and reminded me that Joycee has been through a lot recently and, although she is putting on a brave face, she's dealing with a lot of pain and fear, and she's close to breaking. Sinn doesn't think Joycee should be involved at all. She doesn't think she's ready and she's probably right. I've been so consumed with this case that I hadn't even noticed how high-strung Joycee is. There's nothing I can do about it now, other than watch her, and encourage her.

Wilson thinks her helping with this case is keeping her distracted, which is what he thinks she needs. What happens if we lose? Will that break her? When this is over, I need to have a talk with her about getting some professional help.

Sinn's carrying a hardbound paper copy of the Concordat Book of Laws, not a magical one like mine. She also has a portfolio full of pens, paper, tape, a small stapler, and Post-it flags, a typical lawyer survival pack. I'm carrying a similar portfolio, similarly provisioned.

None of the other members of my team are armed. Sinn told us Concordat Law permits everyone to carry weapons; however, she said it is frowned upon and looked at as a sign of weakness for an Advocate's support staff to be armed. She said typically only judges, Advocates, and the litigants come armed and not their staffs or observers. Armed staffs tend to indicate a coup is in the works. That's not really the message I'm trying to send at my first appearance as an Advocate.

Sinn thinks it's important that we—mainly I—project an image of strength. She's concerned other Advocates are going to test me, and says this will be a lot like a new prisoner's first walk in the yard. Everyone is going to want to measure their dick size against mine. Thank God, I have a big dick; at least that's what my ex-wife used to tell me. Come to think of it, she did lie a lot. I wonder if my ex is the most reliable source of information on that topic?

"Okay, is everyone ready to go?" I ask.

Everyone nods and collectively takes a deep breath. I retrieve my gate pen from my jacket pocket, and use the magical Sharpie to draw the outline of a door and a handle on the wall. I've been practicing opening doors without touching the ring or making any verbal commands. The whole ring touch ritual and verbal thing is hack. The way Whanung opened his gate was way more impressive. It took me a few practice attempts to get it right—now I can do it easily.

"Colt, this gate will open a little differently, because its location is burned into the pen's memory," instructs Sinn.

I furrow my brow in confusion.

"Just ask the pen to open a door to the Magna-Concordat Courthouse and let it do the rest." It feels silly to talk to the pen, but such is my life these days.

"Where's the Courthouse?" I ask.

Sinn smiles, "Rome, of course."

I reach into the brick wall, grab the solid silver handle I just drew, and pull it towards me. The door opens to reveal a gate of shimmering white light. For a moment, I look back at my team with pride. These three individuals, particularly Wilson and Joycee, are about to step through a gate into a Courthouse full of monsters—monsters that don't think twice about killing humans. Sinn assured me that my staff is protected by Concordat traditions so long as I'm breathing, but there's no guarantee I'm going to stay breathing. This might be a one-way trip for all of us. They don't have to do this; they didn't get suckered into being an Advocate, they could leave and live out their lives in relative safety.

"You all don't have to come," I say with trepidation.

"We're coming," they say in near unison.

I smile at their collective bravery; it inspires me and gives me strength. I think about leaving them behind, stepping through and closing the door behind me. This is going to be dangerous, and I don't want any of them to get hurt, but the truth is, I need them. I can't do this alone.

I step through the shimmering gate into the light. It's time to go to Court.

Chapter Thirty-Nine

We step out of the gate into a large enclosed domed building. The entire structure is carved out of a single massive chunk of white marble. I'd be lying if I didn't admit I was impressed. Even though the dome is fully enclosed, it's lit up as bright as the inside of a Las Vegas casino. The light seems to be radiating from the marble itself, which is almost glowing.

The dome is colossal in size, like the Roman Pantheon, except bigger. There are twenty-four small recesses carved into the outer walls, twelve on either side of the dome. In total, they cover about half of the base of the dome. Inside of each small recess is a carved marble door and above each carved door is a rune. Each door has a different rune. The rune above the door we entered through is glowing red. I quickly scan the room. Seven other runes above similar doors are also glowing red. Wilson points down at my hand. The red stone in my ring, which has always appeared to be plain and smooth, has a matching glowing red rune to the one above the door we entered through.

Sinn whispers, "There's one door for each Advocate and the glowing rune above the door signifies their presence."

I nod. Seven glowing runes means seven Advocates are here.

At one end of the dome there are five larger recesses, easily ten times the size of the smaller recesses. Massive doors are carved into the stone of these recesses. I find myself staring in awe and wondering what size creatures need such large doors?

Sinn, who must have seen me staring at the massive doors, taps me on the shoulder. "Those massive doors are where the public enters from. There are public gates in New York, London, Cairo, Mexico City, and Beijing. Colt, stop looking like a kid at a peep show, try and act like it's not your first time"

I clench my jaw shut and try to rein in my tourist-like behavior.

The gates are terrifying. I'd hoped gate travel was rare, maybe even limited to Advocates. The idea that monsters can gate wherever they please is … unsettling. Is anywhere safe for humans?

At the far end of the dome is a massive raised half-moon shaped bench carved out of marble, with seating for twenty-four judges. The middle three seats are occupied. In front of the bench is a massive open well, similar to what you would find in a human courtroom, except bigger. The well is bordered by the judge's bench on one side and two massive marble counsel tables on the other. Lycocide and an unnaturally handsome man are standing at one of the counsel tables. The empty table must be mine.

Slightly in front and between the counsel tables, floating out in a shallow area of the well, facing the judges, is a carved stone podium, partially encircled by a low stone pony wall. This must be where witnesses stand when they're being examined.

About ten feet behind the counsel tables, the bar separates the rest of the courtroom from the gallery. Behind the bar, there are rows of marble benches for the audience. The scale of the courtroom is gigantic. The design is breathtaking and makes me feel small and insignificant.

There are about thirty or so individuals seated in the gallery. Some are human in appearance ... some are not.

Wilson and Joycee take seats in the front row of the gallery, right behind the empty counsel table. Sinn and I, with as much confidence as we can muster, purposefully stride to the empty counsel table and set our things down. It's important to act like you own the courtroom. You want to appear to be the most comfortable person in the room. I spread my pens, sticky tabs, and yellow legal pad out on the table before me. I want it to appear as if I plan on being here a while—as if I moved in. The counsel table is my personal space, and I want it looking lived in, but organized. The last thing you want to do is project messiness to the judge or jury.

Only after the table is arranged to my satisfaction, do I look up at the bench and realize that I know two of the three black-robed individuals seated there. Whanung is seated on the left side and Phulcus is on the right. I'm slightly surprised, but I do my best to suppress any outward indication of my shock. In retrospect, I should have anticipated such shenanigans; the law, even in human courts, is politicized. I should have expected the same of a monster court.

In fact, I'm willing to bet Whanung knew he was a judge on this case when he showed up at my apartment last week. His departing comment about leaving it up to me to disclose our meeting is likely some sort of character or loyalty test. Similarly, Phulcus made his intentions clear on Friday. He's an enemy and is going to vote against me no matter what the evidence is. I'm starting to have doubts about the fairness of this proceeding.

Occupying the center seat is a woman I've never seen before. Her black robe looks simple and faded compared to the richness of her obsidian skin. Her head is shaved and she's wearing gold hoop earrings and a thick gold tribal choker which decorates her long neck. Her features are striking, but are overshadowed by her unnaturally large glowing yellow eyes. She is by far the most physically intimidating of the three judges.

The judges ignore my presence and seem more preoccupied with their cell phones than greeting me. Apparently, the only reception here is cell reception. I wonder if monsters waste as much time on Facebook as humans do?

Sinn leans in close to me and whispers, "That's Whanung on the right; he beats to his own drum. He's not officially affiliated with any faction. He claims he's a Korean demi-god, the father of Korean laws. What I know is that he is long lived and really good with a sword. Pavo liked him; they were drinking buddies, but he did not trust him. Said he was always too clever for his own good."

I nod, prompting her to go on.

Sinn continues to whisper, "In the middle is Sabra, she is the last Night Scorpion, part woman, part scorpion. She's not a were, she can't change her body, she's always trapped between the two species. Her tail—"

"—She has a tail?"

Sinn nods. "Makes it difficult for her to go out in public. She's beautiful, but don't let her beauty fool you—she's deadly. The venom from a single sting from her tail will kill. It's said that night scorpion eggs can only be fertilized by another night scorpion. Without a surviving male, her species is doomed. The last male of her species was killed by a werespider over a hundred years ago. For centuries, night scorpions and werespiders were at war—they hate each other, but that doesn't mean she's on our side. Pavo always said Sabra was a true believer in the rule of law. She could always be counted on to follow the law, regardless of the consequences. Pavo respected her for her principles. I think they may have had a romantic relationship at one point, although he'd never admit it."

I raise one eyebrow at the confession.

Sinn raises hers back in reply. "On the left is Phulcus. You two have already met. I don't like him."

I smile as I turn my attention from the judges' bench to the opposing counsel table. I am constantly amazed by the outfits people wear to court. Flip flops, stripper heels, mini-skirts, tank tops, bandannas, leathers, biker cuts, gang colors, I've seen it all. I mean, for God's sake, your freedoms on the line; please have the courtesy to dress appropriately for the occasion. Lycocide is wearing a red tracksuit with three white stripes running up the sides, and a wife-beater. #WTF. It's comforting to know there are just as many idiot monsters as idiot humans.

On the bright side, Lycocide appears to be unarmed. Then again, he can turn into a nearly indestructible giant spider with knife-like fangs and sword-like appendages. So I guess a weapon would be overkill.

I'm not afraid to admit it; the Advocate standing next to Lycocide is a handsome fellow. Tan, skinny, with long flowing dirty blond hair and piercing blue eyes. He kind of looks like Thor's much shorter brother. He's probably only about five-foot-seven and weighs a buck fifty—perfect Hollywood proportions. Thor's younger brother is wearing white shoes and an expensive royal blue suit with dark blue pinstripes, a white shirt, and a pink tie. There is a razor-sharp silver sword, with a decorative cross pommel hung on his hip. He looks like he just gated in from representing a villain in an episode of medieval *Miami Vice*.

I approach Lycocide's Advocate, while intentionally ignoring Lycocide, and offer my hand in greeting.

"Colt Valentine. Nice to meet you."

Miami Vice grimaces like it is beneath him to touch me. I leave my hand extended, until he accepts it and we shake. I hope I give him warts. I don't have warts; I just hope he gets them.

"Jacob Paul Prestegard," he says, with the pompous flair that only comes from royals and old money. I cringe at the use of his middle name. Right off the bat, I know I'm not going to like this douchebag.

"Mr. Valentine, why don't you do all of us a favor and withdraw the complaint? This is a waste of time. I know you're new to this, but this isn't how things are done." Jacob Paul Prestegard speaks to me in the same way all aristocrats speak to peasants—while holding his nose, and praying my peasant stench doesn't ruin his fancy suit. I really dislike this jerk-off. It's only been thirty seconds, and he's already tried to pull the 'I'm more experienced than you' card. What a dick!

Instead of a witty retort, I wink at him, and then walk back to my table. I firmly believe it's important to try and get into your opponent's head. Zig when they think you're going to zag. Be polite when they expect you to be aggressive. Be a dick over something that should be a non-issue. Be unpredictable.

Just as I reach my table, Judge Sabra's voice echoes through the courtroom. "Advocates, may I please have your appearances."

Jacob Paul Prestegard responds first: "Jacob Paul Prestegard, appearing on behalf of the *falsely* accused Lycocide the werespider."

Shit, is there a formal appearance I need to make, or is it just my name? I probably should have asked Sinn. If I was a United States District Attorney, I'd be Colt Valentine appearing on behalf of the United States. If I was a California District Attorney, I'd be Colt Valentine appearing on behalf of the people of the great State of California. Who or what am I appearing on behalf of? I hate being unprepared. Time to follow the first rule of being a lawyer: when in doubt, make some shit up. "Colt Valentine, appearing on behalf of the Magna-Concordat, and this is my—" oh shit, what do I call Sinn? She isn't an Advocate, but calling her my assistant will probably earn me another swift kick to the nuts. "—my ... colleague, Sinn Palatinus, who will be assisting me today." I point towards Sinn with my left arm. I don't get any disapproving looks from anyone, so I must have said the right thing.

Judge Sabra addresses the courtroom, "Good morning. My name is Judge Sabra. Sitting beside me are Judges Whanung and Phulcus. We are here today because a member of the Concordat has been accused of breaking one of our laws. Without the rule of law, there is only chaos. The Concordat is a joining of different races, with different beliefs, and different values. For more than a thousand years, we Concordat citizens have put our differences aside for the common good and we have lived together, under one set of laws. The Magna-Concordat and its laws are a symbol of our strength and unity. I, for one, am proud to be a Concordat citizen. When one of our citizens breaks one of our laws it harms us all. This Court has always been, and will continue to be, a place of justice. Lycocide the werespider stands before this Court today, accused of crimes against the Magna-Concordat. He will be treated with fairness under the law and be given every opportunity to prove his innocence and to exercise his legal rights. If he is found guilty, he will feel the full punishing weight and force of our law. Mr. Prestegard, is there any reason we should not proceed today?"

Advocate Prestegard clears his throat. "Madame Judge, my client hasn't done anything wrong. This is a case of an Advocate abusing his responsibilities and taking advantage of a citi—"

Judge Sabra interrupts him, "—Advocate Prestegard, I asked if you were ready to proceed. It's a yes or no question. Answer it with a yes or no."

Advocate Prestegard doesn't appear fazed by the scolding whatsoever. "Yes, the defense is ready," he replies.

Sinn whispers to me, "Jacob's a vampire." For some reason, I feel a twinge of jealousy when Sinn says the name 'Jacob.' There's familiarity there, they clearly have some sort of past. I wonder if they dated?

Judge Sabra turns to me; her yellow eyes sparkle with intelligence, "Advocate Valentine, are you ready to proceed?"

"Yes, Your Honor, but there's an issue that needs to be addressed before we begin."

I can feel Sinn's questioning eyes burning holes in the side of my head.

Judge Sabra smiles, showing a mouth full of sharp needle-like teeth. "Advocate Valentine, we don't use the term *Your Honor*. We are equals. I'm an Advocate—just like you. I just happen to be acting as a judge in this matter. You may call me Judge, or if you insist on being more formal, the appropriate appellation for an Advocate, including yourself, is Lord."

Call me new school, but I'm not calling anyone My Lord. "Thank you, Judge," I respond. "As I was saying, there's an issue that needs to be addressed before I begin my case in chief. It's an uncomfortable topic, one that the Court might prefer to address in private?"

Judge Phulcus' inhuman voice cuts through the air like venom infecting a wound. "We don't keep secrets in this courtroom. If you have something to say—say it."

"I'm glad you feel that way, Judge Phulcus," I reply, refusing to be intimidated. "Judges, I apologize for my lack of familiarity with the procedures of this Court, but I need to disclose *ex parte* conversations I had with the judges on this panel about this case."

Judge Phulcus screeches, "He's a liar! He's human. We can't trust anything he has to say! He doesn't understand our ways."

Judge Sabra turns to Judge Phulcus and says in a booming voice, "Let him speak."

Judge Phulcus' hate-filled eyes narrow and home in on me, hurling threats of violence, but he heeds Judge Sabra's command.

The eyes of Judge Whanung, although he maintains his robot-like exterior, are alive. He seems to be thoroughly enjoying this, almost as if he planned it.

I clear my throat and continue, "I met with Advocate Whanung on Friday. At the time, I had no idea he was a judge on this case. He introduced himself and asked me what crime the accused, Lycocide, had committed. I told him it was inappropriate for me to discuss an ongoing case. He accepted my response and that was the end of our discussion in relation to the facts of this case."

"This is entirely inappropriate!" shouts Advocate Prestegard. "Judge Whanung must be excused from overseeing this trial. My client cannot get a fair trial if the prosecution is having secret meetings with a judge. It doesn't matter what the human says they talked about; any contact is inappropriate!"

Phulcus adjusts the aim of his eye daggers from me to Advocate Prestegard. He realizes they've just stepped on a landmine and it's about to blow up in their faces. Unfortunately for him, Prestegard is clueless. Phulcus must not have told him about our meeting.

Judge Whanung speaks, "Advocate Prestegard, I understand your objection. Does your client waive his right to a multi-judge panel?" I catch it. I can tell Phulcus catches it from the look on his face, but Judge Whanung's careful phrasing of the waiver sails completely over Advocate Prestegard's head.

Before Phulcus can intervene, Advocate Prestegard puts an end to any influence he may have had on the outcome of this trial. "Yes, my client waives his right to a multi-judge panel." The smug look on Advocate Prestegard's face is priceless.

Judge Sabra addresses Whanung, "Judge Whanung, do you deny speaking with Advocate Valentine?"

"No, Advocate Valentine spoke truthfully."

"Then you may step down from the bench."

Whanung gives me a knowing smile as he steps down from the bench, crosses the well, and takes a seat in the gallery. It's as if he planned the entire thing. How did he know? I hadn't even met Phulcus yet. Either he got lucky, and I'm giving him way too much credit for this turn of events, or he's playing the game at a whole different level than me. I'm going to have to watch him in the future.

Once Whanung has taken a seat in the gallery, Judge Sabra turns back to me. "Advocate Valentine, you stated that you need to disclose *ex parte* conversations you had with *judges* on this panel about this case. Did I hear that correctly?"

"Yes, Judge. You did."

"Please continue." It's clear that Judge Sabra has also done the math. Three minus two equals one, which means Prestegard is the only one in the dark.

Before I can speak, Judge Phulcus interrupts and addresses the courtroom, "In the interest of justice, I also need to excuse myself. I also met with Mr. Valentine. I don't believe there was any inappropriate *ex parte* communication between myself and Advocate Valentine. I don't recall discussing the case at all, but in light of

Advocate Prestegard's comments about "*any contact,*" and his subsequent *waiver* of a multi-judge panel," Phulcus glares at Prestegard while he speaks, "it is in the best interest of justice for me to step down."

Phulcus is cleverer than I thought. He knows I'm about to drop the boot on him and he has the foresight to crawl out of the way, and to do it in such a manner that he appears like he's the good guy, like he's the one protecting the integrity of this trial. I'm starting to doubt whether or not I'm in the same league as these Advocates, or even playing the same sport. They've had centuries to perfect their craft. I'm basically a child playing a game with adults.

Prestegard finally realizes the trap he's sprung and immediately tries to backtrack. "Wait … if Judge Phulcus says there wasn't any inappropriate communications, his word is good enough for me. There's no reason for him to step down. My client has no objection to him remaining on the bench."

Phulcus' angry look momentarily subsides as he envisions a path to keep him on the panel. With only two judges on the panel, his clutter mate is assured an acquittal. It takes a majority vote to convict someone under the laws of the Concordat.

Seeing the trial slipping from my grasp, I decide to stone cold bluff and push all my chips into the middle. I just hope Sinn doesn't act surprised and give the gambit away. "I have a video from my office internal security cameras. Why don't we all watch the video and then we can decide the appropriateness of the conversation I had with Mr. Phulcus?"

Phulcus' face becomes rage itself. He hisses, "That will not be necessary. I've already stepped down." Phulcus scurries across the well and takes a seat in the gallery.

My bluff worked. Phulcus doesn't want anyone in this courtroom to hear the substance of our discussion. He cares more about protecting himself than his clutter mate. Typical lone-spider mentality.

Prestegard looks befuddled, but he's not done fighting yet. "Lord, my client never agreed to have his case heard by a single judge. We request a continuance and ask the Court to assign a new panel of three judges."

Judge Sabra leans forward across the bench and says with utter disbelief of his claim in her voice, "Advocate Prestegard, did your client not waive his right to a multi-judge panel?"

Advocate Prestegard, in a whiny and defeated tone, answers, "Yeeesss, but—"

"Motion denied," rules Judge Sabra with finality. Judge Sabra then turns back to me. "Advocate Valentine, unless there is anything else, please proceed."

"Thank you, Judge."

Chapter Forty

Sinn gave me the 411 on what I'm expected to do at this trial. It's not all that different from a Grand Jury proceeding or a Probable Cause hearing in human courts. Essentially, I'm the prosecutor, except they call it the accuser, and I need to convince the court that Lycocide committed a crime. I get to present evidence by either calling witnesses and/or publishing exhibits. The defense then may, if it chooses, cross-examine the witnesses I call. At the conclusion of the Accuser's evidence, I may give a closing argument in which I identify the crime that has been committed and summarize how each element of that crime has been proven by the evidence, and then the Court makes an initial determination whether or not I submitted sufficient evidence showing that Lycocide committed a crime against the Magna-Concordat.

If the Court determines that a crime has been committed, then the accused must enter a plea of either guilt or innocence, or elect his right to an Ordeal by Combat.

If Lycocide pleads guilty, he is permitted to make a statement to the Court and then the Court determines his punishment, which I hope is long and painful—even deadly.

If Lycocide pleads innocent, the defense gets to put on its evidentiary case by calling witnesses and/or publishing exhibits, and I can cross-examine those witnesses.

At the conclusion of the defense's evidence, I may present a rebuttal case, meaning I can call witnesses or publish exhibits that rebut any of the evidence presented by the defense.

After the rebuttal case, the defense is given an opportunity to make a closing argument, followed by my rebuttal argument, and then the judge must make a decision of guilt or innocence.

If Lycocide elects not to plead his guilt or innocence, but rather invokes his right to an Ordeal by Combat, the trial is over, and the survivor is the winner. If I die, Lycocide is innocent of all charges. If I live, Lycocide was guilty, but dead. It's all quite final—no appeals or room for error.

"Judge Sabra, I waive my right to an opening remark. I believe the evidence will speak for itself."

I'm not required to give an opening remark so I'm not going to give one. My case is flimsy at best; there's no need to highlight that fact. I'd rather let the evidence speak for itself. I have one goal during my presentation of evidence and that is to introduce sufficient evidence such that the Court believes a crime against the Magna-Concordat has been committed. At that point, the burden will have shifted to the defense to prove Lycocide's innocence. In laymen's terms, I'll have made it out of the first round and I'll have a puncher's chance at shocking the world.

The toughest part of a trial is not letting yourself get overwhelmed by the amount of work you need to do to prove your case. A trial is like running a marathon. If you think about how long it is, how far you still have to run, you won't ever finish; but if you concentrate on the next step, the next stride, or the next mile marker, you will make it across that finish line.

Judge Sabra nods in understanding. "Call your first witness."

Joycee is my first witness. I'm concerned that this is going to be too much for her, but we don't have much of a choice; it's either put her on the stand, or let Lycocide walk, and the only way I'm letting him walk is over my dead body or directly into the path of a truck.

"The Accuser calls forensic computer specialist Joycee Baird to the stand."

Joycee nervously stands up and walks from the gallery bench to the stone witness podium. Her eyes are focused on the ground in front of her. She's trembling, but wearing a brave face. Despite my concerns, I'm really proud of how far she's come in the past week.

When she took the stand in her own case, she was a nervous wreck, afraid of her own shadow and wanted to flee the courtroom at the first chance she got. Today, she bravely stands before a court of monsters, willing to give testimony against a psychopath, who she's watched video butcher more than fifty people. She's an inspiration; seeing her valiantly standing there at the witness podium makes my self-doubts seem small and insignificant. If she can overcome the horrors she's been through—I can do this.

"Judge Sabra, may I enter the well?"

This isn't Texas, so I probably wouldn't have gotten shot for entering the well without asking, and there aren't any bailiffs, at least none that I can see. Then again, Sinn did say this judge had a wicked tail. It's probably smarter to be safe and ask to use the well than be sorry and end up stung by a giant poisonous scorpion tail.

"Yes, you may enter the well," answers Judge Sabra.

"Judge, I also plan on using some video evidence with this witness. May my staff set it up while I begin my examination?"

Judge Sabra answers, "Yes."

Sinn quickly sets up the projector screen and turns on the projector already situated on our counsel table.

I round the counsel table and stand in the well at an angle so that Judge, the witness, the defense, and most of the gallery can all see me. When I reach my destination, I pause for a moment to collect my thoughts. I intend to charge the accused with Treason by Disclosure; that's the only law my team and I think we have a shot at proving. In order to win, I need to prove all of the following:

1. *That the accused disclosed the existence of the Magna-Concordat, or a Citizen to a human(s); and,*

2. *That the disclosure was intentional; and,*

3. *That the disclosure endangered the Magna-Concordat, or the lives of a citizen(s); and,*

4. *That the accused was not justified in his disclosure.*

I don't expect Joycee to be on the stand very long. I mainly need her to explain to the Court what the videos are and where she found them. I need her testimony to help prove, Element (1) *that he disclosed his existence to the human public*; and Element (2) *that it was intentional*; as far as Element (3) *that disclosure endangered the Magna-Concordat*, and Element (4) that the accused was not justified in the disclosure, I'm still working out how to prove them. We're going to need a little help and a lot of luck.

"Ms. Baird, you're good with computers?"

"Yes."

"You're a programmer?"

"Yes."

"Is it true that you currently work for me as a computer consultant?"

"I do."

"Could you tell us a little bit about your professional background?"

"I was a senior programmer at a Silicon Valley tech company for the past four years, and before that, I was in school at Stanford. I graduated Magna Cum Laude with a degree in computer science."

"Did I ask you to assist in the investigation of the accused Lycocide the werespider?"

"You did."

"Could you please tell us what you found, if anything?"

"I found a website where there were thirty-eight videos posted online by a person who went by the internet handle, Wolfspider666."

"Did you watch these videos?"

"I did."

"Is there anyone in the courtroom today who appeared in any of those videos?"

"Yes." Joycee points at Lycocide. "Him. He was in all the videos."

Lycocide hisses and threateningly bears his fangs at Joycee, who begins to tremble.

Judge Sabra smashes her wooden gavel onto the stone bench. A melodic sound pierces through the courtroom. "Advocate Prestegard, please control your client."

Advocate Prestegard shrugs and does absolutely nothing to curtail his client's behavior.

I walk over to my desk and pretend to shuffle through some papers. What I'm really doing is trying to get Joycee's attention, I want to distract her, get her focused on something other than Lycocide's fangs. It works; her eyes follow me all the way to the desk.

Movement can be a powerful tool for a lawyer. Some lawyers pace or move a lot when they're questioning a witness; I think that's stupid. Each time you move, all eyes in the courtroom are going to follow you, to find out what you're going to do. If you remain still, they focus on the witness, which is typically what you want, particularly when it's your witness and they're giving information you want the court to hear. Now that I have Joycee's attention again, I set the papers back down and walk back into the well to continue my questioning.

"Were the thirty-eight videos similar in subject matter?"

"Yes, they were."

"Generally speaking, what was the subject matter of the videos?"

"Terror," she says. "In each of the videos, he changes into a half-spider, half-man, and torments, tortures, kills, and drinks people ... he smiled as his victims screamed."

Lycocide smiles as if he is reliving a warm memory. It's disturbing, and makes me angry, but I try to ignore it. This isn't the time for me to lose my cool.

"Did you count the victims and, if so, how many were there?"

"Fifty-three. There were fifty-three, including children." Joycee starts to tear up. I recognize she needs a break. Time to switch gears for a moment. I turn and face Judge Sabra. "At this point, Judge, I would move the thirty-eight videos into evidence."

Judge Sabra looks to Advocate Prestegard to see if there's an objection. When he doesn't respond, she rules, "Admitted."

I nod politely, signaling my agreement with the Court's ruling. "Judge, I'm not going to play all of the videos; it would take too much time. There are more than forty hours of video in total, and much of it is difficult to watch. I do think it's important for the Court to see and understand the general content of the videos. I've selected about ten minutes of video which I believe fairly summarizes and is representative of the evidence. I would like to play that ten minutes if I may."

Judge Sabra looks to Prestegard again, and asks, "Any objection?" Advocate Prestegard shakes his head no, and then Judge Sabra says to me, "You may."

Sinn plays ten minutes of video for the Court. The clip includes footage of Lycocide changing from a man to a spider; Lycocide torturing; Lycocide killing; Lycocide feeding, and it ends with the clip of Lycocide taunting the parents of the newborn while he drinks the life from it. While the video's playing, I watch the Judge and the gallery. Despite the gruesome nature of the video clips, the mood of the courtroom remains the same. No one turns away, or makes any sounds of disgust. Human death appears to mean nothing to these beings. When the clip ends, I do my best to disguise the disgust I'm feeling for the lack of humanity in the room. There's nothing I can do about it, except continue my examination.

"Ms. Baird, were you able to determine who posted the videos?"

"In part. I was able to trace them back to an IP address."

"What's an IP address?"

"An Internet Protocol address is a numerical label assigned to a computer. Basically, it's your computer's street address."

"What did you do next?"

"I traced the IP address to an actual street address in Redding, California."

"What did you do with the address?"

"I gave it to Wilson Scarborough, an investigator who works for you."

I nod in encouragement, pleased with her responses thus far. "I will ask Mr. Scarborough what he did with that address shortly, but I have a few more questions for you first. What's the name of the website where the videos were posted?"

"X-change."

"How many users are on X-change?"

"That is a difficult question to answer. The number is constantly fluctuating as people connect and then disconnect. I would say a few thousand at any one time."

"Is it true that any of the users could have downloaded those videos just like you did?"

"Yes."

"Could you post a video on there without knowing somebody else could watch it or download it?"

"I don't think so."

"What about thirty-eight videos? Could you post thirty-eight videos onto X-change without knowing others could watch or download them?"

"No."

"How long would it take to upload the thirty-eight videos at issue here?"

"Several hours, if not longer. It depends on numerous factors like internet speed."

"Do you agree, as a computer forensic expert, that it would take an investment of time to upload those videos? It's not something you can do by accident?"

"I agree."

"Is there any way to know how many times those videos were downloaded or watched by others?"

"Not really with any specificity, but I can tell you they were popular on X-change. So, a lot."

"Are they still on the internet today?" Joycee squirms in her chair. I can tell she doesn't want to answer the question, which is confusing, as we've been through this multiple times. I nod, signaling it's okay to answer.

Reluctantly Joycee says, "No, they were there yesterday, but I checked again this morning while I was sitting in the courtroom, and they're gone. They've been scrubbed from the internet. There's no trace of them, which is weird—it's practically impossible to delete something from the internet."

I frown. That's not the answer I expected. Lycocide makes a surprised noise, almost as if he is offended that someone would take down his art. He scowls at his attorney. Prestegard ignores the angry stare; his lips curl up at the edges. It's obvious he had something to do with the removal of the videos and I'm willing to bet that one of the techno mages, like the one who made the app on Pavo's phone, was also involved.

"Thank you, Ms. Baird. I have no further questions at this time."

"Advocate Prestegard, do you have any questions for the witness?" asks Judge Sabra.

Prestegard stands up. "I do," he says and circles his counsel table until he is facing the witness.

"Ms. Baird, you watched all the videos?"

"Yes."

"Other than my client, did you see anyone in any of the videos who wasn't human?"

"I don't know. I don't ... think so."

"It's true, isn't it, that *all* of the victims, every one of them, were human?"

"I don't know. You would have to ask Mr. Scarborough. He investigated their backgrounds."

"I will do that. But as far as you know, that's true, isn't it? They were all human?"

Joycee hesitates, looking to me for guidance, but I remain a statue. She looks down at the floor while she answers, "Yes, as far as I know."

"Let's talk about this website, X-change. That is what it's called, right?"

"Yes."

"Is this a reputable website?"

"I don't understand the question."

"Is this the type of website human parents let their children visit for information?"

Joycee snickers. "No."

"You laughed when you said no. You laughed because X-change is an extremely underground website, an illegal website, where things like child pornography are traded, isn't that right?

"… that's right."

"X-change isn't CNN, MSNBC, or Fox News. The general human public doesn't go there for the news, do they?"

"I guess not."

"You'd agree that a lot of the videos shared on X-change are fake? Fake snuff films, porno's where girls who are eighteen pretend to be minors, stuff like that."

"I guess ... some."

"When you saw the videos for the first time, admit it, you didn't think they were real, did you?"

"Yes, I did. I know exactly what monsters are capable of," answers Joycee with anger in her voice.

Prestegard flinches; he must not know she already knew about monsters, but one misstep isn't going to cause him to back down. "When a user is on X-change they're only identifiable by their online handle like Wolfspider666, correct?"

"Yes."

"You can't tell by their online handle alone if they are human or not. Can you?"

"No, I can't."

"It's possible that every single download of those videos was done by a non-human. Isn't it?"

"No, that's not possible."

Prestegard frowns again. He clearly didn't expect Joycee to put up such a fight. "If you don't know if the users are human or not, how can you know they're not all non-humans?"

Joycee smiles. "For one thing, I'm human and I downloaded them."

Prestegard clenches his fist in frustration. "Other than yourself, you don't know if the downloads were done by humans or not, do you?"

"I ... don't."

"No more questions. Actually, hold on. One more question. How long ago was the first video of my client eating a human posted on X-change?"

"About five years ago."

"*Five* years ago? Did I hear that right?" Prestegard asks.

Joycee quietly answers "yes."

Prestegard smiles, he knows he finished on a high point. "No more questions."

"Advocate Valentine, anything further with this witness?" asks Judge Sabra.

"No, Judge," I answer.

Joycee exits the witness stand and returns to her seat in the gallery. I steal a glance at Sinn. From the look on her face, I can tell she's having the same thought I am—we're fucked. Jacob Paul Prestegard just drove a truck through our theory of the case. I can use Wilson's testimony to prove that Lycocide lived at the address where the videos were posted, thereby proving he posted the videos, but I don't see how, in light of Joycee's testimony that the videos were up there for five years, I can prove <u>Element</u> (3): *That the disclosure endangered the Magna-Concordat, or the lives of a citizen(s).*

That's five years during which the videos never made the news and no humans beat down the doors of Concordat citizens seeking revenge. In short, either no humans have seen the videos, no humans believe the videos are real, or the ones that have seen them just don't care. Now they're off the internet and there's no risk of future discovery. Any way you slice it, the case is dead-on-arrival. Even if I prove all of the *other* elements, I don't see how I can win this. The Court is not going to believe these videos have put the Magna-Concordat or its citizens in danger.

The worst part is the smug look on Jacob Paul Prestegard's face. He knows we're fucked. God, I hate losing, especially to smug, middle-name-using, old-money elitist pricks.

Chapter Forty-One

I wait patiently while Judge Sabra jots down some notes. Finally, she looks up and we make eye contact. "Advocate Valentine, do you have another witness?"

There's nothing I can do at this point but keep going. I'm probably going to have to fold my tent at some point, but I need to find a way to do it in a dignified manner. Better to have the Court toss the case than look like a quitter. "I do, Judge Sabra. The Accuser calls investigator Wilson Scarborough to the stand."

Wilson calmly walks over to me and hands me his old tattered briefcase. "Hold this for me at your desk. We might need to use it later." I don't really want to touch it, at least, not without gloves; but he's insistent, so I take it, making as little skin contact as possible, and quickly set it on the counsel table.

Wilson takes his place at the witness podium, and I take my position in the well. Over the years, Wilson and I have done this dance in dozens of cases. There's nothing to be nervous about. This is just another routine day at the office, absolutely nothing out of the ordinary—other than the fact that the judge has a giant scorpion tail, the defense attorney's a vampire, and the defendant's a werespider who would very much like to rip my head off and drink me dry.

"Your name is Wilson Scarborough and you're an investigator with my office?"

"Yes, I am."

"How long have you been an investigator?"

"Nearly fifteen years."

"Tell us about your training. Did you go to school?"

"No, it's all OJT."

"OJT?" I ask.

"On-the-job training."

"Thank you. Before you became an investigator, were you in the military?"

"Yes."

"What did you do the in the military?"

Wilson smiles. This is familiar ground, an inside joke between the two of us. "You've asked me this before, Mr. Valentine. I'm going to give you the same answer today that I give you every time you ask about my service—it's none of your business."

I return the smile. "Can't blame me for being curious, can you?"

Wilson just keeps on smiling. This back and forth between us may seem innocent and a waste of time, but it's more than that. Levity is important in a courtroom; it helps break-up the monotony of the proceeding and increases cognitive function, by providing rest periods or breaks between the delivery of important information. In other words—it sets the mood.

"We just heard from Ms. Baird. She told us she gave you the address of a location in Redding, California. An address where the videos were posted. Did she in fact do that?"

"Yes, she did.

"What did you do?"

"I drove up to Redding to see who lived there."

"Were you able to determine who the occupant was?"

"Yes, him, the accused." Wilson turns and points at Lycocide. "That dapper fella' in the tracksuit." Lycocide growls. Wilson gives him a wink.

"How do you know that?" I ask.

"He chased me off his property."

"And then?"

"He followed me to a bar in downtown Redding, a real crap-hole, my kind of place."

"What happened next?"

"I feared for my safety, so I called you."

"Then what happened?"

"You showed up, had a discussion with Mr. Tracksuit, during which he admitted he was the person who posted the videos. I think his exact words were, '*I like to share with others. I'm a giver.*'"

"Thank you. I have no further questions at this time." I walk back to my table with my head held high, as if everything is going according to plan; unfortunately, it isn't. That's not a knock-on Wilson; he did his job. The evidence that is already admitted to the Court proves, Element (1) *Lycocide posted the videos*; and Element (2) *he did it intentionally*.

Element (4) *that the accused was not justified in his disclosure* is what we lawyers, and golfers, call a give-me. There is almost never a justification for disclosure. Element (4) is a safety valve for duress. That one-in-a-million case where someone puts a gun to your head and makes you do it; otherwise, like here, it's a freebie. Lycocide is too proud to try to argue that he posted the videos under duress.

The overriding problem is that I still can't prove Element (3) *That the disclosure endangered the Magna-Concordat, or the lives of a citizen(s)*, and I'm out of evidence.

Judge Sabra finishes taking her notes and then asks, "Advocate Prestegard, do you have any questions for the witness?"

"I do."

My head snaps up in surprise. Why is Prestegard asking questions? He's already won. All he has to do is to keep his trap shut and ask the judge for a dismissal. I turn back and scan the gallery, Phulcus is shifting uncomfortably in his seat; clearly, he and I are experiencing the same thought—mainly, that Prestegard is a jackass who likes to hear himself talk more than he likes to win.

"Mr. Scarborough, I understand you did some investigation into the individuals in the video, their backgrounds and such," asks Prestegard.

"I did."

"All of the individuals in the video other than my client were human. Weren't they?"

"As far as I can tell. Yes."

"What type of *humans* were they?"

"I don't understand the question."

"Were they important *humans*? Are they the type of *human* that will be missed? Have there been massive search parties? Have any of the disappearances made the national news?" Each time Prestegard says the word *human*, it sounds like he's trying not to vomit.

Wilson snaps, "No, the disappearances haven't made the news. Nearly all were taken while hiking or camping in Trinity National Forest. The forest's entrance and exit records have been doctored, probably by your client who works there as a ranger. Most of the victims were homeless drifters or out-of-towners on vacation, but they had families, people who loved them. Every human life is important."

"But you admit, they were only *human*," says Prestegard dramatically.

"Yes, they *were* human," answers Wilson, conceding the point. As a professional witness, even though he's angry, he knows better than to fight an important point. Fighting only brings more attention to the point and makes them even more powerful.

Prestegard arrogantly exits the well to stand next to his client. He looks up at the Court. "I have no further questions for this *human*. My Lord, this farce of a trial has gone on long enough. Advocate Valentine is wasting the Court's time. Killing *humans* is not murder—*humans* are food. Lycocide has done nothing wrong. He certainly hasn't committed Treason by Disclosure, which is what I imagine Mr. Valentine is going to try and argue.

"Admittedly, my client, Lycocide, made a poor decision when he posted his feedings on the internet, but no harm came of it. If any harm was going to come of it—it would have already happened. Those videos were up on that website for nearly five years, and the *humans*, if they ever even saw them, ignored them. The Court should dismiss the complaint. This has all been a colossal waste of time." Prestegard glares at me.

Judge Sabra turns and looks at me. "Advocate Valentine, do you have any more evidence?"

Time slows. Judge Sabra's words muffle and elongate until the words are unrecognizable. Something isn't right. My intuition is telling me—I'm missing something. I quickly run through the testimony in my head, looking for something, anything, I can use … and then it hits me. Wilson said something that just might change everything. Time speeds back up, "Judge, I'm not quite through examining this witness."

Prestegard gives me a suspicious sidewise glance. Judge Sabra pauses for a moment, as if considering my statement, and then responds, "Advocate Valentine, you may proceed."

I circle back into the well. There is something itching in my subconscious mind, a scab begging to be picked, the beginning of a plan, and it all starts with something Pavo said to me: "*There are numerous forms of government amongst the different Concordat races. Regardless of the type of government, the Magna-Concordat generically defines them as kingdoms.*" It's so obvious, I can't believe I didn't see it before. I know how to win this case.

"Mr. Scarborough, I just have a few more questions for you."

He nods. I can tell he is a bit uncertain, and has no idea where I'm intending to go, but he's enough of a professional that I'm not worried about it.

"Where did you say the victims were taken from?"

Wilson looks at me with confusion on his face. He hesitates and then answers, "Trinity National Forest."

I smile to reassure him and to let him know he is on the right track. "How do you know that?"

"Well … nearly all the victims either rented campgrounds or signed into the park."

"Why would someone sign in to a National Forest?" I ask.

"When you hike certain trails, it's a good idea to sign in, and give the Rangers an estimate of how long you're going to be out there. Particularly if you're camping overnight. If you don't return by your time estimate, it gives the rangers a heads-up that you might be lost. If you don't sign in, no one will come looking for you."

"How do we know all of the victims were taken from the National Forest?"

"Some of the victims never signed out. So we know those ones were definitely taken in the forest."

"What about the ones that did sign out?" I ask.

"I don't think any did. There were signatures, but they were faked."

"What do you mean?"

"They were all signed out in the exact same handwriting, which is different from the handwriting they used to sign in. I compared the handwriting to Lycocide's and it looks like a match."

"Where did Lycocide work?" I ask.

"At the National Forest. He was a park ranger."

"So, he would have had access to the logs."

"Yes."

"To sum up your testimony, Lycocide's victims were all taken from the National Forest. Do I have that correct?"

"Yes."

"You might say he used the Forest as his personal hunting grounds?" I ask.

"Yes. I guess you could say that," responds Wilson.

"Is Trinity owned by the Government?"

"It is," answers Wilson. "It's a federally designated forest and it's managed by the U.S. Forest Service. It's the largest national forest in California."

"Does the Government allow hunting within the forest?"

Wilson frowns. "Only in specific areas, with a license."

"Does the Government issue a license to hunt humans in Trinity National Forest?"

Wilson chuckles. "No, they don't."

"Thank you. I have no further questions."

Judge Sabra has a thoughtful look on her face. She turns to Advocate Prestegard. "Anything further?"

Prestegard says, "No, I don't know what that was all about, but it didn't change anything. My client is still innocent."

Wilson casually retreats to his seat in the gallery.

"I think it changes everything," I argue while starring directly to Prestegard. "Judge Sabra, the Accuser rests his case. The evidence is clear and undisputed. Lycocide caught, paralyzed, and sucked the life out of those poor souls in those videos. As much as I disagree with the law, and believe in the value of human life, I understand, that the act of killing a human, by itself, is not *currently* a recognized crime under the Magna-Concordat. I don't like the law, but I accept it." I can almost hear Prestegard's smile. "However, it is crime under the Magna-Concordat to trespass against the venison in a Royal Forest. Which is exactly what Lycocide did here."

There's an angry outburst from the back of the gallery where Phulcus is sitting with his cronies. Lycocide screams and hurls threats at me, while Prestegard does everything he can, to hold him back. I should be concerned about Lycocide's claws; instead, I keep wondering how much of this Pavo planned and how much Whanung actually knew. I feel like I was led down this path from the start. Were they working together? Am I still Pavo's pawn or am I being paranoid? Was this all me and my team?

I glance over at Sinn; she hasn't reacted at all. She is either the world's best actress, or was confident I would pull it out the entire time, or maybe she was in on it with Pavo the whole time. She remains a mystery to me.

Judge Sabra yells, "There will be order in this Court!"

Lycocide quiets down, but continues with the threatening body language. Prestegard shouts, "Judge, this is unacceptable! Royal Trespass. That is utter nonsense. That law hasn't been enforced in centuries!"

"That doesn't change the fact that it's the law," I say. "It's in that fancy Concordat Book of Laws right there on your desk. Look it up."

"Judge, this is an outrage!" says Prestegard. "Trinity is not a Royal Forest."

Judge Sabra looks to me for a response.

"Under Magna-Concordat Law, the United States Government is considered a Kingdom. Therefore, under the law, a National Forest is treated the same as a Royal Forest. The facts are undisputed. Lycocide hunted game in a Royal Forest, without first seeking permission. That's against the law. *Humans* are just food, aren't they? Isn't that what you said, Prestegard?"

Lycocide sheds Prestegard and stands nose-to-nose with me. "I am going to kill you, puto."

Judge Sabra yells, "Lycocide, if you touch him—your life is forfeited! That is the law."

Lycocide turns and faces the bench and Judge Sabra. "I want to invoke my right to Ordeal by Combat."

Judge Sabra pauses and then calmly responds, "I haven't even ruled yet. You don't have to make—"

"—I don't care. I invoke my right."

Judge Sabra lets Lycocide finish and then says, "I need you to understand; you do not have to invoke your right to Ordeal by Combat–yet. You can wait for my ruling on whether or not the accuser has met his burden and then you can have some time to talk it over with your advocate."

"No!" shouts Lycocide. "Enough of this already—I want to kill him!"

Prestegard grabs his client and tries to talk some sense into him, but Lycocide pushes him to the floor and shouts at me, "Fight me, mayate! I want to make you scream like I made your secretary scream."

Judge Sabra addresses me, "Advocate Valentine, Lycocide has invoked his right to an Ordeal by Combat. He has issued you a challenge. You can accept and fight him to the death, or you can withdraw your complaint against him."

I look up at the Judge and nod in understanding. A murderous werespider has challenged me to a duel to the death, one I can't possibly win. I can't help but think to myself, how did I get here?

Chapter Forty-Two

The gallery is screaming for blood, and trying to encourage me to accept Lycocide's challenge. Sinn looks concerned, but we discussed this and made a plan. I'm supposed to ask for twenty-four hours to think about it. Joycee is sitting quietly with a look of absolute trust on her face. She believes in me. My eyes drift to Phulcus, and my pulse quickens. No matter what happens, I'm not going to let him get away with murdering Trudy. As far as I am concerned, he was the shooter; Lycocide was merely the gun that killed her. Phulcus is responsible for her death and he is going to pay.

As I scan the rest of the courtroom, I catch Wilson out of the corner of my eye, trying to get my attention. He has a determined look on his face and is subtly trying to point at something with his head. I turn and look in the direction he's pointing and see the tattered briefcase sitting on the counsel table. I look back at Wilson to confirm I am looking at the right thing. He nods.

I unlock the case and open the lid, just enough, so I can peek inside. One look and I immediately know what Wilson's thinking. He clearly has a different opinion than Sinn about how I should handle Lycocide. Wilson may come across as an easy-going, bumbling drunk, but it's all an act. He's sharp, knows how to get things done, and isn't afraid of taking risks. That's probably why I like him so much.

I close my eyes and take a deep breath while I reflect on my situation. I realize I've always known that there has only ever been one way this could end. Only one way those fifty-three people, fifty-four if you count Trudy, get justice. I remember the parting advice Whanung gave me when he visited me in my apartment, 'Werespiders are nearly impossible to kill in their full spider form. Even for a paladin. If you have to kill one, do it quick and do it while it's in its human form.' I open my eyes and look up at the judge and state loud enough for the entire courtroom to hear, "I accept Lycocide's challenge to the death."

Sinn gasps.

I reach into the briefcase and wrap my fingers around the cold metal grip of a Beretta M9, the same one I shot at the range the other day. I spin towards Lycocide and the world begins to slow as my Battle-Sight kicks in. As soon as I have him in my sights, I fire, and keep firing, until all fifteen rounds are spent. I watch the bullets, one after the other, exit the barrel of the gun and cross the distance between us. Bullet after bullet penetrates Lycocide's body, causing it to herk and jerk, and crumple to the floor—in Matrix-like slow motion. It's hard to miss at such close range, and I didn't miss—not even once. Blood oozes and pools on the floor from fifteen separate wounds. As I fired, I closed the distance between us.

The courtroom is silent. Shock has swallowed up all sound. When I reach his body, I calmly tuck the Beretta into the rear waistband of my suit pants and unsheathe my dagger. I grab Lycocide by his hair and lift his head away from his body so his neck is taut. I press my blade against his bare neck and then use some of the kinetic energy stored up inside the blade to heat it up as I saw through his neck. I have been practicing Light-Bringer with silverware at home. The warmed blade slides through his neck and bone like a hot knife through butter. I wipe the bloody blade clean on Lycocide's track pants and sheath the dagger.

I toss Lycocide's head to Prestegard and say, "I hope you got paid in advance." He drops the head in disgust, letting it hit the floor and roll under the desk. I shrug, return to my counsel table, and begin packing up my materials, as if nothing happened, as if I just killed a garden variety spider. I'm feeling pretty good about myself right now. Not

even Johnny Cochran himself ever got to pull a stunt like that in a courtroom.
#I'mInTheBuildingAndI'mFeelingMyself.

It takes about thirty seconds before the shock wears off and the courtroom erupts in chaos. Phulcus is leading the mob and calling for my head. "This is unacceptable. Advocate Valentine has broken the law. He should be stripped of his ring."

We all know the ring won't come off until I am dead, so he's essentially advocating for my death. Seems a bit extreme.

Witnesses in the gallery shout their support for Phulcus' suggestion. I realize I need to get everybody's attention before somebody does something stupid like try to kill me. So, I climb up onto the counsel table and shout, "Quiet!"

A hush falls over the courtroom. "Let me be clear; I have not broken any Concordat laws."

Someone in the gallery shouts, "You murdered Lycocide! We all saw it."

"I did no such thing," I say in a loud enough voice so all can hear me. "Lycocide challenged me to an Ordeal by Combat. I accepted. He lost his head—end of story. It was all completely legal."

Another voice in the gallery shouts, "Weapons weren't selected, a location for the duel wasn't selected. You broke our traditions. You never even gave him a chance!"

"I hold up the Concordat Book of Laws for all to see, and I read out loud, the relevant section: *Ordeal by Combat: Instead of pleading guilt or innocence, an accused may elect Ordeal by Combat and challenge his accuser. If elected by the accused, the accuser must either consent to the Ordeal by Combat or withdraw the charges. Once an Ordeal by Combat is accepted, the parties are to immediately fight to the death. The winner is triumphant and righteous in the eyes of the law.* As you all can plainly see, there is nothing in the law about choosing weapons or choosing locations. The law says the parties are to *immediately* fight to the death. That's what I did."

A hush falls over the courtroom.

"Now, if any Advocate here wants to accuse me of a crime—do it. I dare you. You'll lose, or maybe I'll just kill you." I look directly into Phulcus' black eyes, daring him to challenge me. He stares back, spitting hate in my direction, and then spins and walks toward one of the gates with a blue rune light above it. Prestegard follows him, biting at his master's heels.

"I didn't think so," I call after him.

Judge Sabra addresses the crowd, "This case is adjourned. Advocate Valentine was righteous in the eyes of the law. Mr. Valentine, get off the furniture." Judge Sabra steps down from the bench and heads to one of the other doors.

"Yes, Judge. Sorry about that." I answer as I jump down from the table.

Sinn directs us to "Wait together. The crowds usually clear out of these things quickly. Dangerous beings don't like to spend time together if they don't have to."

My team protectively encircles me while we wait for the courtroom to clear. They all look relieved that I'm alive. I give Joycee a hug and tell her she did a good job. Wilson and I share a look. Some things just don't need to be said. Sinn is, as usual, giving me the cold shoulder. I wonder what I have to do to get her to warm up to me?

Epilogue

Once the courtroom is completely empty, we collectively sigh with relief. I can't believe I'm still alive. Maybe the souls of Lycocide's victims can finally rest. I know killing him doesn't change anything; it doesn't bring them back, but I hope it brings them peace.

"Boss, can we leave this place? It's nice and all, but it's creeping me out. Is someone going to clean this place up?" asks Wilson.

It's only then I realize that Lycocide's headless body is still lying on the floor in a pool of his blood, and his head is still sitting under the desk where it rolled.

I look to Sinn, "Do we need to burn it or anything?"

"No, he's dead." she answers.

"Then I don't know who's going to clean it up, but we're not doing it. Let's get out of here."

As a group, we all walk to the rune door we entered through. When we reach the door, Sinn punches me in the arm. "You're an idiot. That was reckless and stupid. You could have been killed."

I smile from ear to ear. Maybe she does care—at least, a little.

As I retrieve my pen from my pocket, Sinn says, "You don't have to use your pen to open this door. This is your door, that's your rune above it; it's keyed to the ring. Just picture where you want it to open to and it will open."

"Really?"

Sinn smiles. "Yeah, rookie, you still got a lot to learn."

She may be right. All I know is that right now, I'm not thinking about all the things I don't know, or about gangs of mixed bloods moving into my city, or doomsday prophecies, or even about Phulcus and his cronies. Those are all problems for another day. The only thing I'm thinking about right now is gelato. You can't come to Rome and skip out on the gelato, that's a crime punishable by something worse than death—regret.

I bet you can guess where my door opened to.

#GelatoAtTheTreviFountain

Thank You for Reading and I Welcome Your Feedback

Thank you for reading the first of hopefully many Colt Valentine books. Colt has a long and difficult road in front of him. His faith in himself, his friends, his world, and the law are all going to be tested.

Without readers and the encouragement I receive from loved ones, Colt's journey would only exist in my head. It wouldn't be any less real for me, but there's magic in putting a story down on paper. When a character is born on paper and exists outside of an author's head, it grows and takes on a personality of its own and, sometimes, becomes something altogether unexpected. As the author, I naturally have insight into Colt's destinations but, like you, I am excited to discover how he and his friends get there.

In case you're wondering, Book Two, *The Lycanthrope's Lawyer*, is already in the works. I hope to release it sometime in 2019. I'm sorry I can't be more specific, but I am still transcribing Colt's journey from my mind to paper. As you know, Colt has a little bit of OCD and gets upset with me if I don't tell his story exactly right. He can be a real ass—ask Wilson.

Please check my Facebook page (**facebook.com/jasonroseauthor**) for updates on a release date and other insights.

Also, please review my books on Amazon, Goodreads, and your favorite blog, or website reader forums. I read every post, and they deeply matter to me. They also matter to Amazon, which ultimately decides where it places and recommends my book. More reviews can mean better placement and ultimately lead to more people sharing in Colt's journey. Thank you in advance.

Thanks again. You can connect with me online at **facebook.com/jasonroseauthor**, and **instagram.com/jason.rose_author**, I look forward to hearing from you!

Jason Rose

About the Author

I was born at the San Diego Naval hospital in 1978, the son of a Navy service man. Shortly after my birth, my mother was tragically killed in a car accident, and after a short stint living in upstate New York, my family moved across country to Santa Cruz, California. I may not have had the most traditional childhood, but I was surrounded by interesting people who shared their love, wisdom, and diverse world perspectives with me.

The seed for my love of books was planted when I was about eight years old and my second-grade teacher held me back a year because I couldn't read. That summer my uncle began taking me to the public library and we spent nearly every day there. I soon discovered Tolkien, C.S. Lewis, and Lloyd Alexander, among others, and it changed my life forever.

From that summer forward, I became a voracious reader, inhaling books by the bushel. Even in high school when football, basketball and girls dominated my thoughts, I found time at night to read. Reading became my addiction.

After high school, I went on a journey to find myself, which took me to half a dozen different colleges, culminating in a Philosophy degree from California State University, Sacramento in 2005.

I then attended the University of La Verne College of Law ("ULV") where I earned a Law degree and also met my future wife Natasha. I went on to earn a Masters of Law degree in Trial Advocacy and I'm currently a practicing attorney for a Bay Area law firm where I serve as counsel for plaintiffs in personal injury and wrongful death cases.

In 2012, I convinced Natasha to become my wife and in October, 2016, she gave birth to our first child named Ford. In August of 2018 we were blessed with our second child, Porter. As you can imagine, my life now involves changing a lot of dirty diapers, cleaning up toys, going to the park and cutting food up into really small bites.

Thank you for reading!

Natasha, Ford, and Jason

Books by Jason Rose

The Colt Valentine Arcane Justice Series
(an urban fantasy legal mystery)

Book one: *The Knight Advocate*

Book two: *The Lycanthrope's Lawyer*

Learn more about new releases and contact me

I welcome you to visit me and subscribe to my newsletter to be the first to know about upcoming releases.

Facebook: facebook.com/jasonroseauthor

Instagram: instagram.com/jason.rose_author

Excerpt from
The Lycanthrope's Lawyer

(Book Two in the Colt Valentine *Arcane Justice* Series)
Coming soon!

It's a foggy Tuesday morning in the Bay as I drive the empty Oakland streets. The town won't be awake for another hour or so, but I like to get an early start to my day, and I love Oakland in the early morning; it's peaceful and quiet. As I approach my office, a beautiful old red-brick building that reminds me of my Indiana childhood, I notice an old beat-up van parked at the end of the block. It's suspiciously parked on the wrong side of the street, facing the wrong way—towards my office.

The illegally parked job alone probably wouldn't have set off any alarm bells, but there's also a man wearing a suit and an overcoat that look like they cost more than the van itself. He's leaning against the passenger door, watching my office. Smoke is rising from the van's exhaust pipe, so there's probably at least one other person inside trying to keep warm on this cold fall morning. The van has shiny new tires, which is a dead giveaway; no one puts new tires on such a shitty van unless it's more than what it seems. Something about the whole scene makes my skin crawl, and after the month I've had and the things that I've seen, vampires, werespiders, orogs, and witches, you never can be too careful.

I drive right on past my office, past the van and the well-dressed man, and hook a pair of lefts so I can circle around to the other side of my building. As I pass the van, I get a good look at the guy leaning against it; he's a big fella', unnaturally large, with a full beard. He could probably play left tackle for America's team. I try to get a glimpse of the inside of the van, but the windows are tinted. After I park and lock my nondescript Honda, I remove an ornate silver pen from my inner jacket pocket. It resembles a Sharpie, but the most elegant Sharpie ever made, and draw the outline of a door and a handle with living silver ink onto the brick wall. I place the pen back into my pocket, reach into the wall, pull open a magical door, and step through the shimmering light into the center of my dark office. The glowing door closes behind me and disappears. #SomeThingsAreAlwaysCool.

The pen was a gift I inherited, along with a magic book, and a silver ring that won't come off and seems to have a mind of its own, when I killed my uncle, a sixteen-hundred-year-old vampire. I took his place as one of twenty-four Advocates who enforce the Magna-Concordat, a treaty of laws agreed to by all of the supernatural races of Earth, also known as Concordat citizens. All except for humans—who have no rights under the treaty, and are considered by most citizens to be food, or worse.

Once inside my office, I leave the lights off and head straight for the restaurant-grade espresso maker; nothing beats a good latte in the morning, and I hate to face danger before my first dose of caffeine. I was out of pods at home, so I didn't have a cup of joe before the drive and I'm feening. Once the cold milk is warmed into foam, I pour it on top of the double shot of espresso, add two sugar packets, and set it on the conference table in the center of the office, so I can see the front door. I then head over to my investigator Wilson's desk. He's only human, but I wouldn't say that to his face, at least without first buying him a drink.

I reach under Wilson's desk and grab hold of the stock of the Benelli M1 Super 90 with a magazine extension that he stores there—just in case we have unwanted company. I know from prior discussions with Wilson that the tactical shotgun is always loaded for bear, five shots, all silver rounds.

Since the trial of the werespider over a month ago, where I made a bunch of enemies, I've been training in firearms with Wilson once a week, and hand-to-hand combat with Sinn twice a week. We've taken on a few cases here at the firm, but nothing too serious, mainly immigration paperwork and some estate work. Even monsters need lawyers to help with the tedious things like travel, and making sure their children are provided for when they're gone. Besides the fact that all our clients are—for lack of a better term, monsters—and that the Courthouse where we do much of our work is located beneath Rome, this place runs like a typical law office. There's even a lunch cart lady who stops by, peddling sandwiches two afternoons a week—her tuna melt is to die for.

Wilson and Joycee now work here full time with me and my partner Sinn—she's a vampire. Wilson's our chief investigator and Joycee is our tech person. We're looking for a secretary, but so far haven't found anyone. At least no one I both like, and dislike, enough to hire. Despite the fact that we offer good health care coverage, working here isn't necessarily good for your health. You end up exposed to a lot of seedy characters, some human, some not so much.

I set the Benelli down carefully on the table next to my latte; the safety is off and I don't want an accidental discharge. I switch on all the office lights, signaling to the outside world that I'm here. I consider calling Sinn or Wilson, and letting them know about the van, but I decide against it. I can't be afraid of every van or every potential client. I am a Paladin, the last of my kind, and I can defend myself. Plus, Sinn and Wilson will both be here soon. It's not like calling them will get them here any quicker. Unlike me, who has the option of using a magical gateway, they have to drive.

I unlock the front door and step outside into the brisk morning. I stand out front, stretch, and wave hello to the van, letting them know I see them. I prop the front door open and take a seat at the conference table. I rest the Benelli across my lap and take a sip of my latte while I wait for the large bearded man and his friends. I wonder if it will be a consultation or a confrontation. Either way, I've had my first dose of caffeine, and I'm ready to dole out some justice.

Made in the USA
Las Vegas, NV
23 March 2021